BROKEN
BY THE
HORDE KING

ZOEY DRAVEN

Broken by the Horde King

Horde Kings of Dakkar

Book Four

Zoey Draven

Broken by the Horde King

Nine years ago, he broke my heart and never returned. I vowed to forget him…if only I could.

When I was a child, I fell in love with a Dakkari boy. The prince of our clan. *Rukkar*, we called him. For he was destined to become the greatest horde king of our time.

He was Kiran of Rath Okkili. My friend. My strong, unyielding protector. His mischievous smile and golden eyes made my heart flutter and my soul sing. And just when I began to believe he returned my love…he shattered me so completely and never once looked back to see how I'd survived.

Nine years later, he's returned.

Only, he's not a prince anymore.

He's a horde king. Cold and cruel. With molten eyes like sin and a body made for war.

I'd promised myself I'd *never* love him again. I'm older, wiser, and I protect my heart at all costs. But he's driven to prove me wrong for reasons I don't understand.

Because not only does he want my love again…he also demands me as his *queen*.

BEFORE

CHAPTER 1

When I was eight years old, I fell in love with a Dakkari boy.

It hit me fast, like the quick purple lightning that sometimes flashed over *Drukkar's Sea* in the warm season. Fast like the brown *nekkisau* darting for their dark burrows when strange beings strayed too close. Fast like plunging off the tall diving cliffs next to the Okkili outpost, dropping into the chilled sea, the wind slapping at flesh and carrying excited screams and laughter away.

That was what it felt like, falling in love. Frightening and dangerous but wonderful—all at the same time.

I didn't speak until I was eight years old. Not a single word, Dakkari or otherwise. My peers thought I was a mute fool. They would tease and taunt me, jeering at the human girl who didn't look like them, until they made me cry, until fat, clear tears dripped down my face—which delighted them. And still, I never made a single sound. I just stood there, waiting for it to be over, waiting for them to get bored and leave me be. It never occurred to me to walk away...because where would I go?

And this Dakkari boy who I fell in love with?

The clan had always called him *Rukkar*.

Prince.

His father had been a *Vorakkar*, a great *Vorakkar* in his time, roaming Dakkar, living freely on the wildlands until he decided to end his rule and settle permanently. The great hordes of time became outposts—*saruks*, they were called—and the mighty *Vorakkar* had settled his in the South Lands, closest to the beautiful sea, for his *Morakkari* was fond of the coast and the salt breezes that swept in from the Southwest.

That *Vorakkar* became *Sorakkar* to his people. Strong buildings of stone were erected in place of temporary *voliki*. Training grounds and *pyroki* enclosures were made permanent, fortified with Dakkari steel. Walls were built. Roads were laid. His nomadic horde became a clan.

It was there that I had lived the majority of my life, in a *saruk* by the sea.

And the Dakkari boy that I fell in love with was the prince of it all, the only son of the *Sorakkar*. The only son of Rath Okkili.

On a warm day when I was eight years old, a group of my sister's friends cornered me against one of the water wells toward the back of the outpost. Laru, my sister, had been distracted by shimmering baubles at the market, and thus her friends were free to try to make me cry. It was a game to them. A fascinating, terrible little game.

Well, they did make me cry, and like always, I stood there, letting them see my shame and embarrassment and fear until they left, wandering off to find Laru, snickering all the while.

Their words rang in my head as they left.

Ugly, stupid, useless human.

The *Rukkar* found me there, standing with my head down as I tried to will the tears away. He'd been striding past with his private tutor, a swords master, his golden weapon strapped to his hip, on his way to the training grounds.

Even at thirteen years old, the prince was beautiful. Golden eyes that gleamed in sunlight, a sharp nose, a wide, strong jaw, a mischievous smile that made my heart fluttery and my cheeks warm.

That day, he frowned when he saw me, sending his private tutor on ahead with the promise he'd meet him at the training grounds.

"Maeva?" he asked. "What's wrong?"

The *Rukkar* had always been kind to me. I had always suspected it was because he liked my sister, but sometimes I would dream that it was because he liked *me* instead.

I shook my head at his inquiry, and he took my arm gently, his hand hot and wonderful on my skin, and led me away. We slipped out of the outpost, through a secret gate I hadn't known existed, and he led me down a narrow path along the cliff's edge. The path went downhill sharply, but then...

Suddenly, we were in a private place that had a breathtaking view of *Drukkar's Sea*, stretched before us in the glittering afternoon sun. The path led to a wide ledge, big enough to stretch out on, the cliff at our backs. Blue-crested waves crashed against the rocks below, sending salty spray up, misting in my curly hair.

And suddenly, my tears were dried up and my mouth was open in wonderment. When I chanced a peek at the *Rukkar*, his golden eyes were on me and his signature mischievous smile had returned.

"It's a secret," he said, sitting down on the ledge, "so don't tell anyone."

Who would I tell? I thought.

Hesitantly, I sat down next to him, this Dakkari boy who looked more and more like a Dakkari warrior every day, and his tail came to rest in the empty space between us. Silence stretched between us too, and I felt flustered, my tongue tapping restlessly at the roof of my mouth.

"You shouldn't listen to them, Maeva," the *Rukkar* said quietly, his eyes scanning the horizon of the sea. "They only have power over you if you let them. Nothing they say to you is true."

His words sounded final and certain. In awe, I realized this was his power. I realized this was why so many revered him. Why so many believed that he was destined to become one of the greatest *Vorakkar* of our time, surpassing even his father's legacy.

His words had somehow become deeply etched into my mind, and I felt sudden confidence bloom because of it.

Because if the *Rukkar* didn't think I was ugly or stupid or useless, then surely I wasn't.

How could I be when *he* said otherwise?

The *Rukkar* turned to look at me then. Those molten eyes seemed to read every single thought racing through my mind. Those molten eyes darted back and forth between mine, and I wondered what he saw. I wondered what he thought of a scrawny, gangly human girl with brown and freckled skin and curly, long hair that was always left in a tangled mess from the wind. I wondered what he thought of my tailless body and the way my eyes had white in them when his did not. I wondered what he thought of my differentness, of my strangeness.

Desperately, I prayed to Kakkari that he did not see our differences at all. Desperately, I wanted him to think I was pretty, like he no doubt thought of Laru, the great beauty of the horde.

"Do you want to know another secret, Maeva?" the *Rukkar* asked me quietly.

Maeva. It meant *warm winds* in Dakkari. Like the winds the day I was found abandoned in a forest by a Dakkari hunting party when I was three. The day my father and mother and sister had become my father and mother and sister.

I didn't dare breathe, wide eyed, as I nodded my head quickly.

He smiled then, his sharp teeth flashing in the afternoon

sunlight, just as another wave crashed into the cliffs below, sending sea spray between us, misting the air until it sparkled.

"My given name is Kiran," he told me. "I want you to have my name. Because names have power, and if you ever need to use mine, you'll be able to."

Delighted shock went through me, knowing the magnitude of the gift he'd just given me.

Then I did something that shocked the both of us.

"Kiran."

The name left my lips like it had always been waiting there. Like I had always known it. Like I had just been waiting for permission to speak it.

The first word I had ever spoken aloud...and it was his name.

His soft chuckle filled the space between us, and I went dizzy with the sound, my heart fluttering madly, as more spray from the sea coated our skin.

It was then that I gave Kiran of Rath Okkili my heart. That day when I was eight years old. Right there on that sun-dappled cliff overlooking *Drukkar's Sea*, in a private little corner of the world I never knew existed.

Like a fool, I believed he would never break it.

Chapter 2

When I was fifteen, Kiran came of age.

While females came of age at sixteen, Dakkari males came of age when they were twenty. It was something I'd always found amusing, and my mother had told Laru and me that it was because males needed longer to mature. Though, with a sly smile on her face, she said that some never did. My father had chortled in the background when he heard her, as if in agreement.

At twenty, Dakkari males could begin training as *darukkars*, as horde warriors. It meant they could leave the *saruk*, to live and train in *Dothik* among the Dakkari king's, the *Dothikkar's*, warriors.

The *Rukkar's* path was always meant to be different than his peers, however. Not only would Kiran leave his home at twenty to train in *Dothik*, but he would stay beyond that time as well, to begin preparing for the Trials. The *Vorakkar* Trials. They were held every five years, though the Trials did not always produce a new *Vorakkar* because only the strongest of males survived them.

The night before Kiran and the eligible males in our *saruk* were set to ride out, there was a large feast to celebrate, and it was one of my happiest memories.

The music—the throbbing beats of the drums—was so stirring that night. As a *piki* to the *Arakkari*—the queen of the *saruk*, Kiran's mother—my mother was at her side, talking and eating and laughing with her. My father was with his friends at one of the *darukkar* tables, wine flowing freely as boisterous stories passed between them.

My sister and I were dancing in our own little world amid the other clan members. Kiran had come up to us at one point and snuck me a few sips of his wine, another secret between us —one of many. I felt a little sizzle of jealousy when he passed the goblet to Laru and I watched his eyes linger and his grin grow wider when she blushed.

I was used to it, however. My sister was the Dakkari beauty of the *saruk*, with her long, silky black hair, yellow eyes, and sun-honeyed skin. She was sixteen. She'd just come of age at the height of the silver moon. Next year, I would join her.

But then Kiran turned back to me, the only girl he'd given his name to, whose heart he owned, and pulled me into a dance, making me laugh until my cheeks hurt because of my smile.

I felt beautiful that night. *Lomma*, my mother, had made a dress for me that twirled around my legs as I moved. It was the color of the blossoms that sprouted in the meadow during summer, the palest of pinks. At fifteen, I was finally growing into my strange body. I would never be as tall as Dakkari females, but my breasts were larger, my hips wider. While my hair would always be a wild, thick mess, *Lomma* had pinned it back away from my face, threading through a band of gold, decorated with gold-dipped leaves, to keep it secure.

I had hoped to catch Kiran's eyes lingering on me, but he didn't look at me any differently. Still, he danced with me the most that night, and that was enough.

That night, I felt beautiful and I had Kiran's attention and I was happy. After years of not fitting in with the *saruk*, I was finally feeling like I belonged. Like this place was where I was meant to be. Like *he* was where I was meant to be.

At least, until later that night, long after the fires had been extinguished and most of the clan had stumbled to their beds, drunk off wine and food and laughter.

With my heart stuttering in my throat, I was looking for Kiran among the quietness of the *saruk*. The brave, excited part of me wanted to tell him my feelings before he left for *Dothik*. In my foolish little mind, I believed there was a possibility he returned them. I had imagined it over and over in my mind. Imagined it every single way.

I was practically vibrating with nerves and excitement when I went through the secret gate he'd shown me all those years ago, when I walked down the path I'd followed countless times before.

The moon was silver overhead, and as I descended the hill to the cliff's ledge, I saw him. Or at least, the darkened outline of him.

I smiled, hurrying down the path.

"There you are. I—"

My gasp was small, hardly audible, and I could physically feel the blood drain from my face.

Kiran pulled away from the female he had pressed to the cliff's wall, his eyes bewildered when I got closer.

His brow furrowed, his lips parted when he saw me. His gaze seemed panicked, darting to me, then to the female. The female who turned her head toward me, horror in her expression.

Laru.

Kiran was kissing Laru in the secret place he'd shown me, in the place I'd fallen in love with him, in a place that only *we* knew about...or so he'd promised me.

My tongue was doing that tapping thing on the roof of my mouth, and I couldn't form words again. Panic seized me and then squeezed my lungs. I couldn't speak.

"Maeva...*vok*," I heard Kiran say, but I was already running back up the hill to the outpost. "Maeva!"

He managed to catch me just as I reached the hidden gate. Before I could cry out, he wrapped his arms around my waist to keep me in place, even though I struggled in his hold.

He grunted when my elbow caught him in the abdomen. Hot embarrassment and a sense of deep betrayal made familiar tears well up in my eyes. Frantic, panicked sounds were bubbling up in my throat. I needed to get away from him before he saw.

"Stop," he growled, a tone I'd never heard him take with me, catching me by surprise, momentarily stilling my struggles. In that moment, he turned me, holding me in place.

He was tall, even for a Dakkari male. He towered over my smaller frame, completely engulfed my form with his bulk and strength. A sea breeze threaded between us, and even still, I could smell my sister on him—she made her own soaps for bathing. Fragrant and floral. I imagined I smelled the same.

"I'm sorry," he rasped, his voice quiet, but I didn't look at him. "I know she's your sister. And you're my friend, Maeva. I shouldn't have..."

Friend.

That word unstuck my own.

"Is that all I am to you?" I whispered, my vision blurry, the words sounding pathetic even to my own ears.

His friend. Ever since he'd told me his name, I'd never been far away from him. For seven years, he'd been kind to me. Laru had often scolded me for nipping at his heels, following him around, but he never made me feel unwanted. He made me feel less lonely. He let me near him and his friends, and ever since, no one dared to try to make me cry again. I felt protected, I felt safe when I was with him.

That was when I had the courage to look up. My question made him frown, made discomfort cross his features, while I waited with dread curling in my belly.

Finally, he murmured, "You know I care for you, Maeva. I always have."

Hope welled up in my breast and a small smile lifted my lips.

"But you're young," he rumbled, holding my gaze, his words firm. "I want you to understand that. You're young, Maeva. There is much that still awaits you. There is much to learn and experience from this life. The same for me as well."

I shook my head, deaf to his words. "So when I'm older, you might come to care for me the way you care for Laru? When I'm of age?"

The edge of his jaw ticked. He seemed impatient with me at first, his eyes going over my head to peer out at *Drukkar's Sea*. His eyes always went to the sea, as if he could see something that I couldn't.

"Maybe," he finally said, his shoulders sagging a bit even as I felt like I could soar. Suddenly, finding him kissing Laru didn't seem so terrible. Then he sighed, bringing me into him, embracing me. "I will miss you, *seffi*. That much I know for certain. As much as I know nothing will ever be the same."

"I'll miss you too, Kiran," I whispered, seeing Laru tentatively come up the hill from the cliff ledge, her face drawn—and guilty—when she saw us.

Looking back on that moment, I could recognize how selfish and single-minded I'd been. Kiran *had* been on the cusp of a whole new life. He would be leaving home for the unknown, for pain, for anguish, for the Trials. Nothing would ever be easy for him...and I'd been elated that he'd said he *could* care for me like

Laru. That maybe one day, he would want me the way I wanted him.

Then again, I'd been young, just as he'd said...and hopelessly in love with a boy who might never love me back.

Chapter 3

Once, I told my mother that my love for the *Rukkar* seemed more intense when he was gone. To be young and in love…I wouldn't wish it on anyone.

The days dragged, but everything reminded me of him, so I tried to fill my days with things that didn't. The answer to my restlessness came one afternoon when I heard screaming coming from the *mokkira's* home.

There were two healers that served our *saruk,* and the *mokkira* was the master healer, overseeing them with his combined experience.

That afternoon, I peeked inside, eyes wide, and saw a Dakkari female, one of the seamstresses, giving birth. She'd been due for quite some time.

The *mokkira* had seen me watching. His face was drawn, and the seamstress's face was pale, leached of color. Her mate was nowhere to be seen and no other healers were present.

"You," the *mokkira* barked at me, gesturing over to the water basin on the opposite side of the room, "bring me that and help me."

Though I had never seen such a thing in my life, I did as he'd asked, without question. At first, the sight of the seamstress's splayed thighs—and something peeking out from in between them—made my eyes widen and discomfort churn in my belly.

But then she was grabbing my hand, seeking comfort, her eyes wild. And I held on to her hand though I felt my little bones aching and compressing with her grip. I washed away blood until my hands were slippery. I listened to her guttural cries.

When the child was born, squalling into the world, I found tears streaming down my cheeks. The delight and utter joy on the new mother's face was a reward in itself.

I was filled with...*purpose*. A beautiful purpose that felt like Kakkari's touch within me, guiding me to *this*.

Afterward, I watched the *mokkira* with his herbs and tonics, helping her with the pain, until her frantic mate made an appearance, fresh off a hunt.

When I went home that night, with bright eyes and blood on my clothes, I announced to my mother, father, and Laru that I wanted to be a healer.

And in the years that followed, in Kiran's absence, I found a different kind of love in medicine and learning and apprenticeship, though the *mokkira* and the other healers in our *saruk* barely tolerated my constant and no doubt annoying presence. I absorbed everything like a sponge, jotting down notes in the journal *Lomma* made for me until I ran out of room and wrote on anything I could find.

Kiran was allowed to return to the *saruk* every year for a brief stretch of time. During those times, my heart always felt full to bursting. We would go on our runs across the coastline, we would swim in *Drukkar's Sea* if the weather was warm. I would chatter on about all the activity in the *saruk* in his absence, though I wrote to him often with the same gossip and about my apprenticeship, though the *mokkira* had not officially taken me under his tutelage. With time, however, I knew I would wear the elder down.

And Kiran would tell me about *Dothik*, how it was different there, but he would never tell me much more.

Kiran was...changed. In the stretches of time that he returned, he always came home different. Quieter. More... intense. It was more difficult to make him laugh, though he always looked at me with affection, and he still called me his *seffi*. It meant *little bloom* from the beautiful, ancient *okkara* trees that dotted the South Lands.

Kiran was changed, but my love for him was not. It was a steadfast, unshakeable, loyal thing.

The year before the Trials, Kiran didn't come home. My letters to *Dothik* went unanswered, though that was nothing surprising. Kiran had told me his training was regimented and strict. He barely had time alone.

The Trials were different, however. They were dangerous. I remember watching Kiran's mother pace the *saruk*, worried, almost every day of that year, and my mother told me that she hardly ate in her fear.

But I had faith in Kiran. The *Vorakkar* Trials were what he'd been preparing for his entire life, from the moment of his birth.

So, it was no surprise when we learned that Kiran had become the youngest *Vorakkar* in Dakkar's history at twenty-five years, completing the Trials in record time. He would have a moon cycle to rest, and then he would be expected to take to the wildlands, leading a horde all his own, in service to Kakkari, our goddess, and the *Dothikkar*.

That moon cycle, he returned to the *saruk*—he returned home.

But he was not the boy I remembered. He was a *Vorakkar* now. He had scars that he hadn't had before. There was a hardened glint in his gaze that reminded me of his father. There was a cold strength in him that had taken root, that had extinguished the comforting warmth I'd always associated with him.

Now that he was a *Vorakkar*, I wasn't allowed to meet his

gaze. Not directly. The moon cycle when he was home was a strange time. He could no longer be my friend, not the way he'd been before. He could be no one's friend, truly, for *Vorakkar* were supposed to hold themselves away from others.

But if I'd learned one thing in my life, it was that I was stubborn and unwavering. I would try until I failed. And that was exactly what I did.

The week before he was set to return to *Dothik* to gather his horde, he asked me to join it, to join *him* in the wildlands. He promised me that I would have a place as a healer in his horde. Our relationship was shifting—I could feel it. He wanted me to come with him? To leave the *saruk*, my home, my family, to be with him in his new one?

In my mind, I was beginning to believe he returned my feelings. I was twenty then. A woman of mating age, though I was a human. I'd felt his eyes begin to linger on me the way he often looked at other Dakkari females. Soon, he would be choosing a *Morakkari,* a queen and wife, of his own. In my mind, it was possible it *could* be me.

I was older. Maybe this was what we'd both been waiting for.

Even in my excitement, I waited until the celebration feast to give Kiran my answer. At any feast where an unmated *Vorakkar* was present, it was customary for hopeful females to show their interest by presenting him with brew. A goblet of brew, placed on his table, in front of everyone.

That night, I put on my best dress—a long, flowing gown of shimmering bronze that complimented my skin tone, or so Laru had said. *Lomma* plaited half of my wild hair back and decorated the rest with the *seffi* I'd picked from the *okkara* trees in the forest, a morning's run away. I was practically faint with excitement because I knew that night I would declare my feelings for Kiran before the entire *saruk*.

"Are you really going to do this?" Laru asked quietly, brushing her fingers over my cheek. Only she knew that I would be presenting my goblet. We had kept it from *Lomma*.

"*Lysi*," I replied, taking a deep breath, catching her yellow eyes in the reflection of the mirror.

We looked so different, and though we were not related by blood, she would always be my true sister. Just like my parents, who had taken me in when I had no others, when I had truly been alone in the world.

Laru gave me a soft smile and a squeeze on my shoulder. She might have kissed Kiran all those years ago, but she was in love with a *darukkar* of the *saruk* now. An honorable male a few years older, who worshipped the ground she walked on. Any day, we expected him to make her a matehood offering. Maybe even tonight.

"There are my beautiful girls," our father said, appearing in our room, the walls of our home booming with his heavy steps. "Ready?"

A flutter in my belly had me huffing out a sharp breath, and I gave Laru one last smile in the mirror, missing her expression of worry completely.

The feast was grand, as expected. The *Sorakkar* and *Arakkari's* son had just become a *Vorakkar*, after all. The whole *saruk* was in celebration, for it was a victory and an honor for us all.

I couldn't find Kiran before the feast began, but later he slipped into his seat at his parents' sides, taking the place of honor, the place usually reserved for his father. Because as *Vorakkar*, Kiran now outranked his father.

The goblets didn't start arriving until after most of the feasting was over and the drinking began. The *Sorakkar* and *Arakkari* were milling around the tables, and Kiran sat alone, up on the dais, his black hair gleaming in the firelight. My chest ached with his hardened, raw beauty, at the way his full lips seemed perpetually downturned now.

My father mentioned to me once that *Vorakkar* were made, not born. But looking at Kiran right then, watching as the goblets began to arrive on his table, brought to him by beautiful unmated Dakkari females, I thought that Kiran had been both born and made to be a *Vorakkar*.

I gathered my courage close when I saw he drank from no female's goblet. The females left his table disappointed.

I felt Laru's eyes on me as I grabbed my own, still full of brew, and rose from our family's table.

A hushed quiet seemed to descend in my ears as I approached Kiran. I felt like the whole feast slowed when his eyes caught on me.

That frown he wore didn't make me falter, however. Kiran's eyes flickered to the goblet, then back up to me. Though I wasn't allowed to meet his gaze, my eyes never left his.

"Maeva," he murmured, his voice low when I reached his table. "Do not—"

My goblet thudded down onto his table. The sound was final and certain. I swore I heard a snicker behind me, a female's laugh, and saw Kiran's cutting gaze silence it quickly. Then that furious gaze was on me and I felt a ringing begin in my ears.

Dread was curling in my belly, hot and sickening, the longer I stood there. Kiran didn't say a word, his jaw turned resolutely away. His hand didn't move toward my goblet. Suddenly, I felt my skin beginning to warm. My cheeks felt like they were on fire.

"Go, Maeva," Kiran said, his voice firm but quiet, when he realized I wasn't moving.

"Kiran—"

"*Go.*"

The word was sharp, spoken in a tone I'd never heard from him before.

But he was a *Vorakkar* now, and he wouldn't be disobeyed.

I scurried down from the dais, sickening mortification rushing over my head like a wave pulling me under in *Drukkar's Sea*. My chest ached. I bumped into someone and heard a laugh follow. I didn't dare meet anyone's eyes, and when I felt a familiar hand clasp my own, I held on to it. My mother led me back to our table, though she was silent. When I dared to look up at her, her golden skin was flushed but she held her chin high.

With dread, I realized I'd *embarrassed her.* When I met my father's gaze, I saw his jaw was tight and tense. Laru was looking down in her lap. I'd embarrassed us all. My family.

The brew from Laru's goblet—since mine still sat untouched on Kiran's table—tasted like the bitterness of the pain medicine I'd learned to make from the *mokkira*, when before it had tasted sweet and thick.

I didn't know how long I sat there, in a daze, my chest aching. But then I felt *him*, his presence close.

"I need to speak with you," Kiran rasped, taking my arm and guiding me from my seat. "*Now.*"

Like a fool, hope rose in my breast. Even my mother looked surprised, though wary, as Kiran led me from the feast.

I knew where we were going.

Kiran's hand was strong in my own. Calloused in places I didn't remember. I felt a deep scar across the back of it, which I also didn't remember. I had studied those hands dappled in sunlight, clasped around the hilt of his sword, around the reins of his *pyroki*, Roon, so many times. I would've remembered the scars.

He led me out through the secret gate close to the water well. The night was clear, the moon hanging low and sparkling along the sea. I heard the crashing of waves, and I took a wonderful breath of salt air as Kiran led me down the familiar path to the ledge tucked against the cliff, where we'd often spent long afternoons.

His hand left mine, and I pressed my back into the cliff wall, the wind from the sea blowing my dress around my ankles, threading through my hair. A *seffi* came loose with the wind, floating in the air briefly before Kiran snatched it, inspecting it carefully, silently. Then he let it blow away, down into the sea.

He'd always called me *seffi*. His little bloom.

His jaw was tight as he regarded me. "You shouldn't have done that, Maeva."

I swallowed. "Why not?"

Kiran looked away from me, turning his gaze out to the sea. His eyes were always on the horizon line.

"What do you look for?" I asked quietly when he didn't answer me.

"What?" he bit out, turning back to me.

"What is it that you look for? When you look out there?" I asked again, gesturing to the watery expanse before us.

His eyes were surprised, but his facial expression never changed. I wondered when he'd learned to do that. If it was part of his training in *Dothik*. I was beginning to realize that I hated whatever he'd had to learn in *Dothik* because it had chipped away at the warm, kind Dakkari boy I'd come to love.

"I don't know," he answered. Then he said, "Nothing. Nothing at all."

He was massive, standing close to me along the ledge. Strong, broad shoulders. Thick thighs. His tail twitched along the rocks, gleaming with spray from the sea. Thick, golden bands were around his wrists, new and solid, reflecting the light of the moon. His *Vorakkar* cuffs.

He was the *Vorakkar* of Rath Okkili now.

But he'd always be Kiran to me. My Kiran.

"Why did you do it?" he rasped.

The goblet.

"Did it displease you?" I whispered, scared that he would say it did.

But he didn't.

He made a sound in his throat. He turned to me, facing me fully. His golden eyes glowed. "Why did you do it, Maeva?"

"Don't you know why?" I asked softly.

His nostrils flared. The knowledge was there, right in his molten gaze. He knew. He'd always known, hadn't he?

Then I took my chance. Tentatively, like he was a feral beast, I stepped closer. Slowly. Carefully. Kiran held himself still, and his eyes flickered back and forth between mine. He was glaring at me, his mouth turned down into a slight scowl.

But I would always try. Even if I failed. My determination was both a virtue and a fault.

When my hands pressed into his chest, I could feel the steadiness of his heartbeat under my palm. He was so much larger than I was. I didn't think I had ever felt smaller than right then.

Desire started low in my belly, flickering like little flames, licking and consuming.

Something shifted in his gaze. I saw his eyes drop to my lips, briefly. I felt a wave boom against the cliff below, sending sea mist flurrying up around us.

I didn't want to wait anymore.

I went to the tips of my toes and kissed him. Finally.

His lips tasted of *Drukkar's Sea* and sweet wine.

I sighed against him, though it felt more like a desperate gasp. Kiran was frozen at first. I knew it was awkward. I'd never kissed anyone before, and he'd kissed many females, both in the *saruk* and, no doubt, in *Dothik*. I wasn't a fool to believe otherwise.

I moved my lips, brushing them against his. My heart was

beating so loudly that I wondered if he could feel it through my lips.

A sound tore from his throat, guttural and raw.

Then I felt his hands come to my waist, clasping at the thin material of my dress. He began to respond, and my mind did a strange twirl, one that made me feel like I was falling. My spine tingled and pleasure exploded across my flesh.

His lips brushed my own. His heat radiated into me. His hands gripped me tighter.

I knew that he was used to more forward females. Dakkari females had always been bold, and I wanted to be bold. For him. I wanted this.

So when my hands moved to the straps of my dress and tugged at the clasps, the material floated down around me, baring my breasts, though his hands at my waist kept my dress cinched there.

The mist from the sea stung my skin, cold and icy. I felt his brow furrow against me, and then he was pulling back.

His gaze dropped to my exposed breasts, and he stepped away. His released hold made the rest of my dress pool at my feet, leaving me naked and shivering and utterly vulnerable to his gaze.

Kiran's chest was heaving, his nostrils flared, his lips slightly reddened from my kiss.

"What are you doing?" he rasped roughly. "What the *vok* are you doing, Maeva?"

I stumbled back, my shoulders hunching, hearing something in his voice I hadn't expected. Something like...*disgust*. Something that made hurt explode inside me until I felt like I couldn't breathe.

"*Vok*," Kiran cursed, turning from me, raking a hand through his hair. "*Vok!*"

I flinched. "Kiran, what—"

"Put your dress back on," he ordered me. "*Now.*"

Frozen, I didn't move.

He let out another growl and stooped low to pick up my dress. He tossed it into my arms, before turning his back to me so he faced the sea. As if he couldn't stand to look at me. I stared at the broad outline of his dark shoulders, encased in black hide with golden etchings. His black hair whipped in the sudden violence of the wind.

Suddenly, I felt like he was a stranger. Suddenly, I didn't know him at all.

Nausea rose in my belly, and my face was burning as I finally forced my limbs to move. I tugged on my dress with shaking hands, covering my nakedness, only belatedly realizing when I clasped the shoulder straps that I'd put it on backward.

Kiran's voice was firm but quiet. It was nearly carried away with the wind when he said, "I shouldn't have done that."

I knew he meant the kiss. Not getting angry with me afterward. Somehow, that knowledge deflated me even more.

"Th-Then why did you?" I bleated, wrapping my arms around my midsection, feeling my throat burn and my vision blur.

He turned to face me, though I couldn't meet his eyes. All I felt was shame and...disgust. Disgust for myself. Disgust that I'd heard in Kiran's tone, but I had changed it and directed it at myself and I'd made it so much worse.

"Maeva, look at me," he ordered, not even giving me my own sense of privacy.

For years to come, I would never know how I'd found the strength to lift my gaze to his in that moment.

But I did.

I held his eyes while he broke my heart so completely that I knew I would never be the same afterward.

"I do not love you, Maeva," he said, his words slicing through the air like a blade. Coming right at me. "Not in the way you want me to."

The foolish, pathetic words slipped from my lips before I could stop them. I whispered, "But I'm older now. You said that when I was older—"

"*Vok*, Maeva," Kiran cursed. "They were just words. I didn't want to hurt you! But I realize now that I should have been clear from the beginning."

Stunned, I could only stare as another wave boomed against the cliff, wetting my face.

"I love you like I would my own blood, *seffi*," he said, his voice harsh. *Seffi* seemed mocking now, especially considering I'd spent the majority of the morning gathering the flowers dotted through my curly hair. "That is all. I cannot give you what you want."

"You kissed me back," I whispered, tightening my grip around myself.

I wished to Kakkari that I could just disappear. That I could wrap my arms around myself tight enough, pulling harder and harder, that somehow the compression would just make me disappear into nothingness.

"Did you...did you feel sorry for me?" I forced myself to ask. "Is that why?"

Kiran made a rough exhale.

"Maybe," he finally admitted, pinching the space between his brows. "I don't know."

My lungs seized. The whole world seemed to spin.

"You're still so young, Maeva," he continued, raking a hand down his drawn face. His *Vorakkar* cuffs flashed. "But the fault is mine for letting it come to this. I shouldn't have let it come to this. That was why I wanted to speak with you. Because if you join my horde, you must know that our relationship will never be more than what it is. It will not be what *you* want it to be."

He took a step closer to me, his gaze both hard and pleading, and I stumbled back against the cliff wall, sharp rocks jutting into my spine. His words were shards of glass, piercing and tearing right through me. He still wanted me to join his horde? Knowing that he would soon take a *Morakkari*?

He expected me to be able to stand by and watch him love a female that would never be *me*?

Did he think I had no dignity at all? No self-preservation? That I would willingly subject myself to that heartache?

"My father told me once," I whispered, "that a *Vorakkar* had to be cruel in order to lead best. I thought he was wrong. I told him that you would be different. That you didn't have a cruel bone in your body."

His jaw shifted, a muscle ticking there.

"But he was right," I said, my voice soft. Hurt. Raw. Horrified. "I'm beginning to think I don't know you at all."

A sharp huff escaped Kiran's nostrils. They flared wide. His eyes looked...*haunted* by my words. Yet his jaw was set like he'd accepted them as truth.

"I may be young," I continued, licking my lips, shocked when I tasted him there, "and I—I may seem pathetic to you. But I was never afraid to love you, Kiran. And I certainly never felt ashamed that I did. Not until right now."

Not until you made me feel ashamed for loving you.

Not until you showed me your disgust when I revealed my desire for you.

I shivered, my dress getting soaked from the sea spray, molding to my flesh. I didn't want him to see any more of my body. I covered myself as best as I could, in my backward dress. I was heartbroken and miserable and cold. All I wanted was to curl up in my mother's arms. I wanted to feel her stroke my hair like she'd done when I was a child. All I wanted to do was cry and sleep in her lap.

His next question twisted the blade in my chest even more.

"Is that your answer?"

His horde.

He was ripping my heart up, stealing my breath straight out

of my lungs, and he wanted to know if I was joining his horde or not.

A strange numbness descended over me. My gaze left his and turned toward *Drukkar's Sea* beyond him. The dark night sea that had begun to look tumultuous, like a storm was brewing.

I watched a wave build up from the flat surface, crest high, and then shatter below.

How did I say goodbye to someone that I'd known almost my entire life? How did I say goodbye to someone that I'd loved for nearly twelve years—someone I *still* loved, though he was breaking my heart? The pain was like nothing I'd experienced before.

In the end, I didn't say goodbye.

Kiran took my silence as my answer.

"I am sorry, *seffi*," he murmured after a long stretch of silence. "I wish..."

He trailed off.

When he reached out toward me, I backed away, plucking at my damp dress so it wouldn't cling so much. His fist squeezed as it dropped, his lips pressed tight.

"Let me take you back to the feast," he suggested quietly. "Back to your *lomma*."

I shook my head.

"*Go,*" I whispered, tears streaming down my face. I refused to meet his gaze again. "Leave me alone."

He waited another moment, a sharp exhale escaping him. "*Seffi.*"

"*Go!*" I cried, my voice echoing against the cliffs.

Finally, Kiran retreated, back up the hill, back to the *saruk* and the jovial celebration being held in his honor.

Leaving me there, just as I'd asked.

So why did it make me feel more miserable?

Long moments later, Laru found me on the ledge, frozen in place and shivering.

"Oh, Maeva," she gasped, her voice quiet, taking me immediately in her arms. "What happened?"

It was her gentle touch that made me break apart. I came undone in her arms, crying, falling into her until we crashed onto the ledge floor. My sobbing filled the night air, carried away by the wind. Long, deep shudders racked my body, and I cried until I had nothing left in me.

When I calmed down, we were both soaked through to the bone. *Drukkar's Sea* was angry that night.

I lay in my sister's arms, spent and exhausted and numb, and I whispered, "He doesn't love me."

Laru stroked my wet hair.

"Then it is his loss, Maeva, because you have so much to give," my sister told me, pressing a kiss to my cheek. "One day, he will realize that. He will realize his mistake."

Twelve years.

It took him twelve years to break my heart.

It would be nine years before I saw Kiran of Rath Okkili again.

AFTER

Chapter 4

The memory of him rose when I woke. The smell of his sun-golden skin and sweat. The huskiness of his voice, the way he always seemed surprised when he laughed.

Pushing up from my bed, I peered into the early morning darkness of the home I shared with my father. The floors were made of stone and were cold when I settled my feet onto them, shifting out of bed.

I dressed quickly, pulling on my fitted brown trews and wrapping a bandeau, a stretch of soft hide, around my breasts to keep them secure. Then I snatched my white pelt from where it hung against the wall, securing it around my shoulders. I patted my mother's pendant, which lay against my collarbones, to make certain it hadn't come off in the night.

The weather was changing. The mornings were growing colder and colder. Earlier than expected, since we were still in the harvest.

Splashing my face at the water basin on my table, I shook off whatever dream had prompted me to remember Kiran. He crept into my thoughts more than I cared to admit to Laru, but my memories were especially vivid whenever I dreamed of him, when he snuck into my mind when it was most vulnerable.

Unwanted and wonderful. Remembering always made me ache.

It had been nine years since he'd left the *saruk*, since he'd ventured out to the wildlands with a horde of his own. I hadn't seen him—not once—since the night he'd broken my heart on the cliff of *Drukkar's Sea*.

After I patted my face dry, I crept out to the main sitting room, where my father and I usually took our evening meals together. He was gone, however. Off on one of the last hunts of the season. I didn't expect him to return for another week. The hunters in a *saruk* had a more difficult time than hunters in hordes. They had to travel farther. And my father was aging. The longer hunts were becoming more difficult on *him*.

To my surprise, I saw the fire basin was already lit, warming the space.

"What are you doing awake?" I whispered to Laru, though it was a silly question.

"This child won't come until after the cold season passes," my sister complained, her mood sour and grumpy, "and already I feel like this."

Her stomach was slightly swollen. She'd only just discovered the pregnancy, but Laru was prone to sickness. When she'd been pregnant with Rasik, she'd stayed confined to her bed most mornings.

"Here," I said, still feeling the heavy pull of sleepiness as I dragged myself over to my standing chests on the far wall.

I fished out a stoppered vial, the thick blue liquid running up the sides when I shook it. One of my own creations, made of *jenuria* roots and *hakin* blooms—which were hard to come by in the South Lands—simmered over the course of two days and carefully strained.

Many pregnant Dakkari females had begun coming to me for the medicine, which the *mokkira* didn't know about. Word was getting out, however, and I kept a secret stash for Laru, which I'd just made for her two days prior.

"*Kakkira vor,*" she murmured when I brought the vial to her. "Have I ever told you how brilliant you are, sister? How much I love you?"

I kept my chuckle low because I knew Rasik must still be sleeping in Laru's old room. Laru's mate, Nevir, was a *darukkar* —a warrior—for the *saruk.* This time of the year, however, *darukkars* became hunters. He'd left with the same group my father was leading. And whenever the males went hunting, Laru and Rasik stayed with me, though their own home was a short walk away.

"Did the *mokkira* make his decision yet?" Laru asked.

I shook my head, my heart throbbing with the reminder of it. "*Nik.* He said this morning."

Laru squeezed my hand, though her face was a little pale from her nausea. "You'll get it, Maeva. How could you not? Everyone in this *saruk* knows you're a better healer than the other two. The *mokkira* would be an old fool not to choose you."

Pressing my lips together, I nodded at the vial. "Drink that. It'll make you feel better."

I watched Laru tip the vial up and back, letting the thick medicine slide over her tongue. It wasn't pleasant, and she made a face when she was done. But by the time I washed the vial out and returned it to my cabinets, her color had returned, her eyes brighter.

Peeking into Laru's old room, my heart softened when I saw Rasik sleeping on the bed. I'd helped deliver him. I'd listened to my sister's screams for hours, but we'd both been delighted when she held him in her arms for the first time. Even Nevir had looked choked up, and he very rarely showed emotion, unless it was for Laru.

Rasik was three years old, the age I'd been when the hunting party had found me abandoned in the woods and brought me back to the *saruk*. I crept over to his bed and gently brushed my hand through his dark hair. His full cheeks were puffed in sleep, his eyes flickering beneath his dark lids. His tail twitched restlessly, rustling against the furs he'd kicked off.

Pressing a kiss to his forehead, I straightened and left, returning to his mother.

"Is he still asleep?" Laru whispered.

"That boy sleeps like a boulder. Just like you used to."

She cut off her startled chuckle before it *did* wake her son. Rasik was a handful when he was awake, especially with his father gone off hunting, and I knew Laru liked the quiet reprieve in the mornings, even if it was dotted with nausea.

She watched me grab my satchel from the peg at the door. "You're leaving?"

"I wanted to make a run to the forest. To gather more *kioni*. They are falling like mad this time of year, so I need to stock up while I can."

Laru sighed, knowing I was obsessed with *kioni*. They were in the majority of my medicines. Even the *mokkira* had begun to use them in tonics he brewed. Plus, if a horde passed, I could use them to barter with. I was running low on *hakin*.

I pressed a kiss to my sister's cheek. "I'll see you this after-noon, *lysi*?"

"Good luck," she whispered to me. Another shot of nerves curled through me. I gave her a half smile and then left, cold morning air smacking me in the face and filling my lungs.

The *saruk* was always quiet this early in the morning. The violet rays from the sun were *just* beginning to lighten the sky, and I breathed in the crisp, refreshing air, a smile crossing my face. It was my favorite time of day. When the world was slow and peaceful.

Kiran had liked the mornings as well, I remembered. It was when we'd always gone on our runs together.

Taking in a deep breath, I shook my head, darting down the

stairs of our home, the soft soles of my hide boots hitting the stone. The buildings of the *saruk* towered over me as I made my way down the main road of the outpost. Windows were dark, though curls of gray smoke rose from venting holes.

I snuck out of the western gate, nearest the *pyroki* enclosures, passing my hand over a few curious *pyrokis'* sharp snouts when they came to greet me. Then, before me, all I saw was the open beauty of the South Lands with *Drukkar's Sea* winding to my left, as far as I could see.

The Forest of *Isidu* lay to the northeast. That was my destination. My hair was a tangled dark mess, since I hadn't brushed it in my rush this morning, and I wrapped it with a thin cord I always kept with me, keeping it pulled back from my face.

Once it was secured, I started to run, slowly at first, until my muscles warmed and my limbs loosened. My satchel bobbed at my hip. The brown hide bandeau across my breasts kept them tight against me. My boots were light, the soles striking Kakkari's earth gently.

My heart started pumping, quicker and quicker. My smile widened, and I looked up at the brightening sky, feeling lighter than air as I pushed myself faster. My feet hitting the soil of the South Lands matched the throbbing of my heart. Like Dakkar's heartbeat was matching my own.

The forest was rooted a half hour away from the *saruk*, but I took a longer route, winding through the dark bluffs closest to the sea before I cut inland where the cliffs jutted out farther, running over grassy land, the tall stalks of the *runiri* tickling my bare abdomen as I passed.

My delighted laugh was carried away by a strong gust of wind that was blowing in from the west, blowing large strands of my hair out from the cord. Even inland, I could smell the saltiness of the sea, could hear the crashing of the waves, the sound of which seemed to stretch for miles, even to the *Isida* Forest.

Perfection.

How did I ever get so lucky, to live in such a beautiful place?

The South Lands were called Kakkari's haven, after all. Because it was where Kakkari's earth met *Drukkar's Sea.*

Just as the Forest of *Isida* came into view, with its tall black trees that seemed to form a wall across the land, I heard it.

A pained, roaring bellow funneled toward me.

And the sound of a creature I'd never heard before, like a hiss that seemed to shake the ground.

Whatever it was wiped my smile away. My stomach dropped. I froze, scanning the horizon, turning this way and that way as I tried to determine where the noises had come from.

Then, to the far east, I saw a plume of dust kicking up from the ground, dark figures in the distance, though they were too far away to see them clearly.

To my disbelief, what I *did* see clearly was a massive, taloned, scaly creature—a *polkunu*—and then I heard Dakkari male shouts and figures surrounding it.

"*Nik,*" I breathed, fear running hot in my veins when the *polkunu* let out a roaring hiss and slashed at one of the males before rearing back on its long hind legs.

I feared it was the hunting party returning early, though we hadn't expected them for another week.

Father.

Nevir.

Though a ray of sunlight temporarily blinded me, I sprinted toward the group, trying to keep an eye on the *polkunu,* a creature I'd never seen before, though I recognized it by its curved talons alone. My father had always told me they were peaceful beasts, that they were hard to hunt because they spooked easily.

Why is it this far south? I wondered in panic, pushing my

body harder, the group coming into view more clearly. It was so close to the *saruk*.

I saw the glint of a long, golden spear in the sunlight. A Dakkari male roared as he struck the *polkunu* with it. The creature hissed, rearing back again to escape a second jab from the spear, but this time, it began to retreat. It was easily five times the size of a full-grown Dakkari male. It ran on its thick, scaled hind legs, its long neck tucked as it began to race away, blindingly fast.

Back east, away from the *saruk*.

A small blessing at the very least.

"*Darukkars*," came a guttural, dark voice, rising into the sky, "*run it down!*"

The order was followed by the battle cries of horde warriors. Even from this distance, I saw the Dakkari male take off on his *pyroki*, quickly followed by ten Dakkari warriors, also on *pyrokis*. The ground shook with the vibration of them following the *polkunu*.

Not my father. Or Nevir, I realized.

These males were part of a horde. *Darukkars* that were horde-bred, not *saruk*-bred.

I didn't have time to think about why a group of *darukkars* were so close to the Okkili outpost. As far as I knew, no *Vorakkar* had claimed the South Lands for the harvest season, though I guessed these males might be part of a scouting party for the frost.

A pained moan met my ears, and I pumped my arms, racing to the small gathering of males that remained behind. At the edge of the *Isida* Forest, three males were crouching around a *darukkar* lying on the ground, four *pyrokis* hovering close by.

It was the *pyrokis* that announced my presence—kicking and stomping into the earth, one of them beginning to charge at me. I skidded to a halt, holding in a gasp, when one of the *darukkars* unsheathed his sword, approaching me quickly as he nudged his *pyroki* back.

Holding up my hands, I watched as the *darukkar's* brow furrowed when he saw me. No doubt, he hadn't expected a human, and I feared that he'd never seen one before.

"I am a healer at the Okkili *saruk*," I told him quickly, my breath coming out in quick pants as I tried to regain it. "Let me help him."

The male looked away from me, his gaze going west, in the direction I'd come from and where the *saruk* lay, nudged up against the cliffs. We couldn't see it from here, however.

In the distance, I heard the hissing cry from the *polkunu*, heard echoing shouts reverberate over the land as the *darukkars* fought against it. I was thankful they were keeping it away from the *saruk* at the very least.

"*Lysi*," the male finally said, lowering his sword. "Help him."

I nodded, sliding past, my hands already digging through my satchel. It was a lucky thing I had some supplies with me, as I was planning to restock my stores in the *mokkira's soliki* that morning. I was planning to fill the rest of the space with *kioni* from the forest, but that would wait.

"Leave us," the male ordered the remaining two *darukkars*. "Go to the *Vorakkar* and assist him."

Vorakkar?

My brow furrowed at the words, as the two males immediately departed, heading east, but then my attention was drawn to the Dakkari male lying in a pool of black blood.

Dropping to my knees, I ripped off my fur shawl, exposing my shoulders and the flesh my bandeau didn't cover to the cold winds. The male's eyes were wild with pain, his teeth gritted. A large slash ran down his arm, exposing dark bone, an endless flow of blood flooding out from his veins.

"Can you heal him?" the other Dakkari male asked. If he

wasn't the *Vorakkar*, I assumed he was the *pujerak*, the *Vorakkar's* second-in-command, to give orders so easily to the *darukkars*.

One of the first things the *mokkira* had ever taught me was to never make promises when it came to healing. Kakkari wrote the fates of her people long before they came into this world. She could take them as easily as she gave them life.

Like Lomma, I thought, my lips pressing together. Before my mother had died, eight years ago, she had been healthy. Vibrant. One day she was alive, laughing. The next she was dead, cold.

Afterward, the *mokkira* told me Kakkari wanted her back, had called her home. And only after *Lomma* died did he agree to train me as one of his apprentices, though I'd been begging him for years.

Swallowing, I rummaged through my satchel, my hand closing around the vial I recognized by shape.

I didn't answer the male's question.

I *thought* I could heal him. I knew what to do with a wound this deep. But I wouldn't give assurances that might not manifest, especially when it came to Kakkari's will.

The ground began to vibrate again. With a quick glance up, just to ensure the *polkunu* wasn't backtracking toward us, I felt relief when I saw it was just the horde warriors returning on their *pyrokis*, their blades glinting. Squinting, I was forced to look away when the sun reflected off those blades directly into my eyes.

The large group of Dakkari males reached us by the time I tore out the cord holding my hair back, wrapping it around the warrior's thick arm. The cord was slippery with his blood, but my fingers were small, my movements quick, and I tied it tight, knowing it would help stop some of the bleeding.

I sensed the rest of the *darukkars'* presence, heavy and intimidating, as they clustered. I heard the murmurs, heard "*vekkiri*" tossed about—which meant *human* in Dakkari, heard the confusion in their voices.

"Is the *polkunu* dead?"

The question came from the male I assumed was the *pujerak* of the horde, directed at someone among the group.

A grunt was the only response, which I assumed meant *yes*, especially coming from a *darukkar*.

The warrior beneath me groaned, bucking. The pain in his arm probably felt like a hot poker prodding into him. After pushing my unruly hair away from my face, I began to pull dried grass from the earth in thick, fuzzy clumps. Unstopping the vial from my satchel with my teeth, I poured the clear liquid over the grass, drenching it, before stuffing it into the *darukkar's* deep wound.

He cried out, and though I gritted my teeth, I didn't react to his pain. The *mokkira* had taught me to be methodical, stoic, almost bordering on indifference.

The warrior surprised me by lamenting, "A *vokking polkunu* will have killed me. Is this the death Kakkari meant for me? *Vok!*"

A cutting laugh came from the group of *darukkars* as I packed his wound to the brim, stuffing grass against the bone. "You have not been ended yet, brother. There is hope for you yet."

The warrior beneath me met my eyes. His were red, his pupils dilated with the pain.

"Will I die, *vekkiri*?" he asked me. "I'd rather know now."

I hadn't been called *vekkiri* directly in quite some time. The annoyance I felt startled me.

My voice was even and calm, however, when I told him, "I've seen worse. Some of them even *lived*. Those that did, however, usually weren't complaining as I tended to them."

The warrior looked up at me in disbelief as raucous laughs rose from the group of horde-bred *darukkars*.

With my hands bloodied black, I dug into my satchel again, fishing around for the bundle of cleaned and stripped *runiri* I kept inside. I tore off a good amount with my teeth, blowing my curly hair out of my eyes, and used it to tie off the wound, keeping the sliced flesh closed to minimize blood loss.

I blew out a short breath, wiping my forearm over my forehead—feeling the warm smear of blood against my flesh—leaning back onto my heels.

My eyes went up to the *pujerak*, seeing the group of *darukkars* hovering in my vision.

"He is stable for now. Get him to the *saruk* quickly. It's just along the coast." One of the *darukkars* stepped toward the wounded warrior, his heavy footsteps thudding into the earth. "The *mokkira* will—"

My lungs seized, shock stealing whatever words had been poised on my tongue.

It wasn't a *darukkar* that had stepped toward the warrior—toward *me*—at all.

It was a *Vorakkar*.

A *Vorakkar* with familiar golden eyes and a face that haunted my dreams regularly. A face I hadn't seen in almost nine years.

Kiran of Rath Okkili was standing in front of me, blocking out the rays of the sunrise that were cresting behind him.

Half of his black hair was pulled back from his face, emphasizing his sharp, almost regal features, the rest of it swinging down between his shoulder blades, some thicker strands decorated with gold beads and small cuffs. His heavy tail was hovering just off the earth, but I spied the very end of it, tufted in dark hair, twitching, as it'd often done when we were younger.

He was dressed in a brown-and-white mottled pelt that laid across his wide shoulders. He was bare-chested underneath, scars I'd never seen before mapped out across his flesh, telling stories and tales that I was no longer privy to. His strong legs, bigger than some of the tree trunks in the *Isida* Forest, were encased in black hide, his large feet protected by boots. His sword was strapped to his back through an opening in his fur pelt, the hilt peeking out over his right shoulder.

And his face…

If possible, he was more handsome than I remembered him.

His sharp nose led to full lips. Lips too soft for a fierce face such as his. His jaw was wide and strong, a glimmering new scar at the edge of it. His features were composed in a neutral yet intense expression, one that made me want to shiver, as he met my stunned gaze.

His eyes…

Even his eyes looked different.

They were still the same molten gold I remembered, beautiful and mesmerizing. And yet…there was a strange hardness that lurked in their darkened depths, something that had begun during his training in *Dothik* but seemed much more obvious now.

"*Seffi.*"

The quiet word rose from his throat, roughened and deep.

It was *that* word that jolted me from my stupor.

Because it brought a fierce, bitter ache in my belly. It brought longing and hurt so deep I could *burn* with them. It brought a thousand memories and a thousand painful moments. It made me remember how much I'd fought to forget him. It made me remember how much I'd hated him after my mother died, when he hadn't returned to the *saruk* for her burial, even though I had written to him, begging.

It made me remember the betrayal I'd felt. That he'd left the *saruk* in the middle of the night without saying goodbye. Because though our last meeting had been painful, though he'd broken my heart, I had still wanted to say goodbye. Though I had loved him in a way he couldn't reciprocate, it hadn't changed the fact that, next to Laru, he'd been my best friend for close to twelve years.

Kiran of Rath Okkili had left, and he'd never—not once—looked back to see how I'd faired.

Surprisingly, I found that my bitterness and my anger and my longing all slid toward *indifference* the longer I looked at him.

Slowly, I rose from my kneeling position before him. I straightened to my full height. My perusal of him, his greeting to me had taken all of five seconds, but it had felt like a lifetime.

The warrior at my feet groaned, gingerly touching his slashed arm. The *darukkars* behind their *Vorakkar* looked on, waiting for his command. The *pujerak*, however...I could feel his sudden interest in me, the way his eyes narrowed and focused on me, as I looked his *Vorakkar* straight in the eyes. Something that was forbidden. Something that was considered disrespectful.

I held on to that indifference because it felt *good*. For once, I wasn't angry at him. For once, I wasn't hurt. He didn't have power over me anymore. That was enough to celebrate in itself.

The last time I'd spoken to him, I'd been a crying mess.

But I'm not that girl anymore, I thought, seeing Kiran's eyes flicker back and forth between mine. Trying to read me? He'd always been able to before.

Now? I dared him to try.

I was proud when my voice emerged strong.

"Welcome home, *Rukkar*."

CHAPTER 5

"This is the *Vorakkar* of Rath Okkili, *kalles*," Errok, my *pujerak*, grated, his tone firm as he stared down the human woman in front of him. "You will show your respect and greet him as such."

I hardly heard his words. Maeva's dark eyes held mine captive, and I found that it was impossible to look away.

Vok.

My fists clenched at my sides, memories rising between us, suffocating. My heart was pumping furiously in my chest at the mere sight of her.

"He has always been *Rukkar* to me," Maeva said softly. "Our prince has finally returned."

There was a hint of an edge to Maeva's words. Almost mocking.

Her voice was changed, I thought, frowning. Softened and husky. Running my eyes over her, trying to identify remnants of the girl I'd once known, I realized much had changed.

"Don't delay," Maeva said, daring to give orders, further thickening the tension between herself and my *pujerak*, who looked at her in disbelief. "The *runiri* will only hold so long. The *mokkira* needs to mend the wound and quickly."

With that, she turned from us—from me—toward the Forest of *Isida*. With speed that obviously surprised her, my hand shot out and took her forearm, her skin warm and smooth under my calloused grip.

Maeva stilled at my touch, leveling her gaze on me with a neutral expression I couldn't read. It frustrated me.

"The *polkunu* is dead, but it came from the forest," I told her. "You will return to the *saruk* with me. Now."

She tugged her arm out of my grip, reaching down for her white pelt, the ends of the soft fur tipped in black blood from my *darukkar's* wound. A bandeau covered her breasts, wrapped tight—something she'd often done when we'd gone on our morning runs next to *Drukkar's Sea*. Her abdomen was bare, however, and she wore tight trews that encased her hips and thighs like a second skin.

My nostrils flared.

She was more beautiful now than she'd been when we were young. She had the body of a female in her prime, all lush curves that made my claws curl into my palms. She was still the same height—she barely came up to the middle of my chest— but the way she held herself now made her seem taller, her chin tilted high.

Her dark hair, which fell in wind-swept loose ringlets down her back, was longer than I remembered. Her warm brown skin, the freckles that dotted across the bridge of her slim nose and over her high cheekbones, the small scar right below her bottom lip from cliff-diving...these things were hauntingly familiar to me. Things that hadn't changed.

And yet...

I knew on first glance, with *darukkar* blood streaking across her forehead and unreadable eyes, that *this* Maeva was not the same girl I'd left behind. There was a coldness in her face where there had always been warmth and delight and curiosity. There was a quietness in her movements, reminiscent of when she hadn't spoken at all. Her jaw was hard and unyielding, and she didn't shy away from my frown.

She didn't...*care?*

She wasn't happy *or* upset to see me.

My *seffi*, whose laugh and smile were permanently imprinted on my mind, was *indifferent* to my presence, like I was a passing *Vorakkar* she didn't even know.

Something curled in my belly, hot and uncomfortable, the longer she looked at me. Because I'd never been able to hide from her.

Except for the last nine years, I thought gruffly.

"I have a purpose in coming to the forest, and I won't leave until it's done," Maeva told me, straightening and looping her bloodied satchel around her body. The strap cut straight down through the valley of her breasts. "Go to the *saruk* quickly for the sake of your *darukkar*. I trust that you remember the way."

With that, she strode into the *Isida* Forest, leaving me standing there like a fool with my jaw clenched and a growl poised in my throat. The urge to clasp her to my side and force her back to safety was riding me hard.

The sight of her backside greeted me, however. Her hair swayed, the tips of it brushing the swells of her buttocks. Rounded and full, with hips made for mating.

Vok.

Forcing myself to look away, I turned my gaze to my *pujerak*. "Follow her. Make sure she returns to the *saruk* safely."

Errok inclined his head, though he was no doubt wondering why I didn't send one of my *darukkars* in his stead, for his presence was far more important.

I hefted Atevak onto his feet and heard his deep groan as I led him to his *pyroki*.

"The *mokkira* will see you well, *lysi?*" I grunted, my eyes going west, in the direction of the *saruk*.

After nine years...I was finally home.

So why did it feel like I was walking into an *ungira* den?

CHAPTER 6

My wet hands were trembling as I dropped to my knees and began gathering the *kioni* scattered across the forest floor. I'd washed myself in a small pool of water in the forest, scrubbing at my hands and arms, and a *kioni* slipped through my damp fingers.

Kioni were small, no bigger than the tip of my thumb, but crushing their outer shell was near impossible. The nut meat inside was edible, though most Dakkari didn't care for their sweetened taste. I quite liked it, but they were better used for the *mokkira's* potions. *Kioni* were powerful antiseptics and chased away infection if administered quickly.

They only dropped from the tree this time of year, when the meat within was ripe and soft. The stores would have to last us through the frost, so I intended to fill up as many satchels as I could every morning, though I was careful to leave the majority of *kioni* scattered on the ground. Creatures in the forest ate them and needed to make stores of their own.

Luckily, the forest was littered with them.

I sensed a presence behind me, and my lips pressed together. I'd spied Kiran's *pujerak* following me the moment I'd begun winding my way through the trees.

"Who are you, exactly?" came his voice not a moment later.

The Forest of *Isida* was so quiet I could hear a *kioni* dropping from several yards away. His voice was jarring, especially since I was used to the quiet now.

"I am Maeva," I told him.

He made a sound in the back of his throat. "You give your name to a stranger so willingly?"

"I am human," I said. "Everyone in the *saruk* knows my given name."

"*Lysi*, but you obviously grew up among the Dakkari. Why would our customs not apply to you?"

Because they never have. I have always been different from you, I thought, gritting my teeth.

I looked up at him from my kneeling position. Observing him carefully. It seemed to make him fidget.

"I'm assuming you're his *pujerak*," I murmured before shifting my gaze to my satchel, grabbing handfuls of the dark nuts and tossing them in my bag. They clinked against the vials I had stored in there.

"What makes you think so?" he asked. He was leaning against a tree, his arms crossed over his wide chest. Despite his relaxed position, his eyes were shifting through the trees, seeking any possible threat. He was handsome, I recognized, with yellow eyes. He looked around Laru's age—slightly older than me, but younger than Kiran.

"You gave orders to the *darukkars*," I said, shrugging. "And they followed them without hesitation. I don't know much about horde life, but I do know that *darukkars* only listen to their *Vorakkar* and their *pujerak*."

He regarded me in the same manner I'd looked at him. Carefully.

"Who are you, exactly?" he repeated, his voice gruff.

"I already told you."

"*Nik.* Who are you to him?"

Him.

The *kioni* glittered like little black jewels before me, as the sunlight began to dapple through the trees. Morning had arrived, chasing away the dawn. Already I could feel the temperature shift, warming, though my blood still ran hot from the earlier events.

"I am no one to him," I said.

The words...hurt. Oddly enough. But it was a dull kind of ache. I'd learned to live without Kiran. It was obvious to me that he hadn't loved me, not even in a familial way. If he had loved me, if he had cared for me, he might've still broken my heart, but he wouldn't have shattered me so completely.

In my mind, the Kiran I knew was dead and gone. A *Vorakkar* had risen in his place, and it was that *Vorakkar* who was a stranger to me.

"I don't believe that," the *pujerak* said quietly, his features bordering on...disturbed. "No one would speak to him the way you did and not be punished for it. It is obvious to me that—"

"The *Rukkar* and I knew each other as children," I said, cutting off whatever he was about to say because I didn't want to hear his opinions on something he knew nothing about. "If you think we seem familiar to one another, that is why. I have known him almost my entire life, up until he left. As such, we have not seen one another in almost a decade. But I...I will work on being more respectful to his position in the future."

Not that I would see him. I had no idea why Kiran had returned home. Or what he wanted at the *saruk*. I assumed it was to see his parents, the *Sorakkar* and the *Arakkari*.

The *pujerak* went silent, continuing to study me from his place against the tree as I stuffed my satchel full of *kioni*. When I stood and began to exit the forest, he followed after me, his heavy footsteps crunching on the ground.

"You don't have to follow me," I informed him. "I come here almost every morning. I'm in no danger."

"The *Vorakkar* gave me an order to watch over you, and I will see it through," the *pujerak* replied. His words made my belly ache a little. It reminded me of how Kiran had *always* looked out for me. "The *polkunu's* presence is disturbing enough. It charged us as we passed this forest."

"We have never seen one in these lands. I didn't know they ventured this far south," I said, emerging from the tree line, half expecting to see Kiran and his *darukkars* still ringed in a circle, but the land was empty save for a lone *pyroki*, which waited for its master. The rest must've reached the *saruk* already.

"They don't" was all the *pujerak* replied, his voice gruff. His *pyroki* immediately approached, and he took the reins to steady the beast. "Come, *kalles*. I'll help you up."

I bristled at the words, casting him a sharp look. "I know how to mount a *pyroki*. I've been riding since I was a child."

"Of course. I didn't think—"

"And I prefer to run anyway," I said, rolling off my sudden irritation like it had never been, taking a deep breath in through my nostrils. Since Kiran had left, since my mother had died, I'd learned to dampen *everything*. Dampen the pain, the anger, the fear, so it didn't control me. "You can follow me if you'd like."

With that, I secured my satchel and began to run across the land, passing over the bloodied spot where the injured warrior had lain. *I should hurry,* I thought. The *mokkira* might need my assistance.

Though not likely, I thought. I'd been avoiding going to his *soliki* all morning. I couldn't any longer.

Shortly after I began to run, I felt the ground vibrate gently behind me. The *pujerak* was following me, and he followed closely all the way to the *saruk*.

Once we reached the gates, I slipped through, nodding at the two guards posted on duty.

"You should not venture out to the plains, *kalles*," said

Urelli, one of the older guards and a close friend of my father. "There was an attack, and—"

I squeezed Urelli's arm, giving him a small smile. He would worry—and probably tell my father—if I told him I'd seen the attack. "I'll stay within the walls today. I promise."

Good thing I'd washed away the blood already.

Urelli relaxed, and then he straightened when he saw Kiran's *pujerak*. Urelli inclined his head, but I was already striding past, heading toward the *mokkira's soliki*. The outpost, I noticed, was chaotic. The *mrikro* and his apprentices were trying to gather Kiran's and the other *darukkars' pyrokis*, trying to lead them to the enclosure to be fed and watered. The *saruk's* center, which was where most of our feasts and gatherings took place, was bustling with Dakkari.

Excitement filled the air. Most were smiling. Some were whispering together. Their prince turned horde king had returned.

I also noticed that some looks were being tossed my way, and I felt the creeping feeling of shame and embarrassment. Kiran, after all, had rejected me, quite publicly, at his celebration feast. Most in the outpost knew that I'd loved him for many years, had followed him around like a lovesick fool. Most had seen my heartbreak after he left, had been witness to the aftermath.

I lifted my chin. The sooner Kiran left, the better. Life would return to normal, my shame would be forgotten once again. Everything would be fine.

Kiran was nowhere to be seen, though his *darukkars* were being tended to by females, who brought out heaping platters of food for them to pick at. A few *darukkars* inclined their heads at me in recognition as I passed.

Heading up one of the alleys that stemmed away from the *saruk's* center, I ventured between the kitchens and the bathhouse, passing by one of the lesser-used water wells and up a short incline until I reached the back entrance of the *soliki* I spent most of my time at.

I went through the heavy door, the darkness of the potion room greeting me. It had to be dark in here because excess light sometimes changed the potions' quality. Something was bubbling on the fire basin. A pot of bubbling *kioni*, I knew, just from smell alone. I could also tell it'd been boiling through the night. It had taken on a familiar sweetness.

Dumping my satchel on the workbench and shrugging out of my bloodied pelt that needed a scrubbing, I donned my smock, tying it around the back, and slipped into the main room of the *mokkira's soliki*.

It was quiet as I stepped up to the hard slab the wounded *darukkar* was lying on. Unlike in the potion room, the main room was bright, lit from a wide venting hole at the top of the stone building and a plethora of oil lanterns filling the space.

"Maeva," the *mokkira* said, not looking up from the *darukkar's* arm. He'd already untied the *runiri* and unpacked the wound. Thankfully, the *darukkar* was passed out. The *mokkira* must've given him one of his tonics. "I am told this is your handiwork."

Pressing my lips together, my eyes caught on Kiran. I'd sensed he was in the room the moment I'd stepped inside. He'd always had a way of making a room seem...smaller.

The *Vorakkar* was standing with his arms crossed, the side of his pelt bloodied from assisting his *darukkar*. His eyes had fastened on me the moment I stepped inside.

Lingering at the *mokkira's* side was Nebrik. The other healer, Kilen, was absent—he usually assisted the *mokkira* later in the day. Nebrik was the healer who I believed the *mokkira* would give his title to. Because Nebrik was the *mokkira's* nephew. Blood was blood.

"*Lysi, Mokkira*," I murmured, coming to his side. Nebrik was threading fine gold cordage, thin enough to pierce through skin.

They were beginning to stitch the wound, the table a bloodied mess. "The grass was drenched in—"

"*Lysi, lysi*," the *mokkira* murmured, impatient as he always was. "I know. I smelled it."

Kiran shifted, and my eyes flickered to him. I was surprised that he had stayed behind with his *darukkar*. I had expected him to be with his parents.

From across the room, his eyes burned into mine, as if daring me to look away. Nebrik huffed out a small breath, drawing my attention. Nebrik had often made snide comments about Kiran's rejection of me. The male hated my guts because he knew I was his only real competition for his uncle's title— and it made working with him near impossible. He lived to get under my skin.

Addressing the *mokkira*, I began, "Shall I sterilize the—"

But there was a commotion outside and the door to the *mokkira's soliki* opened, blinding us with even more morning light. I heard her voice before I saw her.

"*Rei kassiri*," breathed the *Arakkari* of the outpost at the sight of her son.

"*Lomma*," Kiran murmured quietly, taking his eyes from me before embracing his mother.

The *Arakkari's* eyes were watery with her delight. "You're home!"

The *Arakkari* was still as beautiful as she'd been when I'd first seen her all those years ago. She'd been a queen to her horde for many years, and now she was the queen of the *saruk*, proud and strong. Then again, everyone knew her son was her weakness.

My mother had been a *piki* to the *Arakkari*. One of her close confidants and friends. When I'd been younger, I'd often accompanied my mother as she tended to the *Arakkari*, helping her with her clothes and her jewelry and her hair. I remembered hot afternoons sitting with them in the *saruk's* center or long walks perusing the wares and offerings made by members of the outpost.

After my mother's death, the *Arakkari* had been kind to my sister and me. But since I was unmated—and very likely always would be—she'd taken me under her wing more so than my sister. She'd taught me the universal tongue when I asked it of her. She kept me apprised of the affairs in *Dothik*, news that came in from the capital because she knew it interested me. Though I strongly suspected that she knew I had always been seeking information and news about Kiran.

That had been years ago, however. I no longer met her in private. Every time I tried, her new *piki* turned me away...and eventually I simply stopped asking to meet with her, though I didn't understand it.

"Is something wrong?" the *Arakkari* asked next, taking her son's hands. "I heard about the *polkunu* attack."

The grin he gave her almost stole my breath...because it looked *so* much like the old Kiran, the boy I used to know, the boy I'd fallen in love with. His smile was easy and charming.

"Does something have to be wrong for me to visit?" he asked.

"You have been away for a long while," the *Arakkari* said. She had gone to visit his horde two years ago, had stayed with him for a whole moon cycle before returning to the *saruk*. Still, she missed him sorely. "What brings you back to the South Lands?"

His smile slowly died.

His eyes flickered to me.

I stopped myself from shifting under his gaze, keeping my expression neutral. If he expected me to cower from his eyes like all the rest, he would be sorely disappointed.

"The *mokkira* of my horde passed into the next life a moon cycle ago," he finally grated.

Our *mokkira* made a noise in his throat, never looking up

from the *darukkar's* arm. "I knew him. He was an accomplished healer. He trained in *Dothik, lysi?*"

"*Lysi.* My horde feels the loss of him greatly," Kiran said softly, tilting his chin down. His tail twitched across the floor. "He was training an apprentice, but he is still young and overwhelmed with this new responsibility."

I swallowed, pressing my trembling hands to my thighs.

Kiran continued, mostly speaking to his mother, though I had the sense he was addressing us all.

"I plan to claim part of the South Lands for this next season."

My chest squeezed. Was that panic I felt? Knowing that Kiran would be so close to us for the next few months?

"Truly?" the *Arakkari* breathed, clasping her son's wide wrist, placing her palm right over his *Vorakkar* cuffs, which looked more worn than when I'd last seen them.

Kiran inclined his head, though his eyes were on me. "I come to the *saruk* now to make an offer to one of your healers. I need a new *mokkira* through the coming frost. We have many pregnant females that will give birth soon...one of them human."

Even I couldn't conceal the sharp, surprised breath that escaped me...and I had had plenty of practice hiding my emotions through the years.

Human?

He had humans living among his horde?

So the rumors have been true, I thought in disbelief.

The *Arakkari's* eyes turned to me, golden and glittering in the morning light. Her expression was pensive, knowing. The room suddenly seemed very quiet, heavy, suspended on the cusp of something. Even the *mokkira* had paused in his work.

With his searing gaze still pinning me in place, Kiran murmured, "I know which healer I would like to make the offer to."

Chapter 7

The tension that filled the *soliki* was palpable, and my poor *lomma* was doing everything she could to ignore it.

My father's disapproving stare connected with my unyielding one. Though my mother had come to visit me in my own horde two years prior, I hadn't seen my father since a meeting in *Dothik*, five years ago.

Though it had been five years, my father hadn't changed at all. There were no aging lines on his face. He still wore his pressed Dakkari armor almost daily, his sword always at his side. I knew he still sharpened the blade every night, cleaning it meticulously, though it barely saw use anymore.

"You think that just because you are my son, you can come to *my saruk* to take one of *my* healers?" my father murmured, his voice deceptively soft.

My jaw was clenched tight. For *Lomma's* sake, I kept a tight leash on my temper. Perhaps I was more like my father than I cared to admit.

"Let's not talk of this now," *Lomma* pleaded softly, reaching out to place a soft hand on my father's wrist, right over where his *Vorakkar* cuffs had been. The skin was still lightened where they'd once been. "Eat. Both of you."

My father's gaze never left me, however.

"Get a healer from *Dothik*," my father growled. "I forbid this."

He had four healers going into the frost season. I barely had one. Though *saruks* were larger in population than hordes, four healers still seemed excessive, especially in a time of peace.

The Ghertun under the Dead Mountain had been leashed… for now. Lozza, the Ghertun king, had retreated with his tail tucked between his legs. The Killup were our tentative allies, should tensions begin to rise once more.

My only concern for the frost season were the births of the children and assistance for some of the elder members of my horde, for the frosts were always difficult on them.

"You cannot forbid it," I told my father, lifting my goblet from its place on the wood table.

We were all seated on the floor, our untouched meal spread before us. It was evening. The day had passed by quickly, and already I itched to return to my horde. We had been traveling for two days, and I wanted to be back by the full moon.

"*Neffar?*" my father growled, his temper beginning to snap. *Lomma* squirmed in her seat, her expression one of discomfort. She'd forgotten how often my father and I butted heads. Not a night back home and we were already fighting.

"I don't need your permission, *Sorakkar*," I rasped, holding his eyes.

I had always called him *Sorakkar*. Never *Pattar*. Father.

In this instance, however, my word was meant as a reminder of his rank.

I was a *Vorakkar*. He was not. Not anymore.

As *Vorakkar*, I didn't need his permission to extend an offer to one of his healers. Any members of the *saruk* were free to leave it. Any members were free to make their own decisions.

My father seethed quietly, but I was used to his glare.

I loved my father. I knew he loved me.

But our relationship had never been easy. It never would be, especially now that I was a *Vorakkar*, though it had always been what my father had trained me for.

"Enough," my *lomma* finally snapped, a hint of the *Morakkari* she'd once been shining through. Her eyes were on my father. "Eat. *Now.*"

Leaning forward, I pressed a kiss to her cheek as an apology, and I rose from the table.

The *soliki* had been my home for over fifteen years, ever since my father had settled his horde next to *Drukkar's Sea*. My room was down the back stairwell, closest to the earth, but I had no desire to see it. I would be staying with my *darukkars* and my *pujerak*.

"Sorry, *Lomma*," I murmured. "I need to check on my warriors."

And I need to seek out Maeva, I thought, but I kept that to myself.

If she was not at her *soliki* with her parents, then I had a sneaking suspicion of where I would find her.

The sun had already set when I jogged down the stairs of my parents' *soliki*. It was situated toward the middle of the *saruk,* and I went south, weaving down alleyways and roads that I knew like the back of my hand. *Saruks* would never be as big as *Dothik*, that massive, towering city, but *saruks* were still three or four times larger than hordes. Small cities in their own way, dotted sporadically around Dakkar, if they survived.

And my father's had.

For twenty-five years, it had thrived next to *Drukkar's Sea*.

Returning to the South Lands, however, felt strange. My skin felt tight. The crisp and salt-ridden air—though endlessly familiar and even *comforting*—felt suffocating. I had been a *Vorakkar*, had led my own horde, for nine years now.

Coming back felt like I was jamming myself into a place I no longer fit.

The *saruk* had been my home for most of my life, but not any longer. Not since I left. Now? My horde was my home, no matter where I settled it.

As such, I would be claiming the South Lands for my horde for the coming frost. One morning I had awakened from a dream and I had known. I had known that I would be returning. For nine years, I had purposefully avoided venturing anywhere near here. So when I told Errok, my *pujerak*, to send scouts to the South Lands, to begin laying my claim, he was bewildered.

A part of me knew that Maeva had everything to do with my sudden need to return to the South Lands. A part of me knew that I had avoided *Drukkar's Sea* because of her. My memories of home were so entwined with Maeva. The good and the bad.

When I saw Maeva's *soliki* was dark, I headed west, my booted feet pounding loud on the stone road. I passed a familiar water well and then passed through the secret gate along the far wall.

My chest loosened when the awe-inspiring expanse of *Drukkar's Sea* greeted me. Beautiful and endless. My soul lapped at it hungrily. It fed something inside me that had long been starved, soaking into my very bones, filling my veins.

Perfection.

It always had been.

Boom!

A wave crashed below, and I grinned, that familiar sound comforting like the beating of my own heart. Spray from the sea drifted up, coating my hair and my bare chest.

Winding down the cliff's edge, I found my breaths coming quicker, anticipation rising, *expecting* to see her. In the place I had seen her last.

Her tear-soaked face returned to me, a vivid flash in my mind. Followed by the taste of her, the feel of her warmth underneath my grip and—

The familiar ledge was empty when I stepped onto it.

Maeva wasn't here. Surprised disappointment kept me rooted in place as I turned my gaze to the horizon. Anytime I had sought her out...she'd been here. As if she knew...as if she'd sensed when I needed her.

Boom!

I shut my eyes, feeling the icy spray splatter against my face. Nothing like hot blood. Nothing like the stink of battle. Nothing like the guttural cries of bloodshed and death.

This place was tumultuous and angry and perfect in its own way. It was cold but pure. I didn't hear battle cries. Instead, I heard the tides and the howling wind as it lashed across my flesh.

She isn't here, came the thought.

Maybe she'd never come back.

Maybe she hated me now. She had every right to.

I had only ever wanted to protect her.

Instead, I had betrayed her. I had hurt her more deeply than she'd ever been hurt before that night.

My fists clenched at my sides. My eyes flickered open.

I couldn't stand to be on the ledge. Not if Maeva wasn't here.

When I turned, I froze.

My nostrils flared, my eyes *feasting* on the sight of her like they'd done to *Drukkar's Sea.* Like I'd been starved for her.

Maeva was standing at the top of the cliff, a few paces away. Watching me. The loose white dress she wore was billowing against her ankles, her wild hair whipping across her cheeks, her arms relaxed at her sides.

A goddess in vekkiri *form,* I thought, unable to look away.

And she was furious.

<h1 align="center">Chapter 8</h1>

<hr>

"You have no right," I told Kiran, trying to keep my temper leashed.

I had never been an angry person. Ever since my mother died, however, I needed to work on keeping my emotions in check. It was a constant struggle, every day.

Sometimes it was better to not feel anything at all.

Yet sometimes all I wanted to do was scream until my throat was raw.

He was striding up the hill since I refused to go down to him. I knew I'd find him there. On that ledge. In *our* place.

"No right to do what, *seffi?*" he asked slowly as he approached, his voice carrying easily over the wind, as if even the wind bent its will to him.

To be here.

To come back.

To call me seffi *and act like nothing has changed.*

To make me remember how much I loved you.

To make me remember how much you hurt me.

But in this particular instance, I was speaking of one thing only.

Earlier this evening, long after the *mokkira* successfully closed the wounded warrior's arm, he had taken me into the brewing room and told me his decision in private.

"I have chosen Nebrik to take my place as *mokkira* for the *saruk*," he'd said.

A part of me had feared and perhaps had always known that this would be the outcome. Nebrik was a couple years younger than I was. But I had worked with the *mokkira* longer, had put in the time. My blood. My passion. I had given him everything.

Since Nebrik was younger, it was only logical that he would remain the *mokkira* for the rest of his working days. Years and years.

And me...I'd only ever be a *kerisa*, a healer, bending myself to Nebrik's orders and will. My accomplishments would never manifest into what my goal had always been: *mokkira* of the Okkili *saruk*.

I had dreamed of it for years. Since I had first helped the *mokkira* deliver the child of the seamstress.

And maybe it was because I was human, that I felt I had something to prove. Just because I was human, I could be the most accomplished and experienced healer in one of the most successful outposts on Dakkar.

That had been what I wanted.

That had been what I'd promised my mother and my father.

That I would bring the honor and privilege of the *mokkira* title to our family. Because they had given so much to *me*.

So, earlier this evening, when the *mokkira* had told me his decision, I had asked, "What did I do wrong?"

I hadn't cried since we buried *Lomma*. But I had been on the verge of it then.

The *mokkira* had looked at me carefully, studying me in that particular way of his that always made me feel like I was a wound he was trying to mend.

"The *Vorakkar* spoke to me in private earlier. He made it clear to me that *you* were his choice," he'd admitted quietly. "He doesn't want Nebrik. Or Kilen. He wants you."

"I haven't said I'll take the title," I'd argued. "I don't want it! I want to be *mokkira* of *our saruk.*"

But the *mokkira* had turned from me, discomfort in his features. "I have already made my decision, Maeva. And I know better than to interfere with a *Vorakkar's* will."

It felt like heartbreak all over again.

Everything I'd worked toward, gone in a moment with a few spare words from a *Vorakkar.*

Because it was what *he* wanted.

It had always been about what *he* wanted.

Never about what *I* wanted.

"What did you tell the *mokkira?*" I asked now, my heart thundering in my chest when he came to a stop within arm's reach. The last time I'd been this close to him...I'd been kissing him. Nine years ago. In this very place. Before he'd turned from me in disgust.

Everything about Kiran was rigid and unyielding. Strong. He loomed over me now, his jaw tight, his eyes hard as he studied me. He'd even seemed to grow taller since I last saw him—or perhaps I'd simply *forgotten.* Forgotten him.

"I told him what you already know," Kiran replied, his eyes darting back and forth between my own before he frowned. I watched as his eyes trailed to my lips then downward.

What was he looking for?

"Thanks to you," I breathed, shaking though I tried to make sure he wouldn't see by taking a step away, "the *mokkira* just gave his title to Nebrik. Because *you* told him to release me from the *saruk.*"

"Not in those words explicitly."

"You *implied* them," I said, gritting my jaw so tight I was surprised I didn't break it. "I've worked *so* hard for all these years because that title was to be *mine.* Then you returned. And in a few moments, you took everything."

Again.

That word rang through my mind, and by the way Kiran stiffened, I knew he'd thought it too.

"*Seffi,* I—"

"You will call me *kerisa,*" I said, valiantly trying to keep the bite out of the words. "Nothing more."

His expression darkened considerably.

My words were like a slap in his face, judging from that expression, but I needed to make this clear to him. I wasn't the same girl that had once worshipped the ground he walked on. I'd learned my lesson long ago when it came to him.

That lesson?

Stay far away.

Even still, he was a *Vorakkar.*

Had I been anyone else, surely he would have taken my head for speaking to him in such a manner. I wondered if *anyone* had spoken to him this way in his entire lifetime.

I could see the moment that the *Vorakkar* emerged. His eyes were like glacial chips of ice, the ice that formed in *Drukkar's Sea* during the frost.

"*Kerisa,*" he rasped, making the word somehow seem mocking yet polite, "consider this my formal offer, then. Since you will not be *mokkira* of the Okkili *saruk,* I wish for you to be *mokkira* of the Okkili *vorak.*"

"Through the frost," I reminded him, ignoring the way my belly dipped when he said "the Okkili *vorak.*" The horde of Okkili. How often had I envisioned that title—his title— attached to my own name? "Until you find another from *Dothik.*"

"You can stay as long as you wish. The title is yours until you relinquish it."

Something shifted in my chest at the words. Words that were spoken low and quiet. Words spoken with those golden eyes locked onto mine. Eyes that were so familiar to me I had the strange sense we'd gone back in time, to when we were young.

It had been so easy to love him back then. So why did I feel something stirring in my breast, like—

Nik.

Desperately, I slammed my mind shut on the thought, turning away from him, my arms wrapping around my midsection as I looked out at *Drukkar's Sea.*

He'd always been dangerous to me, hadn't he? Why was I so vulnerable to Kiran of Rath Okkili? Why had I always been?

"You have every right to reject my offer," came his voice. I sensed him stepping into place beside me, so close that I felt his bare, warm arm brush mine. My eyes almost closed at it did, as that small connection sizzled through my blood. His gaze was on the darkened horizon, however. "You have every right to hate me. To be angry with me."

Because he'd broken my heart?

Because he'd turned his back on me and never looked back?

Because he'd never even said goodbye?

Because he hadn't even returned when my mother died, to pay his respects to my family, to my mother who had always treated him like a son?

Slowly, I took in a deep, steadying breath through my nostrils.

I could forgive him for breaking my heart. But I couldn't forgive him for all the rest. He had shown me just how little he truly cared for me.

I only needed to remember that.

Blowing out a small breath, I felt strength return, unyielding and wonderful. I felt my heart harden, the rapid beat of it turning slow. I felt that comforting calmness descend over my mind as I looked out over *Drukkar's Sea*.

Was this what he'd always sought when he'd looked out over the horizon? This sense of power? This sense of peace?

Kiran didn't have the power to hurt me.

Never again.

Not unless I gave it to him.

And I knew I never would.

"I know you, Maeva," came his voice. My name on his lips made me swallow hard. "And I know that a simple title would never be enough for you. You are not a *kerisa* because you want to be *mokkira*. You are a healer because you want to help. You want to take away pain because you can. You feel joy when you help bring new life into this world, and you feel sorrow when you help someone leave it. I know your abilities. I know your skill. I have seen it since we were young. I've witnessed it first-hand, and I know the *mokkira* trained you well. And he is a fool to let you leave so easily, without a fight."

Because he'd already chosen Nebrik and you know it, I told myself.

Kiran offering me the *mokkira* title of his horde only assuaged my mentor's guilt. He'd probably been relieved when Kiran spoke with him...because it had made his decision easier.

When I turned to look at him, I was proud that I felt nothing. No throbbing aches. No pricking of desire. No pitiful little flutters of my treacherous heart.

Maybe I was finally immune to him, I mused, relieved.

"You heal because it is your purpose in this life, because it is your passion, because you cannot imagine doing anything else," he told me, his voice sure. I hated that he knew me so well. That he knew my past like it was inked into the back of his hand. Because he had been very much a part of it. "And there are Dakkari and humans alike in my horde that need help for the coming frost. Don't make this decision based on *us*."

"And if I reject your offer?" I asked quietly, wanting nothing more than to do just that. "There is still time to send for a healer from *Dothik* for your horde."

"There is," he agreed. His eyes seemed to warm, some of that *Vorakkar* chill thawing when he met my gaze. "But Kakkari guided me back home for a reason. I don't believe I'll need to send a *thesper* to *Dothik*. Do you, *rei mokkira?*"

Damn him, I thought, my jaw setting, swallowing *hard.*

My *mokkira,* he'd called me.

"Think it over," he said gruffly, crossing his arms over his wide chest. "I must return to the horde in two days."

Two days?

"This human that's pregnant..." I began.

"Her mate is Dakkari," he said, his tone rough. "Our first hybrid pregnancy in the horde. She will need help, and you have the experience."

My breath left my lungs, my eyes widening. "Not with that."

"Then you will learn."

Always so arrogant. Always so confident.

Perhaps Kiran hadn't changed much after all.

He was asking me to leave my home for a season. The only home I'd ever known. He was asking me to leave my family behind. My father, my sister, *Rasik.*

I couldn't. Surely, I couldn't.

I had never been apart from them.

Then my treacherous mind whispered, *The horde will still be in the South Lands. Not far away. And it is only for the frost, no matter what he says.*

Besides, I'd been ready to leave my family nine years ago, hadn't I? When Kiran asked me to join his horde? I'd been all too eager to leave everything behind for him.

I stiffened, remembering how foolish I'd been.

This was different.

Wasn't it?

Was I really going to leave home, to live at the Rath Okkili horde, whose *Vorakkar* I couldn't stand to look at, whose knowing gaze reminded me of my self-disgust and shame, emotions that had taken me *years* to rid myself of? Was I really going to leave behind everything I'd known to live in a *horde*, on the wildlands?

I feared I already knew.

Mokkira.

It was everything I'd ever wanted, wasn't it?

"I've missed you, *seffi*."

His voice came quietly next to me, like a whisper in my ear. Vulnerable words I felt deep in my belly, like an ache that had never healed.

My fingers twitched at my sides, and I didn't dare meet his gaze. My cheeks felt warm with anger. Perhaps fear and trepidation as well.

"I told you not to call me that," I said, keeping my tone even. After taking a deep breath, I told him, "You can call me *Mokkira* now. For that is all I'll be to you. And only through the frost. Afterward, I'll be returning home."

The *mokkira* of Rath Okkili.

"My father is on a hunt right now. I won't leave until he returns. I won't leave without saying goodbye," I said, my lips pressing together. I prayed he didn't hear the bitterness in my words.

I turned from him, turning my back on *Drukkar's Sea*, my heart heavy with my decision because I would have to speak with Laru.

"There is time for goodbyes, *rei mokkira*," came his delayed reply, spoken when I was already halfway up the cliff's path. "*I must leave in two days, but once the horde is settled in the South Lands, I will send a darukkar for you.*"

"How long do I have?" I asked, relieved, though I didn't turn back to him.

"A week. Maybe more. Then you will join my horde."

"For the frost," I reminded him. "The cold season only."

His hesitation was noticeable.

"*Lysi, kalles,*" he finally said, his voice guttural. "For the frost."

Kakkari help me.

What have I done?

CHAPTER 9

Eleven years ago...

"Let's do the top cliff right now," Maeva suggested. "You promised you'd take me last time you were home. Then you left. Don't think I forgot—I've been waiting almost a year now."

My lips pressed together, already shaking my head. "*Nik.* That's not a good idea."

"Why not?" she demanded, her lips curling in the smile that she *knew* would soften my resolve. "It didn't look so high when I watched you and Safir jump."

"Maeva, *nik*," I told her, keeping my voice firm though I felt amusement threading through my chest at her stubbornness. Being in her presence...it made me feel light and unburdened. It made me forget the hardship and brutality and coldness of *Dothik*. For a little while, at least. "Your *lomma* would have my head if she knew I let you jump from that cliff, *Rukkar* or not. Even Dakkari get injured jumping from there."

That was the wrong thing to say. As soon as the words left my lips, I straightened, realizing it.

Maeva's jaw ticked. She leaned toward me as a breeze from the sea tousled her wild hair about. Briefly, my eyes dropped to her breasts, straining against the material of her white bandeau, before I forced myself to look away, ignoring the sudden, surprising heat in my belly.

I'd returned to the *saruk* for a brief reprieve just two days earlier, but soon, I would need to leave again. Gone for another year. Another year before I would see my home, before I would look upon *Drukkar's Sea*, before I would see my family, before I would see my *seffi* again.

Whenever I returned, I always had the strangest fear that nothing would be the same. With my friends, with my family, with Maeva. In some ways, that fear had begun to manifest. Already I could feel the friends I'd grown up with beginning to shy away from my hardening gaze. Beginning to look at me like the *Vorakkar* I was destined to be. Already I could feel the tension between my father and me growing, could feel my *lomma's* hands linger whenever she embraced me, as if she knew our time together was drawing closed.

But I should never have feared that things with Maeva would change. To outsiders, our friendship might look strange. But it was unwavering and pure. She never looked at me any differently when I returned, though every time I did, I was covered in more scars and it took me longer to smile and laugh.

We always slipped back into how things had been. Like I had never left. Effortlessly. As easy as breathing, I sometimes mused.

Maeva was scowling at me now, the slashes of hair on her brows furrowing. She was a proud little thing. And she didn't like anyone telling her she couldn't do something...especially if it was because she was human.

"Maeva," I growled, watching her stand. "I said *nik*."

But she was already darting up the hill, quick and light on her bare feet, toward the highest cliff that the Dakkari youth used for the most exhilarating of jumps into *Drukkar's Sea* below.

And the most dangerous.

"*Vok*," I cursed, already jumping up from the place where we'd been sitting along the cliffside and sprinting after her. "*Maeva!*"

With dread, I watched her reach the grassy flattened dip of the dark cliff edge, watched her peer over it. The drop into the sea was far. There was one rock, underneath the water on the left side, that would kill her if she jumped toward it. And a human...*vok*, her skin was thin, her bones fragile. She might—

With one last challenging glance at me, Maeva backed up several paces and then sprinted forward.

"*Maeva, nik!*" I roared, watching her feet leave the ground as she jumped, her delighted cry filling that hot afternoon, before she disappeared from sight.

Fear—icy, horrible, sickening fear—like I'd never known shivered up my spine as I sprinted to the cliff's edge. I didn't hesitate. I didn't even take off my boots as I followed after her, diving off the edge, seeing a blue splash below as I did.

The drop was far. The warm air lashed at my cheeks, my stomach dropping, the wind whipping my hair behind me. At any other time, it would be thrilling. Now all I could do was pray to Kakkari that Maeva wasn't injured from the jump.

The impact with the shimmering sea stole my breath. Underneath the water, it was pitch black as I frantically searched for Maeva. When I surfaced, I called out for her, filling my desperate lungs with air as my wild eyes scanned the sea.

I saw her dark head bobbing with the waves, and profound relief went through me. I swam the short distance to her. She was treading water very near the rock that I feared.

She saw me, and her eyes went wide at whatever thunderous expression was across my face. That was when I saw the blood. Red blood, dripping into the sea—a small gash just underneath her bottom lip.

"You foolish creature," I seethed when I reached her, snagging her around the waist and tugging her toward the shore. "You see that?"

I pointed at the tip of the rock jutting from the sea mere feet from where we were when the waves retreated.

Her breath left her when she saw it.

"If you had hit that—"

I didn't even finish that sentence. I was furious with her as I swam us toward the shore, my booted feet heavy under the water, my jaw ticking.

"I—I'm sorry, Kiran," she murmured, helping me kick as more blood poured from her chin, clouding the blue water. "I just wanted—"

"I know what you wanted," I growled. "But you just took years off my life trying to prove something that *doesn't vokking matter.*"

When it was shallow enough to stand, I carried her up the shore, cradled in my arms, as light as a *nekkisau.* I deposited her on the gray sand, leaning her back against one of the boulders that dotted the small shore. It was an enclosed beach, one that disappeared when the tides came in. Just another reason why that particular cliff jump was so dangerous...because this beach was the only way back up toward the *saruk* for miles.

I was shaking, I was so furious. I was shaking, I was so relieved.

Her eyes were watery with tears when they met mine, making me pause, making some of my hot anger melt away... because I couldn't stand to see Maeva cry. Red blood was dripping down her chin in a steady stream now that the sea wasn't washing it away.

"Let me see," I rasped, tilting her face up. Her wide, swirling eyes—all brown and green and golden—tilted up at the corners, and they met mine as my fingers curled under her soft, round chin. "Does it hurt?"

The gash was small but deep.

"It stings a little. Is it bad?"

"You are the healer, not I," I grumbled, knowing how much she haunted the *mokkira's soliki*, though he had not agreed to take her on as an apprentice yet. "What did you hit it on?"

Maeva hesitated. "A wave pushed me into the rock."

A curse left my lips, my anger bursting back to life.

"You will never make that jump again, do you understand me?" I growled.

Even though I was scolding her, her chin lifted slightly. "Were you worried for me?"

"*Lysi!*"

"I was only trying to hold you to your promise," she argued. "Maybe you should have taken me when you said you would."

Disbelief went through me, my eyes widening.

"Impossible creature!" I snapped out, wanting to both shake some sense into her and squeeze her to my chest. "You make me crazed!"

Surprise lit up her eyes. And even though she had blood trailing down her chin, dripping down her neck and across her banded breasts, she grinned.

It was *that* smile. The one she knew I couldn't stay angry at.

Almost shy. Almost sweet.

Already I felt my anger waver.

"Damn you, *seffi*," I rasped. "*Damn you.*"

Her grin widened. She took my hand, her thumb stroking a scar on the back of it, making me shiver. We were both soaked to the bone, but the hot breeze was already threading through our hair, drying our flesh.

"Do you forgive me, Kiran?" she asked quietly.

My jaw clenched, but I felt myself softening toward her. I was weak. Especially when it came to her.

"Only if you promise never to jump from that cliff again," I grumbled, my shoulders loosening. "Promise me, Maeva."

"I promise," she whispered, and I felt myself relax. Because my *seffi* always kept her promises. No matter what. I wouldn't have to worry about her jumping from the cliff again, especially when I returned to *Dothik* in a few short days.

Our eyes connected and held.

Long moments passed as we regarded one another, alone on that stretch of beach that would soon disappear. Slowly, my gaze dropped to her lips. The bottom one was red with her blood.

When I noticed her breath start to come quicker, I stood, discomfort threading through me as I tried to ignore the way my heart had begun to thunder anew, as I tried to ignore the heat in my own blood and the way my trews had begun to tighten. Especially when I noticed her hard nipples pressed against her white bandeau, which clung to the fullness of her breasts.

This is Maeva, I reminded myself.

"Come," I rasped, pulling her up, swallowing, shifting my gaze away. "The *mokkira* needs to tend to your wound."

That brought her up short.

"*Nik,*" she breathed. "Don't bring me to him, Kiran. Please —I couldn't bear it. Especially since he just rejected me as his apprentice again."

"This is your punishment," I growled. "Your pride might be bruised, but at least you'll be healed."

Her shoulders sagged.

"Very well," she grumbled, letting me take her small hand as I led her to the steep, rocky path that would lead us back to the *saruk.*

And despite the circumstances, I felt my lips twitch.

Because these days, only Maeva ever made me smile.

CHAPTER 10

The familiar *soliki* met me as I wound up a small alley from the main stretch of road. The road cut through my father's *saruk*, running from the entrance gate all the way to the edge of the cliff to the walls that protected the back buildings from the sea spray.

It was night. Late. There was a warm glow from inside the *soliki*, illuminating the windows. I heard her laughter—husky and achingly familiar—before I saw her appear in the front window, which I knew was next to a stretch of cabinets.

Maeva was smiling, but when she looked up and caught sight of me standing outside, shifting from one foot to the other, that smile slowly died. Her brow pulled down, her white little teeth disappearing from view.

She said something over her shoulder, unhooked her fur by the door, and came out to meet me. She tugged the door firmly shut behind her—though I thought I caught sight of a child, his tail shifting just out of view.

Maeva's *soliki* was one of the few with stairs that led down to the road. The *solikis* that lay to the south were built into the cliff that abutted the *saruk*, so the stairs were necessary.

She came down those stairs now, her bare feet rasping over

the stone, as she tugged her fur shawl tighter around her shoulders.

"What do you need?" she asked, her voice quiet.

Seeing the child had left me...surprisingly shaken. I peered at her now and forced myself to ask, "Whose child is that?"

Surprise flashed over her face. Discomfort threaded through me, an ache burning deep in my belly, as I waited for her answer. I had never envisioned Maeva with a mate. After everything, I had never given it any thought.

But why hadn't I? Of course it was a very likely possibility. It had been nine years since I last saw her. She wasn't a girl anymore, and I had known, even when we were younger, that there were males in the *saruk* whose gazes lingered on her. Back then, I'd done everything I could to scare them off, to protect her. After I left, however...

Vok.

"The child is Laru's son," Maeva finally said.

The relief I felt should have frightened me. The relief left me, perhaps, even more shaken than how I'd felt seeing the child.

I knew it wouldn't show, however. All Maeva would see was an impassive, hardened expression.

Then again, this was Maeva. She'd always been able to read me better than anyone.

"She lives here?"

"Her mate is out hunting—in the same party as my father," Maeva told me, her gaze sliding past me, her arms tightening around her body when a shiver racked through her. The days were warm, but the nights were beginning to *bite*, another sure sign the frost was approaching soon.

"I've come to pay my respects to your *lomma*," I rasped, not liking the uncertainty that was threading through me...or the fact that she wouldn't meet my eyes.

Her gaze flashed up to mine right then, however—the anger in it cutting and surprising.

Then that anger was gone. As quickly as it'd come. Her eyes dropped away again, and she stepped down from the stairs onto the main road where I was standing.

"It's a little late for that, *Vorakkar*," she murmured. The way she said my title twisted in my belly. My brow furrowed. "Why are you really here?"

I tried to read her, but she wouldn't meet my gaze again. Without thought, my hand reached out to touch her face, to tilt it back so I *could* see it, but she flinched away so quickly I froze.

We stood there as heavy silence stretched between us. In the *soliki* I could hear the child squealing with laughter.

Why am I really here? I thought, repeating her question in my mind.

My tail flicked across the ground restlessly, an anxious tell I'd never been able to quiet.

Because the years have felt endlessly long without you.

That was the simple answer that came to mind. It was an answer, however, that I could not voice. It was an answer that surprised me...but didn't. I felt the ache of it thread through my veins, like it was one long cord that was barely tying me together.

"Look at me," I rasped. When she still wouldn't, I said a word I thought I had forgotten. "*Hanniva*, Maeva."

Please, I'd pleaded.

Maybe it was her surprise that finally drew her gaze to me. But I captured her eyes and I held them, stepping closer.

"We were friends once, Maeva. Can we not be again?"

A *Vorakkar* didn't have friends, however. Not when my days were filled with thoughts of seasons and Ghertun and if our stores would feed my horde through the frost and the *Dothikkar's* ever-changing whims in *Dothik*. The idea of friendship now seemed laughable—especially the type of easy, wonderful friendship Maeva and I had once shared.

"And you showed me just how much you valued that friendship" was what Maeva replied. Even she seemed surprise by the bitterness in her tone.

I deserved her ire, however. I deserved her anger. Nine years ago, I'd left as quickly as I'd arrived. I'd been cruel to her. I'd rejected her. I'd hurt her.

I knew all this. When I remembered her, lying in bed at night, the memory of her tear-stained face haunted me. How many times had I readied my *pyroki* in the thick of night? How many times had I been tempted to ride to the South Lands, to seek her out and make amends to the only true friend I'd ever had?

In the end, I'd always gone back to my *voliki*, back to my bed. I'd steered clear of the South Lands, of *Drukkar's Sea* for a cowardly, shameful reason.

To anyone, nine years was a long time. As *Vorakkar*, nine years seemed like a lifetime.

And now? I didn't recognize the human female in front of me anymore. We were strangers now, tied together by endless memories of who we used to be.

So why do I ache when I look at her? I wondered, gritting my jaw. *Why does it feel so* right *to look at her?*

Because you've always known, came that familiar, nagging whisper in the back of my mind. *Because you've always known and you've tried to fight it all these years.*

I blew out a sharp breath.

"Can this not be repaired between us, Maeva?" I asked quietly.

"*Nik,* Kiran," she said, lifting her chin instead of shying away again. She'd always been a study in dualities. A study in opposites. It was what had drawn me to her in the first place. "I

—I don't think it can. I can't go back. I'm not that person anymore. I'm sure you aren't either."

I'd expected her answer. It still hurt to hear it.

"It's best if we try to forget," she whispered, the words almost lost in the sudden breeze that whipped between us. "Especially if I will be among your horde."

I didn't want to forget. Which made a hypocrite out of me. All I'd done the last nine years had been to try to crush that aching place inside me where Maeva always lived.

When I looked back up at her *soliki*, I saw Laru's child peering at us from the window. A male, his eyes yellow and glowing. Immediately, I knew who the father was. *Nevir.* Once, we'd been friends. We'd sparred together at the training grounds often. I saw Nevir's mischievous expression in his son's face.

Life at the *saruk* had gone on. Suddenly, I felt like an outsider in the place I'd once called home.

My horde is my home now, I knew. *And already I've been away too long.*

With that thought in mind, I turned back to Maeva.

"I leave in the morning. At first light," I told her, my voice hardening. Cold. Detached. Everything that I was used to feeling. "I will send for you in the coming weeks, once my horde is settled in the South Lands."

With that, I left.

She wanted to forget?

For the first time in nine years...I wasn't certain I wanted to anymore.

Laru was watching me when I came through the door, combing through Rasik's growing hair. The little male, though he'd just been bounding with energy before I met with Kiran, was now growing tired, his eyelids heavy. They grew even heavier when his mother began to comb through the little tuft of hair sprouting from the tip of his tail.

Affection flooded my chest as I drank in his sweet, sleepy face.

"Was that..." Laru began quietly, regarding me carefully. "Was that the *Vorakkar*?"

I never knew if Kiran had ever told Laru his given name. Though I'd caught them kissing when Laru had come of age— before Nevir had begun to court her—I never knew the extent of their relationship.

I'd never asked. For good reason. And we'd...we'd simply never spoken of it. Laru had known my feelings for Kiran back then. Once she saw how upset I'd been about their kiss, she'd apologized.

But that had been the last we'd spoken of Kiran. We never even spoke of that night, when she'd found me on the cliff's edge with my dress on backward, with tears streaming down my face and my heart flayed wide open. She'd comforted me, then brought me to my mother, who had comforted me more.

"*Lysi*," I rasped, shrugging off my furs and hanging them by the door. It was warm inside our *soliki*. The fire had been roaring since sundown. As soon as the sun set, the temperature plummeted dramatically.

"What did he want?"

I was careful not to meet her gaze. Instead, I went to my cabinets, in need of a distraction. Inside, there were three rows of carefully organized and labelled vials. All different colors—some clear, some vivid purple—all with different uses. Below the last shelf, I saw the frayed pages of my journal, the one my mother had made me—carefully crafted from hide and strained pulp from fallen trees in the *Isida* Forest.

Running my fingers over the soft brown hide, I murmured, "He's leaving in the morning. He told me he'll send for me soon, after *Pattar* returns from his hunt."

Laru was silent. When I'd broken the news to her last night, after I'd spoken with Kiran at our old private place by the sea, she'd been...quiet. She hadn't broken down into tears, which I had expected of her, given her pregnancy. She hadn't begged me to stay, though I knew she never would. She'd simply said, *Be careful.*

Now? I could sense the inevitable was about to happen.

So, I wasn't surprised when Laru said, "The *Vorakkar* has always held power over you, Maeva."

"Power I willingly gave him," I replied, never taking my eyes from my vials. My gaze was frantic over them, and my hand shook when I reached forward to take Laru's sickness tonic out from its place. I would need to make more for her before I left. I needed to do so many things before I left.

But I was...excited?

I'd never left the *saruk*. Whatever my life had been before I was discovered by the Dakkari hunting party, I would never know. But I would be returning to the wildlands, and there was no denying the anticipation I felt at that knowledge.

"I saw how much he hurt you," Laru said, her voice nothing more than a whisper. When I took a deep breath and turned, I saw Rasik was sleeping on her lap, though she continued to brush his hair. "Everyone did."

My lips pressed together, remembering my shame. Remembering the way the members of the *saruk* had whispered or tittered or looked at me with pity whenever I passed them. My love for Kiran had perhaps been...rather obvious. His rejection of me had been even more obvious.

Then *Lomma* had died.

Then everyone had looked at my family and me with pity.

It had taken a long time for them to look at us any differently. There were still those in the *saruk*—like Nebrik—who would always remember Kiran's rejection. He had been *Rukkar* to the *saruk*. Now he was a *Vorakkar*. That stamp of rejection would be with me always.

"I worry he can hurt you again," Laru confessed.

I sighed. Then I went to her, sitting on the floor cushions next to our blazing fire basin. I watched the shadows flicker over her face, saw the worry in her eyes.

Taking her spare hand, I squeezed softly.

"The *Vorakkar* will never hurt me again," I promised her. I felt those words reverberate in my bones, as if I had cast a spell over myself, as if Kakkari had given me power over those words to make them true. "He told me once that people only have power over you if you let them. I learned my lesson long ago. I had given him too much power over me because I loved him."

I took a small, deep breath, feeling a sudden pang of sadness for the hopeful, foolish girl I'd been back then.

"But I don't love him anymore," I told her. "And I know I can never love him again. I simply don't have the openness to. Not after what he did. Not after how he left. Not after *Lomma.*"

Laru's brow furrowed. "What about *Lomma*?"

I had never told her.

I swallowed and confessed, "I wrote to him after she died."

"You did?" Laru gasped. "What did you say?"

"I sent the letter by *thesper* to his horde, thinking at the time that he would want to pay his respects to her for the burial. Because she loved him, and I knew he was very fond of her as well."

"This was like a second home to him," Laru commented.

"*Lysi*," I whispered. How many times had Kiran been inside this *soliki*? How many times had he taken his meals with us, laughed with us? How many times had he seemed so...*carefree* with us? He hadn't been *Rukkar* in these walls. He'd been...*ours*. "I told him that she died, that we would wait to bury her until I heard from him or until he could return to the *saruk*."

"He never came."

I shook my head. "I thought the *thesper* might have been lost, so I begged the *Arakkari* to send him a letter as well. She must've taken pity on me because she did. She told me a week later that he wouldn't be returning to the *saruk* for *Lomma's* burial. That he sent his *sympathies* to us all."

My lips twisted with that word.

"I realized then that I didn't truly know him anymore. The friend I knew would've come. He would've been there for us... for me," I said quietly, my eyes catching on Rasik's sleeping face. A long breath escaped my nostrils, and I gave my sister a half smile that didn't quite reach my eyes. "He was never going to come home, even though I asked him to. Begged him to. The moment he left here...it was a death in itself. I grieved two beings that I loved when *Lomma* died, not just one. I've accepted that. And I've moved on."

Because I had to.

"I'm different now too," I assured her. "Nine years ago, I was wishing that I'd never met him. Now, I'm willingly going to his horde for the frost. I'm stronger than I was before. And I recognize the *Rukkar* for what he is now...a *Vorakkar*. A *Vorakkar* who will only ever look out for himself and his horde. I'm not going into this blind, so don't worry for me, Laru. I know what I'm doing, and I'm not afraid."

Well, maybe that wasn't entirely true. I wasn't afraid of Kiran. But I was afraid to leave the only home I'd ever truly known. To leave my loved ones, my family, the familiarity of the *saruk*.

Laru released a long breath. Her eyes flitted down to Rasik in her lap, her gaze softening, the space between her brows smoothing the longer she looked at her son.

"You say that you no longer have the openness to love him anymore," Laru whispered, running her hand through Rasik's dark hair, trailing her fingertips over his soft cheek, a cheek I had pressed numerous kisses to tonight as he squealed in delight. "But I wonder if you have the openness to love anyone anymore...the way you loved him."

I stiffened.

When Laru met my eyes, I saw hers were glistening with tears.

"Since he left, since *Lomma* died, you've thrown yourself into your work so completely that it consumes you," Laru commented. "And I know that you love being a *kerisa*. But at what cost? You shied away from males in our *saruk* attempting to court you. You shied away from letting anyone in. You shied away from being vulnerable, and you put these walls up around you that no one could possibly hope to breach."

I frowned, feeling my throat tighten.

"And you always talked of having a family. A mate. Children of your own," Laru continued, sniffling, wiping at some tears that had escaped. "We all know that's possible now. That humans are *Morakkari* now, that they bear their *Vorakkar* children. Doesn't that make you want to build a family of your own? Knowing it's possible?"

Laru couldn't understand. She would never understand what it was like growing up in a Dakkari *saruk* as a human, being bullied and belittled because of it. Never knowing if I could bear offspring of my own. That future seemed laughable to me now.

"I found a new purpose," I told her. "I don't only want to be someone's wife, Laru."

I felt a pang of guilt when I saw her small flinch. I hadn't meant for it to sound that way.

"I don't want that anymore at all. I want something else," I said softly. "I want my work to *mean* something. And at the horde...it just might. If only for a little while, I can help."

Laru squeezed my hand, running the back of her thumb across my palm.

"All I want is your happiness, Maeva," she whispered. "But I worry about you sometimes. I worry that you close yourself off too much."

I gave her a soft smile I didn't feel.

"Don't worry about me," I said gently. Trying to lighten the mood, I said, "Worry about how you will get your blue medicine in the mornings when I'm gone."

Laru groaned, some of the tension between us broken.

And even though the rest of the night passed in peace, that night when I lay in bed, Laru's words and fears kept returning to me.

I wondered if what she'd said was true...if I *could* love a male like I'd loved Kiran. Ever since he left, I'd never given another thought to love. It seemed like such a ridiculous thing in the aftermath of my mother's death and after the *mokkira* had finally decided to take me as one of his apprentices.

In the darkness of my room, with my own thoughts, I could admit that I felt lonely most of the time. Even in the presence of my family, I felt lonely. I'd accepted that it would be a fact of life.

During the day, I masked that loneliness with my work. At night, it was harder to hide from.

Turning over in my bed, I wondered, for the first time, what it would feel like to have my love returned by a male.

I wondered if it was what I needed to not feel so alone anymore.

A week after my father and Nevir returned from their hunt, a week after Laru and Rasik returned to their own *soliki* and it was just my father and me once more, a small group of horde warriors returned to the *saruk* for me.

I had been expecting them, had been watching for them, my satchels long packed with supplies that would see me through the frost, waiting by the door.

It was time.

What I hadn't expected was for Kiran to be among them.

CHAPTER 12

Before the sun had even risen, I was waiting for Maeva near the *pyroki* enclosure, watching intently for her familiar figure striding down the main road.

A crisp breeze ruffled the furs that were draped over my shoulders, prickling my scalp. I turned my attention north, looking past the *saruk's* low gates, toward the direction of the *Isida* Forest.

My fist tightened on my *pyroki's* reins, making Roon shift under me. He was nervous about something. All the *pyrokis* seemed to be, which was part of the reason why I'd returned to my father's *saruk* only a little over a week since I'd left. My horde had laid claim to the South Lands for the season, and no sooner had the first *volikis* been erected, I'd left to come here. Unfathomable. I needed to be with my horde, especially in the first week of being in a new territory.

But I'd been worried. I'd received a report from the *Vorakkar* of Rath Kitala—his *thesper* had found us on the journey to the South Lands—who had claimed part of the East Lands for the frost. His letter had been...disturbing.

As I peered at the walls of my father's *saruk*, waiting for

Maeva, I thought that he should build his walls higher. Make them stronger.

I loosened the reins, stroking my *pyroki's* hard, scaled neck. "We will be home soon," I assured him.

Roon tossed his neck, as if he accepted my promise.

Truthfully, I had returned to the *saruk* for two reasons. One was to speak with my father, to tell him about the contents of Rath Kitala's letter to me, to make sure he began to prepare. Because I had no idea what the letter meant. But there were already stirrings across the land, stirrings we had all begun to feel. The *polkunu* we'd killed so far to the south should've been the first sign that something was amiss.

But according to Rath Kitala, the stirrings had started months ago. So far south, we were just beginning to feel its effects.

My second reason was to escort Maeva to my horde personally. I'd brought four of my best *darukkars*—who were waiting outside the *saruk's* gates—but I hadn't trusted anyone else to see to Maeva's safety. Only I could ensure it. I'd left Errok, my *pujerak*, back with the horde, which was only a day's ride away. If we left soon and didn't stop to rest, we could reach my horde in the early hours of morning.

My ears perked when I heard the soft rasp of footsteps funneling down the main road.

Roon made a chittering little sound in his throat and, without my command, trotted forward. Maeva's smile was soft as she strode the rest of the way, reaching out her palms to stroke Roon's snout.

"How is my favorite *pyroki*?" she whispered.

She hadn't seen Roon when I'd been at the *saruk* last. And Roon considered Maeva just as much his master as he did me, a fact that I had never quite had the heart to break from him.

Maeva had named him, after all. When Roon had been a

newborn, he made long yawning sounds that emulated his namesake.

It had been years since she'd last seen him.

But Roon had remembered her. Of course he did.

Maeva's eyes darted up to mine. I swallowed, dismounting, my booted feet hitting the road hard.

"You said your goodbyes to your family?" I asked quietly. There wasn't a soul awake in the *saruk*, not even the *mrikro*, the *pyroki* master.

"*Lysi*," she whispered.

"They didn't want to see you off?" I asked, quirking a brow in surprise. Maeva had always been especially close with her family.

"I suspect my father didn't want to cry in front of you and your *darukkars*," she told me.

A sharp huff of amusement escaped my nostrils, and I turned to regard her. The teasing comment took me by surprise, reminding me so much of the Maeva I used to know.

I had hoped to meet with her family, but I pushed back my disappointment. The last time I'd seen them, they—her father, especially—had been filled with tension and anger.

Her gaze immediately darted back to Roon, as if she was surprised she'd said it as well.

"I said my goodbyes last night," she said after a lengthy, heavy silence. "I'm ready."

With that, she made to venture toward the *pyroki* enclosure, but I snagged her hand.

Maeva's breath hitched when I pulled her back to me. My jaw tensed, feeling the warmth and softness of her skin. In the darkness, I saw the glassy reflection in her questioning gaze as she tugged her hand from my grip, stepping back to put space between us.

"You will ride with me," I told her, ignoring the way that

simple familiar touch had...shaken me. My palm tingled from it. "There is no need to take a *pyroki*."

"*Neffar?*" she asked. "There's no need for me to ride with you. I'm perfectly capable of riding alone. You know that."

"This has nothing to do with your experience riding. I know you do it well," I told her, taking the two travel sacks from her grip to attach it to Roon's side harness. "Is this all you need?"

Her gaze went to the travel sacks, watching as I clipped them onto Roon's side. "I don't want to ride with you."

"Why not?" I grunted, eyes narrowing. "You are used to riding with me."

"Maybe when I was younger," she said, raking a hand through her hair. A curled strand of it sprang back into her face, which she tucked behind her ear in frustration.

My gaze went to the horizon. Any moment now, the beginnings of the sunrise would start.

"We don't have time to argue, Maeva," I told her. Then my chest tightened with memory. We had always sparred like this, hadn't we? Because it felt as easy as breathing. "We will be pushing the *pyrokis* hard, and we won't be stopping for the night. Are you used to that? Riding as fast as the wind, without rest, without sleep? *Nik*, you are not. But my *darukkars* are. That is why you will ride with me."

Whatever Maeva recognized in my voice, it must've been familiar to her because her lips pressed together and finally she nodded, a small jerk of her head. My tone was unyielding, and she recognized my stubbornness easily. I would not be swayed from this, and she'd always known when to pick her battles.

She knew this was not one she would win.

"Good," I rasped. "We need to leave now."

Without another word, Maeva stepped up to Roon, who dropped his two front legs to accommodate her, something he wouldn't do for anyone else. She mounted him easily, swinging her legs over his wide back. I saw she was wearing her riding pants, the dark material padded around her inner thighs to help with *pyroki* burn.

Roon went to all fours again, straightening. I checked him over one last time, ensuring the travel sacks were secure.

Then I swung up behind Maeva, settling into the natural groove of Roon's back. My *seffi* sat rigid in front of me, holding her spine straight, her muscles tight and tensed. My thighs encased her, bracketing her backside.

When I reached for the golden reins, my arms were braced around her as well.

"Ready, *seffi*?" I murmured. The puff of my words ruffled the mass of her hair in front of me.

"I told you I was," she replied, her tone clipped. "And I told you not to call me that."

Maddening female, I thought, spurring Roon into motion. We trotted through the front gates, meeting up with my *darukkars* stationed just outside them, and Maeva turned to watch the *saruk*. Her face was in profile, but I couldn't read it. Her impassive expression gave away nothing...though she never took her eyes off the *saruk*.

Even when I ordered my *darukkars* and their *pyrokis* with, "*Vir drak ji vorak,*" she never took her eyes away.

It was only when we reached the line of the Forest of *Isida* that she turned forward.

Her head bent low. Against me, I felt a small, shuddering little breath escape her.

I frowned, remembering the first time I'd left the *saruk*, when I went to live with my father's brother in *Dothik* and train among the king's *darukkars* there. I'd felt a deep, aching sadness in my chest then because I knew that nothing would be the same. But I'd also felt excitement and possibility and the knowledge that I was journeying toward something greater, something that I was born for.

"You will see it again," I murmured to Maeva. "It is only for the frost, remember?"

I wasn't used to comforting anyone anymore. The last person I had comforted had probably been *Maeva*, though it had been years and years ago.

Then again, she'd always been my soft spot, as my mother had often observed. I'd never been able to tell if *Lomma* had meant it in a teasing way...or if she'd been concerned about our friendship.

"I know," Maeva said, but her voice was even and unwavering. Her head lifted and she stared straight out at the wildlands beyond the forest. "I've never been past the forest."

"You were once," I reminded her. "You were born in the wildlands. This is just like returning home, *nik?*"

She made a sound in her throat. "I suppose."

A part of me couldn't believe that Maeva was riding Roon with me, like we'd used to when we were younger. A part of me couldn't believe that her familiar hair was fluttering in my vision, that her familiar scent—smelling of the sea and the scented soaps Laru made her—was filling my lungs, that her familiar warmth was pressed into me.

Everything about her was familiar...and yet everything about her seemed different.

"Why did you come back?" she asked softly as we rode parallel with the line of the *Isida* Forest. "I thought you would send *darukkars* for me."

We wouldn't be journeying through the forest, but the line would break soon, tapering off where it ended. That was where the *polkunu* had attacked my *darukkar* last, so we would ride until we were well clear of it—so nothing could take us by surprise.

Unease slid down my chest at her question, remembering Rath Kitala's report.

"I needed to speak with my father," I told her, deciding against telling her anything further. For now.

"About what?"

Of course Maeva wouldn't let it go. She sensed I wasn't being forthcoming, and I would need to tell her something.

"There have been reports of creatures journeying beyond their natural territories," I told her. "I suggested he reinforce the walls of the *saruk* and keep his people away from the forest. To be safe."

Maeva stiffened. "Is this because of the *polkunu?*"

"*Lysi.*"

Partly, I amended to myself.

"But why?" she asked, turning her head to peer into the forest to our left. A forest she had, no doubt, spent much time in over the years. As had I.

"We don't know," I rasped, my fist tightening on the rein.

It wasn't quite a lie. Truthfully, we didn't know what was causing it, only that the Dead Mountain and the events that had transpired there many moon cycles ago—with the heartstone, with the white-haired human sorceress who the *Vorakkar* of Rath Drokka had made his queen—might be the root cause of it.

The *Vorakkar* of Rath Kitala had reported something that was scarcely believable...but I knew the *Vorakkar* was not a liar. I trusted him.

He reported that a dark red mist had blanketed the Dead Lands. Consuming it. Shielding it from view. According to Rath Kitala, even the Dead Mountain—the Ghertun's stronghold and home to Lozza, the Ghertun king—couldn't be seen within this strange mist's depths anymore.

The mist didn't seem to be moving. But it never dissipated, morning or night. It sat there, waiting.

For what? I couldn't help but wonder.

All the *Vorakkar* were on edge. Just when we thought war with the Ghertun could be avoided...they'd unleashed *this.*

Whatever it was. A weapon?

Unless...

Unless it wasn't the Ghertun's doing at all.

Perhaps it was *Kakkari's* doing. And we would all pay—not just the Ghertun.

Huffing out a deep breath, I shifted closer to Maeva, who still held herself rigid on Roon.

"I came to speak with my father...and because I wanted to ensure your safe passage to my horde," I admitted to her gruffly.

A shiver racked down her body, and I realized it was because I'd spoken very close to her ear. She'd always been sensitive there. Sometimes, when we were friends, I'd whisper in her ear just to watch her grin and squirm.

At the very least, I realized some things never changed. I was gladdened by it actually, though watching her shiver from my voice made me highly aware of the flare of desire that heated my belly.

Vok.

"I'm sure your *darukkars* are more than capable of seeing me safely to your horde," she told me, her chin lifting. "You didn't need to come for my sake."

"Then it is a good thing I had to speak with my father," I told her.

"And a *thesper* wouldn't have been enough?"

A small laugh burst from my throat. I knew it would draw my *darukkars'* attention, but I paid them no mind. Up ahead, the forest line was beginning to thin, and then we could unleash the full potential of our *pyrokis'* speed.

"Must you fight me on everything, *seffi?*" I asked her. "In this, you haven't changed."

She stiffened, becoming as still and unmovable as a boulder between my thighs.

"Please don't act like you know me still, *Vorakkar*," she said quietly. "Nine years is a long time. *I* hardly remember who I was back then."

Something discomforting—something that felt like regret and shame and guilt—settled deep and took hold.

Then something defiant rose up in me.

I wanted to make her remember why we'd been so drawn to one another. Why we'd been inseparable—much to my father's irritation.

I wanted to make her understand that she couldn't simply *erase* our past, years of memories because of the events of a single night, the last night I'd seen her.

"Then I will make you remember, Maeva." My words sounded like a threat, even to my own ears. "Because *I* remember that girl, my *seffi*, with her wild hair and her easy smile, and I have been missing her for almost a decade."

Her breath hitched in surprise.

"I will make you remember her," I vowed, "because I can never forget her. No matter how hard I've tried."

CHAPTER 13

I had ridden on *pyrokis* almost all my life. Though, unlike the hordes, the *saruk's pyrokis* were mostly shared with other members since their numbers were limited and we didn't have much need for them.

However, Kiran had been the *Rukkar* and, as such, had his pick of the *pyroki*. I'd been twelve when he'd picked Roon, a newborn from his mother's *pyroki*, for his own.

I remember riding Roon with Kiran during the hot season, when the sun was sizzling even over the South Lands. But Roon would ride fast and the wind would soothe the heat, if only a little. Afterward, we would ride down the slope to the shore and cool off in *Drukkar's Sea*. The salt would dry in my hair, and my skin would smell like the sea for the rest of the day.

Riding Roon felt familiar. But Kiran had been right...the pace at which he and the *darukkars* pushed their *pyrokis* was something I wouldn't have been prepared for on my own. Even with my experience, I felt the muscles in my body screaming. My back ached from holding myself away from Kiran, my arms shook from where they were looped around Roon's long neck, my inner thighs burned—and I was eternally grateful I'd remembered to wear my riding trews.

When the sun was low on the horizon, casting golden light across the beautiful wildlands of the South, Kiran gave a gruff order to his *darukkars* and to Roon. Immediately, our pace lessened. The whipping wind wasn't so loud in my ears, and my cheeks stung and tingled, as did every part of my exposed skin.

"We can keep going," I told Kiran, already sensing that he'd slowed for my sake. We'd stopped twice that day, for brief moments of reprieve and for me to relieve myself behind grassy hills we passed. "I'm fine."

"You are not," he replied. "We will ease our pace."

Part of me breathed a sigh of relief.

The other part knew that the sooner we reached his horde, the better. Because it meant I wouldn't have to be in such close proximity with him. Even now, I felt his thighs tight around my hips. When we were riding, I felt the shifting of his hard body against mine, the way his strong arms tightened around me as he held the reins, though I'd done my best to limit the inevitable contact.

Now that we had slowed to a gentle walking pace—a reprieve that Roon also seemed grateful for—I lifted my hand to my hair, feeling the wild tangle of it. Sighing, I tried to brush through it with my fingers and then started to plait it. Though it was difficult, I managed to braid it and wrapped a piece of cordage I had tucked in my pocket around the end. Even still, wispy tendrils I hadn't managed to tame drifted in front of my eyes, and I tucked those behind my ears.

Belatedly, I realized my mistake. Because, with my hair plaited, most of my back was exposed to him, given I only wore my bandeau wrapped around my breasts. I had taken off my furs and draped them over Roon's neck when the afternoon had heated up.

His touch came. He dragged his fingertip—and his dulled claw—down the jagged, puckered scar that ran down my shoulder blade before disappearing beneath the fabric of my bandeau.

"What is this?" he rasped. I could almost hear his frown.

My jaw clenched tight, and I shifted forward, separating his touch from my body. I ignored the way my skin tingled, how I had to suppress a shiver from his gentleness.

"Nothing," I replied.

I would never tell him how I got it. Not only did I suspect he'd grow livid with the information...the way I'd received the scar had been foolish and dangerous, the decision based on anger and hurt. I was also ashamed of it, just as I was ashamed of my actions—and all the ones surrounding that time of my life, in the year after he'd left.

"You won't tell me how you received it? It looks deep. The wound must have been—"

I still felt that aching, stinging pain sometimes. I didn't need him to tell me how bad the wound had been.

"It was nothing," I said again, my voice hardening.

I felt the sharp, hot breath from his nostrils spread over the back of the scar when he sighed in frustration.

I kept my gaze forward, over the grassy wildlands of the South. The *runiri* were shorter here than the stalks that grew by the sea, but they still swayed with the wind. Perhaps the most uncomfortable observation was that I couldn't *see* the sea. All my life, I had always smelled the salty air, felt the cold fronts that would blow in, heard the crashing of waves against the cliffs—a sound that lured me to sleep most nights.

Though we were still in the South Lands, *Drukkar's Sea* was nowhere to be seen. It had disappeared from view earlier in the afternoon. The air felt warmer, heavier. It even smelled different.

My heart ached with the knowledge I wouldn't return to the sea for a whole season cycle. Already I missed it, just as I missed my family. I had only ever seen my father cry when my mother died. But when I told him that Kiran had offered me the position of *mokkira* in his horde for the frost, that I would be leaving for many moon cycles, he'd been close to tears again.

It had shaken me. My father and I had always been close. It had been *him* that had found me in a wooded area of the wildlands, after all, when he'd been out hunting with his party. He'd heard me crying from the forest's edge, and he'd tracked me. He always told me it had been Kakkari that had led us to one another.

To know that my decision hurt him, to know that he would be alone in the *soliki* he had built with my mother, almost made me reject Kiran's offer. I had told my father so, that if he wanted me to stay, I would.

A few nights ago, however, he had told me he wanted me to go.

He told me that it wasn't for long.

That it would give me the opportunity to learn as *mokkira*, a title that would never be mine in the *saruk*.

That he was proud to call me his daughter, and that Kiran's horde would be lucky to have me, if only through the frost.

It had been all the blessing I'd needed.

Which was how I found myself on the back of Roon, coming to the realization that nothing about the wildlands was familiar and that I already missed my father, Laru, Rasik, Nevir, and *Drukkar's Sea* desperately.

"What are you thinking of?" Kiran suddenly murmured behind me. "I can almost hear your mind turning."

Kiran perhaps understood the sadness that washed over me. For he had loved the *saruk* and the sea when we were younger. Before he'd left for his training in *Dothik*, he'd confided in me how much he hurt at the mere prospect of leaving.

"Does it ever get any easier?" I asked softly, hearing the gentle plod of *pyroki* hooves over the earth from his *darukkars* behind us. "Being away from home?"

Kiran straightened.

"Don't you ever miss it so badly that your whole body aches?" I asked next.

In that brief moment, I *needed* to hear that leaving had hurt him as badly as it'd hurt me. I didn't know why. Maybe I needed some sort of *recognition*. Perhaps I needed to hear a little bit of regret. That it had been hard for him to turn his back on our friendship, regardless of the fact that he'd rejected me romantically.

Because our friendship had still been *real*, hadn't it?

Kiran didn't answer for a long time.

Finally, he grunted, "My horde is my home."

Something hardened further in my chest.

I nodded, but it was almost to myself. The throbbing of *hurt* that I felt at his words surprised me. I thought that by now I would have long been indifferent to him. I thought that by now he wouldn't be able to hurt me anymore.

Perhaps it was proof that Kiran of Rath Okkili would always have the power to hurt me, no matter how much I tried to forget him.

I drew in a long inhale.

I looked out across the *runiri*-covered field. A forest was far in the distance, to the north. Beyond that, I could see the shadowy peaks of mountain ranges, but they looked *weeks* away.

I can do this, I realized, a jolt going through me, followed by a sense of *peace*.

Just as I told Laru, Kiran only had the power to hurt me if I let him.

I liked to think I had thicker skin than I'd had back then. And I *knew* that I'd matured. I'd grown up, moved on.

I knew I could be civil with Kiran—I would have to be, considering he was a *Vorakkar* and I would be a member of his horde. I didn't have to let old pain settle deeper into my bones. I didn't want that.

I just wanted peace.

But I would never be able to have it unless I looked beyond our past.

Could I?

Could I look at Kiran in a different way? Could I see him for the Dakkari horde king he was now—and not as the boy I'd fallen in love with, who had broken my heart not once...but twice?

I will need to, I realized.

A stronger breeze was starting to blow across the southern plains. They quickened the lower the sun drooped in the sky. It was a beautiful sunset with swirls of purple and gold. The light made the *runiri* stalks shimmer as they swayed.

Just then I *thought* I felt the earth tremble.

A moment later, I knew it wasn't my own imaginings because Roon's pace sped dramatically, spooked by something unseen.

"*Vok,*" Kiran rasped, pulling on the golden chains of his *pyroki's* reins. "Roon, *livri!*"

If anything, Roon ignored his master's command because the *pyroki* sped even faster. Behind us, I could hear the *darukkars* pick up their own pace to match ours, keeping close to their *Vorakkar*.

Another tremor rocked the earth, more violent than the last. *That* trembling had been unmistakable. It was something I'd never felt before...like Kakkari was rumbling awake.

My heart sped, and I uttered, "What is that?"

Kiran didn't answer me, and I sensed that he was surveying the land before us. I didn't know what he was looking for, however—most of the land was covered in *runiri* stalks anyway.

He turned in his seat, looking behind him, as I shifted my gaze from side to side. We were in an open field. There was no forest close by for a *polkunu* to surprise us from. There was nothing—

My eyes widened when I saw a massive, dark, deep hole in the ground before us, the tall grass simply gone from it in an almost perfect circle...and we were racing right toward it.

Acting on instinct, I jerked Roon's left rein hard, shifting it from Kiran's hand, and the *pyroki* pivoted, letting out a displeased, loud chuff as he did.

If not for Kiran's strong thighs keeping me in place, I might've fallen off Roon's back entirely. Behind me, I heard the *Vorakkar's* curse, heard the *darukkars'* yells of alarm when they saw the giant hole in the ground.

The ground trembled again. The *pyrokis* let out keening wails, and to my disbelief, a giant beast, long and sand-colored and slithering, burst from the hole. An ear-ringing shrill cry, one that made me wince and cover my ears, filled the field.

"Hold, *darukkars*!" Kiran ordered, his voice muffled and dulled. "Stand down!"

The beast was *massive*, whatever it was. It could crush us all with its weight. Its wormlike body was ridged, the flesh thick and wiggly as it pushed itself from its dark den in the earth. I didn't see any limbs, but it reared up. The fading sunlight bounced off its body, but it blocked out the entirety of the sunset as the *darukkars* urged their *pyrokis* away.

But *we* weren't quick enough. Roon, in the confusion, back-tracked the way we'd come before Kiran was able to correct him. A long claw began to uncurl from the beast's belly, dagger-like and sharp and glittering black. We were too close. That sharp, ear-splitting scream seemed to become louder and louder.

"Kiran," I breathed, my eyes wide, my heartbeat thundering in my throat.

Kiran's dark gaze met mine, grim realization etched in his

features as I saw the flash of the black claw extending toward us, as the beast thrust itself in our direction, wailing in the wind.

At the last moment, Kiran managed to get hold of Roon's reins and turn the *pyroki*—so Kiran's back was to the beast.

"*Nik!*" I cried, realization going through me. Kiran managed to spur Roon into a run, but I heard the *squelch* of the claw as it made contact with the *Vorakkar's* back.

I felt his body jerk against me. I heard his grunt, his raspy curse.

With a wild look behind me, I saw the claw retract, black with Kiran's blood.

"*Draki,*" Kiran growled to Roon, his voice thick and husky, teeth gritted in pain.

As Roon sped at his master's command, I saw the slithering beast begin to give chase behind us.

"It stopped," I breathed. "It finally stopped."

Kiran was rigid behind me. I was turned in my seat, craning my neck to look past his bulky form, tracking the wormlike beast across the grassy field. It had stopped and began to slither back the way it'd come, its wailing, keening, high-pitched cry continuing to carry across the wind.

When my gaze met his, I knew he was in pain. His eyes were hard, his mouth pressed into a firm line. He'd broken a bone once during training. I remembered sitting with him in the *mokkira's soliki* as the elder male set it. I remembered that Kiran hadn't made a sound, though his bone was protruding from his flesh. But his eyes had been cold and he'd been clenching his jaw so tightly I was surprised the bone didn't disintegrate.

He still wore the long scar on his forearm, just one of his many scars.

"We need to stop so I can look at the wound," I murmured, spying black blood dripping over Roon's side.

"Another few moments," he said tightly. "We need to clear the *ungira's* territory. There may be more."

An ungira? I thought in disbelief.

"But...but *ungira* live far to the east," I whispered. I didn't think my *father*, a seasoned hunter, had ever seen one. Perhaps when the *saruk* had been a horde he had, when Kiran's father had been *Vorakkar*.

This is why he came back, I knew. To warn his father that creatures were crossing territories.

I just hadn't realized how dangerous those implications were. Not until I'd stared down into the darkness of an *ungira* den less than a day's ride from the *saruk*, from my family.

"Kiran." I felt a familiar sense of calm descend over me. I met his eyes and didn't look away. "I need to look at the wound. *Now.*"

Just then, a *darukkar* called out, "There is a grouping of hills up ahead. They should be safe."

I didn't think anyone had ever given this *Vorakkar* an order since he'd risen to his rank. His nostrils had flared at my words, his eyes burning into mine, though his dark pupils were dilated with pain.

Then, without breaking my gaze, he ordered his *darukkars,* "Patrol the area. Make sure there are no more dens nearby. We will camp here for the night."

A chorus of, "*Lysi, Vorakkar,*" came, and then the *darukkars' pyrokis* picked up their speed, fanning out in all directions, pounding the earth with their clawed hooves.

Kiran and I were alone, and he urged Roon into a gentle pace, turning him in the direction of the hills. They were slightly sloped with mostly flattened crests. If we made camp at the top, we would have a view of the grassy fields below and could see any *ungira*—or other beasts—that approached.

When we reached the base, Roon climbed the hill effortlessly until we reached the first plateau. I slid off Roon's back easily, landing on the surprisingly spongy ground. It was soft and gave very easily. Taking Roon's leads from Kiran's hand, I watched the *Vorakkar* carefully as he dismounted.

When he turned, my jaw tightened, my fingers squeezing into my fists.

Like me, he'd taken off his furs earlier that afternoon, but he still wore a black hide tunic that molded to his chest. It had given him some protection from the *ungira*, but not enough.

The back of the tunic was slashed from the base of his neck to his lower back. It was a black and bloody mess. I couldn't see the depth of the wound, but the way his blood glinted in the sunset's light made my stomach coil with nausea—and I had never been sick from the sight of blood before.

But this is Kiran, I thought.

Blood had begun to drip down his black tail, sliding down the long, flexible appendage.

When Kiran turned to regard me, my face gave nothing away. I realized now why the *mokkira* always looked so *impassive*. Because he couldn't give his true thoughts away. He was duty bound to help heal whoever sought his aid.

Even in his pain, I saw the corner of Kiran's mouth quirk.

"That bad, *seffi?*" he asked.

He's lucky to be alive, I realized, my brow furrowing, not certain I liked the churning in my gut at *that* realization. That he'd come very close to death today.

That if he hadn't turned in that split second...it would have been *me* that had taken the *ungira's* attack. And I probably wouldn't have survived it.

Swallowing, I went to one of my travel sacks that Kiran had attached to Roon's side earlier that morning.

Inhaling a deep breath, I closed my eyes momentarily.

I ran through the supplies I needed in my head, envisioning them all. *Boiled water. Clean cloth.* Uudun *salve.* Kioni *pulp mixed with* jenuria *extract.*

Judging by the depth of the wound, I would also need to stitch it closed.

When I opened my eyes, I felt more centered. I felt focused.

Determined. Detached. Sometimes I had to remove emotion from the equation. Sometimes a body just became a body. Just flesh and muscle and sinew and blood.

"I need to get a fire started," I told him.

"I'll do it," he voiced.

"*Nik*," I murmured, already snagging the shallow fire basin from Roon's other side. "Sit down."

Before I could protest, he took it from my grip, and I pressed my lips together. He was stubborn, just like me. Deciding I wouldn't waste time arguing, I rummaged through my travel sack, quickly pulling out everything I would need as I heard him pouring in the fire fuel.

When I turned around, he lit the fuel with a spark from his sword—creating a fire far more quickly than I ever could—and *then* sat down. I laid a pot in the basin, nestled among the fire fuel, and filled it with water from the water skins. Hopefully it would begin to boil soon.

I maneuvered behind him. Strangely, I felt him tense up. Thinking it was due to the pain, I gave him a vial of the *mokki-ra's* potion, mixed from boiled down *terruni* leaves and mashed and fermented *pova* roots. *Begalia* would be better for the pain—at least for a Dakkari—but I didn't have any on hand.

"Drink this," I murmured, moving his hair away to drape over his front, exposing the expanse of his back. I felt him stiffen further. "What's wrong?"

He took the vial from my fingertips, but he didn't move to drink it. He brought his knees up to his chest and draped his arms over the tops of them. Next to me, his tail flicked wildly, splattering drops of blood across the springy hill.

"I am not used to it anymore," he finally told me, his voice gruff.

"Used to what?" I asked. "Getting slashed by *ungira* talons? This has happened before?"

He chuffed out a breath. He twirled the vial between his fingertips, and the golden liquid flashed in the fire's light.

"Having anyone at my back," he said.

My fingers paused at the straps of his tunic, his words making my chest pinch, making some of my carefully curated detachment float away. Desperately, I tried to draw it back around me, like a shawl around my shoulders and a calming balm for my mind.

Once he left for *Dothik*, even before the Trials had happened, he always returned home changed. He started pulling away from his male peers that he'd trained with daily, from the childhood friends he'd grown up with. Everyone except me. Partly because…I suspected I didn't *let* him pull away from me.

But his words just now revealed that he'd built up walls around himself too. Not just me.

I didn't reply. I wasn't even sure what I would say.

Tugging at the straps of his tunic, I released them and then took a sharp, slim blade from its sheath, one that my father had given me when the *mokkira* had taken me on as an apprentice. I used it to cut the tunic from his back and then slid the material down his arms and away.

The wreckage of his flesh met me. But it wasn't the *ungira* wound that momentarily made me freeze, that made burning horror rush up my throat, the bile stinging it.

It was his *Vorakkar* markings.

Hundreds of whipping scars, some long—running from his shoulder blades to his tail—some short, though they looked deeper.

In my mind, I knew *this* was a mark all *Vorakkar* wore. The last test of the Trials in *Dothik*. Only the strongest survived, and I never had any doubt that Kiran would.

But to *see* it…knowing the pain that the whipping marks would have caused, knowing the burning agony that Kiran must've endured, knowing that he'd always been *meant* for this pain...

It ripped my feeling of detachment clean away until my hands trembled and I had to focus on breathing through my nostrils.

One breath in, one breath out.

"I never wanted you to see them," came his guttural rasp.

His words jolted me from my stupor, and I swallowed, my eyes tracking to the *ungira* wound, the wound I *could* heal.

He'd never wanted me to see the scars?

His words were strangely...vulnerable. Intimate.

They shook something in me. Grabbed at my heart that had been broken and haphazardly patched together again. His words threatened all the hard work I'd done to *forget* him and forget the overwhelming feelings he'd always stirred in me.

Earlier that morning, he'd threatened to make me remember the girl I once was. His *seffi*.

I had almost laughed in his face. But now...

Now I began to fear that he might manifest that girl back into existence. At least the memory of her.

Nik, I thought, snapping back the warmth that had begun to spread.

I grappled for control, and I looked away from his back, down to my travel sack of supplies. I laid out everything I would need next to me in even rows and then snagged the water skin.

His body stiffened when I poured the water down his back. It wasn't boiled, but I needed to see the depth of the wound.

My lips pressed together. The cut was deep. I would need to stitch the line of it down the entirety of his back and make sure infection didn't take root.

"You're not asking me if you'll live, like most I see with injures like this," I commented softly, if only to take my mind off the warmth that had threatened to explode in my chest. I scooted my knees forward, not caring that they were now damp with his blood. "Turn your back toward the fire."

Kiran shifted. He murmured, "Have you always been like this? Or did I simply forget how demanding you are?"

"You are a *Vorakkar* now," I told him. "Maybe you simply forgot how to take orders."

He huffed out a sharp breath from his nostrils. "My *darukkars* are out patrolling. If you wanted to end my life right now, you would be able to, *rei mokkira*. I know the wound is not deep enough to kill me—I feel it—but I could bleed out."

My hands stilled before I ever even touched his flesh. "Why would you say something like that?" I whispered.

His head turned to regard me over his shoulder. His expression revealed nothing, but I understood what he was asking.

"You think I want you dead?" I asked him, frowning, disturbed.

He shrugged his shoulder, though the skin around his wound pulled. More blood leaked out, and I washed it away again, using the cloth I had to press the wound tight.

He didn't even flinch. And I suddenly knew that when he'd been whipped for his *Vorakkar* marks, he hadn't made a single sound then either.

My heart threatened to break at that thought.

"I hurt you, left you," he murmured. "Maybe you do wish me dead."

I clenched my jaw tight, perhaps the only change in my expression.

"It was a long time ago, *Vorakkar*," I told him, keeping my voice even. "I don't think of it anymore."

A lie.

His eyes flashed, his brow furrowing, as if he couldn't figure me out.

"Do you have a mate now?" he asked gruffly.

A strangled sound rose from my throat, and I saw his

expression change. It lightened, his brow smoothing. *Relieved? Nik*, that couldn't be right.

"Why does it matter?" I asked, incredulous, watching the cloth bloom black, already soaked with his blood. I peeled it away carefully, casting my gaze to the pot in the fire basin, little bubbles rising.

"You do not," he said, his tone dismissive. He turned forward, and I stared at the back of his neck.

A bubble of uncomfortable emotion rose within me. A mixture of shame, of self-consciousness, of embarrassment that I hadn't felt in years.

My cheeks burned with it. Then I grew angry.

Because the truth was...for years after he left, I'd been filled with a sense of self-disgust. I remembered Kiran's expression the night I'd undressed for him on the cliffside. I remembered that thunderous look in his eyes, the way his mouth pulled down when he saw my naked body. I'd been the most vulnerable I'd ever been with another being.

And he had been *disgusted*.

After that night, after he left, I'd taken his disgust and directed it at myself. I'd multiplied it until it had threatened to drown me. I'd been in such a dark place. Because back then, I didn't have the self-esteem to realize that just because Kiran didn't desire me, I could still desire myself. *Others* could still desire me because I was *worth* it.

It took me years to realize I had a lot to give someone else, a partner, a mate. Now? There was a sense of *pride* that I'd been able to love someone so completely and utterly.

Of course, I had never allowed myself to love that deeply again.

But at least I knew I was capable of it. At least I had experienced it.

Laru had been right, however. I'd loved deeply...and then I built my walls up, high and impenetrable. There were males in the *saruk* that had expressed interest in me over the years, males I'd grown up with all my life.

But I didn't desire them. It was like that part of me had died and any hope for a mated life, for children and love had died with it.

In the end, I didn't reply to Kiran, not that he'd asked me a question. I didn't know why he was interested in whether I had a mate or not. It wasn't his business. It wasn't his concern, and I strongly suspected he'd asked the question to unsettle me.

The water began to boil, and I retrieved it, using the bloodied cloths to keep the handle from burning my palm. I set it down next to me to cool.

"I *do* have a mate," I informed him, staring at the blood on his back, at the deep wound he'd taken when he'd shielded me from the *ungira* attack.

He stiffened, his head whipping toward me, the muscles in his arms bunching and tightening.

"I've chosen myself," I said. "And *only* myself."

I didn't need Kiran anymore to make me feel whole. Or any male for that matter.

I made myself into who I was.

And *that* was something I took great pride in.

"Now turn, *Vorakkar*," I ordered, keeping my voice hard. "I need to clean your wound before you *do* bleed out."

"I've upset you," I grunted, the knowledge making me more uncomfortable than the wound on my back.

Maeva's silence was thunderous behind me. It felt heavy.

"I always seem to have a way of doing so," I commented, pressing my lips together, leaning forward, feeling the sizzling heat of my wound zip up my spine.

"I'm not upset," she informed me. And to her credit, she didn't sound upset.

But I knew Maeva, regardless of what she might've thought.

In the distance, I saw a plume of earth kick up around my *darukkars' pyrokis.* They had spread out, going in all directions from the hill to ensure that we hadn't unwittingly stumbled onto an *ungira* nesting ground.

I saw them begin to return, finding nothing, and some of the tension in my shoulders eased.

"You saved us, Maeva."

I felt her hands still on my back. She'd dipped a cloth into the hot water next to her, and she'd begun cleaning the wound, making me grit my teeth.

"I did not see the *ungira* den. If you hadn't taken the reins, we would've dropped inside," I continued.

"You were turned in your seat," Maeva said quietly after another moment, her hands resuming over my heated flesh. "You would've seen it had you been facing forward—perhaps far sooner than I had."

"I am trying to thank you, *seffi*," I said. Despite the situation, despite the furious frustration I directed at myself—I'd come to protect Maeva as we journeyed to my horde, and instead, I'd almost gotten us killed—I felt amusement curl in my chest.

"If that is the case, I haven't heard a *kakkira vor* from your lips at all," she informed me as she concentrated at her work.

A low rumbling chuckle rose in my throat, emerging before I realized it. I was glad my *darukkars* were not here. If they'd heard me laugh, they'd have probably shit themselves.

"*Kakkira vor*, Maeva," I purred gently. "Does that satisfy you?"

She didn't answer my teasing question.

Instead, she said softly, "*Kakkira vor, Vorakkar.*"

That surprised me.

"For what?"

"For taking this," she said, pressing the cloth to my wound. "I wouldn't have...I wouldn't have survived this."

My gaze lingered on the flickering fire, my body tightening. *Nik*, she wouldn't have. But why was she thanking me? Surely she knew that I would do anything to keep her safe.

Then again...maybe she didn't. Not anymore.

I felt a hot puff of breath drift across the back of my neck. I barely suppressed my shiver, stiffening slightly, my nostrils flaring.

This was no time to feel desire and heat tighten my *deva*, given the situation.

But it had been almost a year since I'd last rutted a female. The most frustrating part of it all was I didn't know *why* I had suddenly imposed this stretch of celibacy on myself.

Errok, my *pujerak*, snickered constantly at my situation. It amused him to no end that *I* would willingly subject myself to this. Dakkari were lustful beings. We liked to fuck. We liked to touch and lick and kiss and stroke.

So why was I doing this?

I thought I knew, however.

I strongly suspected my newfound celibacy had to do with Maeva. With Kakkari. With the dream the goddess had given me. With the memories that rose within me afterward.

I cursed under my breath, cutting off my thoughts as I grappled for control.

"Did that hurt?" Maeva asked, briefly pausing in her work. Belatedly, I realized she'd been in the process of cleaning out the deepest part of the fresh wound. She thought my curse was in reaction to pain.

If only she knew the direction of my thoughts…

"*Nik.*"

My stiff word made her resume. I told myself to focus on her touch. I forced myself to focus on the way the cloth dragged over sensitive flesh, scraping at me from the inside. *That* was better than remembering Kakkari's dream.

Once Maeva was done cleaning out the wound, she rinsed it and then set about packing it with *uudun*—I'd recognize the sharp smell of it anywhere—and another mixture I couldn't identify, though it felt warm and hot.

Her soft voice came to me after a long stretch of silence.

"You didn't want to kill the *ungira*," she commented. "Why?"

My arms squeezed tighter where they were wrapped around my drawn-up knees.

"We were not hunting. My horde has plenty of food stores for the frost already," I told her.

"You killed the *polkunu*," she pointed out.

Blowing out a sharp breath, I raked a hand through my hair,

my tail twitching. It felt stiff with my drying blood, and it brushed her leg.

"The *polkunu* was close to the *saruk*," I said. "If I let it live, it would have been a danger."

"The *saruk's* protection isn't your concern," she said, though there was no bite in her words—merely an observation. "Any other *Vorakkar* would've let it go."

"Perhaps," I replied. "But many that live in the *saruk*...I care about them and their protection."

Maeva didn't reply to *that*.

"It was us that surprised the *ungira* this evening," I said. "And *ungira* are territorial beasts. They build their dens in the ground before the frost to lay their eggs. That was likely a mother protecting her young from potential threats."

I heard Maeva swallow as I felt the coolness of the *uudun* slide down the inside of my wound. I wondered what she thought of the wreckage of my back. I wondered if the scars frightened or disgusted her.

I'd told her the truth. Ever since I'd received them during the *Vorakkar* Trials, I never wanted her to see them.

It was a little late for that now.

"Another beast has left its natural territory of the East Lands," she commented softly.

My lips pressed together.

Lysi, another instance. One of many. And these were only the creatures we'd spotted in the South. There was no telling where other creatures had scattered, as they fled from the Dead Lands and the East.

I would need to report these to the other *Vorakkar*. Likely, we would all need to convene in *Dothik* once more. The *Dothikkar*, perhaps, didn't know of these new disturbing changes yet. But he would. And we would need to decide what *could* be done, especially concerning this red mist that had begun to spread.

"What has happened in the East to drive them away?" she asked, though I sensed it was a question more to herself. "Have the stories been true? About the human sorceress who wielded Kakkari's power under the Dead Mountain?"

"*Lysi*," I rasped. "The stories have been true. The *Vorakkar* of Rath Kitala witnessed it, as did the *Vorakkar* of Rath Drokka, who later made the *vekkiri* his queen."

She went quiet, though I could almost *hear* the thousands of questions bubbling in her mind.

"She almost died, didn't she?" Maeva asked after another silence.

"*Lysi*," I said, my voice gruff. "The *Vorakkar* of Rath Drokka almost went mad when she would not wake. He tried to use the heartstone to save her life, though it would have been at the cost of his own."

"He loves her?"

Something about her question made my throat tighten with regret. Her innocent question made me remember just how much of a romantic optimist Maeva had been.

Now?

There was a hardened indifference to her, one that cut me to witness it, especially when it was directed toward me.

"*Lysi*, very much," I said, my tone rough from the sudden tightness of my throat. "Why else would he make her his *Morakkari*?"

A charged silence followed. A silence that made me aware of her, of every movement she made, of every brush of her fingers against my ravaged flesh.

"There are many reasons," she said, clearing her throat. "Power and the future of the horde, for one. Among the hordes' histories, there have been many *Vorakkar* who chose queens not based on love but on position and connections. In fact, choosing a *Morakkari* on the basis of love might be the worst decision a *Vorakkar* can make."

My jaw clenched.

Frustration threaded through my veins.

I hated her speaking like this. Before, she'd always sighed with adoration and giggled with delight when she heard the great love stories of our history. She'd always declared that she wanted a love like what her parents shared.

I'd always loved that about her…that her heart had been so open that it was practically bursting.

"And what of my parents?" I couldn't help but ask, my voice gruff.

"It proves my point," she said, stoppering her jars once she finished packing the wound. "Your father chose his *Morakkari* because she was the daughter of his *pujerak*. Because her line extends for generations across the wildlands, because she was suited to be his queen. And because her father was his *pujerak,* it would only make their ties stronger. Their love came with time—and it was a happy discovery, I'm sure—but the relationship did not start with it. I admire that."

"You would so easily dismiss those *Vorakkar* who decided to choose love over convenience?" I asked.

For a moment, I thought she would ignore me. She was already beginning to clean out the salves she'd layered inside my back. They only needed to sit for a short while to help prevent infection, which meant the wound was deep enough to require stitching.

"Love ends," she said simply. Quietly. "Maybe it's better to choose stability."

I barely concealed my flinch.

I felt her words hit me like a strike across the face.

In my anger, I rasped, "Perhaps I will take *you* as my *Morakkari,* then."

She stiffened.

"To secure a skilled *mokkira* for my horde, to keep you past the frost and not let you leave. Isn't that the *stability* you speak of?"

I wanted her to get angry. I wanted her to feel the bite of sadness and regret and the deep sense of loss I felt now. I wanted to peel back the layers of practical indifference she had wrapped herself in like Dakkari steeled armor. I wanted to see a glimmer of the girl whose emotions I could read as clearly as dark ink across parchment.

She didn't prepare me when she began stitching my wound. The sharp pinch of the needle through my flesh made me grit my jaw, but my heart was still pounding furiously fast from her words…and, perhaps, from the vision of her as my *Morakkari*.

Vok.

"You can certainly try, though it would be a waste of your time," she said, her voice even. Then came the bite of it when she continued, "Because I wouldn't have you, *Vorakkar*."

At her declaration, I felt something spark in my chest. That low, sizzling burn that felt frighteningly like *determination*.

There was nothing more that I hated than being told I couldn't accomplish something.

Maeva knew that.

She knew exactly what her words would ignite.

She'd done it to frustrate me.

Well, it had worked.

My body was tight. A strange mixture of anger, of madness, of thick, choking lust, and of biting amusement took hold.

"You would have had me once, *seffi*," I purred, though my words sounded mocking even to my own ears. I hadn't meant for them to sound that way, but I heard the shocked exhale that left Maeva's lips. "Perhaps I can have you again."

Her hands trembled as she dug the needle into my flesh, perhaps deeper and harder than necessary.

As the tense silence stretched, I immediately regretted my words.

"Maeva—" I started, but she cut me off.

"You're cruel, Kiran," she whispered. "Have you ever realized just how much?"

I stiffened.

"Nine years is a long time," she continued, "but I don't think you've changed at all."

I was saved from replying when my *darukkars* returned, climbing up the short incline of the hill and beginning to make camp for the night after informing me that the land was clear.

All the while, Maeva was silent behind me and she hurried to finished stitching my wound closed, as if the sooner she finished, the sooner she could be rid of me.

Long after she was done, long after the moon had risen and my *darukkars* had taken to their sleeping pallets, her words continued to echo in my mind.

You're cruel, Kiran. Have you ever realized just how much?

She'd said something similar to me the last night I saw her.

What she didn't realize was...I knew how cruel I could be. I *knew.* I'd begun to recognize it in *Dothik,* when I began training for the Trials. I'd begun to recognize it in the way I had to detach from those around me to best lead. I'd begun to recognize it in the bitter coldness in my chest, that sometimes felt like it would never leave me.

I knew that I was cruel and selfish, that I could be ruthless to get what I wanted, that I could kill without flinching, that I could bury my emotions so deep that I hardly ever felt them.

I was a *Vorakkar.* A horde king of Dakkar. And I had sacrificed much for it.

What I also knew was that I had *never* wanted to hurt Maeva. Next to my *lomma,* she was the last being I had ever wanted to hurt.

I'd done so anyway. It had haunted me ever since.

For the rest of the night on that hill in the South Lands, with

Kakkari's stars shining bright overhead, with luminous ancient constellations that told ancient stories, stories I had once recited to my *seffi*...Maeva didn't meet my gaze once.

CHAPTER 16

"We have arrived," Kiran said quietly, close to my ear.

I nodded, holding myself stiffly on Roon's back. With the exception of when I'd checked his wound earlier that morning, Kiran and I had barely spoken as we continued on our journey.

His words sparked a drumming of nerves and anticipation and curiosity within me.

From a distance, his horde looked like a massive sprawl of hide-covered, light brown, domed tents that I knew were called *volikis*. I spied figures, tall and imposing, bustling around the front of the horde. A wall was being erected, one made of dark wood and reinforced with Dakkari steel beams, which glinted in the bright afternoon sunlight.

As we drew closer, I determined the horde was much larger than I'd originally anticipated. I had my first jolt of fear. What if I couldn't handle being a *mokkira* to a horde this size? For some strange reason, I thought the horde would be smaller, more intimate, more *manageable*.

But the sheer sprawl of it, the noise from voices and laughter, the clanging of metal, the chatter that filled the air like a buzzing...I had my first stab of doubt.

Then I set my jaw, determination coursing through me, pushing out that doubt.

I can do this, I thought. *I will* do this, *and then I will return home.*

The desire to return to the *saruk* had plagued me all night, keeping me tossing and turning, especially after the exchange with Kiran—of heated words, of the stinging hurt and throbbing remembrance they had awakened.

But this was a new day.

Kiran might still have the power to hurt me. Perhaps he always would, given our history. I needed to accept that, recognize it, so that I could control my emotions better.

Lomma had told me that acceptance was the first step toward healing. From my own experience, I knew that to be true. It had taken me a long time to accept that she was gone, buried in the ground, her spirit firmly with Kakkari once more... but it wasn't until I did that I finally felt some anger and hurt and grief release from me.

I would use the same approach with Kiran. I had been doing the opposite by pretending that I was indifferent to his presence, by pretending that he hadn't hurt me as much as he did, by pretending that I wasn't disappointed or really *vokking* angry with him over the years.

But maybe I needed to accept those emotions, feel them deeply, and then release them. Maybe then I would truly be free of them. Free of *him.*

Last night, as I stared up at Kakkari's stars, very aware that Kiran was sleeping only a short distance away, I'd come to this decision. The decision that I wouldn't hold a grudge against him, that I would take advantage of my time in his horde, that I would take advantage of the opportunity to be a *mokkira,* a master healer—what I'd always wanted.

It didn't matter that Kiran could still hurt me, that he mocked me with his words.

It didn't matter.

Because I didn't trust him.

As such, I would never be in danger of loving him again.

I would come to his horde, I would be useful to the horde members in whatever way I could through the frost, I would help bring new life into this world, and—perhaps most exciting of all—I'd be able to interact with beings of my own *race*.

Humans lived among his horde.

That was enough reason to journey here.

The half-finished horde gates were drawing nearer and nearer. One of the workers spied us in the distance, and a loud cry of greeting echoed over the land. More heads snapped up, more voices joined in. Around us, Kiran's *darukkars* responded with a greeting call of their own, though the *Vorakkar* was silent at my back. As if sensing that he was home, Roon sped faster.

The horde was close to a forest whose name I didn't know. And as we rounded the line of the trees, I felt a jolt of surprise and delight when I spied what I thought was *Drukkar's Sea*, only it lay in the wrong direction. Behind it, jagged black mountains sat tall and proud, so high that I couldn't see the tops of them in the cloud covering.

"Is that the sea?" I asked in my surprise.

"*Nik,*" Kiran said. "It is called a lake. The water that comes down from the mountains feeds it."

A lake?

I didn't know the South Lands could look like this. Beautifully majestic, with shimmering water, deep, dark forests, and mountains, all within view. Of course, a large part of me missed the sea, missed the familiar air it swept in along the coast...but at least there was water here.

I felt some tension release from my shoulders. Seeing this lake was like greeting a familiar friend.

I will be okay here, I thought.

Kiran led his *darukkars* through the gates of his horde. To my surprise, I saw it had a similar layout—at least from the portion I could see—to the *saruk*. There was a large gathering space for feasts and celebrations at the front, next to a training enclosure where I saw *darukkars* sparring with one another, their golden blades flashing in the sunlight. A wide path ran north, which looked like the main road of the *saruk*, and I assumed it connected most of the *volikis*.

Though, instead of the tall buildings made of stone like I was used to, these domed tents were low to the ground, stuck to the earth. Some were much larger than others, so I assumed that they served different purposes.

As for the horde members themselves, various Dakkari, old and young alike, came to greet their *Vorakkar*. They made a path for us, lining the main road, as Kiran led Roon to the *pyroki* enclosure, situated toward the back of the horde.

There, I received another shock. Nothing prepared me for the sheer amount of *pyrokis* or the sheer size of the massive enclosure. I saw warriors in the enclosure, a *mrikro*—the *pyroki* master—giving orders as they built them nests for the coming frost. A huge endeavor, considering there were over a hundred creatures.

Kiran brought Roon to a stop, and I slid off the *pyroki*, stroking his snout, highly aware of the crowd of Dakkari that had formed, following us from the main road.

I felt their eyes on me, heard the whispers, some of which I could make out.

"*Why does he bring a* vekkiri *back home with him?*"

"*Why is she dressed in* saruk *adornments?*"

"*Look at her pendant. It is Dothik made. Look at how small it is. She dares to wear that here?*"

As that last statement reached my ears, my hand drifted to the valley of my breasts and I felt a burning in my throat. Though small, my mother's pendant was heavy and comforting.

The Dakkari who spoke about it was a female, tall and imposing and beautiful. Her dark skin was a similar shade to my own, though that was where our similarities ended. She had piercing golden eyes and long, silky black hair that reached her wide hips.

Her tail flicked across the ground, and she was dressed in a long dress that brushed the tops of her feet, that molded to her flesh. Through the thin material, I could see her nipples, painted gold, something I knew horde females did often, especially if they were searching for mates.

My back straightened. I'd learned from a young age that if I didn't stand up for myself, then I would always be seen as weak. Coming to Kiran's horde, I needed to make my new rank known. Because a *mokkira* was held in the same respect as all the masters in the horde were, and I expected to be treated as such.

"It was my *lomma's*," I voiced, bringing my gaze to the Dakkari female, seeing her golden eyes widen with a bit of surprise. Suddenly, the whispering ceased, a hush quieting the crowd. "And it is not *Dothik* made. It was made by a talented goldsmith in the *saruk* of Rath Okkili."

I heard the shocked murmurs at my declaration.

"She speaks our tongue?"

"Who is she?"

The female dropped her gaze away from my mine, and I felt my chin lift further. When I looked behind me, I saw Kiran had dismounted from Roon. His eyes lowered to the pendant, nestled between my breasts, his jaw clenching, before his eyes returned to mine in question.

Remembering that we were in his horde, in front of a large crowd of his people, I dropped my own gaze. Though I disliked him, I still had to show my respect for his position, especially since I expected others to show their respect for mine.

To distract myself, I patted Roon's snout, who chuffed and

nuzzled against my hand. At least until the *mrikro* appeared at my side, the older male giving me a disapproving frown as he led Roon away, into the enclosure for much needed food and rest.

Am I not allowed to touch Roon when we are in the horde? I wondered. For the first time, I regretted not asking my father more about horde life, about the customs and signs of respect that weren't necessarily adhered to in a *saruk*.

Kiran handed me my travel sacks, which I took, sliding the straps over my shoulder, the heavy weight of them comforting against my side. Something of home, in this strange new place.

Then Kiran lifted his gaze to the crowd that had formed, that cold, hard expression etched into his features. Nothing like the smiling boy I'd once known.

"After the passing of our *mokkira*," Kiran started, and I heard a wave of murmurs rumble its way through the crowd, "we were in desperate need of a skilled healer for the frost. Instead of bringing one in from *Dothik*, I took the best healer from the *saruk* of my father. She is to be our *mokkira* from this day forward, and I expect the same respect given to her as you gave our last *mokkira*."

From this day forward?

I pressed my lips together, keeping my gaze steady and my face carefully blank as I scanned the crowd of Dakkari.

I saw expressions of surprise, expressions of worry. Some, however, didn't seem too concerned, which made me feel hopeful. There was a crowd of maybe fifty gathered, though I knew this wasn't the whole population of Kiran's horde. But word would spread if this place was anything like a *saruk*. There were sure to be plenty of gossips. Everyone would know that their *Vorakkar* had brought in a *vekkiri mokkira* by the end of the night.

When Kiran glanced down at me, silence stretched out, thin yet heavy.

Clearing my throat, I regarded the crowd once more and said, "It will be my honor to serve the horde of Rath Okkili, just as I served the *saruk* of Rath Okkili."

That was when my gaze caught on someone that made me still with surprise.

A female.

A *human* female.

She was lingering on the edge of the crowd, leaning against one of the *volikis* that lay closest to the *pyroki* enclosure. Her belly was swollen with child, and I knew that *this* was one of the females Kiran had spoken of. The one with a Dakkari male as her mate, with a hybrid child in her womb.

Another jolt of doubt went through me as I met her eyes. They were like *mine*. Though her skin was lighter in color and she had brown eyes instead of my hazel ones, her eyes were slightly tilted up at the corners like mine. She had whites surrounding her irises, like mine. She had hairs over her brow bones, no tail jutted out from underneath her flowing dress, and the tips of her ears weren't pointed, like mine.

When she nibbled her lip, I saw the flash of her white, dull teeth, and I felt something strange in my chest. Something I'd never felt before. Something like kinship and recognition.

I'd never seen a human before, except for my own face peering back at me in reflections. I didn't remember my parents. I didn't remember the village I must've come from. I didn't remember ever seeing another face that looked like mine...until now.

Then, with blood rushing in my ears, I saw another. A human male came up next to her, and they bent their heads, speaking. I studied the male, my heart thudding in my chest, and a frown formed on my face.

This male had hair the color of dark fire and skin so light that it seemed translucent. His eyes were *blue*, a color I'd never seen before, except when it was reflected in *Drukkar's*

Sea. He wore black hide pants and a brown tunic over his lithe form.

I saw another human approach. Another male, with gray hair and dark eyes. They were all looking at me, and I met their gazes with a kind of stunned realization.

Belatedly, I realized that Kiran was speaking, and I exhaled a breath sharply, turning my eyes back toward the crowd.

"—and a feast will be held to celebrate her arrival and our new home in the South Lands for the frost. In two nights."

A feast?

The crowd gradually began to disperse once it was clear that that was all Kiran was going to say on the matter, though many lingered and watched.

Not unlike a saruk *after all,* I thought. Perhaps everyone in a horde was always in one another's business as well.

A shadow fell over me, and when I looked up, I saw that it was the Dakkari female, the one that had spoken about my pendant. She was looking at me with a slight frown, her eyes narrowed as she studied me more closely. Raising my brow in expectation, I met her gaze readily, which I could tell she hadn't expected.

She reminded me of Laru's friends, the friends that, when we'd been young, had always tried to make me cry because I was different. They were all grown now, with young children of their own, but even now...I sometimes still remembered the ugly things they used to lob at me.

It wasn't me she wished to speak to, however. Her expression softened, her eyes sparking when she turned to regard Kiran.

Of course, I thought, pressing my lips together in annoyance.

"Can I speak with you a moment, *Vorakkar*?" the female asked, her voice low and purring. "In private?"

The female was beautiful. Her hair glittered in the sun, her curves were on full display, and her nipples were tight and pebbled through the almost-translucent material of her dress. I'd always known that Dakkari were not shy about nudity...but ever since I'd disrobed for Kiran that night on the cliff, I had always avoided being exposed for too long.

Kiran barely spared her a glance. In reading his expression, I swore I spied a hint of his annoyance, a slight ticking of his left jaw muscle, which always meant he was impatient.

"Later," he bit out gruffly. "I must see the *mokkira* settled and then find my *pujerak*."

The female barely held in her pout, her hand lifting as if to touch his arm before remembering herself. Seeing that movement, I realized that they'd been intimate once. She had almost dared to touch him in front of the crowd that were still gathered.

Something uncomfortable burned in my chest at the thought. I swallowed. I sensed Kiran's dark eyes on me before I felt his hand pressing into the small of my back, leading me away.

Stiffening, I stepped away from his touch, giving him a glare over my shoulder. His expression lightened. I swore I saw a brief twitch of his lips before his face smoothed. Already the Dakkari female was looking after us, a dark, furious frown on her lips.

We set out on the path away from the *pyroki* enclosure. A female stepped in our way before gasping and apologizing, lowering her head.

"*Kallo,*" Kiran said to her. It was a term of respect for a horde member, I knew. "Will you follow us? I have a task for you."

"*Lysi, Vorakkar,*" the female squeaked, her eyes widening when she glanced up, as if shocked Kiran had spoken directly to her.

The dark-haired female fell into step behind us as we wound our way through the encampment. Kiran nodded his head to the horde members we passed, but his expression invited no further conversation. Finally, toward the back of the encampment we stopped in front of a *voliki*.

"This will be yours," Kiran said, gesturing toward it. "For now."

For now?

I frowned, wondering why his words sounded so strange. As if he expected me to be in a different place soon.

"You may rest if you wish. I can have a bath sent in," Kiran said, meeting my gaze.

I swallowed, shaking my head. "I'd like to see where I'll be working, to set up my supplies. I don't need rest."

Kiran studied me. I was all too aware of his gaze hovering over my features. I saw it lower, back to the pendant between my breasts.

"Very well," he rasped. He nodded to the female lingering on the edge of my vision. "Your *piki* will show you."

Piki?

I gasped, outrage filling my breast, especially when I heard the Dakkari female make a trilling sound of surprise in the back of her throat.

A *piki* was one of the higher positions in a horde and a *saruk*. Because a *piki* was the companion to a *Morakkari*. A companion and helper to the queen of the horde, a trusted confidant and friend.

"*Don't* do that," I hissed softly, keeping my voice low so that even the female wouldn't be able to hear.

"Do what?" Kiran challenged.

"Do not say things like that because your horde members will actually believe them," I told him.

If his people believed that Kiran had just assigned me a *piki*, then they would assume that I was his future *Morakkari*. The one he'd chosen for himself.

Which was *ridiculous*. I didn't understand why he would do such a thing.

Unless...

Nik.

He wasn't serious last night. He'd been mocking me when he told me he'd take me as his queen, rubbing salt into an old wound because he could.

And now? He was just furthering that ache.

"You dare to give a *Vorakkar* an order?" he rasped quietly, angling his head down, close to mine. My breath hitched. His eyes were so warm, dancing with something I didn't want to identify. "Only a *Morakkari* can do that. You are only confirming it, *seffi*."

My eyes flashed up to his. I didn't care that others would see me glaring at him. He deserved my ire.

"There's *nothing* to confirm," I hissed, suddenly more angry at myself than I was at him. Because I was letting him get under my skin again when I had promised myself that I wouldn't let my reactions get the best of me. "I told you I wouldn't have you, and I *meant it.*"

His brow quirked.

All arrogance.

All Kiran.

Even he heard my nervous swallow.

"Your *piki* will guide you around the horde, to let you get your bearings," Kiran said again, raising his voice, *daring* me to refute him. "And then she will show you the *mokkira's voliki*. Your apprentice will be waiting for you there."

A little flash of excitement battled with my irritation.

My own apprentice.

My own *voliki*.

My own horde.

My glare never lessened, but I came to the decision to let it go. It would be Kiran's humiliation if he let everyone believe I would be his *Morakkari*. Because I would be leaving. And I wouldn't look back when I did.

I meant what I'd said.

I would never love him again.

That knowledge dampened a bit of my rage.

"*Lysi?*" Kiran rasped, his molten eyes darting back and forth between mine.

I took in a deep breath, setting my shoulders back.

"*Lysi,*" I replied, giving him a small smile that I hoped had a little bite to it. "You may leave, *Vorakkar.* I have work to do."

His sudden smile disarmed me, made me doubt myself as my heart hammered in my chest. His smile always had a way of doing that to me. His smile made the whole world go dizzy, though it made me feel rooted, made me feel *home.*

I hated that it still had that effect on me, after all these years.

He reached out to stroke my cheek, tucking stray hairs behind my ear. My flesh tingled where he touched me. I barely stopped myself from closing my eyes.

"I like when you give me orders, *seffi.*"

Between us, a thousand memories rose, and those memories, most of them wonderful, threatened to choke me.

Then he turned...and he was gone.

"And this is the *bikkus' voliki*," the soft-spoken Dakkari female murmured, coming to a stop in front of another massive domed hide tent.

Above it, I could see black smoke rising into the sky, a venting hole allowing it to escape. The scent in the air around the *voliki*—one of fatty grilled meat—made my mouth water.

This *voliki*, unlike many of the others, had flaps on the side of the tent, like windows. They lowered, revealing thin netting that kept dust and debris out of the cooking space while also letting a cool breeze inside—because I was certain it was as hot in there as it was in the weapons master's *voliki*...and he had a forge.

"If there is not a feast or a celebration, the *bikkus* will deliver your meals around set times. Or if you get hungry before then, you can send me to get you a meal," the female finished.

"You don't do your own cooking here?" I asked, cocking my head to the side. "They cook everyone's meals?"

"*Lysi*," my *piki* said, frowning. "Of course."

"In the *saruk*, we cooked almost all our own meals," I explained.

Another thing I would have to get used to, considering I

quite liked cooking. I thought it was like mixing medicines and tonics. Finding the right ingredients and experimenting with them until you produced something perfect.

She continued to frown, as if confused, and we moved on, making our way to the front of the horde. Earlier, she'd explained that they'd just settled in the South Lands a week before and that they were still preparing for the frost. But to me, everything seemed like it worked and flowed seamlessly. Horde members had their tasks, did their duties, contributed to the horde...and somehow it worked.

As we walked, her words returned to me.

"You don't have to get me anything, you know," I said, feeling that sense of strange discomfort through my chest. Lowering my voice when we passed a group of *darukkars* who looked our way, I said, "The *Vorakkar* was just...he was jesting when he spoke of you being my *piki*. I am not going to be his *Morakkari*. Ever."

Her words struck me as being *very* careful as she said, "Even still, *missiki*—"

I drew in a sharp breath at the title. It meant *mistress*, a position of power.

"If the *Vorakkar* assigned me as your *piki*, that is how I will serve you until he orders me otherwise," she said. Her tone was cautious...almost *apologetic*.

"How about you call me Maeva instead of *missiki*?" I suggested hurriedly. I understood what she was saying. She was duty bound to serve me, as if I *were* the *Morakkari*. I didn't want to get her in trouble with the *Vorakkar*, for she was a member of his horde and was loyal to him, though he would certainly hear about *my* profound irritation with him sooner rather than later.

The female let out a little gasp, her eyes going wide. "*Missiki*, you should not give me your—"

"Name, *lysi*, I know," I said quickly, waving my hand. "But please, I do not care for such things. If you do not wish to call me by my name, then please call me *Mokkira* instead. Not *missiki*."

Her hesitation was palpable. It stretched between us before she finally nodded. "*Lysi, Mokkira.*"

"And what should I call you? *Lirilla*?" I asked.

Lirilla was the term for a female acquaintance, though not quite a friend. Yet. It was a respectful term, however, so I knew she wouldn't find offense in it.

"You may call me by my name, since I am your *piki*, after all," she finally said softly. Her eyes darted to mine, and I saw a hesitant little smile cross her lips. She looked to be a little younger than me but not by too many years. "My name is Hinna."

I knew I wouldn't win on the whole *piki* issue. But I would take it up with Kiran, not with her.

"Hinna," I said softly, inclining my head.

"*Lysi.*"

I gave her a small smile. Though we had just met, I liked her. I thought we could become friends during my time here. She seemed patient and kind as she guided me through the horde.

"Would you like me to show you the *mokkira's voliki* now?" Hinna asked. "*Your voliki?*"

My smile widened.

Lysi, we would get on just fine.

"Lead the way."

The Dakkari boy was sweating and looked at us wild-eyed when Hinna and I stepped into the *voliki* that would be mine to oversee.

I blew out a breath, my eyes flickering over the untidy surfaces, the spilled jars of medicine and brews, the dust that floated in the shaft of light that speared down from the venting hole at the top of the domed structure.

The boy looked bewildered, frowning, but then blushed when he saw Hinna. I didn't think I'd ever *seen* a Dakkari blush, but the color of his golden, ruddy cheeks bloomed darker.

"*Lysi?* Do you... Are you unwell?" the boy asked.

There was a dark green stain on the parchment-colored apron that was tied around his waist. His fingers were stained with what I believed to be the root that made *uudun* salve. His dark black hair reached his shoulders and was haphazardly tied behind him, strands escaping and sticking to the sweat at his temples.

It *was* quite warm in the *voliki*. Just like the *bikkus' voliki*, I saw that there were ties that lowered part of the hide on the inside, to make windows. I went to them, unknotting them and lowering the flaps. Immediately, a breeze swept in, cooling and necessary.

"What—what are you doing?" the boy asked. "*Nik*, the *mokkira* always said when making the brews, the windows stay closed. The wind—"

"That batch of *uudun* is spoiled already. I can smell it," I told the boy, gesturing to the pot that was bubbling over the fire. I went to it, peering down at its contents. "*Lysi*, the color is all wrong. Did you blanch them first?"

The boy blinked rapidly, the frown never leaving his face. His eyes flittered to Hinna and then back to me. "I skinned them."

"*Nik*," I said. "You always blanch first. Then separate the skin. Then mash them, but only in the complete darkness."

The boy wasn't *quite* a boy, but his features were soft, his form slim. I guessed he was close to Hinna's age, a few years younger than me. His eyes had a slight red tinge to them. His tail was black, dragging across the *voliki* floor.

"You're..." the Dakkari male started, peering at me. "Are you the new *mokkira*? The one the *Vorakkar* sent for?"

"*Lysi*," I murmured, inclining my head.

The relief on his face was palpable. For a moment, I thought the boy might start crying.

"I'm assuming the *mokkira* had just taken you on as his apprentice before his passing?" I asked gently.

The boy swallowed hard, the thick golden column of his throat bobbing. "*Lysi*. Only a few moon cycles before."

Poor boy. No wonder.

I nodded, reaching out to touch his forearm. "That's a large burden to carry. But don't worry, I'm here to help you now. *Lysi?*"

He looked at me with new eyes. He didn't even seem to notice that I was a *vekkiri*. He didn't question my presence there. The lines on his forehead smoothed, and he let out a shuddering breath. That was when he seemed to realize the disarray in the *voliki*.

"I had meant to clean before your arrival," he said sheepishly, pushing a strand of hair off his face. "But then I realized our stocks of *uudun* were depleted. It slipped my mind. A female had come to me with sickness, and I forgot—"

"It's all right," I told him, looking around the *voliki*. "We will clean today, get everything sorted and organized. I have extra *uudun* with me in case we need it. But we will focus on replenishing the stores tomorrow, *lysi?*"

From behind me, Hinna asked softly, "Would you like me to get fresh water and cloth, *Missi—Mokkira?*"

I didn't comment on her slight slip of the tongue. Instead, I nodded. "That would be very helpful, *kakkira vor.*"

"I will assist you," the Dakkari boy hurriedly said, that dark blush back on his cheeks when Hinna looked at him. A small smile crossed my lips, but I hoped his little crush wouldn't serve as a distraction. "If that is agreeable to you, *Mokkira*," he added.

"*Lysi*, please help her. We will need a lot of water and cloth to get this *voliki* back to its rightful state," I told him.

His blush deepened.

Before he left, he inclined his head. Quietly, he said, "My given name is Essir, *Mokkira*. It is my honor for you to have it. It will be my honor to learn from you as your apprentice."

Something bubbled up in my throat, thick and wonderful. I'd never had the opportunity to teach anyone before. I'd always wanted this. I'd always worked toward this.

Determination burned inside me. I had only so much time to teach Essir, but I would ensure that he would be able to handle whatever the horde threw at him.

"*Kakkira vor*, Essir," I murmured, inclining my head toward him. "Now go. We have much work to do today."

"*Lysi, Mokkira*," he replied, and then he left the *voliki*, holding the entrance flap open for Hinna.

When I was alone, I sighed. Then I breathed in the various scents, identifying ingredients that lingered, some that might have been forever imprinted in the hide of the structure.

Sturdy work benches lined the walls of the *voliki*, curved to follow the circular shape. It was massive inside—more room, even, than we'd had in the *saruk*. A few support columns stood in the very middle, surrounding the venting hole at the top. And on the left side of the *voliki*, there was a thick flap that covered at entire section of the structure, cutting it off from the rest of the space.

When I went to inspect it, it was as I suspected. This was where the previous *mokkira* had brewed his potions and tonics. No light reached here, just like in the back room at the *saruk*. Unlike the rest of the *voliki*, this space looked relatively clean. Practically untouched, I assumed, since the *mokkira's* death.

I ran my fingers over the black pot that sat on the work

bench there. It was clean, though dust ridden. I went back out to the main section. A Dakkari-steel cot was to the right of the tent, nearest the venting hole. For the more serious wounds, the ones that bled. Dakkari steel cleaned up quite easily, leaving no stains on its surface.

Tall columns of cabinets and drawers were flush against the far-right wall, where I assumed the medicines and supplies were kept.

I blew out a breath, listening to the quiet of the *voliki*, which mixed with the sounds of Kiran's horde drifting in through the open, netted windows.

This will be my home, if only for a little while, I thought.

And I would make the best of it.

CHAPTER 18

"An *ungira*?" my *pujerak*, Errok, breathed. His brow furrowed. He went silent for a brief moment.

"Half a day's ride from here," I finished, spreading my hands over the hip-height table before us in my council's *voliki*. The elders were not present, nor were the masters. It was just Errok and me, and we spoke in low tones. I pointed down at the map of Dakkar splayed out on the table, the tip of my claw grazing over the South Lands. "Around here."

"You think our gates will not be enough?" Errok asked next. "Already I have heard rumblings from the males. Asking why they need to use so many materials since we are in the South Lands. They believe we are safe here."

At any other time, that would very well be the case. The South Lands were often seen as peaceful. Unlike the East, where larger beasts like the *ungira* roamed because they liked the heat, the South Lands didn't have such predators.

The stitching on my back pulled, making my teeth grit. Maeva had put fresh bandages on it that morning, before we'd left to journey to my horde, but the pain was a constant discomfort.

"I think the gates will need to be reinforced with the last of our steel stores," I admitted.

"The weapons master will not be happy about that," Errok pointed out. "Some of the warriors need new swords."

"I know," I growled, blowing out a sharp breath. "I need to send messages to Rath Kitala and Rath Drokka. Have the *thespers* come back?"

"Only one," Errok said.

So I'd only be able to send one message. *Vok.*

"We need to meet in *Dothik*," I knew, frustrated.

"Rath Drokka will be loath to leave his *Morakkari* at this time," Errok countered. "His white-haired sorceress just gave birth to their children. He will not journey all the way to *Dothik*, especially when the frost draws nearer."

"Whatever is happening in the East Lands," I began softly, my eyes straying to the Dead Mountain on the map, "it is beyond anything we've ever seen before. I fear if we wait too long to understand what this is, it will be too late."

"And the *Dothikkar*?"

"*Vok*," I hissed. "Like he would do anything about this?"

Errok pressed his lips together.

"*Nik*, he will let his hordes take care of his problems, as he's always done," I finished. "He will keep his army behind his walls."

"But Rath Kitala told him of the red mist?" Errok asked softly.

"*Lysi.* He sent a messenger to *Dothik*, not a *thesper*."

"Then perhaps he will call on all of you to journey to *Dothik* and Rath Drokka will not have a choice in the matter."

That was likely what would happen, which was frustrating in itself. I needed to be *here*, in my horde, not journeying around Dakkar at the whims of the *Dothikkar*.

I went silent, my eyes flickering over the map. My gaze drifted to the *saruk*, perched at the edge of *Drukkar's Sea*. I could almost feel the breeze across my face and taste the salt in the air.

"The weapons master will need to make do with what he has for the new swords," I decided. "The gates will be important for the frost. If I am called to *Dothik*, I will bring steel back with me, but we will use what we have here for reinforcements."

"I will inform the builders," Errok said.

I nodded. "Is there anything that needs my attention after my absence?"

"*Nik*, everything has been running smoothly."

"Good."

Errok asked, "The new *mokkira* is settled, then?"

I felt Errok's heavy gaze on me. I met his eyes. "*Lysi.* She is."

"Are you going to tell me about her?" Errok asked next. "Or is that a secret you keep for yourself, one you've kept for so long?"

"I don't know what you mean."

Errok barked out a short laugh. "I have known you since our training days in *Dothik*, Kiran. Almost fifteen years now. Don't play that game with me."

My chest felt tight when I looked back down to the map.

"Is it *her*?" he asked next.

My jaw clenched. My swallow was hard and loud in the *voliki.*

I had never explicitly told Errok about Maeva. We'd met when I left the *saruk*, when I went to live with my uncle in *Dothik* to train among the *Dothikkar's* warriors for the upcoming Trials. I returned home, back to the *saruk*, every year for a short time. Then I would return to *Dothik.*

That went on for some time until I completed the Trials, until I was made *Vorakkar* with my blood and pain, until I took to the wildlands and formed a horde of my own, with Errok as my chosen *pujerak.*

"She told me you have known one another since you were children," Errok continued after my silence stretched out.

My head snapped up. "What else did she say?"

"Nothing," he said. "Well, she told me her name."

"*Vok,*" I rasped, a short chuffing laugh falling from my lips. "Of course she did."

"You were lovers?" Errok guessed.

I froze.

"Never," I finally murmured.

My *pujerak* raised a brow in surprise. "Truly?"

I growled, my hands clenching into fists on the table.

"We were..." I trailed off, not knowing how to explain the complexities of it. But his words made me remember every single time I had *wanted* Maeva to be my lover, though those moments had been later in our friendship. "Complicated."

"*Vok,*" Errok rasped, his eyes widening in surprise. "It *is* her, isn't it? The female that's *vokking haunted* you all these years."

"I don't want to speak of this," I finally snapped.

"You mean you don't want to speak of *her,*" Errok amended.

"It doesn't matter," I rasped. "She loathes me now. For good reason."

"Yet you brought her to your horde," Errok said, crossing his arms over his wide chest. "For what purpose? You intend to win her back? Make her your *Morakkari*?"

My mind flashed to the dream Kakkari had given me. A vision?

What I knew for certain was when I was with Maeva, even when she was furious with me or cursing me silently...I felt that peace that I had been searching for ever since I'd left the *saruk* all those years ago.

It had been her. It had always been her. I'd found her when I was thirteen years old, and I'd fought against her pull ever since. I'd hurt her, rejected her, humiliated her...when all she'd ever done was care for me. Love me.

She was right to hate me. I would hate me, had our positions been reversed.

In the end, I didn't respond to Errok. I'd leave the bastard guessing because it would serve him right for meddling.

"I'll be at the training grounds," I said, pushing back from the table. "Prepare the *thesper* for me. I'll send the message to Rath Kitala by the end of the night."

A gentle glow spread out from underneath the entrance flap of Maeva's *voliki*.

Anticipation had been building inside me all day. I'd gone almost nine years without laying eyes on her once, but now that she was back in my life...I could hardly go a single afternoon.

"*Seffi*," I grunted out, keeping my ears perked for sounds inside, and I stepped forward.

A small gasp met me.

Maeva had been undressing. My gaze caught on the skin of her back, smooth save for the jagged, deep scar that ran down her shoulder—a scar she wouldn't tell me about.

Though I'd seen plenty of naked females before in my life—Maeva included, for that matter—I growled in surprise. She was still wearing her riding trews from earlier in the day, and a small bathing tub was wedged up against the side of the *voliki*, steam curling off its surface.

She'd been about to bathe, and I'd interrupted her.

The sight of her skin disappeared from my view as she hurriedly tugged her bandeau back down over her breasts.

Maeva turned to glare at me, her jaw ticking. My nostrils flared as I studied her face like I'd been starved for a mere glimpse of it. Even frowning at me, she was beautiful.

"You cannot just enter my dwelling," she informed me, her tone clipped yet restrained.

"Actually, I can," I grunted, fists clenched at my sides. "We are not in a *saruk*, Maeva. And I am your *Vorakkar*. You need to remember that."

She wanted to say something, wanted to argue with me. I saw it. It was the way her mouth pinched, how the space between her brow squeezed...before everything smoothed out. Before her frustration and anger disappeared entirely and I was left with her indifference again.

It felt like a punch in the gut, just like it had the previous night. But I had promised myself that I would make amends for my hurtful words, lobbed at her in frustration and longing and melancholy.

"And if you wish to bathe, you should tie off the entrance with these," I informed her, gesturing to the slim cords that ran down the sides of the flap. "If you want your privacy."

Her eyes flickered to the ties. After a moment, she nodded, casting me a speculative look that made the *voliki* seem three sizes too small.

"What do you need, *Vorakkar*?" she asked.

My body tightened at the question. Distracting myself, I ran my eyes over her travel sacks, which were sprawled out across her bed of furs. I frowned, seeing she hadn't brought much. My eyes went to her storage chests but saw they were open and empty.

"Where is the rest of your clothing?" I asked.

She slid her gaze to the bed. "I have enough for the cold season. My fur serves me well," she added, gesturing to the while pelt that was still slightly stained with the *darukkar's* blood, the one she'd helped after the *polkunu* attack.

My frown turned into a scowl. She didn't know how brutal the frost could be in the wildlands. *Voliki* were not *soliki*. They didn't provide as much insulation. The nights would be cold, and she didn't have a mate to warm her.

Yet, I mused.

Then again, Maeva had never needed much. While the other females in the *saruk* had cooed over baubles and trinkets that our tradesmith would bring from *Dothik*, Maeva only had eyes for the sea. And the forest. And her family. And...me.

She'd never cared about new dresses or adornments. Or jewelry—which was why I found her mother's pendant so curious now. When we were young, she'd risen early in the mornings, threaded a brush through her unruly hair once or twice—much to the dismay of her mother and Laru—and gone outside, where she loved it most. With the breeze across her cheeks and the salt air filling her lungs.

The frost had always been hard on her. Though it was more mild along the coast, the cold season kept many inside their *solikis*. And for Maeva, that was the cruelest of tortures.

"You will need more than this," I told her, my voice gruff. Why hadn't her parents told her about the cold season among a horde? Surely they would've told her to bring more supplies. "I will have your *piki*"—she sucked in a breath—"procure more for you."

"I'm actually glad you're here," Maeva started, ignoring my criticism about her packing, "because we need to talk about that."

"About what?" I asked, raising a brow, crossing my arms over my chest. Her gaze flickered down to it, to the scar that lay right over my pectoral. Despite the chill in the night air, I'd just come from the training grounds and had left my furs back at my *voliki*. My blood was running hot. I hardly felt the cold.

"I know you're jesting about it," she continued, meeting my gaze again, "but you really shouldn't call her that. Others will overhear and assume something that isn't true. I would think you would know better, considering this is your horde. You know how rumors circulate."

"She is your *piki*," I murmured softly. "She has a *piki's* duties. She will attend to you until you dismiss her for the day. She will assist you when you need it. She will help you dress and adorn yourself. She will—"

"Why?" Maeva asked. "Because I'm not presentable enough for your horde? I don't need help *dressing*, Kiran."

She must really be angry with me to use my given name.

"*Nik*," I said softly, keeping her eyes. "You have always been beautiful."

Those brown eyes—with mesmerizing flecks of green and threads of gold—widened slightly.

"And I don't care what you wear. But you are new to a horde," I remarked. "New to a horde going into the frost. You will need help. And I want to ensure that you are taken care of while you're here."

"The other humans were new to your horde as well," she countered. "Did you give them all *pikis* too?"

My lips twitched, hearing the slight sarcasm in her tone, though she kept her voice light and even. No one else would notice it except me. And maybe Laru.

"I gave them guides as they adjusted, *lysi*, though they were not assigned *pikis*."

Frustration lit her eyes up before she seemed to extinguish it. "Then she is my guide."

She settled on that word, and I knew she preferred it over *piki.*

I couldn't help the dark grin that stole over my face, one that made her lips press together and her hands fidget at her sides.

She's not as unaffected by me as she appears, I realized. Relief filled me at the thought. I always felt like I was waiting when it came to her. Waiting for something. A sign, perhaps, before I would take the final plunge, make the final decision.

"*Nik*," I said. "She is your *piki*. Not your guide."

Maeva glared. "What's the difference?"

Her words were soft but clipped, and she raised a brow to highlight her point.

I stepped toward her. It was already small in the *voliki*, made smaller by the presence of the bathing tub. I heard her breath quicken as I approached, until I was next to her bed and staring down at her. I could lift my hand and touch her cheek, we were that close.

"What do you think?" I whispered.

"You've taken it into your mind now," she said, her eyes flickering back and forth between mine, realization spreading. "I told you I wouldn't have you, and now you're determined to prove me wrong. You really haven't changed at all, have you?"

"It was always in my mind," I rasped out roughly. I let her process those vague words as she saw fit. Simply hearing them made her lips downturn. "And you are the same way, Maeva. You cannot deny that you are as stubborn as I am."

"*Fine*," she snapped. "If you want her to be my *piki*, then that is what she'll be. But it will be *you* who will look like a fool once I leave after the frost. Not me. Not again."

She hadn't meant to say that.

Her expression became stricken at the last words—my own chest tightened until I couldn't breathe—and I caught her chin, clasping her face gently when she began to turn from me. To hide?

"You are *not* a fool, Maeva," I said, my tone bordering on savage, as angry as it was. "And you never were."

For a moment—for the briefest and most wonderful of moments—her guard dropped. The walls melted away, and I caught sight of the girl I'd loved a thousand different ways.

And then she was *here*.

Vulnerable and expressive and opening herself up to me in a way that humbled me. Showing me her hurt and her frustration and...our memories.

Right here.

My heart began to pound in my chest, so loudly that I thought she would be able to hear it. Those twin dark orbs staring back at me went a little glassy. She seemed to be holding her breath as my thumb stroked the softness of her cheek.

"*Seffi,*" I whispered, not trusting my own voice in that moment.

Then something flashed in her eyes. I felt her retreat as if it was a physical thing.

Then she slammed that wall back into place, cutting me off again, and it made me go cold.

I had promised to make her remember. Remember me. Remember the girl she'd once been. Remember everything.

But she didn't want to. She refused to.

Because I'd hurt her and I'd done it knowingly. Purposefully. Cruelly.

Because she hated me.

Until that moment, however, until she showed me a glimmer of what we'd once had together, until she snatched it back away...until that moment, I hadn't realized how *deep* that hatred ran.

She didn't want anything to do with me.

Which is problematic, I mused, a deep, brooding scowl forming across my features.

Because I was beginning to suspect that she was *mine*...and that she always had been.

CHAPTER 19

"Hinna," I murmured quietly, so Essir wouldn't overhear her given name.

My *"piki"* turned her gaze to me, expectant and hopeful. It was obvious the poor female was bored out of her mind, sitting in the *mokkira voliki* with nothing to do, while Essir and I brewed a batch of *uudun* salve.

Essir, I'd found, had a great memory, but at times, he could become easily distracted. Earlier, he'd memorized the recipe for *uudun* quite quickly, repeating all the necessary steps in perfect order, yet he'd caught sight of Hinna briefly and he'd added too many roots to the pot.

When I'd gently corrected him, he'd been mortified, almost plunging his hand under the boiling surface of the water to fetch the last root before I caught his wrist. He got flustered easily, which wouldn't make him a great healer. But he was young too. Perhaps calm would come with time and with confidence.

Because the last *mokkira* hadn't taught him nearly enough.

It was clear I had my work cut out for me.

"Lysi, Mokkira?" Hinna asked, rising quickly from her spot

on the floor cushion. She'd already washed all the surfaces in the *voliki* for the second time that morning. Everything was fresh and clean, not a speck of dust or blood or earth anywhere.

I bit my lip, looking down at the *kioni* I was mashing in my mortar. She came to my side, her form lingering in my periphery.

"Do you know where the *Vorakkar* is?" I asked.

"He usually trains in the morning. He might still be on the training grounds with the *darukkars*. Or he might be in with his council. They've been meeting a lot lately."

I thought of the *ungira's* den we'd nearly tumbled into and pressed my lips together. There was no doubt in my mind that they were meeting more than usual, but I wondered how much the horde knew of the stirrings in the East.

"Will you go find him for me?" I requested. "He was injured on our journey, and I need to take out the stitchings today."

She almost choked. "You want me to...to summon the *Vorakkar?*"

I turned my gaze to her, pausing in my work, the muscles in my arm burning from the repetitive motion.

"*Lysi,*" I said. "It's important."

Hinna swallowed, then dropped her head in a slight bow of respect.

"*Lysi, Missi—Mokkira,*" she corrected hurriedly. "I will find him for you."

"*Kakkira vor.*"

My "*piki*" left the tent, briefly letting in a stray shaft of light, piercing across the workbench I was working at. Essir wasn't visible. He was behind the thick curtain that separated the dark area where we could brew the more sensitive medicines. I'd tasked him with watching the pot of *uudun,* and I knew that he was probably counting the simmering bubbles. He was eager to learn, and I admired that. I could work with that.

I had just finished mashing the *kioni*, my heart thudding in my chest knowing I would have to see Kiran that day, when that shaft of light appeared next to my hand again.

Already? I wondered, frowning, turning.

But it wasn't Hinna. Or Kiran.

It was the human female. The pregnant one. The one that I'd seen yesterday when I'd arrived at the horde. And behind her, coming into the *voliki*, was the human male with dark red hair that almost looked black.

"Hello," the human female said as I stared in surprise. "I hope we are not interrupting."

She spoke in the universal tongue, not in Dakkari, and for the first time, I thanked Kiran's mother in my mind for teaching it to me, sending that prayer of thanks up to Kakkari, where it was in her hands.

It had taken almost daily instruction for four years before Kiran's *lomma* had considered me fluent. Though my pronunciation was not perfect, I could speak and understand the language that my birth parents would've spoken. The language *I* would have spoken had I not been abandoned by them.

An expression of hesitation came over the human female's features, and she glanced at the male next to her, who was studying me carefully.

"Do you...do you not speak our language?" she asked.

"*Lysi,*" I said in a rush. "Yes. Yes, I do. My apologies."

Relief was palpable in her expression though she commented, "Your accent is like theirs. Different."

I thought it strange. That she was calling the *Dakkari* different when it had been *me*, all my life, that had been the strange one among them.

I swallowed.

"My name is Addie," the female said. She waved to the male standing next to her, who gave me a lopsided grin, his blue eyes seeming to sparkle in the light. "And this is my friend, Gabe. We...we wanted to come meet you."

I looked between them. Gabe glanced down at Addie when she introduced him. The expression on his face was one of... affection and admiration.

Perhaps I'd been mistaken. Kiran had told me there was a human female in the horde that was pregnant with a Dakkari male's child, but perhaps it was not this one.

"Is he the father of the child?" I asked, nodding down to her belly. She was carrying low and looked to be mere weeks from giving birth.

Addie's eyes widened, a choke emerging from her throat. "*Gabe?* No."

To his credit, Gabe didn't take her words as an insult. At least, I didn't think so. His smile dropped briefly before it lit up his face again. Then he crossed his arms, leaning against one of the stabilizing columns near the entrance of the *voliki.*

"She wouldn't have me," came his voice. His words were in jest, I thought.

"My husband is Dakkari," Addie said softly, a pleased flush coming over her cheeks. I remembered a time when my features formed a similar expression. All I had to do back then was *think* about Kiran and it was like entering a dreamland.

"I understand," I said, stepping closer, my hand skimming the steel table that was set up near the middle of the *voliki.* "The *Vorakkar* told me about you."

She swallowed, blinking up at me with brown eyes as I studied her features, seeing similarities there that made me feel...dizzy. No tail. Rounded ears. Whites in her eyes around the irises. A slim nose that gave way to lips that were like my own. A similar softened face shape, unlike the sharpness of Dakkari features.

And her build was like my own, save for her pregnancy. We were almost the same height. I was only ever the same height as

Dakkari females when they had not yet gone through their final growth.

And the male...

The dark-haired human male was taller than I was, a little broader. But he didn't possess the sheer strength of Dakkari males, with their wide chests, thick thighs, and towering builds.

We all stood staring at one another, silence stretching between us. I began to shift on my feet when the male laughed, husky and deep, surprising me with its richness.

His eyes were bright and amused when he asked, "You've never seen other humans before, have you?"

I blinked. Addie slapped the back of her hand across his abdomen, making him wheeze out a rough breath. Though her own gaze was curious.

"*Nik,*" I murmured. I cleared my throat. "No. I have not."

Gabe cocked his head to the side. Unlike Dakkari males, his hair was cut short to his scalp. It was only long enough to curl around his ears.

"Where did you come from?" he wondered.

"If you speak of a human village," I started, the words strange on my tongue, "then I am not certain. I was found in a forest when I was young. My home is the *saruk* of Rath Okkili. By *Drukkar's Sea.* That is where I was raised."

"So...you grew up among the Dakkari?" Addie asked. "Truly?"

"*Lysi.*"

"Wow," she rasped, but I didn't understand that word's meaning. Kiran's *lomma* hadn't taught me that one. Though I guessed it was a kind of exclamation, given her widened eyes. "That's...surprising."

I caught motion out of the corner of my eye and saw that Essir was eavesdropping on our conversation, though I wasn't certain he knew the universal tongue.

In Dakkari, with a raised brow I asked him, "Has the *uudun* begun to separate yet?"

His expression turned sheepish, and he scuttled back into the darkened area. I heard, "*Nik, Mokkira.* Soon."

I turned my attention back on Addie when she asked, "What is your name?"

I hesitated, thinking of Essir in earshot, and how I quite liked him calling me *Mokkira*. That seemed like a silly, selfish thing though.

"Or," she started, her expression dropping slightly, embarrassed, "do you not wish for us to have your name? I'm sorry. I forget sometimes, even though my husband always—"

"It's all right," I said. "My name is Maeva."

"Maeva," she repeated, her embarrassment turning into a pleased, shy expression. "It's nice to meet you."

My eyes went to Gabe. I felt a strange flush threaten to crawl up my neck when I saw his eyes flickering over me, dragging over my shoulders, my breasts, my hips, my legs, my feet, before he met my eyes. He didn't seem embarrassed to be caught. Instead, he gave me a wide, teasing grin that made me freeze. That made me swallow hard. Because it reminded me entirely too much of Kiran's. All confidence and charm.

Nik.

Averting my gaze to Addie, in an effort to distract myself, I asked, "Will you come lie on the table since you are here? I would like to check the child."

Addie bit her lip but nodded, waddling over to the steel table. It was quite high up for her, but Gabe assisted her before he retreated back toward the entrance, giving us space.

Just then another shaft of light entered the *voliki*. Hinna returned, seeming startled by the presence of the two newcomers before her expression smoothed. She came to me. In Dakkari, she said, "The *Vorakkar* is meeting with his council. He told me that he will come when he is able to."

I nodded, relief sizzling through me, which made me ashamed. I didn't want to be a coward when it came to Kiran... but last night was still swimming in my mind, and I didn't know if I had recomposed myself quite yet. I didn't know if I was ready to see him again so soon.

Hinna retreated back to her place on the floor cushion, next to a stretch of cabinets that I'd organized my medicines, potions, tonics, and ingredients in.

Placing my hands on Addie's growing belly, I pressed, feeling for her organs and anything abnormal.

"When did you learn of the pregnancy?" I asked, concentrating closely, looking at the steel of the table.

"About three moon cycles ago," she said. "I think. I don't know how long before then...we didn't realize it until my bleeding time stopped."

I nodded, though her answer filled me with doubt. I had never encountered a hybrid pregnancy. Everything I knew about birthing might not apply here, and that filled me with discomfort. I wondered if the last *mokkira* had kept any notes. If he had, I hadn't found any in the *voliki* when we'd cleaned and organized it yesterday.

"When did you come to the horde?" I asked, frowning.

"Six moon cycles?" she asked. I sensed her turning her head, regarding Gabe. "You think?"

"About that," he replied, his voice gruff.

They'd been here that long? Had the events of the Dead Mountain been that long ago already?

I pressed deeper, feeling for the child, a small bulk that felt familiar yet different.

"Any pain?" I asked Addie quietly.

"No," she said.

"Any sickness?"

She hesitated. "Sometimes. It's gotten better."

"I have something you can take for the nausea," I told her. "My sister depends on it when she is pregnant. It will help."

"Your sister?" she asked. "There is another human in your *saruk*?"

My eyes flashed up in surprise. "*Nik*. My sister is Dakkari. We are not of the same blood, but she is my sister nonetheless."

Addie's cheeks flushed. "Of course. I'm sorry for assuming..."

She trailed off, and silence stretched between us.

She cleared her throat. "Thank you. For offering to help with the sickness. It can be brutal some mornings."

I nodded, keeping the frown off my features when I felt the child in the wrong position.

Vok.

Another thread of doubt reached me. The safest way for Dakkari females to give birth was with the child facing head down. But what about humans? Was this position normal?

Addie's child was head up. At least, that was what I believed.

"Did the *mokkira* say when he believed you would give birth?" I asked.

"He thought I was a moon cycle or two away. That was before his passing though." She studied me, swallowing. "Is everything all right?"

"*Lysi*," I murmured, giving her a small smile when I pulled my hands away. "I will be honest though. I have never delivered a hybrid child."

Addie swallowed, her gaze drifting down to her belly. "Yes, the last *mokkira* told me that as well."

I didn't like the uncertainty and fear that had drifted into her voice. I reached forward, squeezing her forearm.

"But there are others that have," I told her. "In other hordes."

I knew that for certain.

"Truly?" Addie whispered.

"I will write to the healers. To learn what I can about their experiences, *lysi*?"

You have nothing to fear was poised on the tip of my tongue. But my training prevented me from saying it. Never give false hope. That was what my *mokkira* had always ingrained in me.

She nodded, hope springing into her gaze. "But...the child feels all right now?"

Again, I didn't want to lie to her.

"The child might be in the wrong position," I admitted. Her face paled. "But I believe I can turn him. Or her. I would prefer to write to the other healers first, however. To be certain."

She nodded. "Yes. Please."

"For now, let me get you the tonic for the morning sickness. Just take a sip of it if you're feeling any nausea."

"Thank you," came her small voice, watching as I went to my cabinets and procured the blue tonic that was of my own creation, the one that Laru had practically hoarded during her last pregnancy.

Thinking of her, knowing that I wasn't there to help her, hit me with a pang of guilt and longing. I'd dreamed of her last night, a senseless dream, though I'd known Laru had been there. A comforting, familiar presence.

I blew out a long breath and handed Addie the tonic, the blue liquid sloshing in the large vial.

Helping her down off the table, I led her back to where Gabe was standing. My eyes went to him, and then I remembered the older human male that had approached them the day before.

"How many humans are in the horde?" I asked, wondering if they had all come from the Dead Mountain...if they had all been imprisoned slaves of the Ghertun.

"Only six," Gabe said. He inclined his head to me, a smile dancing on his lips. "Seven, now."

Addie cut in and asked, "Will you be coming to the feast tomorrow night?"

The feast?

Oh, *lysi*, I remembered Kiran announcing that yesterday. I'd almost forgotten.

"I suppose so," I said, giving her another smile.

"Then I guess we'll see you there," she said softly. "We can introduce you to the others then."

I nodded. "I'd like that."

Addie waved, a flutter of her hand, as she stepped out into the cooling afternoon. Gabe was slower to leave.

I felt his fingers brush mine. I blinked when he winked at me.

"Save me a dance tomorrow night, will you, Maeva?" he asked, that self-confident grin on his handsome face.

A dance?

Then he was gone, slipping through the entrance, disappearing from view though I heard their footsteps retreat.

I heard Addie's fading voice. "You're smitten with her, Gabe," came her teasing.

His laugh was his only response, and then I couldn't hear them anymore.

I'd been courted before. By Dakkari males who gave me gifts and laughed and flirted and touched. Once it had happened when I was younger, though his courtship had suddenly stopped. Another time had been a couple years after my mother died, but I had ignored his advances. Another was a year after that, which ended the same way.

I remembered Laru's fears, her quiet confession to me…that she worried I'd never love another male again. That I didn't have the openness or the will to. That I would never lower my guard, that I would never be vulnerable around another again to *allow* myself to love.

Laru might have been right, though I found that I desperately wanted her to be wrong.

Gabe wanted me to save him a dance?

I just...might, I thought to myself.

"*Mokkira,*" came Essir's voice, making me jump. "The *uudun*
is beginning to separate."

Inhaling a deep breath, I nodded.

"I'll be right there."

CHAPTER 20

"*M*okkira," came the voice.

In the privacy and emptiness of my *voliki*, I jumped, my heart beginning to throb, half expecting to see Kiran ducking his way inside.

It was night. Darkness had long fallen, and I was sitting on my bed after my bath, brushing through the wild locks of my hair.

But it wasn't Kiran's voice.

"*Lysi?* You may enter," I called out.

A head ducked inside. It was a *darukkar*. His red eyes regarded me before his head dropped in a slight nod of respect.

"The *Vorakkar* requests your presence at his *voliki*," the *darukkar* said. "I will lead you to him."

I stood from my bed, dropping the brush onto the low table that I'd taken my evening meal at. I'd waited for Kiran all afternoon and into the early evening, for him to make an appearance after I'd requested *his* presence. I'd dismissed Essir and Hinna once it grew dark...and still, I'd waited, perched on a stool in the *mokkira's voliki*.

Annoyance stretched tight inside me, but I gathered my supplies and followed the *darukkar*. We weaved through the encampment, heading toward the back of it until we came to a large *voliki* that was separate from all the rest.

Light filtered through a small slit in the entrance flap, and the *darukkar* hung back as I stepped forward.

"He is waiting."

So did I, I couldn't help but think. *All day.*

I pressed my fingertips to my chest, just over my heart, and felt the rapid throb of it. Taking a deep breath, I pushed my way into the *voliki*, not bothering to announce my presence.

Kiran's *voliki* was everything I'd imagined a *Vorakkar's voliki* to be. Almost regal with its expert-crafted furnishings, though the carpets that lined the floor seemed well-worn with age. His *voliki* was a similar size to the *mokkira's*, though it didn't smell like boiled *uudun* and everything about it was more inviting.

It smelled of Kiran. A scent that always reminded me of summertime and the salty, warm wind that blew in from the far west. Of heat and the earthy fragrance of *runiri* when they were just beginning to sprout, pushing up from the rich, dark soil.

That was what Kiran smelled like—an addicting scent I'd gone without for quite some time.

How was it that a certain smell could trigger a rush of memories?

Nik, I would not think of them, I decided. Instead, I inspected the rest of his *voliki* quickly, getting my bearings.

Like the *mokkira's voliki*, Kiran's had stabilizing columns toward the middle, which surrounded the venting hole at the top of the hide. A bathing tub was just to my left. A darkened area at the back of *voliki* was where his storage chests lay. A tall cabinet was to my right. Just next to it hung a blade and a few daggers, their golden tips glinting with the fire light from the basin, which was placed in front of the cabinet. Intricate designs were carved into the gold of the basin, beautiful and eye catching.

His bed, large and imposing, was piled high with furs,

though they were mussed and askew. I wondered how many females had known its softness and warmth before I pushed the thought away, especially when it made my stomach sour.

And in front of the bed, in front of me, near the middle of the tent was a low table, laden with platters of food. It was *there* that Kiran was sitting. Eating. His gaze had flicked up to me when I'd entered, and now he was watching me with those golden, knowing eyes.

He'd bathed, I noticed. The tips of his dark hair were wet, stray droplets of water trailing down his bare, wide, scarred chest. His legs were bare as well, though he was wearing a fur loincloth that covered his lower region.

I swallowed, flicking my gaze away from *that* part of him.

The expanse of his golden flesh was on full display, however, luminous and difficult not to appreciate. Slabs of muscles shifted, muscles that humans didn't even possess, when he leaned forward, beckoning me closer, watching me from his place on the floor, seated on a cushion.

With such a large *voliki*, I would have thought it would make Kiran seem smaller. But I'd have been sorely mistaken. The *voliki* seemed smaller with *him* in it, not the other way around. His mere presence was...commanding.

The fire in the basin sparked, and I nearly jumped out of my skin.

Thankfully, Kiran didn't comment on it and instead asked, "Have you eaten?"

"*Lysi,*" I replied, coming forward though he hadn't given me permission. The sooner I finished unstitching his wound, the sooner I could return to my own *voliki*. The sooner I could get away from him and his warm flesh and the quiet press of the air around us, making it difficult to breathe.

Kiran caught my wrist when I attempted to slide past him. The shocking warmth of his palm momentarily fizzled any thought from my mind, giving him time to pull me down next to him, so close that my knee brushed the fur of the cloth covering his cock.

I stiffened, beginning to pull away, but Kiran held me.

"Sit with me a while, *seffi*," he murmured. I'd have said his tone was soft, but Kiran's voice was too deep and raspy to be anything but commanding.

I licked my lips, my shoulders sagging when I realized I wouldn't be able to escape quickly. But I wouldn't let him intimidate me either. If he wanted me to stay, fine. But I would make certain he knew it was an inconvenience.

"Will you look at me?"

I set my jaw. Mentally preparing myself for our next battle.

"*Seffi.*"

I bit my tongue and then leveled my gaze on him.

"I am looking at you," I remarked.

On the table, I saw his hand clench. Something dimmed in his gaze, and he shook his head. Frustrated?

"Not like you used to," he commented, the words heavy, choking the air around us.

Suddenly, I realized how tired he looked.

How *exhausted*.

And I felt it then.

A little thread of worry slid like a worm through my belly, uncomfortable and unwanted...but *there*.

Kiran scrubbed a hand over his face, over the lines that pulled around his constant scowl, that never used to be there. If anything, the lines had been there before because he'd smiled and laughed too much.

"Have you been sleeping?" I couldn't help but ask. I told myself it was the healer in me. Sleep was important, especially when the body was recovering from a wound.

"Some," he replied.

"You need to rest more, *Vorakkar*," I said. "Your wound will not—"

"I do not want to fight tonight, *seffi. Lysi?*" came that tired voice.

Swallowing whatever words had been perched on my tongue, I grew quiet. In my lap, I fidgeted with the strap of my satchel that contained my supplies.

When the silence stretched too long, I murmured, "I should check your back."

"*Nik*, not yet," he grunted. "I just want to look at you right now."

I frowned and then stilled when his hand bridged the gap between us. We were already sitting close to one another, so he only had to lift his hand before I felt his hot palm clasp my cheek. His hands were so big that his fingers threaded through my hair as his thumb brushed the tip of my nose.

"Your face is as familiar to me as my own," he murmured. "Isn't that strange?"

Not really. I could draw Kiran's face from memory—at least the face he'd had nine years ago. His features had sharpened over the years, his jaw widening, a few new scars covering his flesh.

But I understood what he meant. I only barely suppressed a shiver when he brushed the tip of my nose again...when his thumb lowered and I felt the tip of his claw rest against my bottom lip.

My heart was speeding in my chest, my eyes locked on his. What was he doing?

Then he was leaning forward, and for a brief, searing moment, I thought that he would kiss me. Only he pressed his nose just below my ear, and this time I couldn't suppress my shiver. He knew my ears were sensitive—they always had been. And when he inhaled gently, bumps exploded across my flesh, down my arms, a sizzle of pleasure racing down my spine, blooming around my tail bone.

"And you still smell like my *seffi*," he murmured in my ear. He pulled back just enough to meet my gaze, and I saw the familiar swirling threads of gold through his eyes. "Like *Drukkar's Sea* and the *felliki* soaps Laru always made you. Does she still?"

The back of my throat began to tighten as the warmth of his breath hit my cheek. So, so familiar.

What I hadn't expected—and what made my hands begin to shake—was the lightning bolt of desire that struck me fast and hard when I found *his* scent was all around me.

Desire.

Wanting.

Longing.

I had cut myself off from feeling it. Whenever it began to bloom and warm in my belly, whether it was from a dream of Kiran I couldn't help or a memory, I distracted myself until it disappeared. I threw myself into my work. I went for long runs along the coast. Anything to dampen the feeling—or to extinguish it completely.

But there was nowhere to run in here. Kiran had my face in his grip and his eyes were pinning me in place. I felt the fur of his loincloth brush my thigh, and suddenly, the tension between us was so suffocating that I couldn't breathe.

"*Lysi,*" I managed to rasp, my voice surprisingly husky as I answered his question. "She does."

Kiran's eyes flashed at the sound of my voice. The air shifted. Becoming hotter. Especially when his gaze trailed over my face and settled on my lips. Especially when his thumb moved and he brushed the bottom one.

I didn't understand what was happening.

I thought I had rid myself of desire for him.

I thought I was long past it.

And here he was, proving me wrong again. Proving to me that he still had control over me, control that might always be his.

Stop this! my mind screamed—though for a moment, I was tempted to lean into him. Which was madness. That was the power he had over me. Even still. Even after all these years.

Clearing my throat, I tore myself away, standing. It was like coming up for air, the first relieving gasp after being under water for so long.

My hands were trembling, and Kiran was watching me, all golden, warm flesh and beckoning desire. My eyes caught on something, though I looked away quickly. The furs that covered his cock seemed lifted, raised.

I didn't dwell on *that*.

Instead, I moved behind him, not daring to speak, dropping to my knees.

For a moment, I froze, desperate anger sliding inside me, a welcome relief to dampen my inconvenient desire. I'd forgotten about his back. The once perfect, smooth flesh was now littered with so much scar tissue that it was a wonder how the *ungira* had pierced him with its talon at all.

"Maeva," came his rasping voice. It was edged in something thick I didn't want to identify.

Peeling back the bandages, I saw that the wound was healing nicely—a welcome relief. Dakkari were always quick to heal. Whereas for me, it had taken nearly two weeks before the *mokkira* had taken the stitchings out from the back of my shoulder.

I discarded the used bandages and rummaged through my satchel for my blade to cut the threads, all too aware of the heavy silence and the way Kiran's body was tight, his muscles bunched.

"Relax," I whispered to him. "It will make it harder for me to remove them if you don't."

I heard his sharp exhale. I placed my fingertips on his back, feeling the tendons and sinew release, ever so slightly.

"I dream of you all the time, Maeva."

A shuddered gasp escaped my lips before I could stop it. Surely I hadn't heard him correctly.

"*Neffar?*"

His voice had been quiet yet guttural as he'd spoken the words.

"Even before I left the *saruk*. In *Dothik*, I would dream of you."

I was frozen behind him, an unmoving statue as I stared at the scars weaving the memory of unspeakable pain across his back.

"Why are you telling me this?" I asked softly.

A rough shake of his head came.

"So you know that I have never forgotten you," he rasped. "Not for a single day, a single moment."

Except when I needed you most, came the sad thought, creeping into my head like poison, painful and slow. But the thought didn't have its usual bite of fury. Only sadness. Only disappointment.

"I know it doesn't matter much now," he said. "I know your hatred of me is warranted. But I have always remembered. I wanted you to know that."

Hatred? I wondered, my brow furrowing, a sharp pang resounding in my chest.

Had I ever *hated* him?

True, consuming, dark hatred?

Nik. Never.

Even when he was breaking my heart. Even when he didn't say goodbye. Even when he'd turned his back on me.

I had felt betrayed by him, certainly. I had felt hurt by him. I had wished that I'd never met him on some particularly bad days.

But I had always realized that I was thankful for our friendship. There had been good there. Good that had come before the bad. Almost every good, happy memory I had growing up...they had always involved Kiran or my family.

"I don't hate you, Kiran," I told him softly, taking my blade in my hand, starting at the top stitch, popping it open with the sharp tip. "I never have."

I just...can't go back to how we were before, I finished quietly in my mind. *It would break me.*

Kiran didn't reply to that. He said nothing as I finished taking the stitches from his back, inspecting the closed wound that would further scar his already-scarred flesh.

I bit my lip, tearing my gaze away from one whipping lash that hadn't scarred well. I washed the flesh, applied a fresh coat of *uudun*, and then bandaged it again.

"It will heal well," I told him softly when I finished. "You can take the bandage off in the morning, but keep *uudun* on it for another few days, *lysi*?"

I fished a pot of the salve from my satchel and set it on the low table, next to the almost-empty platters of his evening meal.

He inclined his head. Then he asked, "Are you settling in well? Do you need any further supplies for the *mokkira's voliki*?"

I was surprised he'd asked, but I shook my head, meeting his gaze when I stepped around him, looping my satchel over my shoulder.

"I have everything I need," I told him.

Kiran stood to his full height, and I had to crane my neck back to keep his gaze. He looked even more massive with most of his clothes off, and I tried to hide how hard I swallowed at that realization.

"Actually, there is something," I said quickly, remembering.

"*Lysi?*" he grunted, stepping around the table until we were standing within arm's reach of one another.

"I need a *thesper*," I told him.

He frowned. "You wish to send a message to the *saruk*?"

"*Nik,*" I said. "I need to send a message to the horde of Rath Kitala. And hopefully to Rath Tuviri as well."

"Why?"

"I met one of the human females today," I said softly, lowering my gaze to the notch of his golden throat. "The pregnant female."

Kiran inclined his head. "Addie."

"*Lysi,*" I said. "Since her child is both Dakkari and human, I was hoping to correspond with the healers of both hordes, since I know they've had experience with delivering hybrid offspring."

Kiran's jaw tightened. "There are no *thespers* available for your use at present, *seffi.* We have two only. One has not returned from the horde of Rath Drokka, and I just sent one last night to Rath Kitala."

I blew out a breath. "She is due within a moon cycle. And I fear the child is in the wrong position. I need a *thesper.*"

"And we have none," he rasped. "I am sorry, *seffi.* Until one of the *thespers* returns, your message will have to wait."

I was afraid it couldn't.

"Then I need to travel to one of the hordes myself," I told him. "Which one is closest?"

"You will do no such thing," he growled, those eyes sparking. "I forbid it."

My shoulders went back and I lifted my chin. "Why?"

"I should not have to tell you that, *rei mokkira,*" he said, his tone unyielding. "You have a responsibility here. The frost comes soon, and there is much to be done. Not to mention the fact that the wildlands have become unpredictable. You have seen firsthand how dangerous they can be. *Nik,* you stay in the horde, where you can be protected, where you are safe."

"Kiran," I breathed, needing him to understand. "I—I don't

know what I'm doing. I don't know what to *expect* from a hybrid pregnancy, and I won't have Addie pay the price if I cannot help her because of my inexperience."

His nostrils flared.

"*Hanniva,*" I whispered. "I need to help her. *Hanniva.*"

I saw the defeat in his gaze before I saw it in the drop of his shoulders. His jaw was tight. I had forgotten how often I'd gotten my way with him.

"The nearest horde is Rath Tuviri's," he finally voiced. "But you will not leave. I will send a *darukkar* for you, *lysi?* He will be slower than a *thesper,* but he can reach the horde and return in a little under a week."

Relief and gratitude filled my chest.

"*Kakkira vor,*" I said quietly.

"Write out your message and get it to me," he said. "I'll send the *darukkar* out the morning after the feast."

"I will."

He sighed, studying me. The fire in the basin popped again, crackling.

Goose bumps broke out over my arms again when he rasped, "I *had* forgotten how I could never say *nik* to you, especially when you looked at me like that."

His words mirrored my own thoughts.

"Like what?" I whispered.

A huff burst from his nostrils. He shook his head, keeping whatever he thought to himself.

I turned to leave. "If you cannot say *nik* to me, *Vorakkar,* then I suggest you get some sleep. It will do you some good."

"I'll keep that in mind, *rei mokkira,*" came his response.

I ignored the way my belly fluttered as I stepped from his *voliki,* a cool breeze threading through my hair. I took in a deep breath and felt it sting my lungs.

Overhead, a bright star streaked across the sky, and I froze as I watched its trail.

Kakkari's guiding light?

A sign?

Nik, it couldn't be.

Swallowing, I averted my gaze and ignored it, just as I ignored my speeding heart and flushed cheeks.

It would only mean trouble.

CHAPTER 21

Errok laughed, the boisterous sound filling the empty clearing, carrying over the cold air that stung our flesh that early in the morning. He laughed, even though he wiped the blood away from his split lip.

"That was a dishonorable shot," he growled.

I grinned. "We were always taught to strike. No matter how."

Without warning, Errok retaliated, slamming the hilt of his sword into my thigh. Before I could react, he slugged me across the face, making me stumble back a couple feet.

"Like that?" he asked, raising a brow. His chest was heaving. As was mine. We had been in the training enclosure since the first rays of dawn had broken across the sky. Behind us, the horde was still sleeping. Most of it. It was beginning to stir, fires being lit, smoke curling from *volikis*.

"Again," I growled, wiping at the blood at my temple.

Errok was the only one who could get away with something like that. And only because he was my *pujerak*. Only because we'd known each other in *Dothik*, had trained together with the *Dothikkar's darukkars*.

As we did every morning, we trained together. Because we were almost a perfect match for one another's strength and blade skill. We had been the best in *Dothik*, after all. We had both worked hard to be the best. I knew that Errok had always had his sights on being a *Vorakkar*. But the *Dothikkar* had not allowed him into the Trials because he had no line, no ancestry to account for.

I knew that it always ate at him. Sometimes we butted heads, him needing to submit to my position when he had the soul of a *Vorakkar*.

It was something I knew he'd always hold against me. That I had been chosen and not him. Because of who my father was.

Still, we were friends.

Still, we had worked together from the very beginning to build this horde. He was my second-in-command, and the horde treated him with the respect he deserved, the respect he'd earned.

"There is your female," came Errok's gruff voice, the ringing of our clashing blades filling the clearing.

"*Neffar?*" I asked, turning my head to where he'd nodded.

I caught sight of dark curls and smooth flesh.

That was *all* I saw before Errok sliced a thin line through my hide trews, black blood beginning to leak over the material. I hardly felt the pain, knowing that had he been an enemy, he could've gone for a killing blow.

"The oldest mistake in history, my friend," Errok rasped, backing away. "Getting distracted by a female. Didn't our general in *Dothik* beat that out of you?"

I grunted. I'd just come of age when I went to *Dothik* that first time. There had been a girl, a Dakkari beauty with black hair and yellow eyes, that supplied the training *darukkars* with food three times a day. The general had caught me fucking her in an alleyway and had proceeded to beat the shit out of me.

Darukkars in training weren't allowed to take females. The general had believed the aggression from the lack of release would fuel us, would fuel our skill, as was tradition.

Of course, none of the *darukkars* in training had abided by that particular rule. Errok himself had fucked half the *Dothikkar's* keep during his time there. Then again, he'd always been the more charming one of the two of us.

"He really should have beat it out of *you*," I retorted, my eyes already on Maeva as she walked up to the training grounds enclosure.

The training grounds themselves were close to the front of the encampment. The weapons master's *voliki* was the only one around the area. It was an empty space surrounded by a wooden fence, which was where Maeva stopped.

"Unlike you, my friend," Errok said, a smirk in his voice, "I never got caught."

When I glanced back at him, I saw his gaze was on Maeva, a familiar expression sliding over his face that made my jaw grit. Because it usually meant trouble.

"Maeva," my *pujerak* murmured, walking to her, his eyes pinned to her in a way that made a fire burn in my chest. Especially when he used her given name, a name she'd so easily given him. "Tell me, did the *Vorakkar* here tup the whole *saruk* when you two were younger?"

Something flashed in Maeva's eyes, and I felt my dread spread as I sheathed my sword.

Errok leaned his forearms against the fence, leaning closer to her, and continued, "Because we were just discussing our time together in *Dothik*. About how he'd gotten caught by our general mating a female though it was forbidden. He got caught quite a lot actually. It's a wonder—"

I grabbed Errok's arm and pulled him away.

Vokking bastard.

"What the *vok* are you doing?" I hissed to him.

He grinned, blood still dripping from his lip where I'd struck him. He *vokking* knew that Maeva was important to me. And maybe he didn't know the extent of our complicated friendship, but he should've known better than to meddle in something that was none of his business.

"I caught him with my own sister once," Maeva said, her voice deceptively calm. "So I can believe it."

Errok turned to look at her, and I barely held in my wince.

She was looking at me. To anyone else, she might have seemed unaffected by Errok's words...or her own admission.

But not to me. I saw the way her jaw was tight. The way her eyes were too bright.

I remembered that night, remembered the devastation on her face when she stumbled upon Laru and me. I'd just come of age. Though we'd only kissed, it had been a *vokking* monstrous thing to do to Maeva, especially when I'd known her feelings toward me, though I hadn't reciprocated them. At least not *then*.

But I'd been young and foolish, thinking more with my cock than my head. A part of me had hoped that Maeva would find out. So that maybe it would make her hate me. So that maybe it would drive her away. Because once I left for *Dothik*, nothing would ever be the same.

I'd been cruel, just as she'd told me.

"Your sister?" Errok asked, brow raised. His look of genuine surprise made my gut churn, made me feel like even more of a monster when he turned to look at me as if to verify it.

"Leave us," I ordered him, my voice hard, my eyes like shards of ice.

I was pissed at him, but I would speak to him later. This wasn't an unusual occurrence. Errok was testing his limits again. It was something he'd always done, even from the beginning.

Only now, he'd pressed against a vulnerable place. Possibly my most vulnerable place. *Her.*

Errok flashed her another grin.

"Put some *uudun* on that cut, *pujerak*," Maeva ordered softly.

"Maybe you can do it for me, *Mokkira*," came his reply, making my body stiffen.

"It's small enough," she said, her voice deceptively light and airy, filling my chest with relief. "I'm sure you can manage yourself and not waste my time."

A small smile softened her firm words. A flash of surprise came over Errok's face. She'd shocked him. That surprise melted swiftly, morphing into a frown as his gaze flickered over her. Trying to read her?

Good luck, Errok. I have known her for years and even I cannot read her sometimes, I thought.

She raised her brow at him the longer he stared.

A low chuckle tumbled from his throat.

"My apologies, *Mokkira*. You are quite right," he said, inclining his head in a show of respect, chastened.

Errok strode from the training grounds, leaving only the two of us. Maeva pulled her furs—still blood-stained at the bottom, I noticed—tighter around her shoulders. The mornings were growing icier by the day, the afternoons cooler.

"I am sorry, Maeva," I said quietly, stepping toward her. "He should not have said anything. It didn't...it didn't mean anything."

She cocked her head to the side, regarding me. "You are free to do whatever you please, *Vorakkar*. Why do you feel the need to apologize to me?"

A part of her was pissed. Hurt.

I'd never told her about the females in *Dothik*. It was a part of my life that I'd kept entirely separate from her...because I'd known that it would upset her. Because I'd always known how she felt about me.

Because a part of me had always felt...*unfaithful* to her.

Like what I'd been doing was wrong...even though every Dakkari male went through a rutting period when they wanted to bed every female that caught their eye.

There had been females in the *saruk*, of course. Females that Maeva had no doubt heard about. But of those females, it was Laru that I had always regretted most.

I had betrayed Maeva's trust so many times that it was a wonder she'd stayed my friend at all.

I couldn't change who I'd been, however. The decisions I'd made when I was a mere boy. But I was making decisions *now* that would reveal the path for the rest of my life.

Decisions that very much included her. At least...I hoped so.

Though my hand was slightly bloody, I reached forward and caught her face in my palm.

"Maeva," I rasped, my eyes flickering back and forth between hers, "there have been no others. Not for a while."

Her gaze flashed, fury burning so brightly there. One of the few unguarded emotions I'd seen from her since I returned. It *almost* felt like a relief. To know that she wasn't as indifferent to me as she wanted to be.

She turned her face away.

"You know," she said softly, "sometimes I wish that I'd accepted Ojinu's courtship when we were younger. Maybe then I wouldn't have wasted so much time—"

She cut herself off abruptly, her jaw gritting, her nostrils flaring.

A dark frown had formed on my features. I knew exactly what she spoke of, and though she'd be furious at me—again— I told her, "He wouldn't have dared continue his courtship."

"Why?" she bit out. "Are you saying he didn't even like me?"

Ojinu had been a male at our *saruk*. Last I'd heard, he lived in *Dothik* now—good riddance. But he'd been attracted to Maeva, had begun his courtship of her...

I needed to be honest with her, though she might hate me even more for it, despite her assurances last night that she didn't.

"I told him to stop," I told her, meeting her shocked, widened eyes. "I scared him off of his pursuit of you."

Then her eyes narrowed. "You *what?*"

"He wasn't good enough for you, *seffi,*" I said, my voice gruff.

She stared at me.

"You...you had no *right* to do that," she whispered, her fists clenching at her sides. "Especially *you!*"

"He was courting you but bedding others, making *them* promises he had no intention of keeping," I argued, brow furrowed. "He was a dishonorable male and wasn't even worthy of your time."

Not to mention the disgusting things he'd said about bedding a human...that he would be the first to fuck Maeva, that he would tell the other Dakkari what it was like. He'd said those things when I'd been in earshot—his last mistake—and I'd jumped at him in my fury, nearly beating him senseless. It took five males to pull me off him.

After that, he'd never looked at Maeva again.

"I won't apologize for protecting you," I grated. "I will *never* apologize for that, even if you hate me for it."

She was breathing hard, staring at me like she'd never seen me before.

Her hand flashed out. I thought she would slap me across the face, but she ended up slapping something against my chest.

It dropped to the ground between us. A rolled piece of parchment, tied neatly with gold string.

When I scooped it up, I realized it was her message for the

mokkira of Rath Tuviri's horde, the horde I would be sending the messenger to tomorrow morning.

When I straightened and looked at her, she met my gaze steadily, her chin lifting. She wiped the rage off her features, though traces of it lingered in her pressed lips and hardened eyes.

"I'm not ashamed that I loved you, Kiran."

I froze, the world seeming to quiet around us.

Maeva continued, "I know you think that love was silly and foolish."

I frowned. "*Nik*, Maeva, I—"

"But I'm not ashamed of it. Because I loved you as best as I could. And as young as I was...what I felt for you was still pure. My mother told me that. That I should be proud that my heart had been open enough to love you like that, without fear."

Words bubbled up on my tongue, words that I couldn't form.

"But I *am* ashamed that I wasted so much time loving you," she said. My chest tightened, a dull, throbbing, familiar ache spreading. "So much of my life."

I would be the first to tell anyone that I'd never deserved her love. I knew that. It was why I had pushed her away so much toward the end of it all.

"The last thing I *ever* wanted was to hurt you," I said quietly, the lines of my face drawn, the cut on my thigh beginning to throb.

"I know. I believe that," she whispered. "But you did it anyway, Kiran. And you made it hurt so much worse."

I flinched, another aching pain threading through my chest.

"Please make sure that gets delivered," she said, nodding to the scroll clenched in my fist. "It's important to me."

She turned away but then paused.

"I meant what I said, Kiran," she murmured, her back to me.

"It's best if we try to forget. Everything. That's the only way this will work."

Then she strode away, her words souring my belly.

"Maeva," I called, my voice guttural. "Maeva!"

She didn't stop. She continued on her way, ignoring my calls.

I tilted my head back to the sky and blew out a long breath.

"*Vok.*"

"Are you all right, *Mokkira*?" Hinna asked softly. "You have been so quiet today."

"I'm usually quiet," I noted, giving her a small smile as I sat perched on the edge of my bed. That hadn't always been the case, however. When I was younger, Laru and my mother had often joked that I could carry on a conversation with myself for days if given the opportunity.

"Perhaps," Hinna said, frowning as she brushed through my hair, trying to make the curls submit. "But you seem *more* quiet today. I couldn't help but notice. Even your apprentice mentioned something to me."

They had been speaking of me? Though I strongly suspected that Essir would take any opportunity he was presented to speak with Hinna in private, including to gossip about me.

I blew out a breath. This was all Kiran's fault. Of course.

"I'm fine," I assured her, making an effort to lighten my expression. "I think I'm just nervous about the feast."

Not a complete lie, though I'd been to more Dakkari feasts in my lifetime than I could count. But this was my first feast at the horde. I wanted to make a good impression on the beings that I would come to know well during my time here.

And naturally, my mood was soured. Had been soured since this morning. And I didn't know how to feel about it, didn't know how to process all the ugly emotions our conversation had brought to the forefront.

But this is the process, isn't it? I pondered.

Like a broken bone. If it didn't heal properly the first time, it had to be broken again.

Well, Kiran had broken me. Then *I* had broken me. And I hadn't healed properly, from either of those times.

Being at the horde, being so near to Kiran...it felt like I was breaking myself all over again, deconstructing myself into my baser parts.

Breaking that bone...well, it wasn't meant to be pleasant. It had to hurt. It had to dredge everything up that had been festering inside me for so long.

Looking down in my lap, I queried hesitantly, "Can I ask you something, Hinna?"

"Of course," came her instant reply.

I played with the light material of the dress that Hinna had brought me earlier to wear. A beautiful shade of light purple. The color of *Drukkar's Sea* in the early morning, when the tides were calm.

"Why hasn't the *Vorakkar* taken a *Morakkari* yet?" came the soft question.

Her hand paused in my hair.

"I do not know," Hinna replied, just as softly. "Females in our horde have made their interest clear. Females from strong lines. But beyond a single night, he does not seem to return their interest."

A single night.

How many females in his horde *had* he bedded?

And why did that question send such searing, aching hurt through me?

"He has not taken a female in quite a long time. Since before the Dead Mountain," Hinna said. "At least that is what the rumors have been. It is strange for a *Vorakkar*, *lysi*?"

I cleared my throat. "I wouldn't know. I've never lived in a horde. And our *Sorakkar* was always true to his queen."

And tonight at the feast, I would no doubt have to witness dozens upon dozens of unmated, hopeful females presenting their goblets at his table.

Once, I'd been one of them. Hopeful. Confident.

A fool.

"Forget I asked," I told her, shooting her a small, tight smile over my shoulder. "I just expected him to be mated by now."

Her hesitation was palpable, her fingers sliding through my hair.

"Have you known the *Vorakkar* long?"

I made a sound in the back of my throat.

"Nearly my whole life," I replied. "We were good friends."

That sounded like a lie. We'd been *great* friends, the best of them. Once. And I'd always wanted more...though a part of me had perhaps always been aware of Kiran's hesitation.

I blew out a breath. I had been unfair to him too. One couldn't help who they loved, obviously. And one couldn't help who they *didn't*.

"I thought as much," Hinna said softly.

A laugh bubbled from my throat. "Anyone who saw us now would think we were strangers."

"*Nik*," she said, shaking her head. "I don't believe that. It was apparent to me that you were connected in some way. It would be apparent to anyone."

Sighing, I brought my hand up, clasping my mother's pendant. My dress was cut low, exposing the valley between my breasts. The necklace was on full display, and I squeezed it tight.

If *Lomma* was still alive, I wondered what she'd say. What she'd think of the male Kiran had become.

"You can ask me anything, *Mokkira*," Hinna told me when silence stretched between us. "I know you don't wish it, but I am your *piki*. It brings me great honor to hold such a title, and as such, I am in your strictest confidence."

I understood what she was saying.

"I can ask you to be my spy, then?" I teased.

A small chuckle fell from her lips. "If you wish it, I can be. No one ever notices me, which is a useful trait for a spy."

I frowned when I heard a tiny bite of bitterness in her tone. With a pang of guilt, I realized that I didn't know much about my new friend. I had been so consumed with setting up my place as *mokkira* that I hadn't asked anything of her life.

"Do you have a family?" I asked. "A mate?"

"My *Lomma* is a *bikku*," Hinna told me. "I was working to deliver meals before the *Vorakkar* asked me to be your *piki*. My father was a *darukkar*—and a great one at that—but he died a long time ago."

"I'm sorry," I whispered, turning to meet her gaze, especially when I heard her sadness mingling with her pride. "I lost my mother. It was one of the worst things in the world to endure."

Understanding went through her gaze, and she nodded. "I still miss him terribly. Some days are worse than others."

A wave of grief washed through me because I understood exactly what she meant. Sometimes, if I saw something that I thought my mother would like or find amusing, my first instinct was to run and tell her...only to remember. Even after all this time. Sometimes...it still *stunned* me that she was gone. Sometimes it still robbed me of my breath.

I blinked back the sudden blurriness in my vision and reached forward to squeeze Hinna's hand.

She let out a shuddering breath, shifting her shoulders in a way that made me think she was trying to move past her words.

"No mate though," she said. "Not yet."

"You want one?"

"Oh *lysi*," she said, finishing up with my hair. She'd managed to pin half of it back and knot it in an intricate braid I could never hope to replicate. "I want a horde of children too."

I laughed. "A horde?"

"*Lysi*. But no male has shown interest."

I pondered that. "That's not true. My apprentice seems quite taken with you."

"*Essir?*" she asked, her tone bewildered.

So she knew his given name.

"I've known him a long time," she said, her tone dismissive. "I do not see him as a potential mate."

Unrequited love, then.

I had more experience with that than I cared for.

Hinna put the last touches on my hair, decorating it with gold-plated flowers that she must have gotten somewhere in the horde, since they certainly weren't mine.

I stood from the bed, smoothing my dress, which flowed to my ankles. Though the night was cool, I knew I wouldn't need my fur shawl. The fires would be lit, and we would be drinking and dancing and feasting. That would keep me well warm.

"Let's go," I said, leading us both from my *voliki*. I heard the drums, the music, toward the front of the horde. The feast had already begun.

Out of the corner of my eye, I caught movement.

Sighing, I saw it was the *darukkar* who'd I'd begun to notice this afternoon. Always close to me, always watching, though he tried to keep out of sight.

Kiran had stuck a guard on me.

Shaking off my frown, I trudged forward, ignoring the guard.

I didn't get nervous too often, but my nerves were beginning to creep up on me. And as I always did, I inhaled long breaths and squeezed my mother's pendant for comfort. It gave me just enough to arrive at the feast with my chin held high and a small smile hovering over my lips.

I was determined to enjoy the feast. I was determined to forget the exchange Kiran and I had had this morning. Everything would be fine.

I heard the greetings as we wound our way through the thick crowd of Dakkari horde members.

My title was murmured in respect as we passed, and I inclined my head, giving a small smile in return to whoever greeted me. Their eyes eventually strayed to Hinna, no doubt wondering why the Dakkari female had been trailing me almost constantly since my arrival.

The drums were loud, pounding out a primal, familiar beat, one that had been played in the *saruk*. The feast was held in the open area I'd spied my first day. A raised dais was to the right, overlooking the dancing and the various tables laden with heaping platters of food and fermented brew in golden goblets that were spread on the outskirts.

Dozens and dozens of gyrating bodies were moving to the drums' beats already. I saw that we were a little late to the feast, as most were in the middle of eating or just finishing up. Most were deep into their goblets.

And though I tried not to look, my gaze tracked and stuck on the raised dais as we continued to wind our way through the crowd—to the large, golden, throne-like chair that oversaw all.

Kiran sat there. Alone. Apart.

His handsome, rough features were set into a deep, brooding expression. His elbow was perched on the arm of the throne, his hand cupped underneath his jaw. His other hand was tapping on the other arm of the throne. Restless. About what?

He was finished eating, I saw. When a *bikku* approached the dais with another platter, piled high with *wrissan* and *lobbas* roots, he waved her away.

Kiran was scanning the large crowd in front of him, watching the dancing, watching his horde members feast and laugh and drink.

For the first time, I wondered if he was lonely. If being *Vorakkar* was a lonely thing to be, especially when he hadn't yet taken a *Morakkari*.

I imagined it felt...isolating. To lead a horde and not truly be a part of it.

His eyes found mine, and I saw him straighten on his throne, his hand drifting away from his jaw. He leaned forward, those eyes pinning mine, almost making me freeze in place.

"*Mokkira*," came a familiar voice, and I looked away, a long breath releasing from me as I did, to see Addie waving me over to a full table.

Hinna hesitated for a moment before she changed directions and led me over to the pregnant human female, who was currently perched in the lap of who I assumed was her Dakkari mate.

Most of the table was filled with humans, I noticed. Obviously I had met Addie and Gabe, who gave me a wide grin. The four other humans in Kiran's horde, however, I had not met, and my eyes raked over them curiously as Addie made the introductions.

"*Mokkira*," she said, waving her hand down the table, "meet Cass, Seb, Jeremiah, and Lysa—the others I told you about."

Hinna stiffened at my side, no doubt because Addie had announced all their names without their permission. But humans, I suspected, didn't have the same aversion to introductions with their given names as Dakkari did.

Thankfully, Addie had used my title or else Hinna would've fallen over in shock—and then probably reported it to Kiran.

My eyes trailed over the humans, attaching their names with their faces. I smiled at all of them, lowering my head in respect.

Cass and Lysa were the two females of the group. Seb and Jeremiah were the males. In fact, Lysa and Jeremiah looked to be mated as they were leaning into one another, Jeremiah's arm slung around Lysa's shoulders. They were an older couple, with graying hair. Jeremiah was the male I'd seen when I first arrived.

Cass was younger than Lysa and Jeremiah, though I guessed she was ten or so years older than me. She was just beginning to gray, and she sat quietly at the end of the table, looking at me with suspicion, though she returned my nod when I glanced at her.

Seb looked to be a little younger than Cass. The lines of his face were weathered, his skin dark. Like Gabe, he looked strong but lithe, so unlike the brute strength of Dakkari males, the corded muscle and hefty bulk that I'd seen all my life.

All the humans inspected me just as curiously as I inspected them. No doubt, Addie had told them about me, about what we'd discussed in my *voliki*.

"And this is my mate," Addie said, as if it weren't obvious enough. She patted the Dakkari male's bulky shoulder, stroking the smooth flesh there. "He is a *darukkar* here."

In Dakkari, I murmured a greeting to him, lowering my head in respect for his title, which he mirrored.

"Come, sit," Addie ordered, earning her a murmured word from her Dakkari mate in reprimand. She wasn't allowed to give me orders. I answered only to the *Vorakkar*, but I didn't take offense. Still, she flashed a look of apology to me. "Will you come sit and eat? Both of you?"

"*Lysi,*" I said, casting a look at Hinna. "We will. Unless you wished to sit with your *lomma*."

Hinna bit her lip and shook her head. "We can stay here, *Mokkira.*"

I nodded as Gabe stood from his stool, shuffling around stools at the end of the table to bring two empty ones over. He flashed me another grin, taking my hand, catching me by surprise.

"*Kakkira vor,*" I murmured, a little confused as he helped me sit. Hinna cast him a look of disapproval, her spine straight, as she sat in her own stool.

All the while, I felt Kiran's burning gaze. When I flashed a look up at the dais, I saw his darkened expression around the *bikku* that was currently refilling his goblet of fermented brew.

My own goblet was pushed in front of me, and I took a sip as platters were shuffled down from the end of the table so we could eat.

"You don't water yours down?" Addie asked, chuckling.

I frowned in confusion before I realized she meant the brew. "*Nik.* Why?"

Hinna took a sip from her own goblet as I set mine down.

"It is pretty strong stuff for humans," Gabe said next to me, leaning closer until our shoulders bumped together.

"Is it?" I asked, my gaze meeting his. "I wouldn't know. I've had it nearly all my life."

Gabe blinked, his cheeks going a little red, the color matching his hair. Even though the other humans had probably watered theirs down, we were a little late to the feast, and the way his eyes shone told me that he'd probably had a goblet or two of his own already.

"What is it?" I asked him, watching that flush bloom across his skin in a way that reminded me of my apprentice, Essir, when he spoke with Hinna.

He shook his head, the dark curls brushing the tips of his ears. "Nothing. You're just very..."

"Very what?" I asked, frowning, wondering if I'd done something wrong.

"Beautiful."

I swallowed, nearly rearing back. It was on the tip of my tongue to deny his words. I'd never been called *beautiful* in my life. The compliment was thoroughly strange, especially when I'd grown up in a Dakkari *saruk*, where I had *always* been different, been strange looking.

Discomfort flooded my belly even though I was pleased with the compliment. My gaze flashed up to Kiran again—his jaw was tight, his eyes pinned on Gabe and me—before I looked away. Kiran had certainly never thought I was beautiful. I remembered his disgust at my bared body well enough.

Enjoy this night, I reminded myself.

Gabe was still blushing as though he was waiting for my reaction, and I gave him a smile, my teeth flashing.

The vain creature in me wondered if I was considered beautiful among humans. The vain creature in me *hoped* that I was because I had been so strange for so long.

"*Kakkira vor,*" I said. "Thank you."

His grin was wider than mine, and he reached for the platter of food, bringing it in front of me. "Here. Eat."

I nodded and nudged the platter toward Hinna as well as we started to dig in. I wasn't all that hungry—the exchange with Kiran earlier had soured my appetite for most of the day —but as I began to eat, my hunger suddenly made itself known.

I was content to listen to the conversation around us as we ate our fill. A few *darukkars*, friends of Addie's mate, were sitting at the table as well, and the mixture of Dakkari and the universal tongue was interesting, though confusing. Addie knew a little Dakkari, but most of the humans didn't, including Gabe.

But it was fun to listen to new voices and try to pick apart the threads of conversation as I ate and drank. If I didn't understand something—Jeremiah and Gabe were discussing something about the soil, and my confusion must've shown on my face—Gabe would lean over and try to fill me in. I discovered that Jeremiah and Gabe assisted with the crops for the horde.

They were sowing the frost crops, but the soil in the South Lands was more compact than they were used to.

"Frost crops don't really take in the South Lands," I told him. "Maybe if we were more north. Those in my *saruk* don't even bother with planting until the ground thaws again. We eat a lot of dried meat in the cold season."

Gabe took another sip of his brew, and I was fascinated by the red flush that had been steadily creeping up his neck since we'd arrived. I was almost concerned about it until Addie poked fun at him.

"Maybe you can help us with the plantings once the ground thaws," Gabe teased softly, giving me a small smile that didn't reveal his teeth.

I blinked. I felt the brew warming my belly. I was beginning to feel...light. Happier.

"If I'm here that long," I said, flashing him a smile and not entirely sure why.

"Maybe you'll find a reason to stay," he remarked, raising one of his brows, looking at me, his gaze flickering back and forth between my eyes.

He was pleasing to look at, I realized. Perhaps not as pleasing as some other males I'd seen—one in particular—but I liked looking at his features. And Hinna seemed to as well, considering how many times she'd glanced over at him throughout the evening.

A smile was on my lips, a retort poised on the tip of my tongue, and then I saw movement behind Gabe, near the dais.

And then my smile died, if only for a brief moment. My belly soured in memory as I saw the first of the brave females begin to approach Kiran's empty table.

It was the female who'd made the comment about my mother's pendant the day I arrived at the horde. Her inky, silky black hair swayed past her hips as she climbed the stairs to the dais. She wore a hide skirt, exposing the lengths of her golden legs, and a backless top with golden beads woven into the material.

A goblet was resting in her hands, and I watched with a sickening feeling as she set it on Kiran's table. The crowd had started to hush. I remembered those giddy nerves, the night I'd presented my goblet to Kiran when I was young. That rush of excitement and confidence...only to crumble to ash when his rejection was obvious.

I almost cringed, thinking about how foolish and hopeful and naive I'd been. But it was my past, I reminded myself. I had nothing to be ashamed of. It had been okay to be hopeful and excited. I'd snapped out of it eventually, hadn't I?

Maybe I haven't, I thought, feeling bile rise in my throat when I saw the female's hand drop to Kiran's forearm as she spoke with him.

I turned forward again, staring down at my almost empty goblet. As if hearing my thoughts, a *bikku* came around with a jug and refilled it, the golden liquid sloshing around inside.

I took another long draw from it and felt Gabe's eyes on me.

When I met them, he asked, "Will you dance with me now?"

Briefly, my gaze flickered to Kiran. I saw his carefully blank expression as he spoke to the female, though his eyes strayed back to mine.

I wanted to forget.

"*Lysi,*" I said, standing. "I will."

This feast, I found, was a special kind of hell.

I wondered why the *vok* I'd announced it when the frost feast was to come soon anyway, but I knew. I had wanted the horde to celebrate Maeva's arrival and our arrival to the South Lands.

In a foul mood, I could hardly keep from scowling at the fifth female that had presented her goblet to my table. I kept my expression neutral though my eyes strayed to the female that I really wanted to approach me.

This female—her given name was Tiunu, and she worked as a seamstress—kept her hopeful gaze on me as she propositioned what all the rest had.

"I am not seeking an *alukkiri* for the cold season," I murmured to her, seeing her shoulders sink ever so slightly. My gaze flickered to Maeva, my jaw tightening when I saw the human male's hand graze her bare shoulder as they danced.

Tiunu bowed her head in respect. "If you change your mind, *Vorakkar*, I would be most willing."

I bit out a sigh of frustration as the female descended the steps of the dais. I saw another female begin to come forward, and all I wanted was for Maeva to approach.

Though I was still furious with him, my *pujerak* cut off the sixth female's path and strode up the dais himself.

"You look like you want to do battle," Errok commented, snagging one of the goblets that littered my table and taking a hefty swallow. His gaze scanned the crowd, landing on Maeva dancing. "Ah."

"You forget your place sometimes, Errok," I rasped, cutting my eyes back to him, standing from my seat.

"Are you still angry about this morning?" he asked, frowning. "I was just jesting, Kiran. Surely you—"

"When it comes to *her*," I growled, stepping closer, "stay away. You know nothing of what our relationship is or was. *Lysi?*"

Errok looked at me steadily. He clasped his hand on my shoulder, squeezing. Quietly, he said, "With all due respect, friend, I have a feeling you do not either."

His words hit me hard. My body was tense and tight. Not even the brew could help loosen it.

"I know you, Kiran," Errok voiced. "I have known about her for a long time, though you never said her name. You never needed to. She was with you. Always. And now you finally have her near. And what are you doing? What the *vok* are you doing? Because if I had a female I wanted above all else, you better believe I wouldn't watch her dance and smile and laugh with another male."

He was...*right*.

What the vok *am I doing?* I questioned, squeezing my fists.

I wasn't like this.

I was a *Vorakkar*.

If I wanted something, I took it.

And Maeva?

Well, she wasn't a *something*. She was everything.

When I looked past Errok, I caught sight of Maeva. In a dress that reminded me of the one she'd worn the night I pushed her out of my life. A light purple that made her skin gleam. The golden flowers in her hair made her curls shimmer in tandem with the firelight.

She was laughing, her head thrown back, a bright smile—one I missed desperately—on her features. I'd always loved watching her dance. Because when she danced, it was mesmerizing. She was graceful and soft and sensual.

The first time I'd wanted her—the first time I'd desired her in my furs—had been when I'd watched her dancing at one of the *saruk's* feasts. We'd both been young then, and afterward, I'd been ashamed. Because Maeva had been my friend. I'd felt strange about the realization that I'd desired her in that way because it felt like I'd been breaking an unspoken agreement between us.

We aren't children anymore, I thought.

She was a beautiful female. I was a Dakkari male in my prime.

And I *vokking* wanted her in *my* furs and in no one else's. I wanted to slide deep inside her and hold there. I wanted to catch her gasps with my lips and do every wicked thing to her I'd fantasized about for years.

She'd claimed she would never have me.

I wanted to make a liar out of her.

I wanted to show her that I *had* been worthy of her love all those years ago. Because her love had been the most beautiful thing in my life. I knew that now. I wished I'd known it then.

The human male, Gabe, made her smile. Seeing her so open and unguarded with another male made my chest ache with regret and longing. It made it difficult to breathe. It made jealousy burn me up from the inside out.

I felt Errok squeeze my shoulder again.

"I'll hold down the dais while you're gone," he teased. When I turned to look at him, his brow raised. "Unlike you, I *am* looking for an *alukkiri* for the cold season. The nights are long, or have you forgotten?"

A breath chuffed out of me. "I haven't forgotten."

His head tilted out to where Maeva was, and I inclined my head, knowing that he spoke the truth. We might've butted heads often, but he'd always had my back when I needed him most. It was why I'd chosen him as my *pujerak*. It was why he made an even better friend.

With that, I strode off the dais, my booted feet falling heavily, drawing the gazes of my horde. But I only had eyes for Maeva, and I never took them off her as I approached.

I had been waiting for her to give me a sign. A sign that there was still hope for us, that she might come to care for me again if I gave her reason to.

But I was done waiting.

Because I *knew* she could care for me again. I would *make* her remember. Everything. I was going to make her mine because she'd *always* been mine.

But I couldn't make her remember when she was in the arms of another male.

When I reached where they were dancing, it was Gabe that saw me first. His expression flickered into one of confusion, the smile dying off his face, his hand trailing off Maeva's waist.

I jerked my chin at him, nodding to the table where they'd been sitting for the feast. His brow furrowed, and his gaze immediately went down to the female in front of him, though he didn't move.

Maeva stiffened, as if sensing my presence. When she turned, I saw a light flush on her cheeks from her exertion, her breaths coming quick. The drums came louder, seeming to throb in time with my steady heartbeat, seeming to vibrate my whole body when our eyes connected.

I stepped closer. When I was looking at her, all I saw was

her. I didn't notice the hush of my horde. I didn't notice the sea of gazes.

Maybe it was the goblet of brew I'd watched her drink, but there was a challenge in Maeva's eyes. Her brow was cocked, her lips pursed.

Out of the corner of my eye, I saw Gabe begin to fall back. Away. As if he knew he wouldn't—or couldn't—challenge me.

When it was just the two of us in our small circle, I snaked my arm out, wrapping it around Maeva's waist.

A gasp—so quiet I was the only one who heard it—fell from her lips when I dragged her close. Her waist was small, flaring out to wide hips I wanted to grip.

Maeva's bravado fell away quickly, replaced by something that looked like...trepidation.

"Dance with me, *seffi*," I rumbled, lowering my head until my lips brushed her ear. "Because I should be the only male who gets to put his hands on you."

The ragged gasp that escaped her this time was louder. Angrier.

I grinned, feral and dark, anticipation coiling in my chest.

"What are you *doing*?" she whispered.

Laying my claim, I thought, determination pulsing through me. But I had a feeling if I said the words out loud, she'd slap me across the face.

Our bodies pressed closer. The silk of her dress brushed across my bare chest. The fur hide of my trews touched her thigh, bared by the slit that ran up her dress. When I angled my head down, I spied her nipples, hard and tight, straining against the material that covered them.

Desire made me stiffen. I imagined leaning down, taking that nipple between my lips, and suckling on it in front of the entire horde. Then they would all know she was *mine*.

A rough breath tore from my throat. Against me, I felt her heartbeat pick up, heard her breathing quicken, her chest rising and falling. Without a doubt, she felt my cock, hard and thick, pressing into her belly.

"I was waiting for you, *seffi*," I murmured. "Waiting for your goblet to reach my table."

That made Maeva stiffen. Belatedly, I knew it was the wrong thing to say.

"Are you...are you *mocking* me?" she breathed, her eyes wide. In that moment, she couldn't hide her hurt. I saw it, striking me like a blade in the chest, before she covered it with an expression of detachment.

Nik.

Detachment was the *last* thing I ever wanted to see on her face again. I would rather she be *infuriated* with me, her eyes glowing like hot embers, striking me in the chest with her fists and screaming at me, than see her *vokking* indifference.

I couldn't bear it.

"Never," I growled.

But of course, she would have never approached me. She'd approached me with her goblet once before. The night I left her standing on that windy cliff. The last time I ever saw her, with her wet eyes and slouched shoulders.

I'd humiliated her. Torn out her heart like the callous bastard I was and left her to pick up the pieces once I was gone.

Of course she would never approach me again.

"Maeva," I rasped, hearing the drums beat louder, sensing bodies shifting around us, dancing, though I felt their gazes too. "*Seffi*, let me—"

She tore out of my arms faster than I thought possible, pushing through the crowd of Dakkari that surrounded us.

With a clenched jaw, I watched her go until I lost sight of her at the edge of the feast. I would give her time.

But if she thought I would pull back, pull away from her again, she was mistaken.

I wouldn't let her go this time.

Chapter 24

I don't know if I can do this, I thought, pushing through the crowd of Dakkari still gathered at the feast.

I tried to keep my expression neutral, knowing that the eyes of the horde were upon me. I waited until I reached the soothing edge of the darkness, between two *voliki* where the fire light from the feast didn't reach, and then my face crumbled. Tears threatened to sting my eyes, and I hadn't cried since my mother died.

Why does he make me feel this way? Still? After all this time?

I didn't want to go back to my *voliki*. I would go mad there, trapped in that confining place.

What I really wanted to do was go running across the plains. I wanted to feel *Drukkar's Sea* mist on my face and breathe in that nourishing air.

But I was far from the sea here. Encased by land. On all sides. Trapped.

Longing for home hit me hard. For my *pattar*. For Laru. For Rasik. Even for Nevir. For nights together, riddled with laughter. For our evening meals that we cooked. For the way my father would watch us all, the quiet sadness in his gaze because he wished *Lomma* could've met Rasik, could've seen what our family had become.

My throat was closing up so tightly, and I made for the gates of the horde, needing to see the stretch of the plains. I was confined by walls here. By protective gates that were built high. I needed to see something other than *walls*.

There were no guards at the gate entrance—everyone was at the feast—and I slipped past. The moment I was free, I bunched up my dress so it wouldn't tangle around my ankles and I started to run.

I knew where I was going. The moonlight reflected off its surface, shimmering and silver. The lake that I'd spied on my first day stretched far to the northern mountain range. It almost seemed like the sea. It looked like it had no end.

My bare feet hit the earth hard. My breath began to come quicker, my lungs filling with crisp air that somehow seemed more wonderful now that I could see beyond the walls. My blood felt like it was throbbing, warm and alive, underneath my skin. It was in part because of the fermented brew I'd had at the feast and partly because I was running, *free*, Kakkari's air nourishing me in a way I desperately missed.

When I reached the edge of the lake, I realized I was crying.

And somehow it felt like a betrayal.

I hadn't cried since my mother's burial. Because *that* had been the worst moment of my life. I had thought I'd cried enough in the days surrounding her death that I had simply depleted my store for the remainder of my days.

Yet here I was.

In a strange horde, away from home, away from my family.

Near Kiran.

Kiran, who could still make me feel too much.

It felt like a betrayal somehow, and I didn't know why. Why waste tears on him, on loneliness, and homesickness...when tears were for things like burials and heartbreak and death?

Behind me, I could still hear the throbbing of the drums from the feast and the delighted cries of Dakkari horde members as they danced and feasted and laughed.

I'd never felt more alone in my entire life. I didn't remember my life before the *saruk*. I didn't remember the forest I'd been found in. I didn't remember my birth mother or father, though I had often wondered why they hadn't wanted me.

Even still, I knew that this loneliness was deep. I'd felt it even before I'd left home. And that knowledge, that secret I'd never told even Laru—how *vokking lonely* I was—made more tears blur my vision as I stepped into the lake.

The water was shockingly cool. Almost frigid. But it felt good. A chill raced through my bones and cooled my hot blood. It reminded me that I was alive. That I was *here*. That this was my choice and no one else's. I needed to remember that.

I stepped deeper into the lake, needing to feel that chill *more*.

Beneath my toes was a silky sand, similar to the sea. The inky blackness of the depth didn't frighten me. I didn't wonder what creatures might lurk beneath the surface. I'd never worried about that in *Drukkar's Sea*, and wading into the lake felt like coming home. If only for a little bit.

Or maybe I simply drank too much at the feast, I mused, wading in deeper.

I tilted my face back to the moon and closed my eyes, feeling its light drift across my cheeks. Breathing in a long breath and savoring the notes I found there. The heady, musky scent from the forest. The crisp scent from the lake. The tinge of smoke that drifted from the fire basins at the feast.

And the sounds.

The festivities were muted. Out here on the plains, I heard creatures tittering and scurrying in the trees to my left. I heard the breeze rustling through my hair. I heard the small waves of the lake lapping at my legs.

And I heard something else.

Footsteps approaching me from behind, nearing the edge of the lake I was knee-deep in.

"*Seffi*, come out from there," came his voice. A voice that slid through me like silk and warmed brew. "Your bones will freeze."

"Maybe I want them to."

When I opened my eyes and turned, I saw his brows furrow, no doubt seeing the tears reflected in the same moonlight that cut across his face and made him seem all the more dangerous.

His own feet—though he wore his thick boots—were already in the water, wading toward me. His bare chest gleamed, every scar glinting silver. His long hair, decorated with golden beads and clasps, rustled in the breeze. His golden eyes never left me.

"Can't you just leave me alone, Kiran?" I whispered, a shiver racking through me. I curled my arms around myself, hugging my midsection tight. "*Hanniva*. I'm begging you."

He hesitated, studying me. Then something came over his face and he continued forward, reaching out for me. His hand was hot and shocking against my cold, goose-bumped flesh. Already I felt my muscles relax at that touch...and I was miserable that they did.

"My guard said you went beyond the gate," Kiran said, his voice gruff, pulling me toward him. "It's dangerous right now, *seffi*. You know that. And your safety will always come first."

"Why?" I whispered. "I just wanted to see the wildlands. I just wanted to see something beyond all those walls."

Understanding crossed his expression. He would understand. We'd gone running across the plains almost every morning, laughing into the breeze, far beyond the *saruk*. The wonderful lightness, the *freedom* of it was unparalleled.

"Let's go running in the morning," he murmured, drawing me toward him as I shivered more. "*Lysi?* I will take you far, but at least I can protect you if we come across any wandering beasts."

An intense burst of longing went through me. One that almost made me say yes to his suggestion.

When he pulled me to the lake's edge again, my flesh began to chill from where it'd been under the water, now exposed to the punishing breeze. When he had me out of the lake, his hands came to my face, brushing my tears away. His expression was grim, focused on his task.

We were close. His heat was pulsing off him in waves, sinking into me.

I might regret this in the morning. I might regret letting him so close again. But I studied his eyes, and all I felt was a deep sadness. Not anger and bitterness. Just sadness, one that made more tears replace the ones he wiped away.

And I could blame it on the brew in the morning, but truthfully, my next words were long overdue and I just wanted an explanation. Finally. I just needed to know *why*.

"You didn't even say goodbye," I whispered.

Kiran stiffened, his eyes flashing to mine from where they'd been focused on my cheeks, darting back and forth.

"I was hurt that night on our cliff," I continued, my shoulders sagging. "*Of course* I was. But I didn't think that *that* was the last time I would see you. You were my friend, Kiran. And you didn't even say goodbye when you left the *saruk*."

"I did try," he said quietly, his voice rough and low yet still soft. It bordered on *gentle*.

"*Neffar?*" I whispered.

He swallowed, looking past me at the lake for a brief moment, seeming to collect his thoughts, before his eyes returned to mine.

"Your father wouldn't let me anywhere near you. *Vorakkar* or not."

My father?

A small breath whistled from his nostrils.

"I was expected in *Dothik*. I *had* to leave, Maeva. You wouldn't come out from your *soliki,* but I wanted, *needed* to speak with you again before I left. I needed…" He blew out a rough breath. "I needed to know you were all right. I can't count how many times I came to your *soliki*. Your father was camping on the stairs, almost night and day at that point."

My brow furrowed.

The corner of his lips lifted briefly before they smoothed into a solemn line. "He struck me across the face so hard he made me bleed when I tried to push past him."

My blood chilled further. Kiran had been a *Vorakkar* at that point. If my *pattar* had struck him, it would've meant punishment. Maybe even his *death*.

"Your father loves you," Kiran continued gruffly. "I don't have to tell you that, *seffi*. And he told me that the only way I would speak to you again was if I killed him right there… because he wasn't going to let me anywhere near you again."

He wiped at more tears that streaked down my face, his jaw tightening as he saw them, as if he couldn't *stand* to see them.

"I did try," he said. He swallowed. "But I always regretted not trying harder. And as the years passed…it was just easier to stay away. To not stir up the past. I thought…I thought that you hated me. That you never wanted to see me again. I thought it was best if I stayed lost in the wildlands."

That confession whistled out of him, and it struck me like a blade to the chest.

Processing his words, I was forced to confront the fact that they angered me. It was not directed at Kiran, however, but at my *pattar*.

How many times had he heard me cry in the months after Kiran's departure? How many times had he heard me sob that my friend hadn't even said goodbye?

And all along, it had been his doing. *He* had kept Kiran away from me. While I knew it was done with love, that he thought it was what I wanted, that he thought it would protect my heart further...I had still *needed* to say goodbye. To have that closure.

Instead, that hurt had lingered. Aching and raw.

"And what about after?" I asked, my toes digging into the soft sand of the lake's shoreline, needing it to ground me. "The year after you left?"

His brow furrowed. His hand drifted to his hair and raked through it. "The first year was difficult. New hordes always are. I thought about returning to the *saruk* often, thought about seeing you, but there was always something that needed to be done."

I shook my head, wrapping my arms around myself tighter.

Quietly, I said, "It was important to me that you were there, Kiran."

I had never said those words out loud. I had never told Laru or my *pattar* about how hurt I'd been when he hadn't come for my mother's burial. It had further deepened an already festering wound, spreading like an infection.

"Maeva, you knew I was a *Vorakkar*," he said, even as a flash of hurt and guilt crossed his usually cold expression. "I was not going to stay in the *saruk* forever. I had to leave, to make my mark, to lead my horde."

My nostrils flared as I desperately tried to get air into my lungs.

"Not at the *saruk*," I voiced, my brows dropping, my lips turning down.

Obviously, I had always known he had to leave. Then again, I had always believed I would go with him.

"At her *burial*. You never came. I had written to you, begging you to come, and then you ignored me and instead told your mother to give us your regards? As if we were strangers to you? *It hurt*, Kiran. It always has and it always will."

"What are you talking about?" he asked quietly, his eyes suddenly rapt and intense. "*Whose* burial?"

Something seemed to burst inside me. All the emotion, perhaps, that I had kept bottled up and buried for so long. All coming the surface.

"My mother's!" I cried, tears swimming in my eyes as I stumbled away from his grip, which had suddenly loosened.

"*Neffar?*" he rasped, frozen in place, his lips parting. "What are you talking about, Maeva?"

His reaction made me hesitate. It didn't make sense. Kiran wasn't a liar. Why would he pretend he didn't know?

Nik, I thought, my resolve hardening. He had to have known. Even if my own message hadn't reached him, his mother had written to him and received his prompt reply by *thesper.* She'd read his letter to me herself.

"Don't do this, Kiran," I pleaded, my voice shaking. "*Please* don't do this to me! Don't tell me you don't even remember, or I will truly *never* forgive you for it."

An intense expression flashed over his face.

Realization. Disbelief. Grief. Anger. Guilt.

All combined into one aching look that made my chest *crumble.* That made me stumble away because all at once, I felt my whole world tilt. I felt my reality twist and become something else.

All at once, I had to look away. I spun, my breath coming quick and hard, my vision beginning to sway. I stared out at the lake. Unseeing. Then I crumbled to the ground, falling to the sandy bank in a heap as my legs gave out on me.

Then I said the words that were somehow the truth. I had seen them in his expression, and though it had been nine years, I still *knew him.* They were the truth, though I didn't know *how.* Or why.

"You didn't know," I said quietly. I envisioned my words drifting across the surface of the lake. "*You didn't know.*"

I didn't know where my words would end up. How far would they go? How far could they drift across the lake?

Silence stretched between us, heavy and tense.

And even though I had already cried for the first time in eight years that night, I felt my shoulders begin to shake. I felt my body vibrate, like it was coming to life, like it was trying to purge every deep-rooted emotion within me, emotions that felt poisonous and hateful.

My breath was short, coming quick. I couldn't *vokking* breathe.

Then the tears came, a flood of them, breaking from me. Then came the sobs, deep, aching, rasping things that felt like they were ripping my body apart.

"*Seffi*," came his voice. I felt him drop to his knees behind me, right at my back. I felt his arms come around me, felt him pull me deep into his chest until I was cocooned in his embrace. Until all I could feel was his heat and his heartbeat throbbing against my spine. And his scent, warm and familiar, all around me. "*Seffi*."

His forehead dropped to the back of my head, and I felt his breath on my neck as he tried to steady his own.

"*Seffi*, I am sorry," he murmured to me, his arms tightening when he felt my sobs come harder. "I am so sorry for your *lomma*."

I couldn't see anything through my tears, so I simply closed my eyes. My hand lifted from where it was clenched in the sand, and I gripped his forearm, my fingers brushing the hot metal of his *Vorakkar* cuff, wide on his wrist. My nails dug into his flesh, but it was only to hold him to me.

I wasn't capable of any more words.

Only tears. And maybe those tears were enough. Maybe those tears were like words, falling down my face like a difficult conversation, a conversation long overdue.

I cried on the edge of that lake, with his arms around me, with the moon over us.

I cried until I couldn't anymore.

CHAPTER 25

Sitting on the edge of the bank, I clutched Maeva in my arms tighter, though I was careful not to wake her.

Behind me, my horde was quiet. The gentle glow from the fires was nearly extinguished as my horde members stumbled back to their beds—or someone else's—drunk on brew and feasting and dancing.

But I was right where I wanted to be.

Maeva was draped across my lap, one of her cheeks pressed against my bare chest, right below my right pectoral. My arms were tight around her, as if I feared she'd leave, even in her sleep.

The tears that streaked her face had long dried, though I could still see the tracks of them. She didn't move, though her breaths were even and slow. I kept her warm enough, though I worried about the brisk, frigid air that would freeze the material of her dress that had gotten wet in the lake.

My own boots were soaked. I knew I needed to bring us back to the horde soon, but I couldn't bring myself to move.

Instead, I stroked Maeva's dark hair—hair I'd always loved, hair that got everywhere, that went wild in the wind, and dried even more curled from *Drukkar's Sea*. I listened to her soft breaths and tried to keep my grief gentle and tamed, though I felt it roving inside me like a beast.

Grief that was both for Maeva and for her mother. Grief that was for me.

I couldn't understand it.

But everything suddenly made sense.

About her piercing anger that would sometimes unleash before she covered it up. About the deep hurt that I sensed inside her. About her mother's pendant—one I recognized, one I knew Maeva's *puttar* had gifted her *lomma*, one that her *lomma* had always thought special and cherished. About the way my *seffi* sometimes couldn't meet my eyes.

I had thought her hatred of me had stemmed from my rejection of her. From rejecting the love she had so freely and openly and bravely offered me once.

Now I knew her hatred ran deeper. Her *hurt* ran deeper. Because it was coated with betrayal and disappointment and confusion *and* grief. *Loss.*

I blew out a breath, swallowing hard as I stared out over the lake, my gaze tracking every rippling wave that came toward us with the breeze. Beyond it, I looked to the mountains. Next to us lay the forest, dark and quiet, though I was certain to keep an ear out for any beasts that might be within.

I'd meant to give her time. But when one of the *darukkars*— one I'd assigned to keep an eye out for Maeva—had come to me, reporting she'd gone beyond the gates, I'd immediately followed.

When I stumbled upon her, she'd been half inside the frigid lake, her dress drifting out around her like a cloud, her hair tumbled down her back. She'd seemed like a goddess to me then, lit by silvery moonlight, standing tall and beautiful. Mesmerizing.

Then she'd turned and I saw her face streaked with tears. Maeva had always been quick to tears when we were younger.

Her emotions were always close to the surface. With me, she'd never been embarrassed about her tears, though I knew she didn't like others to see her cry.

But *this* Maeva broke something inside me while simultaneously bringing something back to life.

I'd felt this *thing* shift inside me. My heartbeat came quicker, though my breath became deeper, more full.

And perhaps this *thing* was more of a decision. One I'd always been aware of. One I'd made long ago.

And that decision was that I never wanted to leave Maeva's side again...and I never wanted her to leave mine.

It had been hard enough the first time, leaving the *saruk*, leaving her behind. As a *Vorakkar*, I learned from my mistakes. I didn't make the same one twice.

So, right then, I decided that I would make Maeva love me again. Whatever it took. I decided that I would make her my *Morakkari*. That I would claim her in the old way. That she would be my *kassikari*, my love, my mate, my queen.

It had always been her. It always would be.

After that decision flowed through me, *pure relief* followed. Like a breath of air when I'd been submerged for so long. A weight off my shoulders.

Errok had always wondered why I hadn't taken a queen long ago, as was expected. Most *Vorakkar* took a *Morakkari* within the first few years of the horde's birth, if only to strengthen it.

But I had never shown any interest. Every time I'd thought of it, my stomach had churned and I'd growled at Errok to stop asking me about it.

Because I'd always known? Because I'd always known that deep in my heart, I'd chosen a *Morakkari* long ago and that she hated me because I hadn't realized it sooner?

But now it was so much more than that.

I hadn't been there for her when she'd needed me most. I

knew how much Maeva loved her *lomma*. I'd witnessed that love so often. And I'd loved her mother in my own way as well. Maeva's *lomma* had never looked at me any differently because I was *Rukkar* to the *saruk*. She'd treated me like her own because she'd been a loving and open being, traits that were rooted in her daughter.

And she is gone from this life. And I hadn't even known, I thought, regret and sorrow mingling with my guilt.

What I didn't want to face was that if what Maeva said was true, then my own mother had had a hand in my ignorance.

Blowing out a deep breath, I stopped stroking Maeva's hair. The breeze was picking up, and I didn't want her chilled because of it, though my flesh could keep her warm enough. Carefully, I stood, keeping her cradled in my arms, adjusting her so she rested more easily within them.

Looking down at her tear-streaked face, my chest *vokking* ached like mad. Our conversation wasn't over. Not nearly, not even close to being over. But she was exhausted. I got the sense that she'd been overwhelmed with everything that had come to light that night and it had simply been too much.

While I had so many questions, they would wait. They'd waited *years*. They could wait for another night.

Once she was secured in my arms, I took one last look at the lake and peered into the depths of the forest beside us, listening. When I heard nothing, I took us back to the horde.

When I reached the gates, the two *darukkars* who were taking the first night watch were there, tired though alert after the feast. Their eyes went to Maeva cradled in my arms, to her wet dress and my own squelching boots, though they said nothing.

I merely nodded at them when they greeted me, and I ordered quietly, "Close and secure the gates."

"*Lysi, Vorakkar,*" said one, and he went to do just as I'd bidden.

The horde was quiet as I wound my way through the *volikis*, taking the shortest route toward the back of the encampment. Within some *volikis* I passed, I heard slumbering snores. In others, breathy moans and slapping flesh. In others, quiet laughter and whispered words.

And when I happened upon Maeva's own *voliki*, I barely glanced at it as I strode past. I set my jaw in determination.

Quietly, I murmured, "You belong with me, *seffi*. In my furs. It is there that you will sleep from now on."

My words sounded like an oath, even to my own ears. A promise. They filled me with peace. They filled me with *rightness*, as if Kakkari had always meant for this. And perhaps she had. She had shown me the dream after all.

When I reached my *voliki*, I ducked inside the quiet darkness.

And finally, I brought my female to our bed.

When I opened my eyes, I experienced the dizzying sensation of not knowing where I was. Then last night returned to me all at once...at the same time I smelled Kiran's scent *everywhere*.

I winced when I sat up in a bed that was definitely not my own. A headache was throbbing behind my left eye. I suspected it was there more from the crying and the emotional release of last night than from the brew I'd consumed at the feast.

My face felt puffy and swollen. My eyes felt tight, my mouth dry. And when I braved looking around the *voliki*, searching for the male that it belonged to, I let out a little breath when he was nowhere to be seen.

Next to me, there was an indentation of a large body. When I reached out to touch it, I found it cold. The furs were mussed on that side, though they were snug around me.

Had he *covered* me?

Swallowing, I dropped my face in my hands and scrubbed them over my face.

Last night, I must've fallen asleep at the lake. Kiran had obviously brought me back to his *voliki,* but he could've just as easily deposited me into my own.

Just when I was deciding that I should leave before he returned—and take a much-needed bath—the *voliki* entrance flapped back and Kiran ducked inside.

Heart stuttering in my chest, I saw his face do something strange—an expression I'd never seen before and couldn't identify, but one that made my breath quicken with *awareness*. Awareness that I was in his furs. That I could smell him all over me.

Before he could say anything, I said quietly, "About last night, we should—"

He threw something on the foot of the bed, cutting off my words. He came to stand against one of the stabilizing poles that jutted up at the center of his *voliki*.

The thing he'd thrown was a satchel. A familiar satchel. When I dragged it toward me, I saw some of my clothes were inside it.

I blinked down at them before looking back at Kiran. "*Kakkira vor,*" I said, though my words were hesitant.

Tucking a strand of unruly hair behind my ear—which popped right back out—I saw he'd brought me my bandeau, a tunic, and clean trews, in addition to my flat sandals that I preferred because they were less heavy than my boots.

"Get dressed, *seffi,*" he rasped, watching me with those intense golden eyes, his arms crossed against the black hide of his own tunic, one that hugged the muscles of his body tight. "I told you I would take you beyond the gates this morning."

I hadn't thought he was serious. I thought he'd promised it to get me out of that freezing lake last night.

Still, I wasn't certain I should go. I had a pounding headache, my brain felt all fuzzy, and I was still so confused about what had happened between us last night.

Confused about everything, truthfully. I wasn't sure I was ready to *face* what had happened.

Then again, just thinking about the fresh morning air filling my lungs, about the view of the shimmering lake and the black mountains, about that feeling of wonderful lightness as my feet met the soil of Kakkari's planet, as though she was reverberating inside me...I didn't know if I could pass up the opportunity. Despite everything.

Kiran knew that too. He knew I wouldn't say *nik* to him if he asked me to go running.

"How early is it?" I asked, to buy time.

"The fires have yet to be lit" was his response. So I guessed dawn had just broken.

When I pushed off the furs, I was highly aware of his gaze as it followed my movements. Thankfully, I was still in my dress from the night before, though the bottom of it was stiff and stained from the lake water. A strange gray color that matched the color of the sand at the banks.

When Kiran didn't turn to leave so I could undress in privacy, I licked my dry lips and picked up my satchel. "I'll dress at my own *voliki*."

A grunt emerged from his throat.

"*Nik*, dress here," he ordered, moving away from the stabilizing pole. "I'll wait for you outside."

Then before I could say anything, he was gone, ducking underneath the entrance and out of direct sight.

I couldn't read him this morning. I couldn't read what he thought of last night. I couldn't read *why* he'd brought me to his bed.

Even when we were younger, back at the *saruk*, we'd never slept beside one another through a night. Once, we'd dozed together on a cool cliffside one afternoon, but it hadn't been for long. It had been during the hot season. When I'd awakened, he'd been watching me and had gruffly said he had to return to the *saruk*. He hadn't met my eyes for the rest of the day, which had confused me.

But now it was dawn and I'd woken in his bed. And he'd certainly met my eyes *this* morning.

My face flamed when I realized I was grateful for the early hour. I did not want to be seen leaving the *voliki* of a horde king the night after a feast. Then another thought occurred to me. What if someone had seen him bringing me to his *voliki* last night? He would have been carrying me since I didn't remember waking.

"*Vok*," I whispered.

Frowning, I knew it couldn't be helped. I would still have to deal with the embarrassment of leaving the feast early after storming away from Kiran. I'd tried to keep my expression impassive, but I didn't think I had accomplished that. His horde would know something had transpired between us, and I'd disrespected their *Vorakkar* by turning my back on him.

With one last look at the entrance, I turned and unclasped my stiff dress, letting it pool on the floor. Then, quickly, I tugged on the clothes that Kiran had brought me.

When I was fully dressed, I found one last item at the bottom of the satchel. My fingers drifted over the strip of dark, shimmering fabric. He'd even remembered to bring me a tie for my hair.

I stared down at it, feeling my chest tighten. Upon waking and thus far, I had avoided thinking about last night. About the realization that somehow, some way, Kiran *hadn't* known about my mother's death. About her burial.

Maybe I have been poisoned against him for so long...for a reason that was a lie, I thought, swallowing. Because I'd always known that I could forgive him for breaking my heart—it wasn't his fault if he didn't love me the way I'd loved him, after all.

But I had never been able to forgive him for leaving and not saying goodbye...and for turning his back on me when my *lomma* died.

Both of which I now knew to be untrue.

Guilt swarmed me. Shame lodged itself in my chest, and I breathed deeply, pressing against my breastbone to try to loosen it.

I can make this right, I thought.

First, I owed him an apology. We would have to discuss it. Again. No matter how painful last night had been.

It didn't stop me from feeling like a fool though.

But how could I have known?

I believed words that had been fed to me. First by my own father. Then by Kiran's mother. Two people I had trusted and cared for had lied to me.

Pressing my lips together, I quickly plaited my hair and secured it with the tie. Then I went out to meet Kiran.

The chill in the air made bumps spread over my flesh, but it also filled my lungs with brightness. Almost immediately, I felt some of the pain from my headache begin to fade as my cheeks stung, and I couldn't help the small curl of my lips.

Kiran was watching me, and that smile slowly died. I tucked invisible strands of hair behind my ear due to my nerves.

"Will you be cold, *seffi?*" he murmured, shortening the distance between us, standing before me, all broadness and muscle.

I shook my head. "*Nik,* I'll be fine."

He inclined his head, and I took the opportunity to scan the encampment in front of us, searching for anyone that might be awake at this hour. But there was no soul in sight.

Kiran's hand on my hip shocked me as he led me away from his *voliki*. His warmth spread beneath my trews and, as if sensing I would pull away in surprise, his grip tightened.

"How are you feeling this morning?"

As we passed quiet *volikis*, I licked my lips, peering down at the ground briefly before replying softly, "Like a fool."

His grip on my hip tightened, making me swallow.

Kiran said, "We will discuss it later, *lysi*? Let's enjoy the wildlands first."

I bit my lip, nodding, knowing it was inevitable.

"And you are not—and never have been—a fool. I've told you before, *seffi*."

His tone was so authoritative, as if his words were an order, that it almost made my lips quirk. As if he could drive any doubt from my mind with mere *words*.

But that was Kiran. Charmingly arrogant.

We were quiet the rest of the way and didn't encounter a single soul until we reached the gates. Two *darukkars* were posted there, and they opened them at Kiran's nod. And when we stepped from the encampment, my reaction was just like the previous night, though it felt much stronger.

The beauty of this part of the South Lands was easy to see. The landscape was so different than my *saruk* by the sea. My eyes feasted on the black-tipped mountains and the endless hills and multi-colored plains dotted with various foliage that was beginning to die and recede for the coming frost.

The lake was in front of us, all calm black water this morning, and the dense forest was to our left, curving around the lake on that side like it was its protector.

In the distance, toward the mountains, I saw a plume of dust kicking up.

"What is that?" I asked, worry jolting me.

"My *darukkar*," Kiran replied, his eyes on me. "I promised to send him to Rath Tuviri, *lysi*?"

"Oh," I said quietly as gratitude swarmed through me. Was that why he'd been up so early? "*Kakkira vor.*"

His lips quirked ever so slightly, making my heart speed in my chest. His eyes were warm, intense. *Like benuva,* I thought. The sweet, thick, delicious sap from *bunu* trees. Looking at him felt like *benuva* bursting over my tongue, sliding down my throat, and warming my belly.

Swallowing, I forced myself to look away. Clearing my throat, I asked, "Which way?"

"What were you thinking just now?" he asked, stepping closer.

Surprise jolted me, my eyes widening on him.

"Nothing," I said quickly.

"Then what is this, *seffi*?" he rasped, reaching out to brush his fingers over the front of my throat.

A sharp hitch in my breath came at the unexpected contact. I tilted my head back to look up at him and felt the side of his claw drag across my sensitive skin. I barely suppressed my shiver, but I could do nothing about the way my nipples pebbled tight under my tunic...and the *zinging* heat that pooled low.

"You are getting flushed, and we have not even started yet," he purred. His eyes were watchful, his voice deep and husky.

Why did those words sound so...*wicked*?

Silence stretched as we regarded one another.

"Nothing," I said again, the word coming out a little breathless. "What are *you* thinking right now? Because—"

"I'm thinking how much I enjoy looking at you," he replied, making me blink, the rough, calloused tip of his thumb dragging down to the notch in my throat.

It bobbed against his finger when I swallowed hard.

My first instinct, as it always was when it came to compliments, was to deny his words. I didn't know what he was doing or why, but I wasn't so naive as to think he was attracted to me, though his words and his touch would make any other female believe he was.

Kiran had never been attracted to me.

I wouldn't fool myself into thinking that he'd suddenly changed his mind.

Clearing my throat *again*, I stepped away from his touch.

I didn't want to go down this path again.

I couldn't.

"Shall we?" I asked quietly, turning my burning face away.

Kiran waited a moment before he blew out a rough sigh and said, "*Lysi.*"

Then a calculating expression came over his face and the left side of his mouth quirked.

"Race you to the end of the lake, *seffi*," he murmured, jerking his chin behind me.

"*Neffar?*" I frowned.

Kiran took off in a steady run.

Realization made my eyes widen, made my heart skip a beat. "Not fair!"

His deep, rumbling chuckle wound its way back to me.

For a moment, I forgot. It was like nine years had been erased in a single moment as I sprinted after him.

I shook my head, smiling as my hair blew back and my feet pounded harder and harder on the earth.

It felt nice to forget. If only for a moment. It felt nice to remember that before everything happened, I had always loved Kiran as my *friend* first. He'd been the one who'd comforted me when he found me crying. The one who'd always made me feel special and important to him.

But I needed to remember that this male was dangerous to me. That he made it all too easy for me to love him.

I would never love him again.

I couldn't.

Because if I did, it might destroy me completely this time around.

My brow was furrowed in concentration. Keeping my hand steady, I plucked the last of the debris from the *darukkar's* open wound and dropped it onto the table beside him.

"*Ruhna,*" I said, which was the *Dakkari* word for *apprentice,* nodding at Essir, "it's clean. Close it and then apply the *uudun.*"

Essir looked nervous. As did the *darukkar,* suddenly. But my apprentice didn't dare voice any of his concerns after I'd given him an order, and he nodded, moving to my side.

Hinna was watching, looking a little pale from the sight of the wound, her normally healthy, golden complexion going a little gray. Luckily, she stayed as far away from the well-lit table as possible and was slowly edging her way to the entrance flap.

Taking pity on her, I asked, "Will you go get some more water? In a fresh basin, *hanniva?*"

"*Lysi, Mokkira,*" Hinna replied quickly, inclining her head before darting from the *voliki.* My lips quirked, and I turned my attention back to Essir. He was wrapping the needle with thread, and I took it from him, showing him how to knot it tighter before handing it back. "Quickly."

Essir nodded, his hand shaking ever so slightly as he brought the needle to the *darukkar's* flesh.

"Would you not rather close it, *Mokkira?*" the *darukkar* asked hurriedly.

"My *ruhna* is quite capable, I promise you," I told him, giving him what I hoped was a comforting smile. Essir glanced sideways at me, his eyes wide. Then he gave me a little bashful grin, his shoulders straightening, before his expression morphed into one of extreme concentration and he made the first stitch.

The *darukkar* jumped as if he'd gotten slashed with a broad sword rather than a tiny needle, but Essir didn't comment on it and the warrior slowly relaxed, gritting his jaw, as my apprentice made quick work of the small wound. A training accident during sparring practice that afternoon.

Something that I'd learned happened all too often, especially among some of the more inexperienced *darukkars*.

Once the *darukkar* was stitched and bandaged, he left. The moment he did, Essir gave me a triumphant smile though his bloody hand shook as he said, "I did it!"

"The last *mokkira* never let you close wounds?" I asked. I'd guessed as much, but it still puzzled me. My very first day as my own *mokkira's* apprentice, he'd had me close a nasty, deep leg wound on a *pyroki* of all things. Later, I realized he'd done it to test me, to see how I responded under pressure when I knew next to nothing.

I must've passed his little test.

"*Nik*, never," Essir replied, sighing as he went to scrub his hands in the dirtied basin to get most of the blood off. Shortly after, Hinna returned, balancing a fresh one, and he smiled at her when she dropped it onto one of the empty benches on the far wall.

"Thank Kakkari he's gone," Hinna sighed, her shoulders sagging. "I was certain I would faint any moment."

I hid my smile, going to my cabinet to put away the supplies. The air in the *voliki* smelled of simmering *kuniri*, an earthy scent with a tinge of sweetness.

"You might see a lot worse," I commented. "Maybe you should hope that the *Vorakkar* assigns you a new position soon. Especially before the birthings begin."

"*Nik*," Hinna said quietly. "I do not wish that. My duty is to you, *Mokkira*. I am most honored to serve you."

I heard the honesty in her voice, and it made my own throat tighten with emotion. With gratitude. I reached out to squeeze her hand when she assisted me with putting away my supplies.

"*Kakkira vor*," I said to her. "You will get used to the blood."

"I have no choice," she said, giving me a small smile. "I will get better."

"What *did* the *Vorakkar* assign you to do exactly, Hinna?" Essir asked, using her given name.

Hinna looked to Essir. Then she looked back at me, biting her lip.

I sighed, my shoulders dropping ever so slightly. It would dishonor Hinna if I told her to lie. In her eyes, the *Vorakkar* had given her a very respectable and prominent position in his horde, though his reasoning for it still didn't make sense to me.

When I inclined my head to her, Hinna answered Essir proudly and immediately, as if she'd been *dying* to tell anyone at all.

"The *Vorakkar* assigned me as her *piki*."

The silence was deafening before Essir choked out, "*N-Neffar?*"

Hinna tried to keep her smile from being *too* wide. A valiant effort, though she failed, which almost made me chuckle.

When Essir turned his wide eyes on mine, he asked boldly, "You will be the *Vorakkar's Morakkari?*"

His question sobered me. For a brief moment, I allowed myself to remember earlier that morning. Running on the shores of the lake with Kiran, my heart pounding with excitement. We hadn't run on the path that edged up to the forest. I knew it was because Kiran was still wary of beasts that might've wandered too far. Though he'd seemed to enjoy the run, he'd always been on alert, a long dagger sheathed at his hip.

We hadn't talked. We'd just been in one another's presence. We hadn't *needed* to talk. It had been...strangely wonderful.

Afterward, I had surprised myself by asking if we could do it again the next morning.

Kiran had looked at me, that mouth curving into a secretive, maddening grin.

"*Lysi, seffi,*" he'd said. "You know I can never deny you anything."

I would be lying to myself if I said his words hadn't brought a rush of adrenaline and pleasure with them.

Then he'd left me at the entrance to the *mokkira's voliki*, just as the horde began to rouse, as the sun shone bright and golden, coming up over the plains, and said he would see me later tonight.

"*Nik,*" I finally replied to Essir. "The *Vorakkar* was only ensuring that I felt comfortable in the horde when he assigned our Hinna here as my *piki.*"

Essir frowned. Hinna purposefully fiddled with something on the workbench. Even I heard his thoughts. Even I knew that Essir didn't believe me. Because *pikis* were—and always would be—solely for the *Morakkari* of the horde.

I sighed.

"It's getting late," I said once I finished organizing my cabinets. "Both of you should return to your *volikis* and take your evening meals. I'll clean up here, *lysi?*"

It took a little while to convince them both, but eventually, I found that I had the *mokkira's voliki* all to myself. I took comfort in tidying it and pride in cleaning it. For the frost, it was all mine. For the frost, I could make my mark in this horde.

But it will come to an end, came my treacherous thought.

All the more reason to savor it, I knew.

Once I finished, the sky was dark and the fires were blaring throughout the horde. More and more of the fire basins were being fed throughout the day as the chill started to stick. I shivered, wrapping my furs around me tighter, as I made my way toward my *voliki.*

The Dakkari that I passed inclined their heads, murmuring my title in respect, and I returned their greetings with a small smile. I wasn't used to the attention, especially since back at the *saruk,* I'd been nothing more than an apprentice. No one had looked at me twice, though most had been friendly enough.

I'd only been at the horde a handful of days, but my feet led me to my *voliki,* as if I'd walked that path all my life.

Only...my *voliki* wasn't there.

Frowning, I spun around, flicking my gaze at my surroundings.

Nik, this was definitely where my *voliki* was supposed to be. Though it was dark, I spied the outline of it on the earth, a round dome in that glaringly empty place.

Neffar?

What was happening?

I sensed movement behind me. When I turned, I saw the *darukkar* that had been trailing me lingering behind the nearest *voliki.* I sighed. I knew that Kiran had assigned him to look out for me, and I had known I was being tailed since the second day at the horde.

And this *darukkar* wasn't exactly discreet.

"Do you know where my *voliki* is?" I called out, feeling a little ridiculous since the warrior was obviously trying to hide from me.

After a brief moment of silence, the male shuffled out from

behind the nearest *voliki*, his shoulders going back, though I spied a tinge of embarrassment on his features.

"The *Vorakkar*" was his response.

My frown deepened. "The *Vorakkar*?"

"*Lysi*," the *darukkar* replied. "He had your *voliki* dismantled this afternoon."

He *what*?

But *why*?

I swallowed, confusion furrowing my brow. "Then where are my things?"

The *darukkar* jerked his head in the direction of the back of the encampment. And there, on a slight incline, was Kiran's own *voliki*. Underneath the entrance flap, I saw a glow from within. Through the venting hole at the top, dark smoke swirled upward toward the clear night sky.

My heart leapt in my throat.

Every time I thought I had him figured out again...he went and did something like this.

As I'd realized this morning, Kiran was charmingly arrogant. Only, right now, I didn't find him quite so charming. Especially since he'd *dismantled* my *voliki* and hadn't *told me*.

And I intended to tell him so right when I figured out what the *vok* was going on.

With that thought in mind, I straightened my shoulders and stalked toward his *voliki*.

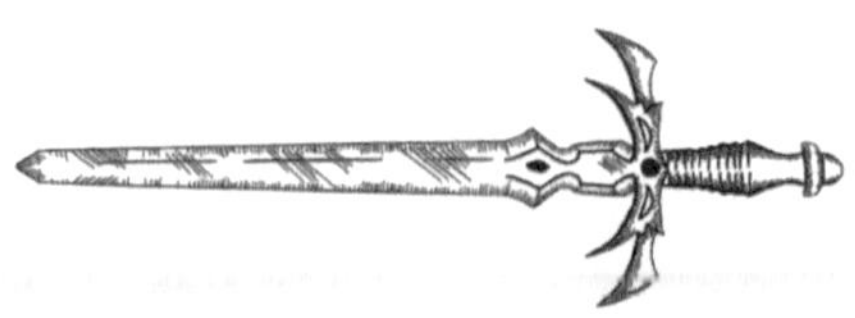

CHAPTER 28

Licking my lips, I prepared myself for a fight when I heard angry, quick strides approaching my *voliki*.

Blowing out a long breath, I leaned farther back in the bathing tub, my arms draped along the edges, as I fixed my gaze on the entrance flap in anticipation. Beneath the water of my bath, my cock hardened, resting against my belly.

She didn't bother to announce herself, as was expected. Anyone else would've been punished for it, and she knew that.

Instead, she pushed underneath the entrance, her gaze flicking around my *voliki*, a frown on her lips.

Then she froze, her eyes going wide, when she found me lounging in the bath, my gaze fastened on her, waiting for her to speak.

But she surprised me.

I'd expected her to spin around in embarrassment. While Dakkari were not shy about nudity, Maeva had always been so, though she'd been raised Dakkari.

Except she didn't break my gaze. Instead, she acted as if she hadn't stormed into my *voliki* while I was bathing and, after clearing her throat, demanded quietly, "Where is my *voliki*?"

My *seffi* wasn't so unaffected by me, however. I spied that dark flush rising in her neck. The same one I'd commented on earlier this morning, when I'd stroked her soft skin there and tormented myself with thoughts of licking her there, of *biting* her there, marking her as my own.

"I had it taken down," I murmured, shifting slightly in the bath, drawing her gaze to my chest.

"But *why?*" she asked, blinking, frowning. A knot of tension loosened in my chest at her presence. Just looking at her pleased me.

Vok, she was beautiful. Her expression was maddeningly bewildered and innocent. As if she hadn't yet realized my intentions.

"Go eat, *seffi*," I said, gesturing over to the low table filled with platters of food. "You must be hungry."

She was still wearing the clothes she'd gone running in, though she also wore her furs, which Hinna must've retrieved for her before I had her *voliki* dismantled.

"*Nik*," she said slowly, her eyes barely gliding over the table before returning to me. "I want to know what's happening."

I blew out a short breath, raking a hand through my wet hair. I had been asking myself how to tell her without her wanting to kill me in response. Maeva was independent, which I had always admired. While she'd always had a streak of independence growing up, it had morphed into something entirely different now, and I wasn't sure how to go about this.

"Are you...are you sending me away?" she asked softly.

A sound of disbelief left my throat.

"*Nik*," I growled, my body tensing at the words.

Just the thought of her leaving sent discomfort shooting through my chest. On the rim of the bathing tub, my fists clenched.

"Then..." She trailed off, licking her lips. "*Neffar?*"

"I'm debating how to tell you in a way that won't cost me

my *deva* when you cut them from me," I informed her, the corner of my lips ticking up.

Her flush deepened though she demanded, "Tell me *now*."

"You dare to give a *Vorakkar* an order?" I purred, the way her soft lips pursed in determination making my cock even harder. "Good thing you are the only one allowed to."

A huff of impatience left her, reminding me of the old Maeva.

"Kiran, where am I supposed to *sleep* if you got rid of my *voliki?*"

Knowing I couldn't put this off any longer, I stood from the bathing tub, water sluicing off my body as I watched her. Maeva blinked, a small sound emerging from her throat that reminded me of a startled *privixi* as her eyes fastened on my cock.

Again, she surprised me. She didn't turn away. And her gaze was all wary curiosity, curiosity that almost made me groan out loud. How had I not given in to her that night on the cliff, nine years ago? She'd bared herself to me, offered herself to me freely, and I'd rejected her advances.

And how many times over the years had I cursed myself for it?

But our friendship had been more important than sex then. I hadn't wanted to ruin that. And I'd feared that if I allowed myself to love her as I wanted to, to be with her the way I wanted to, in the end she would realize that I hadn't been worth it after all.

Maeva's love then had been so pure, so complete, that it had *frightened* me. But I wasn't afraid anymore.

I had been...foolish. Cowardly.

But I'd been young.

Now I had been a *Vorakkar* for nine years and I had experienced the hardships of this life, of life in the wildlands, and the responsibilities that came with leading a horde that depended on me to be strong. I wasn't that young, *saruk*-bred boy anymore, who had been barely old enough to lead.

Now I knew what I wanted, and she was standing right in front of me, looking at me in a way that made me want to toss her onto the furs and mate her in the way I'd craved for *vokking* years.

I didn't bother to dry off. I stepped out of the bathing tub and stepped toward her.

She wanted to know where she would sleep?

Beside me. Where she belongs, I thought.

Gesturing to my furs, I rasped, "*This* is where you will sleep, *seffi*."

She blinked again, though her gaze seemed a little unfocused.

"*Neffar?*" she asked quietly, as if she hadn't *heard* me.

"With me," I rumbled, drawing closer.

"*Neffar?*" she asked, jerking in surprise, her voice rising. "Kiran—"

We were close, so close that I could feel her heat. Between us my cock was hard and thick, and I heard her breath hitch when her eyes caught on it. Her hands curled at her sides.

A rumbling groan fell from my throat, and I purred quietly, "What do you want, *rei seffi*?"

Do you want to touch me? Feel me? Kiss me the way you did nine years ago?

My question seemed to jerk her out of whatever she'd been thinking. She physically jumped, her breath tumbling out of her in rough pants.

"*W-What* are you doing, Kiran?" she whispered, her eyes wide in shock.

Reaching past her, I snagged my fur cloth and donned it, one that tied at my waist and concealed my cock. I slept naked and didn't see the point in wrestling on trews after my washing.

But her next unguarded, strangely vulnerable words made me freeze.

"You...you don't want me like that. You never have," she said quietly. "So what are you *doing?*"

A sound of disbelief, rough and almost *angry*, tore from my throat.

"What the *vok* are you talking about?" I asked, my tone low but soft.

Her face was burning, the darkest it had ever been before.

She turned away from me, going over to the fire basin, showing me her back.

"Tell me," I murmured, trying to keep my voice steady. I had a suspicion of what she'd meant by the words. Approaching her, I questioned, "Because of that night?"

A ragged breath whistled through her nostrils.

"You just...you never wanted me."

I hated how brittle her words sounded. How uncertain they were. My brave, confident Maeva.

I had hurt her so many times that she carried some wounds I wasn't even aware of.

My jaw tensed as determination coursed through me. That was our past, however. And I would damn well make sure that I showed her just how much I wanted her, how much I desired her.

How much I'd needed her all these years.

"I watched you for so long," she whispered, still not meeting my gaze. "I knew there were other females. What your *pujerak* said didn't surprise me. And I—I knew that you didn't return my feelings."

"Maeva..." I rasped, raking back my wet hair, feeling the droplets run down my chest. *Vok.*

"You never gave me any indication that you wanted me," she whispered, and I could hear the mortification in her tone. This wasn't easy for her. But it was that same strength that I knew she possessed that was bringing these words to the surface. Because my Maeva didn't back down from anything. "So I thought that I could be bold, like the females you had liked in the *saruk*. But that night, on the cliff, you..."

"I rejected you," I finished for her.

She shook her head. Then my brave Maeva turned and she met my eyes, letting me witness her embarrassment. I frowned when I saw it coupled with shame.

"It wasn't just about the rejection," she said, her chin lifting. "I remember the way you looked at me. I've always remembered it."

I frowned. I didn't know what she was talking about. I didn't remember feeling anything that night but punishing desire and shame for my own actions—at hurting her, at realizing that I would only disappoint her.

"I don't understand, *seffi*," I admitted, shaking my head.

"You were disgusted."

That was certainly not what I expected, and I barely stopped myself from reeling back in surprise.

Then came the anger, flashing through my chest like lightning, my body tensing tight.

"I threw myself at you," Maeva whispered, blinking, swallowing, her breaths coming quick. "I bared myself to you. And all I remember is the way you looked at me. Like my body repulsed you. Like *I* did. And I knew then that you truly didn't desire me...though I had hoped you would. For so long."

Vok.

Vok, vok, vok.

I was such a *vokking* fool.

Chest tight with regret, I moved to step toward her just as I heard someone striding up to my *voliki*.

"Maeva," I said, my voice low and tight. I was barely holding onto my control. "*Vok*, I've *always*—"

"*Vorakkar*," came a male voice from outside.

I cursed loudly, looking at Maeva, a deep scowl etched into my features, though she was looking toward the entrance of my *voliki*. In *relief*.

"*Neffar?*" I snarled to the intruder outside, raising my voice so he would be able to hear it.

A *darukkar* ducked his head inside, one that I'd posted at the gates for the night watch. His eyes flickered to Maeva, and she turned her head away, putting space between us as if embarrassed to be caught in the *Vorakkar's voliki*.

"What is it?" I growled, tension and anger thrumming tight inside me.

The sooner he left, the sooner I could make this right between Maeva and me. The sooner I could inform her that I'd never *stopped* wanting her, that I had tried and failed to dull my desire and memories of her over the last nine years, distracting myself with females whose faces I couldn't even remember, and slaughtering any Ghertun packs we'd crossed, perhaps a little too viciously, and moving from one place to the next, though staying far from the South Lands, far from *her*.

The *darukkar* seemed out of breath.

"The *Vorakkar* of Rath Rowin is at the gates seeking entry to the horde."

I inhaled a sharp breath and jerked my head to the other male.

"*Neffar?*" I rasped.

"He says he brings urgent news from *Dothik*."

"*Vok,*" I murmured tightly, already reaching for my fur pelt, swinging it over my shoulders. I didn't bother to pull on trews, but I did stuff my feet into my hide boots. At the last moment, I decided not to strap on my sword. The *Vorakkar* of Rath Rowin was a friend. One of the few *Vorakkar* I actually liked.

When my gaze cut to Maeva, she was looking down into the flickering flames of the fire in the golden basin. The light cast her skin in warmth and beauty.

With a heavy heart, I told her quietly, "We will continue our discussion once I return. But you will sleep here for the night, *lysi?*"

She didn't answer me. She didn't look at me.

Unable to help myself, I brushed my fingers underneath her jaw, turning her toward me until those swirling, dark eyes were on me.

"Eat, *seffi*," I ordered her. "I'll come back to you soon."

She seemed to realize I wouldn't leave until she gave me an answer. Finally, after a tense, long silence, she nodded.

Relieved, my touch drifted away.

Then I turned, nodding at the *darukkar*.

"Let Rath Rowin pass. I'll meet with him now."

CHAPTER 29

"You come at a very inconvenient time, my friend," I growled to the *Vorakkar* of Rath Rowin, stalking into my council's *voliki* only to see Errok already there, his arms crossed over his chest.

Rath Rowin smirked, though it didn't reach his eyes. He took in my state of undress and assumed that I'd been with a female.

While I had been, it hadn't been in the way I craved.

"My apologies, Rath Okkili," Rath Rowin grunted. "Next time, I'll be certain to schedule my visits around your nightly amusements."

Errok caught my gaze. His brow lifted. I hadn't seen him since we sparred on the training grounds after my run with Maeva this morning. He'd gone off with some hunters to patrol the surrounding lands for more trespassing beasts.

I clasped Rath Rowin on the shoulder, and he did the same to me.

"What news do you bring from *Dothik*?" I asked, my tone low.

Rath Rowin had always been intense. He'd always taken his

duties as *Vorakkar* with the utmost seriousness. At times, he could be unbending and rigid in his rules. Severe, even.

Some would call him cruel.

Almost a year ago, the *Vorakkar* of Rath Kitala had encountered a Ghertun spy close to his horde. He'd had the Ghertun imprisoned and then brought him to trial before his horde.

If the circumstances had been different, Rath Rowin would've cut the Ghertun's head from its shoulders before it could utter a single word and walk away unbothered.

Most *Vorakkar* would hesitate.

Rath Rowin never did.

Though we were friends, I would be lying if I said his presence at my horde didn't make me uneasy. He'd come alone as well. He hadn't even brought *darukkars* to accompany him, probably because he didn't like to leave his horde unprotected in the slightest. Every sword was valuable, after all.

"The *Dothikkar* wants us all to meet in the Dead Lands" was what he replied.

"*Neffar?*" I growled. "Tell me, did Rath Kitala's messages finally reach him?"

"About this red mist?" Rath Rowin asked, his brow raising. "*Lysi.*"

"And he will actually leave *Dothik*, take to the wildlands for the first time in his reign, to meet us there?"

Rath Rowin leveled me a knowing look. "Of course not. He will remain in *Dothik* behind his walls. He wants us to report back. And as we all thought, he is panicking about this mist. He is even going to advance the next Trials."

"*Vok,*" I cursed, even as a derisive laugh almost fell from my lips. "But the last Trials just barely ended. *That Vorakkar* has not even taken to the wildlands yet, and the *Dothikkar* wants another Trial so soon?"

Out of the corner of my eye, I saw Errok straighten.

"When will he set them?" my *pujerak* asked.

"After the frost. He reasons that more *Vorakkar* are needed to keep the wildlands safe," Rath Rowin remarked. He huffed a deep sigh. "And I must say, I am beginning to agree with him."

I sobered, my jaw ticking. I walked to the table in the center of the brightly lit *voliki*, with the map of Dakkar spread out on its surface, my gaze straying to the Dead Lands.

"We face more threats now than we ever have in our history. It is not only Dakkari that live here now. We have *vekkiri*, Ghertun, Nrunteng, and Killup now too," Rath Rowin continued. "Not to mention that the hordes of Rath Dulia and Rath Loppar are coming to their end. New hordes must rise to take their place."

He was right. Of course he was right.

Good riddance to Rath Dulia—that spineless bastard. But Rath Loppar was an honorable male, a natural-born leader who would most likely settle down in his elder years to create a *saruk* of his own. Just like my father.

I had the same aspirations, once my time as *Vorakkar* was over.

Maybe a *saruk* by the sea—just like where we'd grown up— since Maeva was so fond of the coast.

Swallowing, I looked up from the map to meet Errok's gaze.

My *pujerak* asked, "Has Rath Kitala had any more updates about the dark fog? Has it grown?"

Rath Rowin shook his head. "I haven't heard any more from him. Rath Tuviri would be the first to, I suppose, since their hordes are closest to one another."

"I sent a messenger to Rath Tuviri this morning," I said, which seemed to surprise Errok. Looking at Rath Rowin, I said, "My *mokkira* had a request for their healer. And our *thespers* have not yet returned."

Rath Rowin nodded.

"When does the *Dothikkar* expect us to meet in the Dead

Lands? The frost is coming soon. Surely he cannot expect us to leave now," I murmured quietly.

There was still so much to be done in the horde.

A truth that no doubt frustrated Rath Rowin too, since he'd been tasked with calling the *Vorakkar* to this meeting, leading him away from his own horde at such a precarious time.

"He does," Rath Rowin replied. "In one week's time. Right on the cusp of the season."

I blew out a rough breath, rubbing at my temple, which had begun to throb.

"I do not have much time to inform the others," Rath Rowin said. "And so I must leave soon. I hope to reach Rath Tuviri by tomorrow if I travel quickly."

"Stay the night, at least," I suggested. "*Ungira* have moved into the South Lands. I got a talon to the back not long ago."

"I do not fear *ungira*," Rath Rowin said, his tone matter-of-fact, his brow raised.

"And yet it is hard to see their dens in the dark," I reasoned. "Leave at dawn, Rowin. My *mrikro* will see your *pyroki* well fed and rested. I have no spare *volikis,* but I can have a bed brought into this one."

Rath Rowin sighed, deep but short.

"A rested *pyroki* travels faster," he finally said, "and mine deserves the break. I will take your offer and leave at dawn. You have my thanks, Okkili."

I clasped Rath Rowin's shoulder once more and turned my gaze to meet Errok's. His expression was pensive, and I knew exactly what had captured his interest during the conversation.

The advancement of the next Trials.

Pressing my lips together, I nodded at him, giving him the signal to send for the *Vorakkar's* accommodations, and he exited the *voliki* quickly.

Rath Rowin watched him go before his gaze sharpened back to mine.

"This is the first time in a long time that the hordes have been close to one another for the season," Rath Rowin commented. "All have settled within a week's ride of one another. Do you think that is a coincidence? Or has Kakkari signaled something within all of us to stay close?"

"I have always believed that if we listen to Kakkari, our lives will unfold just as they are meant to," I told him quietly. "So *nik*…I do not think it is a coincidence."

"What do you think it is?" Rath Rowin questioned next. "This mist? This fog that blankets the Dead Lands? Do you think it's a punishment from Kakkari, meant for the Ghertun?"

My nostrils flared. "I do not think it is only meant for the Ghertun."

"Why?" he grunted.

"Because this fog is driving Dakkari-bred beasts from their natural homes," I said. "It is frightening them away. They seem to sense something, and because of it, they are more dangerous, more easily aggravated. A *polkunu* nearly killed one of my *darukkars* near my father's *saruk*."

"All the way down by *Drukkar's Sea*?" he asked, his tone quiet yet pensive.

"*Lysi*," I rasped. "So I do not think it is a warning for the Ghertun. I think it is a warning to us all. And I intend to ensure that the *Dothikkar* knows this after we meet. For too long, he has sat on that throne and done nothing. For too long, he has let us deal with the sufferings that have never before existed in the wildlands, sufferings that we hardly have time to deal with ourselves."

The suffering of the *vekkiri*, the Nrunteng, and the Killup specifically. Though most Killup had left the East already, venturing north.

"Maybe this is what it takes for him to finally see," Rath Rowin added softly. "A warning from Kakkari herself."

"He will reason it is for the Ghertun, however," I already

knew. "Because this fog is not over *Dothik*. And as such, it is not his problem."

"But it frightens him," Rath Rowin said. "That is something."

"True," I voiced.

"*Vorakkar*," came a voice from outside the *voliki*.

At the same time, Rath Rowin and I barked out, "*Lysi?*"

We exchanged looks, and a smirk crossed the other male's features just as two warriors entered with a large bathing tub.

"My apologies, Okkili," Rath Rowin said. "For a moment, I forgot my place."

I clapped him on the back. "I'll leave you to rest. We will speak in the morning before you depart."

The *Vorakkar* nodded. With a knowing look, he added, "Go back to your female. I'm sure my brief interruption left her wanting."

That was exactly what I intended to do.

But first, I needed to make certain the gates were secured and then I needed to speak with Errok. No matter how terribly I needed to return to Maeva, I would always be a *Vorakkar* first.

I woke to movement, my lids heavy like boulders. For the second time that day, I didn't realize where I was until I smelled Kiran. Until I realized I'd woken in his bed, a place I'd never intended to be.

My belly grumbled with hunger, but I'd been too upset and embarrassed earlier to eat. And now, Kiran's bulk was dipping the bed, making a small crater that brought me closer to his body.

I still didn't know why he'd had my *voliki* dismantled. I still didn't know why he demanded that I sleep here.

He blew out a deep sigh, and I felt him shift, felt him turn toward me. It was darker in the *voliki*, the last of the embers in the fire basin glowing low. He must've been gone a long time and I must've inadvertently fallen asleep.

When his arms wrapped tight around me from behind, I didn't stiffen or pull away. In fact, I was *surprised* by how my body responded. My eyes closed for a brief moment, fluttering shut, relaxing in his unexpected hold. Kiran had touched me often enough—Dakkari were very affectionate creatures. But as Kiran aged, as the time had drawn closer and closer to his purpose in *Dothik*, he had begun to withhold his embrace, which had always come so easily from him.

I missed this, I thought quietly. I missed being hugged by him. Because whenever he hugged me, whenever I smelled him or felt the tight squeeze of his large arms, I felt safe. Protected.

Loved.

Even though it wasn't the type of love I'd wanted from him. He'd loved me like a sister. He'd told me so himself.

Which was what made tonight all the more confusing.

And I was so *vokking* tired of *thinking* all the time.

So, I let him hold me because it simply felt good and I was too tired to fight it, to pull away when I didn't even *want* to.

When he breathed, warm air rustled the tiny hairs at the nape of my neck. I felt the sharp tip of his nose burrow into my hair, and bumps exploded across my arms when he inhaled deeply.

Underneath the furs, his legs tucked against mine, all warm, hard flesh that heated me quickly. I wondered if he was naked, and the thought jolted something *deep* within me.

"You were a child when we became friends, *seffi*," he murmured.

My brow furrowed, and I stared across the furs, across the bed, across the *voliki* to his chests that lay in a darkened corner. I wondered if they were his *deviri*, his gifts to his chosen *Morakkari*, gifts he might have been collecting for her even when he'd lived in the *saruk*.

That thought made jealousy burn in my chest, though it was more of a deep, melancholic ache than a sharp, punishing sting.

"A child," he whispered. "Then again, so was I, though I was older than you. For years and years, all I wanted was to watch over you. Protect you. Make you laugh and smile because I loved it when you did."

His voice was soft, but I heard the truth in it. The soft reverence in it, like he held on to those memories of our childhood just like I did. Because they'd been special—not many were lucky enough to experience a friendship like ours—and we'd both known that.

"And for a long time," he continued, "I did not see you as a female of age."

I inhaled a long breath and blew it out. His head shifted, his warm hand slid across my waist, draping over my hips. My heart picked up speed.

His lips were against my ear when he murmured, "But I remember one of the first times I wanted you. One of the first times I saw you as a female in your prime, a female I wanted to take to my furs and keep there."

My lips parted, and I barely suppressed a shiver.

"The storm over *Drukkar's Sea*," he said, and I swallowed, my mind already going to that night because I knew exactly the moment he was talking about. "Do you remember?"

I was reeling, my thoughts of that night flowing fast. Kiran had snuck me out of my *soliki*, long after the *saruk* slept, because a storm had blown in off the coast. The moon had been full, though we'd hardly been able to see through the black clouds. And purple lightning had struck across the sea, thunderous loud *booms* following in its wake.

Kiran had already been to *Dothik* then. But he'd returned to the *saruk* for a little while, on a short break from his *darukkar* training at the capital.

"I remember. The rains came, and we got soaked to the bone," I whispered. "It was beautiful that night."

"*Lysi*," he murmured, his voice gruff in agreement. "The rains came and soaked your nightdress straight through."

I blinked, heat coiling up my throat, making it difficult to swallow.

"And you were bared to me," he growled in my ear. "All of you."

My nipples went tight, my breasts heavy with the *desire* I heard in that rich voice.

Surprise jolted me when that big, heavy hand slid again, as the back of his claws brushed my tight nipples, a strangled sound falling from my throat. Gentle enough that it might have been a mistake...but Kiran didn't do anything by accident.

"And these," he rasped, "were pebbled hard and straining against that *vokking* dress. And all I wanted to do was lay you down on that coastal cliff and suckle on them as the rain pelted us."

His claws dragged against my left nipple, more deliberately this time, and I couldn't contain my gasp. I couldn't help the sound that fell from my throat, a shocking sizzle of pleasure from that tiny touch *completely consuming me.*

It frightened me, the depth of it. I had deprived myself of a male's touch for so long, and now that Kiran—the only male I'd ever truly desired—was stroking me, it was *overwhelming.*

"K-Kiran," I whispered, gripping his wrist and squeezing, keeping those claws away even as my legs tensed and a sharp throbbing began between them.

"And your smile that night, *seffi,*" he continued, his voice sounding *dazed.* Far away, as if he hadn't heard me say his name. "*Vok,* you were laughing and running along the cliffs. We were such a mess from the mud and the *runiri* pollen. But you didn't care. You were delighted. I'd never seen you so happy, and you were happy so often, Maeva."

I...*had been.* Kiran had always made me happy, even when he made me want to scream.

"You don't know how *vokking* close I came to claiming you that night," he confessed.

Blood rushed in my ears at the pronouncement as disbelief mingled with my lust, as my lust mingled with my memories. And everything, *everything* was always mingled with Kiran.

"I would have let you," I whispered, my throat stinging and

aching. Because I'd wanted him so much. Because I'd loved him so much then.

"I know," he growled.

Licking my lips, not entirely sure I wanted to know the answer, I asked, "Then why didn't you?"

I heard his deep swallow. I heard his rough breaths. He went quiet for a little while, though he broke free of my hold on his wrist and trailed his big hand down my soft belly. I was only wearing my tunic. He stopped before he reached the junction of my thighs but only just barely, and he spread his fingers wide until his large hand covered the entirety of my abdomen.

"Because I was always supposed to protect you," came his quiet answer. "Even if it was from *me*."

My brow furrowed.

"There were other males that wanted you, Maeva," he told me. "Males that weren't worthy of you."

"You mean Ojinu?" I asked, my voice quiet.

He'd mentioned something about scaring off Ojinu from his courtship of me.

Kiran stiffened. "Among others."

"No one ever approached me," I said.

"Because I didn't let them," came his gruff reply. "They were vile males, not worthy of your time."

"What is it?" I asked, because there was something he wasn't telling me. I was certain.

He hesitated.

"Kiran."

Finally, as his arm tightened around me, he said, "Ojinu always bragged to the other *darukkars* in training that he would be the first to mate you. That he would be the first to—"

He broke off, a curse falling from his lips.

I swallowed. "That he'd be the first to mate a human, you mean."

Kiran sighed and his forehead dropped into my hair. "*Lysi.*

We fought. I told him to never *look* at you again or I'd kill him. And I meant it. I'd never been so angry, Maeva, when I heard him."

"I don't remember that," I whispered, my eyes wide. I'd been furious—and hurt—when he told me about Ojinu when I met him at the training grounds. Now I felt the opposite.

"I didn't want you to know," Kiran grunted. "And after that, the other males who desired you never dared to try their luck either. I was still *Rukkar*, after all. They wouldn't dare."

Closing my eyes, I blew out a breath. "For years, I thought no one was attracted to me. Because I was *vekkiri*. And now you're telling me that many were *because* of it?"

The thought sickened me. That Ojinu had only begun a courtship so he could see what mating a human was like. And what if I'd eventually given in to him, because I was young and stupid and impulsive and would've wanted to see if it made Kiran jealous? He would've bragged about it to the rest of the males afterward.

But Kiran had saved me from that humiliation, from that shame.

Gratitude spread through me.

"What does this have to do with the night of the storm?" I whispered.

"Because I thought that maybe I was no better than *they* were," he admitted.

His quiet confession made me more confused. And though I wanted to stay turned away from him—because somehow it made talking about these things easier—his eyes would tell me what I needed to know. I knew that for certain.

Shifting in his arms, I turned so that I faced him, my cheek pressing into the soft cushions underneath my head. His hands never left me. They went around my back, and I felt one settle on the swell of my buttocks—a possessive, intimate touch, as if we'd done this a million times before.

Those golden eyes were rapt and intense on me. Pinning me in place. Kiran was never afraid of anything. He wasn't afraid of this conversation, so I didn't want to be either.

His eyes trailed down to my breasts, and his grip tightened when he saw my hardened nipples underneath the thin tunic. I gasped when he moved his hand to cup the side of my breast, its weight in his palm, his eyes going dark with hunger.

"Y-You thought that because you wanted me, you were like the others you scared away from me?" I asked.

"I had always promised to protect you," he repeated. "I thought that I was *worse* than them. Because you were my *seffi*, my Maeva. And suddenly, all I thought about was fucking you, mating you. Because I wanted you for my own and I wanted every inch of you. And in my mind, I could *never* have you. It felt like I was betraying you. It felt like I was dishonoring the trust you had in me, breaking an unspoken promise between us."

"But I loved you then, Kiran," I whispered, feeling my nose sting. My tears came more easily than they had for the past eight years. Like a gate had been opened. "All I wanted was you. Surely you knew that."

"You were everything that was good in my life, *seffi*," he told me. "*Vok*, when I was in *Dothik*, I *ached* to see you again because you made me *feel*. I didn't want to destroy that, destroy *you* in the process. Because I might have."

The tears blurred my vision. I couldn't believe what he was telling me. So many things that had been kept hidden, secrets that I would have never known about.

"And *Dothik*," he whispered, his eyes looking dazed again. "*Vokking Dothik*. That place ate at me. It made me...cold. It made it easier to detach. Made it easier to forget."

I had known that. Every time Kiran returned to the *saruk*, he was changed. Hardened. But that cold exterior had always softened for *me*. That was why I'd been so certain he'd begun to return my feelings.

And from what he was saying...it was possible he *had*. But then he'd pushed me away.

"And that night?" I asked, my voice ragged. "That night on the cliff after the feast? The last night I saw you?"

One of his hands came up to cup my jaw, spreading wide. His thumb brushed the thumping flesh of my throat, right over my fluttering heartbeat.

"I always told you that you were young, Maeva. But truthfully, it was *me* that wasn't prepared for what would come. I was on the cusp of something *more*. My time as *Vorakkar* hadn't even begun yet. I wasn't..."

He trailed off, a deep sigh escaping him.

"I wasn't thinking of anyone but myself," he confessed. "I was scared to take to the wildlands. I didn't tell a soul that— not even you. I doubted my ability to lead a horde. I doubted everything. The *last thing* I was thinking about was taking a *Morakkari*, Maeva. Not then."

I swallowed. I could remember the hopeful, delighted girl I'd been before that night. The dizzying belief that Kiran *would* make me his wife. Because I'd been the only one he'd asked to join his horde, after all.

"But if I could change it, I would," he told me. And I heard the truth in his voice. "I think about that night all the time. And if I could change it, I would have claimed you on that cliffside and stolen you away to my horde before you could change your mind about me."

All the breath whistled out from my lungs.

"You think I would've changed my mind?" I asked in disbelief. "When I had loved you for over twelve years?"

The corner of his mouth lifted as his heat pulsed into me. When he shifted closer, I felt the press of his cock against my belly, and I was astonished how *hot* he was. His cock felt like a sizzling brand against my flesh.

"Undoubtedly," he murmured gently. "You would've realized eventually that I wasn't good enough for you. That I didn't deserve you or your *vokking* beautiful smiles or the way you looked at me when we ran the coast together."

Everything crumbled around me. Every belief that I had had in the last nine years had all but disintegrated in the course of two nights.

I didn't know *what* to believe anymore.

"I can't change what happened between us that night," he said, his voice dropping low again. Gruff. "But I'm not that male anymore, Maeva. I'm not afraid anymore. I might not be worthy of your love, *seffi*—truthfully, I might not ever be—but I can promise that I am the best male for you in this entire universe. And I will prove it to you."

I had to remind myself to breathe.

I didn't know what he was asking. Or if he was even asking anything. I didn't know *what the* vok *was happening right now.*

"It's been a long time," I whispered. "I don't love you anymore, Kiran. Not the way I used to. I don't think I'm capable of it anymore."

If I expected my words to deter him, I should've known better. This was Kiran of Rath Okkili, after all.

His dark grin made my stomach flip and my skin tingle.

"That's a lie, *seffi*," he murmured. "You've just buried it so deep you've forgotten it. But I promised I'd make you remember, didn't I?"

"Is that why you came back?" I asked, the strange, sudden thought shifting something into place. Perfectly. "Is *this* why you came back? After all this time? Why now?"

It seemed ludicrous. Ridiculous.

A strange expression went over his face. He said, "Because for nine years, when I lay in my bed, I would think of you. The years passed and all I could think of was you, *seffi*. It has always been unfinished between us."

"So you came to finish it?" I asked, fear swimming through

my chest. Fear that Kiran *could* swing back into my life and make me love him again like he'd never left. If anyone could do it, he could.

"*Nik*, not to finish it," he rasped, tucking a strand of my hair behind my ear. "To *start* it."

Start what? came the hysterical thought.

His cock pressed harder against me when he murmured in my ear, "Give me the frost, Maeva."

The frost?

"Give me that time to convince you to stay. As mine," he growled, his lips brushing the sensitive shell of my ear, making me shiver.

Heat bloomed in my belly. Desires I'd long ignored came roaring back to life. The desire for touch, for sex, to know what it was like to be kissed and held and *wanted*. To know what it was like for a male to be deep inside me, to feel his heat and weight on top of me.

My mouth moved, though I didn't think it was connected to my brain. "You want me as your *alukkiri*?"

A lover for the frost. Someone to pass the frigid, long nights with. It was an unmated *Vorakkar's* right to take one every season.

A small, deep, rumbling chuckle rolled from him. The sound filled my ears. His hand drifted down from my jaw, went back to my buttocks where he *squeezed* hard, and another strangled small sound emerged from my throat as my nipples tightened so hard they almost *hurt*.

"*Nik*," he purred. "You will be my *Morakkari, rei seffi*."

He pulled back so my eyes met his. His golden gaze tracked over my face, taking in my stunned surprise with something that resembled *determination*.

My knees would've quivered had I been standing up. Because I knew that look on his face. I *knew* that determination.

"I'll be returning to the *saruk* after the frost," I said quickly. "I-I will be. Don't look at me like that."

Kiran grinned.

"You will be my *Morakkari*, Maeva," he vowed. "And I will convince you to accept me as your mate. *Any way possible.*"

I almost whimpered at that, my gaze flicking wildly between his eyes, panicked, uncertain.

"In the meantime," he rasped, his hand squeezing my backside again, making a small sound escape from my throat, "you'll warm my furs."

His knowing smile almost *undid* me.

"You'll know my touch, my kiss," he purred, "my cock."

Ragged breaths tore from me. My hands curled against his chest, my nails unconsciously digging into his warm flesh.

Because *for Kakkari's light*, I *wanted* him. At least, I wanted to experience him in *that* way. If only to *know* what it would be like. If only for the memory of it.

"And I'll know you," he continued, making me swallow. "Every part of you, *seffi*. The way it *always* should have been between us, had I not been such a coward."

"Kiran," I whispered.

"Tell me you'll have me, Maeva," he rasped, brushing his lips across my cheeks, my nose, leaving tingling sensations in his wake.

I wasn't prepared for this. He wasn't playing fair. He knew all my weakest places because he knew me so well.

"Tell me you'll have me for the frost, at the very least," he said when I didn't answer.

It was reckless. It was probably the most foolish decision I would ever make if I said yes.

And while I would never be his *Morakkari*—because I *would* be returning home, to my father, to my sister, and to my nephew who I wanted to see grow—*maybe* I could be his lover. For a little while.

He'd been the only male to stoke my desire so high. The only male I thought about when I pressed my fingers between my thighs on lonelier nights. The only male I had ever truly *craved*.

I hadn't been reckless or stupid in a long time. The last form of it had resulted in the long scar that ran down my shoulder. Then again...that was the last time I'd ever felt the thrill of adrenaline and the thrill of being *alive*.

After Kiran left, after *Lomma's* death, for so long, I'd been numb.

And maybe I *did* want to remember the girl I'd once been. The one who'd been *excited* about the possibilities of this life. Who'd laughed and sprinted along the cliffside during a rain storm. Who'd loved purely and completely. Who hadn't been afraid.

Because sometimes I missed her. I missed that girl.

"*Seffi*," he murmured.

Kiran was warm and strong against me. Waiting for my answer.

I'd make him wait a little longer, however.

"I'll think about it," I said, brow rising. "But it might take a little more than a night for you to convince me."

My challenge spread in his gaze. I saw it. And I realized that I knew *exactly* how to deal with Kiran. I knew what surprised him. I knew what made him angry. I knew what made him chuckle. I knew what intrigued him.

"You expect to be courted—as you should," he rasped. My breath whistled from my lungs, a little gasp that I couldn't hide, when his palm shifted again and he brushed my peaked nipple beneath my tunic. His eyes went *molten*.

We might've just started the most dangerous game of all between us.

"But don't worry, *rei seffi*. You will be."

CHAPTER 31

His hands were on me when I woke in his bed.

My eyes were half-lidded with drowsiness, but I noticed that my skin was tingling and an aching heat had built up between my thighs.

Those big hands moved, squeezing and stroking.

"Kiran," I whispered, realization piercing the dreaminess of the early morning.

"Mmm," came the rough, husky sound in my ear. He was behind me, his legs pressed against mine, his hard cock at my back—he *definitely* slept naked—and his head was tucked into my neck. His nose dragged against my skin, and his hand slid up to my breast, all possessive and proprietorial.

A ragged gasp tore from my throat.

"It drives me to madness," he growled in my ear.

"*N-Neffar?*" I whispered.

"Your scent," he voiced, deep and low. That voice spread through my body and lit it up from the inside. "Knowing you're in my bed. Waking beside you. So *vokking right, seffi.*"

My lips parted and a moan tumbled from them. A startled moan because his hand dipped beneath my tunic—and then that calloused, rough, delicious touch found my breast. Those fingers closed around my taut nipple, and I squirmed, my hips jerking, my back arching.

"*Vok*," he rasped. "So sensitive, *lysi*?"

I couldn't speak. Foreign sensations rained down on me. The heat of his hand on my flesh. The pleasure he elicited. The way his hips rolled against my back, grinding against me. The long, hard press of his massive, warm, strong body.

We'd done a lot of things with one another, but we'd never done *this*.

He'd never touched me like *this*.

He'd never spoken to me like *this*.

"You were moving against me while you slept," he growled, his thick, dark hair tickling my neck where it was entwined with my own. "I could smell how aroused you were. I could smell you all over me."

Hazily, I remembered fragments of a dream. Of Kiran. Of tingling heat, right on the verge of exploding—

"Do you want me to stop?" he rasped in my ear. There was an edge to his tone, one of strained amusement but mostly desperate need. "Or do you want more, *rei seffi*?"

More, my treacherous mind decided almost immediately.

When I finally found my tongue, my tone was breathless yet husky as I said, "Is this how you courted other females, *Vorakkar*?"

His dark chuckle filled my ears as he stroked my nipple. That magnificent laugh spread over my body, lifting little hairs in its wake like it was electric.

"I have never courted a female before, Maeva," he murmured. "It will only be you."

I didn't know why that filled me with such pleasure, why my heart did little flips at those words.

Then again, he is a Vorakkar. *He never needed to court a female. They needed to court* him, I thought.

"You want me to touch you?" he questioned.

Before, my words had held a bit of bravado in them, but all I really wanted to do was whimper and squirm against him, to try and get his hand where I *really* wanted it to be.

It was strange. Like I was outside my body. My blood was rushing, but there was still that thin veil of a dreamlike state. Like this wasn't really happening.

But Kiran was all hot flesh and musky, tantalizing heat against me. This *was* real. And maybe this was the start of what would come next for us.

Was I ready for it?

"*Lysi,*" I whispered.

I felt his rough exhale across the back of my neck. Then he was shifting, rising onto his elbow so he could look down at my face. When those eyes found mine, I wondered what he saw. I felt flushed and overheated. I was certain my hair was a wild mess from sleep.

"*Rinavi leika,*" he said, his voice gruff though the words were sweet.

Words that I wanted to immediately deny because I was unused to compliments about my appearance.

You are beautiful, he'd said.

And maybe it was the quiet reverence I heard in his voice—or the small part of me that would always trust him, trust that he wouldn't lie to me about something like this—but I actually believed him.

Kiran of Rath Okkili thought I was beautiful.

When I swallowed, my throat felt tight. *Nik,* this wasn't about love or our past or anything that had happened between us.

This was about sex and intimacy and touch—things I'd never experienced but *needed* to.

I needed to keep them separate in my mind if I ever had a chance of coming out of this *whole.*

"Touch me," I ordered him.

Those golden eyes sparked.

He leaned down, and I let out two little sighs as he pressed kisses to my neck. Then I gasped when he bit at the sensitive column of my throat, not hard enough to hurt but hard enough to leave a mark. My body felt like it was his when he laved at the mark with his dark tongue to soothe it.

Underneath the furs, I felt his tail move, felt it wrap around my thigh and hold it fast. Dakkari tails were strong, almost all muscle, though they were incredibly flexible. I wouldn't have been able to break his hold even if I wanted to.

He kept me on my side and used his tail to lift my leg—and a ragged moan tore from me when the very tip of his tail stroked the slick cleft between my thighs.

"Here, *seffi?*" he murmured, that voice like sin and silk. I felt a rush of wetness.

Wicked, wicked male, I thought in disbelief.

"*Nik?*" he rasped, his tone too rough to be teasing.

"*Lysi,*" I whispered. "*There.*"

Kiran's hands moved in an instant. Those strong, calloused fingers delved beneath the furs, running over my hip from behind before trailing down.

When his touch found my aching sex for the first time, I felt my whole body jolt with the sensation of it. Like a bolt of Drukkar's purple lightning had zapped through me, from head to toe. Kiran groaned, that delicious sound making my heartrate climb higher and higher.

His fingers stroked my wet slit until I parted for him. I heard slick, small sounds that would've embarrassed me had I not been so aroused, had I not been so utterly focused on his dizzying touch.

Kiran had pulled away from my neck to watch my face. When he found my clit, that hidden, sensitive bead, my hips rolled, my body tightening.

Already I felt on the verge of orgasming and he'd only just begun to touch me.

"There?" he asked.

My clit, he meant.

Lips parting, I realized that Kiran was trying to learn what I liked. Where to touch me. How hard, how soft.

Because he'd never been with a human female before.

"*Lysi,*" I answered him, feeling his cock grind into my backside harder.

Hot and hard and thick and long, I thought. I wanted to touch him too, but I didn't know what to do.

But he groaned, rolling those hips perfectly against me, as he continued to stroke my clit. And when he explored lower? When he wedged one of his fingers into my sex?

"*Vok,*" he cursed, his brow furrowing, those eyes registering disbelief. "You're so tight, *seffi.*"

I bit my lip, feeling his finger stretch me, which made his thumb put more pressure on my clit. My breaths came quicker, my hips rocking, trying to get him *deeper*, and I cried out when I felt my body begin to tighten.

"*Kiran,*" I cried out in a ragged, hoarse voice.

"*Lysi,*" he breathed as I tightened around him. "*Lysi,* come for me, Maeva. Let me feel you."

My orgasm was powerful and hit me *hard*, stealing my breath and making me freeze.

My back arched as I felt Kiran's other hand curl around my throat, keeping my head still so he could watch me, so he could see every expression that passed over my face. I felt my heartbeat thrumming against his palm like a drum. I kept his eyes with my own until the pleasure forced me to close them.

The waves felt punishing, rolling through my body violently. Kiran's touch prolonged them. And I never wanted them to end. I never wanted to leave this bed. I only ever wanted to stay here, in this pleasure.

But all too soon, it began to disappear and I grew too sensitive. I reached down to push his fingers away, my breath ragged.

When I met his eyes, I marveled at how *intense* he looked. To anyone else, he would've looked angry. But I knew that expression. I knew he was processing what had happened, I knew he wanted more, I knew he was trying to work out how he could get *more*.

As for me, I felt surprisingly relaxed, given that the Dakkari male I'd loved and loathed most of my life had just brought me to an *amazing* orgasm. I was—surprisingly—calm about it.

"Kiran," I said softly, my voice hoarse from my cries.

His name seemed to shake him from his thoughts. I still felt him hard and throbbing at my back, though his hips had stopped rolling and grinding. My torso was twisted toward him. His tail was still wrapped around my thigh. His hand was still curled around my throat.

When his head dipped, a jolt of panic went through me, erasing whatever calm I'd felt. Right when I felt his breath drift across my lips, I shifted my head, turning it away. His lips landed on my cheek instead.

Kiran made a rough sound in the back of his throat but kept his lips at my cheek, brushing a kiss over it. I didn't want him to kiss me. Not the way he'd been about to. Because I'd kissed him like that once. And the beginning of it had been wonderful. But the end of it had left me in pieces with a shattered heart.

If he kissed me again, it would blur the lines of what this was. I couldn't risk that.

When Kiran pulled away from my cheek, his eyes darted back and forth between mine, a slight frown on his features. But he didn't comment on what I'd just done. Or ask me why.

Though it couldn't yet be dawn, I heard footsteps approach the *voliki* from the outside, crunching over the earth as if a thin layer of ice was upon it. The mornings were getting colder.

"*Vorakkar*," came the voice.

"*Lysi?*" Kiran grunted.

A *darukkar* ducked his head inside the tent, but I didn't flinch. Kiran kept my eyes, as if testing to see if I would turn away, prevent myself from being seen in his bed. My body was covered, but the *darukkar* saw me, nonetheless. Saw Kiran hovering over me.

The *darukkar* inclined his head in respect.

"The *Vorakkar* of Rath Rowin is preparing to leave," the warrior announced. "Will you be seeing him off?"

"*Lysi,*" Kiran rasped. "I will be there."

My breath hitched when, all at once, his touch was gone from me. His hand uncurled from my throat, his other hand pulled away from where it'd been resting above my sex, his tail uncurled from my thigh.

My body felt cold when he left the bed. As he stood, I saw his cock and my eyes went wide. It was flushed a dark color and pulsing against his abdomen. So hard and rigid that it looked *painful*.

The *darukkar* was already gone when I looked back to the entrance. Hesitantly, I sat up in the bed, the lingerings of my own orgasm still pulsing gently through my sex. I watched as Kiran went to a basin of clean water perched on one of his taller chests. He leaned over it, splashing his face, leaning his arms across the basin as water dripped from his face.

I heard his deep breaths. Was he trying to...get control of himself?

He stayed there for a brief moment before he straightened and dried his face. Snagging a pair of trews from one of the chests, he dragged them on, though he had trouble tying the laces with his massive erection.

Kiran was watching me as he finished dressing. The tension in the *voliki* was strange. It was quiet but charged, though there was no strain to it.

It held the edges of a promise. Like Kiran intended to return and finish what we'd started. Whether that was the kiss I hadn't accepted or if he wanted me to finish *him*, I didn't know.

"I have a gift for you," came his words.

I blinked in confusion. A gift? That wasn't what I'd expected.

Though my curiosity was piqued.

I'd never been one who needed material things. I owned a small chest of clothes that were practical and durable. I had one brush for my hair, which I honestly felt sorry for more times than not. I had my mother's pendant, which was my most prized possession, and my healer's kit, which my father had given me when the *mokkira* had taken me on as his apprentice.

But I didn't need anything else. I didn't need much at all.

Kiran went over to the smaller chests tucked against the back wall of the *voliki*. The chests I'd always assumed were his *deviri*, his marriage gift for his chosen *Morakkari*.

From one of the chests, he pulled something golden and shimmering. Tucking a piece of my hair behind my ear, I watched him approach. It was hard to believe that just moments before, his fingers had been between my thighs and he'd been stroking me to orgasm.

Kiran sat on the edge of the bed, fully dressed, as I shivered a little in my thin tunic. He held something up before me.

My breath quickened. It was a simple necklace but beautiful and intricate in its design. The chain was slim and interwoven with various colors of Kakkari's gold. Small golden beads were threaded through the chain—

Nik, not beads. *Flowers.* Tiny gold flowers.

Seffi flowers, I realized, my heart speeding with the knowledge. Beautifully and expertly made. So small that they were impossible to see unless one was looking closely.

And hanging from the bottom of the golden chain was a small pendant. A clear circular locket made of glass with the edges bordered in shimmering gold. And inside the locket, I could see sand. Light gray sand. Sand I would know anywhere because it was sand from home. From the shores of the *saruk*, from the shores of *Drukkar's Sea*.

My eyes started to sting, and I looked back at Kiran in surprise.

"This is…" I said quietly. "This is from…"

"I had it made for you a long time ago," he admitted, his eyes flickering back to the swinging pendant in his grip. He unclasped it and leaned forward to settle it around my neck.

His scent was dizzying, and I felt the weight of the pendant settle slightly above my mother's necklace, the one I always wore. Kiran secured it, then leaned back, fixing his gaze on it before his eyes returned to mine.

"*Leika,*" he whispered.

I was still reeling.

"When…when did you have this made?" I asked.

He raked a hand through his hair.

"After I completed the Trials," he told me. "I had it made in *Dothik* before I returned to the *saruk.*"

A sharp exhale released from my lungs.

"I had hoped you would accept my offer," he admitted quietly. "To join my horde. And I knew how you would miss home, how you would miss the sea. I wanted you to have a piece of it after we left."

But then I'd stayed behind, I knew. I'd never joined his horde, never left with him.

My throat was tightening, and I didn't trust that my voice wouldn't shake if I opened my mouth.

"I know you miss home now," he finished.

"And you've kept it all this time?" I whispered, reaching up to touch the pendant though my eyes never left him.

In his deviri *chests,* I thought, but I wouldn't dwell on that now. I knew from the tiny gold *seffi* flowers that he'd had it made for me alone. He wouldn't have given it to anyone else. I knew that with certainty.

His expression grew shadowed. He reached forward to touch the necklace, his fingers lingering over my skin.

"I wanted to give it to you before I left," he admitted.

But my father wouldn't let you see me, I thought.

"And when I didn't see you, I took it with me because..."

He trailed off and a deep sigh burst from him. His jaw tightened, briefly.

"Because?" I whispered.

"Because I always knew that one day I would give it to you," he said quietly. "That I would see you again, *rei seffi*."

Fear bloomed deep in my chest, but it wasn't sharp or alarming. It was...calm. It was fear that I accepted as my reality because it made me remember how easy it had been to love Kiran.

And I felt the lingerings of that love. Right then. Whispers of it inside me. Traces of it, as if that love had been stamped into my bones, as if that love might never be gone.

Maybe he was right. Maybe I had never stopped loving him, and all I'd done instead was bury it so deep that I couldn't feel it anymore.

I hoped that wasn't true.

Because it meant that all Kiran had to do was dig inside me to uncover it, to bring it bursting to life again.

I imagined dirt and earth packed tight and hard inside me, choking me. And with his gift and the meaning and sentiment behind it, I felt some of that dirt loosen, soften. I imagined his strong hands delving into that soft earth, assured and determined, reaching inside me, reaching places I thought long gone.

That was the fear that came to me right then.

Clearing my throat, I looked down at the necklace. If I wore it among the horde, everyone would know it was a gift from him. It was much too exquisite, much too expensive for anyone else but a horde king to give.

And maybe I wasn't immune to material things. Especially if they were this beautiful. Because even with the risk that his horde would know about us, I didn't want to take it off. It was a piece of home.

"It's beautiful, Kiran," I finally told him, meeting his eyes again. "*Kakkira vor.*"

He nodded and his hand slid away from my neck. I watched him stand, watched him move to the fire basin and light it up for me. The fire flared to life, and already I felt the warmth from it creeping across the *voliki.*

"I'll send your *piki* in to attend to you," he said, his small, knowing smile catching me off guard.

"Kiran—" I sighed.

But he was gone, ducking beneath the entrance so I couldn't argue.

I sighed again, the quietness of the *voliki* reaching me. It seemed so much larger now that Kiran was gone. He'd filled it so completely that I acutely felt his absence...

Or maybe he'd just captured so much of my attention, held onto it like the sly, wicked, arrogant creature he was, that I hardly noticed anything else.

"I might be in trouble," I whispered, stroking the pendant, desperately wishing Laru was here.

I had been so certain I could do this, that I wasn't at risk of loving him again.

It had taken Kiran a single morning to make me doubt everything.

CHAPTER 32

"Oh, it's beautiful, *missiki*," Hinna breathed. Then she blinked at me guiltily and corrected, "*Mokkira*."

I sighed, suddenly feeling like I was fighting a losing battle, especially since Hinna was brushing through my wet hair. She'd tried to help me wash my hair in the bath—which was a traditional duty of a *piki*—but I'd firmly put a stop to her advances, and she'd sat, worrying her lip as if she was *failing*, as she watched me finish rinsing off.

I'd felt a little guilty, so when she picked up my brush with a hopeful expression—the brush which I'd found among the rest of my possessions that Kiran had taken from my *voliki*—I didn't protest.

When she'd first set foot into the *voliki* this morning, she'd looked so excited she could explode. She'd confessed she'd never been inside the *Vorakkar's voliki* and had peered around discreetly with wide eyes while I'd bathed.

And thankfully, she didn't ask why I was suddenly sleeping in the *Vorakkar's* bed because I wasn't even certain I could give her an answer.

Now she was admiring the necklace that Kiran had given me in the mirror. I was seated on a low stool, and Hinna was standing behind me. It felt nice to have someone brush my hair. My *lomma* had often brushed it at night before I went to bed.

A pang went through me, and I breathed through it. It always hurt to remember, to ache with the memory of her and to know that we would never make any more together.

Blinking back the tears that were rising, which were always close to the surface these past two days, I cleared my throat.

"Hinna, can I ask you something?"

"Of course, *Mokkira*," she said, frowning.

Swallowing, I asked something that had been on my mind since...well, since I'd arrived, truthfully.

"Has the *Vorakkar* been with a lot of females in the horde?"

Her hand paused in my hair for a brief moment before she resumed.

"It is hard to say for certain," Hinna finally answered, hesitation in her voice, which made my chest clench, a sharp sting of jealousy I thought I'd been over. "In fact, the *Vorakkar* has always been private about these things."

"Private about what things?" I asked, frowning, staring into the mirror at the pendant that hung from my neck. Little *seffi* flowers twinkled in the fire's light in the basin next to us.

"It is strange," Hinna went on, "because the *Vorakkar* has never shown interest in taking a *Morakkari*. Until now."

I swallowed.

"I mean," she stated quickly, "that...he has...he never—"

"It's all right, Hinna," I said softly.

She took a breath.

"So he never announced he would begin his search for a queen?" I asked.

"*Nik,*" Hinna said. "And whenever there were feasts, he never drank from the goblets that the females brought to him."

I looked down in my lap, saw that my fingers were fidgeting, and I pressed them against my thighs to still them. Thighs that Kiran had stroked just this morning.

My breath went a little shallow, and I tried not to think of *that*. A part of me still believed those erotic, wonderful moments had been some sort of weird dream, even though I knew they'd happened. I'd found the beginnings of Kiran's seed on the back of my tunic, where he'd ground into me, when I'd undressed for my bath.

A deep flush started at my neck, but I cleared my throat again, trying to focus.

Hinna continued, not seeming to realize the direction of my thoughts, "But there were some females. In the horde."

My jaw tightened.

"There was a female," I said quietly, "who was there when I arrived at the horde. She asked to speak with the *Vorakkar* in private. I got the sense they'd been together before."

"I remember. Her given name is Jinir," Hinna confided in me.

I met her eyes in the mirror.

"And was she one of the females?" I asked.

"So she claims," Hinna told me, and I felt that jealousy pierce me again. But of course Kiran would've had sex with other females. It had been nine years. There had never been promises made between us, and he was a *Vorakkar* in his prime. "It was a couple years ago. She told her companions, so naturally the entire horde knows. The *Vorakkar* was not...pleased about it. She has been trying to get back into his furs since. Unsuccessfully."

My lips pressed together. *Nik*, Kiran would not have been pleased that she'd gone around the horde bragging about their bed play. Kiran had always been private. As *Vorakkar*, I imagined he was even more so.

"And you said it has been some time since his last female?" I asked quietly.

Hinna's voice lowered. "None I can remember hearing of since before the last frost."

Over a year?

No wonder he'd looked frustrated this morning. I remembered his angry, flushed cock, which made me nibble on my lip.

"*Kakkira vor*, for telling me," I finally said, getting control of my rapid heartbeat.

I realized it didn't matter. Not truly. It was, perhaps, my own insecurity and nerves that made me ask in the first place. Because Kiran was experienced in these things—in mating and sex— and the truth was that I *wasn't*.

It was strange for a female my age, at least among the Dakkari, to be untried. A virgin. I'd almost had sex once. After Kiran had left and I'd still been so hurt and angry. I'd kissed a handful of males in the *saruk* after he'd gone—though thankfully not Ojinu—as if he'd know and it would make him jealous. *Foolish.*

And one male had gotten me out of my trews before I'd known it—but I had stopped him, suddenly panicked, suddenly so *vokking* sad and angry that Kiran had gone, that I'd burst into tears. The male had left me, and I never kissed another male again.

Now I looked back on that sad girl I'd been and all I wanted to do was hug her. Embrace her. Tell her that everything would be fine, that her purpose in life was different, greater than a single male.

It had been my mother who embraced me back then, however.

"You can ask me anything, *Mokkira*," Hinna said quietly, giving me a small smile in the mirror. Her gaze went to my necklace again. "What are the flowers called? I have never seen them."

I touched the chain.

"*Seffi*," I told her quietly. "They grow on *okkara* trees. In the ancient forests. In the warm season, they bloom across the branches and when the winds come, they float down like a waterfall of flowers. The ground gets covered in them."

"They sound lovely," Hinna breathed.

"They are," I said softly. "The trees only grow in the South Lands. Maybe you'll get to see them while you are here."

"Oh, I doubt that," Hinna said quietly.

"Why?" I asked.

"The *Vorakkar* said the South Lands have been unsafe," she said quietly. "We usually never build walls this strong. When we were in the West, we didn't build walls at all. He does not want us out in the wildlands."

He hadn't told them about the dark mist in the East?

I frowned.

"Do you know why?" she asked, her voice so soft that I almost didn't hear her.

I didn't want to lie to her. But I also knew that this was Kiran's horde. I couldn't interfere with his decisions, and he'd obviously kept the red mist a secret for a reason. Surely, he must have one. And surely, he would tell his horde soon.

"The South has been strange lately," I told her. "For now, maybe it's best to stay within the walls."

She wasn't entirely satisfied with my answer, but she nodded and continued to brush out my hair.

"*Lysi*, that is probably best," she said.

"*Nik*, try again," I ordered Essir. "Like this."

I showed him the correct stitching on a *lobbas* root again. The brown root had thick skin and was how I'd learned to suture most wounds with efficiency, a tip from my own *mokkira*. My poor family had eaten *lobbas* for weeks as I practiced, so we didn't waste the food.

It was a quiet afternoon, so I thought it was a perfect time to help teach Essir more suturing techniques. We'd already refilled our stock of *uudun*, I'd boiled *kuniri* and mashed it for preservation, and we had the last of my *hakin* blooms and *jenuria* root simmering on the fire. With the babies that would be coming during the frost—and the babies that would be *made* during the frost—I thought having extra stores of the potion for morning sickness would be a good idea.

Since it was a cool afternoon, we had the window coverings lifted, letting in more light and a nice, refreshing breeze. As Essir practiced on the next *lobbas* root, which I'd asked Hinna to procure from the *bikkus*, I looked out the windows.

I saw a flash of red hair, vibrant in the sunlight. Gabe. Walking next to him was Addie, and they were chatting animatedly, Addie waving her hands and smiling up at him. I'd last seen them at the feast, but it looked like Addie's belly had grown even rounder in that short time.

Then I heard a Dakkari male call out. Addie turned, her smile wide, and she laughed when her mate suddenly appeared from around another *voliki*, tugging her into his arms.

Addie stared up at him, all adoration. Behind her, Gabe lingered, a strange expression on his face though his gaze was turned away.

Something about his expression stuck in my chest, made my throat tighten with understanding. Something I'd caught hints of before.

Before I knew it, I told Essir, "I'll be right back. Continue practicing, *lysi*?"

"*Lysi, Mokkira*," came my apprentice's reply, and I ducked from the *voliki* just in time to wave at Addie as she passed with her mate, his arm around her. They were heading in the direction of the *bikku* tent, but Gabe wasn't following.

It felt strange to call out his given name, but I knew that he would not take offense.

"Gabe!"

He'd been turning in the opposite direction, but when he heard his name, he smiled wide.

"Good afternoon," he greeted, walking toward me. "I thought I'd never see you again," he teased.

He meant after the way I'd left the feast.

"I apologize for that," I told him, inspecting his face carefully. His eyes were rapt on me, his smile charming. "Too much brew, I suspect."

His smile died slightly. "You sure it wasn't the *Vorakkar* cutting in? The way he looked at me almost made *me* sick."

I frowned. Had Kiran been scaring Gabe away that night? Had he approached us when we were dancing to send a deliberate message to the human male?

Sighing, I said, "Regardless, I shouldn't have disappeared like that. I'm sorry. I've been meaning to come find you, but..."

"The duties of a *mokkira* are important," he assured me, placing his hand on my arm. His palm was warm. Nice. But I didn't get all shivery and my heart didn't speed when Gabe touched me. "I understand."

I didn't want to lead Gabe on...because I knew how unfair it was. How frustrating it was. But I at least thought it fair to give him an explanation.

"Gabe," I said, clearing my throat, "I...I know that you have an interest in me. And—"

"Is it that obvious?" he teased, his smile widening, though his cheeks flushed a little.

I bit my lip, and my uncertainty must've shown on my face because I saw a muscle in his jaw jump. I saw his smile falter a little.

He blew out a breath. "I see."

I didn't know how to do this. I'd never *had* to do this, but I wanted to be direct and honest.

"Is it the *Vorakkar*?" he asked quietly.

I sighed, not knowing how to explain but wanting to. A

Dakkari female passed, carrying a bucket of water, and I moved closer to Gabe so we wouldn't be overheard.

Gabe took my silence for my answer. His smile was bright, but I could see his discomfort, his embarrassment.

"Human men cannot compete with Dakkari males," he finally said softly. "I think I've known that for a while."

My brow furrowed. "That's not it at all."

"I saw the way he looked at you," he confessed. "That was why I backed off at the feast. Because if a human cannot compete with a Dakkari, you better believe that *no one* can compete with a horde king."

"Come with me," I said, frustrated when another horde member passed.

He sighed, and I led him to a more private place in the encampment, winding my way through the *volikis* until we reached the edges of the *pyroki* enclosure. Not many ventured here during the day, probably due to the stink. But I didn't mind it.

The nests for the frost were built for the *pyroki*, I saw. Only the *mrikro* was around, and he was inside the pen, mucking it out.

I leaned against the fence, pressing my belly into it as I draped my arms across. The breeze felt nice, and it kept most of the smell away since it blew north.

"Gabe," I said quietly, "the *Vorakkar* and I have known each other since we were children."

He nodded hesitantly. "Yes, you said you grew up in his father's...village?"

"A *saruk*," I corrected. "But *lysi*, very similar to a village, I suppose."

"Were you...together?" he asked quietly.

I sighed again and turned to look at him.

"*Nik*, never," I told him. My shoulders went back a little as I said, "But I did love him. For a very long time."

His brow furrowed. His gaze strayed past me to the enclosure, his jaw tight, pondering something.

"We were friends. Very close friends," I continued. "And when he became a *Vorakkar*...well, I didn't see him for close to ten years. Not until recently."

Gabe swallowed.

"He didn't love you back?" he asked.

My lips pressed, and I said slowly, carefully, "I know what it feels like to love someone who does not feel the same way. How much it hurts."

His shoulders stiffened, but he turned to face me, studying my expression with wariness.

I reached out to touch his forearm, squeezing. He didn't have to tell me if he didn't want to, but I liked Gabe. And I hoped that we could become friends during my time here.

His shoulders sagged all at once, and he slumped against the fence.

"Is it that obvious?" he asked, repeating words he'd said earlier, but this time, his tone was miserable, not teasing.

"I'm sorry. I know how painful it can be," I said quietly. "How long have you loved her?"

A sharp exhale, bitter and short, escaped him.

"We met under the Dead Mountain" was what he said.

I swallowed. I'd known about the Ghertun taking slaves. I couldn't imagine what that must've been like, to live in that dark place, walls all around, suffocating.

"Addie was from another village. She'd been there longer than me," he whispered. "I had only been a slave for a...month before we got saved."

"How long was she there?" I asked, throat tight. I'd heard stories of what the Ghertun did to their slaves.

"Almost a year," he told me. "She was so different than she is now. She was quiet, withdrawn. I did what I could whenever I saw her, to try to make her smile. But those were few and far between. Then we came here, and it was here that she began to heal. Her mate helped her with that. Her mate brought her back to life, it seemed. And how selfish am I that I wish it had been *me*?"

"Oh, Gabe," I whispered, squeezing his arm again, my chest aching.

He shook his head. "We don't talk about it. None of us do. We all just want to forget. And maybe that's why Addie could never love me. Because I remind her of that place."

"But you're her friend," I argued. "And she seems so happy when you're around."

"That took time," he said. "But yes, we are friends. And that's all I can ever hope for. That's all we'll ever be to one another. Especially now."

Out of the corner of my eye, I saw a *pyroki* approach, heard a chuffing sound emerge from its throat.

Roon stuck his snout right next to my face, and I couldn't stop a small smile.

"*Rei kassiri*," I whispered softly, stroking Roon's nose.

"What does that mean?" Gabe asked, looking at the *pyroki* with wariness.

"My love," I translated.

"Isn't that the *Vorakkar's pyroki*?" Gabe asked, seeing the golden marking that decorated the beast's black scales, wide strokes and swirls of glimmering paint.

"*Lysi*," I told him.

"Does it have a name?"

"*Lysi*," I said, giving him a small smile, "but I cannot tell you it. The *Vorakkar* would be displeased if I did. I don't even think the *mrikro* knows it."

"You do," Gabe pointed out, raising a brow, seemingly relieved that we were done talking about Addie.

I pressed a kiss to Roon's long snout, and I saw the *mrikro* looking over at me, his eyes basically popping out of his skull in disbelief, a mucking shovel in his grip.

"That's because I named him," I informed Gabe.

When the *mrikro* approached, Roon stomped his long legs, flicking his tail. The creature let out a ferocious snarl when the *mrikro* reached out to take him away from the fence, a snarl that had both the *pyroki* master and Gabe backing away.

"*Nik*," I murmured, grabbing Roon's neck. "Don't do that, *kassiri*. Go with the *mrikro*."

Roon stomped his feet.

"I'll come visit you later, I promise. Maybe I can convince your master to take you out on the wildlands, *lysi*?" I cooed softly to the irritated beast, pushing his snout toward the *pyroki* master.

As if Roon knew what I was saying, the fickle beast seemed pleased with the words and finally allowed the *mrikro* to lead him away, back to where he was being fed.

When I turned back to Gabe, who had jumped back from the fence, my gaze focused behind him and I saw Kiran standing there, his wide arms crossed over his chest.

All at once, my heart tripled its beats. Kiran's gaze burned into mine, even from that far a distance. His *pujerak* was with him and a *darukkar* I didn't recognize, who was speaking to them both. Though Kiran's attention was only on me.

Swallowing hard, I let my gaze drift over him. All thick thighs encased in tight hide. A broad chest that seemed to stretch endlessly. Strong cords of muscle that ran down his arms. His black hair was loose, that tail was flicking ever so slightly behind him, and those full lips were curving into a small smirk. A maddening smirk when he saw me studying him.

Arrogant male, I thought, breaking his gaze. Feeling heated and flustered as I recalled the way his fingers had moved between my thighs this morning and the gruff, ragged sounds that had torn from his throat as he ground his cock into me.

Kakkari help me, I pleaded.

I turned back to Gabe, who was still frowning into the *pyroki* enclosure.

"Shall we head back?" I suggested, wanting to get away from Kiran's knowing gaze. "You want to help me grind *pova* roots? I could use your strength. Don't tell my apprentice this but he's not as strong as he looks," I joked.

Gabe chuckled, rubbing the back of his neck.

Blowing out a breath, he smiled and said, "Why not?"

CHAPTER 33

"A storm is blowing in," Errok said, striding into the council's *voliki* later that night. "Or so the scouts you sent out report. A storm that might bring the frost."

"They returned just now?" I asked, looking down at the message from the *thesper* that finally returned from Rath Kitala's horde.

"*Lysi,*" Errok replied. "When will you leave for the Dead Lands?"

If the frost was moving in, I didn't want to get caught up in a storm traveling to Rath Kitala's horde. Then again, I still had a week before I had to meet with the others.

"How far off is it?"

"The storm?" Errok questioned. "Three or four days' ride, though it might blow in sooner, depending on its speed."

I grunted, rereading the message scrawled in Rath Kitala's hand.

"What does it say?" Errok asked, coming to stand on the opposite side of the table, spreading his hands down on top of it.

"Nothing of importance," I said, handing the letter to him, blowing out a sigh of frustration. "The fog is stable. It hasn't moved. Rath Kitala has *darukkars* posted at the Dead Lands that send him daily reports."

Errok made a sound in the back of his throat as he scanned the message quickly.

"He says the land is quiet," I murmured softly. "Very quiet. Eerie, even."

Errok met my gaze from across the table.

"Do you want to send a *thesper* back? To confirm the meeting with all the *Vorakkar*?"

"The *thesper* is exhausted," I told him, thinking of the poor winged beast that had nearly dropped from the sky on its return. The *mrikro* was charged with overseeing our *thespers'* care. "She's getting much needed rest."

"The *thesper* is that tired from that short distance?" Errok asked, incredulous.

Which was another troubling thing.

Grimly, I nodded.

"Is she sick?"

"She doesn't appear to be, but I told the *mrikro* to watch her carefully. She's eating and drinking, at least. And she was in perfect health before we sent her to the East Lands."

"You think this mist is responsible?" Errok asked, narrowing his gaze. "Do you think that is why creatures are leaving those lands? Because it's making them sick?"

"I don't know," I said, the frustration evident in my voice.

"And what of the horde?" Errok asked. "When are you planning to tell them about the mist?"

"Soon," I said, nostrils flaring. "But I might wait until I return from the East. When I have more news."

Errok didn't like that decision. "They have a right to know what's happening, Kiran."

"I know," I growled. "But do you truly want me to tell them right before I leave? You want to handle the chaos after that? What can we say? That there is a strange red fog that blankets the land and that Dakkari-bred beasts are becoming more hostile and dangerous? They will want to know *why,* and until I meet with the others, until I see this place for myself, what more can I give them?"

Errok's jaw was tight.

"As *Vorakkar*, Errok," I growled, "you must weigh the choices carefully and decide on what will lead to the best outcome. Telling them now will induce panic and questions because we know *nothing*. Those with family and loved ones in the East will fear for them. Many may want to leave for *Dothik* right as the frost comes, which will only make that journey more dangerous. Meaning I will have to spare more *darukkars* to see them safely there. *Darukkars* we might *need*. Panic and fear are the last things we want right now. They might have a right to know, Errok, but right now it is my responsibility to keep my horde safe, and that is what I am doing."

"I understand," Errok rasped, though I felt the tension thrumming tightly between us.

There was still something unspoken between us. Last night, after Rath Rowin arrived, I hadn't been able to find Errok. And this was the first time all day that we'd been alone together.

"You intend to try your hand at the next Trials, do you not?" I asked. "Now that the *Dothikkar* is holding another so soon after the last?"

Errok's jaw tightened.

Silence stretched between us.

"I have not decided" was what he finally said. I heard the truth in his voice, the hesitation.

My fists clenched on the table. We were in an abnormal situation, one that had happened a few times in Dakkar's history but not often. Errok had not been eligible for the Trials when I first offered him the position of *pujerak*...but according to our laws, he would be now.

He'd been rejected the first time because of his lineage—or

rather, his lack of lineage. But since he'd been a *pujerak* for these long years, he'd be accepted readily and without question.

It wasn't often that a *pujerak* broke away from his horde to try for one of his own. Then again, Errok had the soul of a *Vorakkar*, not a *pujerak*. At times, I knew how it grated to heed my orders, especially when they challenged his own wishes.

But this was my horde. Not Errok's. And as such, he always had to obey me.

For someone such as Errok...it wasn't easy. Being my *pujerak* had not been easy on him—I knew that. But he'd stayed for me. He'd stayed for our friendship. He'd stayed for his position.

Now that there was another path opening to him, however, one I knew he'd always craved...it would change everything between us.

"As your *Vorakkar*," I started quietly, "I would do anything to sway you from this decision. It will disrupt the horde at such a precarious time, a horde that has come to depend on you, as I have."

Errok's brow pulled. His lips pressed.

"I know," he said.

Taking a deep breath, I carefully measured out my next words.

"But as your friend, Errok," I continued, "I will tell you to go."

Errok straightened across the table, looking at me in barely concealed surprise.

"*Neffar?*" he rasped.

"We always knew," I said. "We both knew when I asked you to be my *pujerak* that you were meant to lead, not to follow. And now...the *Dothikkar* will accept you at the Trials. And if you do not go, you will regret it for the rest of your life."

Errok already knew this. If he'd had no loyalty to me, if he'd had no loyalty to the horde, he would've already left for *Dothik*, though the Trials would not take place until after the frost.

"What about the horde?" he asked quietly. "With what is happening in the East...you are right, Kiran. I cannot leave now."

"Leave after the frost," I growled at him, making his shoulders go back. "Or I will banish you from the horde myself."

A short huff left his nostrils as he stared at me across the table. I swallowed a curse and instead shook my head, giving him a half smile.

"Don't worry about the horde, my friend," I told him. "The horde is my responsibility. You will learn that soon enough because I have no doubt in my mind that you will emerge from the Trials triumphant. I will find another *pujerak*. But you will never get this opportunity again. So *take it*."

At my words, it seemed like a weight had been lifted from him. It had been heavy, no doubt. Torn between his duty and his future.

Errok inclined his head once. It was the answer I needed.

I looked down at the table, at the map of Dakkar. I would be sorry to see him gone. He'd been my friend and advisor since before the horde began.

"That's settled, then," I said gruffly, straightening.

Then I turned, intending to return to my *voliki*, where I hoped Maeva would be.

"Kiran."

I looked over my shoulder, brow raised.

"*Kakkira vor*," he said quietly. "You've always been a good friend to me. I will never forget that."

I inclined my head to him. He wouldn't leave for another few months, but I already knew it would come too soon.

"Get some rest, *pujerak*," I rasped. "We have much to do tomorrow."

"You too, *Vorakkar*," he returned. "Don't let your *kalles* keep you up all night, *lysi*?"

I barked out a laugh.

It might be the other way around, I thought, striding from the *voliki* and walking to the back of the quiet encampment. Anticipation rose in my chest, anticipation that had been building since the moment I'd left her early this morning.

I wouldn't be able to keep my hands off her. Not when she'd stoked the wild beast that lay within me, the beast that wanted to do wicked, wicked things to her, things I'd fantasized about for *years*.

When I reached the *voliki*, I stepped within, eagerly seeking her out.

When I saw her, I froze, a growl escaping my throat as my cock seemed to harden with lightning quickness. All the blood in my body seemed to rush down to my cock, leaving me dizzy as I straightened.

But *vok*, she was beautiful. And waiting for me.

Warm light drenched her as she sat on the edge of the bed, facing the entrance. She was alone, her *piki* already dismissed for the night. And she seemed to be *anticipating* my own arrival, looking at the flap of the domed *voliki* with expectation, her foot tapping on the rug beneath her bare toes.

When I met her gaze, I realized that we both knew what we wanted. Maeva knew what she wanted from me, dressed in a thin, short nightdress that made my cock pulse in my trews. And I definitely knew what I wanted...though I wanted much, much more than she was willing to give.

Yet, I added. She would give me everything. I would demand nothing less. I'd show her that she craved it, that she still wanted me, that she still *vokking* loved me. She would be my *Morakkari*. She just didn't know it yet.

And in return, I'd give her everything that I had inside me, laid out at her feet like I was making an offering to an altar of Kakkari.

My *seffi* deserved nothing less than to have her *Vorakkar* on his knees in front of her.

Vok, I'd beg if I had to.

Maeva was perched on the edge of the bed, her legs crossed. Her hair was in coiled ringlets down her back, tamed yet still wild. Beautiful. My pendant was still around her neck, along with her mother's. And that dress...

I spied her nipples straining beneath it, free of her usual bandeau. The material was thin, so thin. If she stood in front of the fire, it would be near translucent. And I wanted to *vokking* rip it off her, my fists squeezing at my sides as I threw off the furs draped around my shoulders.

Those hazel eyes looked like mirrors as she stared at me across the *voliki*. Mirrors that traveled down my body as I uncovered it for her.

Her breathing went shallow when my hands went to the laces of my trews. She shifted forward, uncrossing her long legs. I nearly groaned at the curiosity I saw in her gaze, curiosity I intended to assuage tonight.

"Lie back on the furs, *seffi*, and take off that dress if you do not want it destroyed," I growled. "We aren't waiting anymore, *lysi*?"

CHAPTER 34

"I'd rather not take the dress off," I murmured, hoping my voice sounded calm and strong. The opposite of what I truly felt.

I was surprised my hand didn't tremble as he stalked toward me. Slowly. Like a predator circling its prey. His hands went to his chest, tearing at the strap that held his sword at his back.

Followed shortly by his boots...his tunic...

Then his hands returned to the laces of his trews, half of them undone.

"Take it off," he rasped. "Are you going to make me beg, *seffi?*"

"Would you?" I couldn't help but ask.

"Undoubtedly," he growled, those eyes shimmering wickedly, though his expression was so drawn and intense that he looked angry.

Ignoring the way my heart was attempting to pound its way from my chest, I watched as he tore through the hide laces of his trews and peeled them efficiently down his legs. When he straightened, completely and utterly naked, my breath left me.

Golden, warm flesh that looked like velvet in the fire's light.

All hardened muscle, dipping and rising, casting shadows across his skin. Glinting scars winking as he approached.

And his *kakkiva*. His *cock*. It was thick and pulsing. That angry, flushed head was slick with the beginnings of his seed, dripping down the length. His *deva* were drawn tight underneath him, and though I couldn't see his *dakke*—the sensitive bump above the root of his cock—I knew it would be hard and aching too.

Magnificent male, I thought, barely concealing a whimper.

Kiran came to stand in front of me, towering over me. His knees brushed my thighs, and the bed was at the right height so his cock was right in front of me. Up close, I saw the golden tattoos swirling across the flesh. Most Dakkari males who intended to take a mate had them. A promise to their mate.

Quicker than I could blink, Kiran's hand reached down and he tore the dress clean from my body.

"*Kiran!*" I gasped, too shocked to realize that I now sat naked in front of him, watching as the scraps of the dress that Hinna had brought to me were now in tatters next to the bed.

"I warned you," he rumbled in reply, his voice so dark and guttural it was almost unrecognizable.

Then he pushed me back on the furs, and *that* was when I realized the position I found myself in.

In a *Vorakkar's* bed. At his mercy. Naked and exposed to him. The flesh between my thighs was slick and aching and tingling. I might've been uncertain about this before, but my body knew what it wanted…and it wanted Kiran. It always had.

"*Vok,*" Kiran rasped, staring down at me. Looking like the dangerous, dark king he was, his face slightly shadowed, as his gaze trailed over my body. My first instinct was to cover myself —an old habit—but when I moved my hands, he snapped, "*Nik.*"

That word made me freeze, made my hands drift hesitantly down to my sides.

That was when I realized I *liked* the way he was looking at me. It made me shiver. I swore I could feel the heat of his gaze as it traveled over my body, running over my breasts, my waist, my hips, my sex, my legs.

Kiran looked at me like he *owned* me. Like I was his to do with whatever he pleased.

"You want me on my knees before you, *seffi?*"

There was something happening here. Something I wasn't sure I understood, but his words felt like a challenge. Like a struggle for power, power that he was *giving* to me. He wanted to see if I would take it.

My chest was heaving as I looked up at him.

"*Lysi.*"

Kiran didn't keep me waiting. He lowered himself down to the floor of the *voliki,* and when his hands came to my thighs, parting them, they felt like a brand over my skin. Searing and hot.

A small exhale escaped me when he pulled me right to the edge. Anticipation rose in my belly. Laru had told me about this. How a male could pleasure a female like this. I'd always been curious about what it felt like.

"You are never allowed to wear anything to our bed again, *seffi,*" he rasped, so close that I felt his breath across my sex. "Not a scrap of cloth. *Lysi?*"

Our bed? I thought.

Then Kiran lowered his head and all thoughts flew from my mind like a gust of wind had just blown through it.

Oh goddess.

A harsh growl ripped from his throat, and I felt the vibration of it across my sensitive flesh. Then came his tongue, long and hot, and I felt his claws prick my inner thighs, as if he'd forgotten how hard he was gripping me, as if he'd forgotten himself.

But that little prick of pain didn't bother me. Especially

when sharp *zings* of pleasure pulsed through my blood. When the most wonderful sensation made the back of my neck tingle.

A moan tumbled from my throat, and Kiran gripped me harder at the sound. His tongue licked and laved the slick slit between my thighs, dipping into my sex, seemingly ravenous for my taste.

And when that tongue lapped its way upward? When his tongue lashed at my clit, that sensitive little bead he'd discovered earlier this morning?

My eyes flashed down to him in disbelief, my back arching off the furs, hips rolling. Golden eyes looked back me. Kiran's brows were pulled down—as if *he* couldn't believe the pleasure of this—and those pupils flickered all over me, watching me, reading me.

All at once, that little ball of fear returned to me.

This is too intimate, I thought, and it felt like a scream in my mind. *Too much.*

I couldn't let him do this again. Couldn't let him inside again. But I wanted this. I wanted to experience this pleasure.

As a compromise, I closed my eyes and tilted my head back, breaking his gaze. In that darkness, all I could feel was his tongue and his kiss. All I could feel was the pleasure he was expertly wringing from me, making my hips roll into his mouth, making him grip me harder to keep me in place.

I focused on the pleasure he was bringing *me.* Not on Kiran himself. Not on the gruff sounds he was making between my thighs or the way his tantalizing scent drifted through my hair, my nostrils, my skin.

"I need this every night. I need a taste of your cunt every night," he growled, making me moan. "I swear on Kakkari, I won't be right without it, *seffi.*"

Please stop talking, I pleaded with him silently, feeling my control begin to slip, the illusion I'd spun beginning to fade.

I could be selfish, couldn't I? I *needed* this to be about me. Not him.

He groaned when I gasped. Because he lightly suckled on my clit and I swore that lightning struck my body when he did. My eyes flew open, and I stared up at the ceiling of the *voliki* in disbelief, as the beginnings of a strong orgasm began to rise. Through the venting hole at the top, I could see the stars glimmering. It was a clear night, beautiful and calm.

When my orgasm hit me, I cried out, screwing my eyes tightly shut. Blood was rushing so loudly in my ears that I could only hear my own furious heartbeat. My hips rocked and rolled, feeling that tongue never leave me, feeling it lap at the essence that was leaking down my thighs. That tongue...all over me.

Kakkari help me, I pleaded, the thought clear and loud.

Because I didn't think I would be able to survive *this*. Whatever *this* was.

Finally, it was over and I sensed Kiran moving. Rising. When I widened my half-lidded gaze, I saw him crawling up the bed, dragging me up with him so our legs weren't hanging off the side.

He lowered his head again, but I turned mine away, feeling his lips land on my jaw. A rough sound tore from his throat, but he wasn't dissuaded. He kissed a line down my throat, over where he'd bitten my neck this morning, and he added another mark there. A little collection, just for him.

I swore I felt my nipples tingle as he did, felt the pulsing of my previous orgasm continue.

His cock was thick and heavy against my naked belly. When he pushed his hips down, his cock seared a line from my sex all the way up past my belly button.

"I'm already wanting to lick your cunt again," he growled, trailing his lips down toward my breasts. "*Vok*, I want your scent all over me. I'd *bathe* in it if I could."

I swallowed, the wicked words making me squirm underneath him.

"*Oh*," I breathed when his tongue flicked against one of my nipples, then he did the other. "*Lysi.*"

A small, ragged sound burst from his throat, and his lips closed over my breast. My mind swirled when he sucked *hard*, the tingling between my thighs returning tenfold. Like he was sucking there again.

When I was wet there and my nipple was straining and hard, he turned to the other, giving it similar treatment. But he rolled the first between his fingers, plucking and gently thrumming his claws over the peaked, sensitive tip.

"But I can be patient, *rei seffi*," he continued after releasing my breast with a loud *pop*. Then, as my chest heaved, I felt those eyes on me, peering up at me. "Because I know you'll feel my tongue between your thighs again before the night is done."

I whimpered, the little sound surprising but not entirely unexpected.

Wicked, wicked male.

That small smirk almost made me want to close my eyes again.

"For now, I want you," he rasped, rising from me, going to his knees between my slightly splayed thighs, peering down at my swollen, flushed breasts. His handiwork. "And I intend to have you, Maeva."

There was a heaviness in my mind as I watched him. A comfortable heaviness, strangely enough. Like I knew that what would happen next was inevitable. That it might have always been inevitable. That it had just needed time to come to fruition but it was *always* meant to happen.

Swallowing, I wondered if he felt it too as he widened my thighs, as his tail curled around him. It brushed my foot before wrapping around my ankle, tightening around it like a vice. Tethering me to him.

I'd always wondered if I'd had a tail, would mine unconsciously hold on to him, seeking him out in any way it could? The Dakkari always said that the tail was the mind—the thoughts and feelings of it—they couldn't hide. Because it acted on instinct, on want. Not on reason or logic.

A ragged gasp tore from my throat when Kiran let his cock slide over my slit, letting the heat and heaviness of it rest there. Letting me feel it. Letting me feel what it would mean to take him inside me, letting that cock fill every spare inch of me.

He squeezed the very root of his cock, the calloused knuckles of his hand lightening with his hard grip.

"I swear I could come just looking at you, *seffi*," he growled.

I'd purposefully avoided his eyes, but when I looked into them right then, I had the sensation of falling. Like jumping off the cliffs of the coast. Belly flipping, excitement and nerves and trepidation coiling tightly together until I couldn't distinguish one from the other.

Then Kiran was moving again.

Moving into me.

Suddenly, I was frightened. This was a line. A line that had always been between us. A line we couldn't *uncross*.

"Kiran," I whispered, my eyes wide.

But he was certain now.

When he hadn't been before.

I saw it in his eyes as they gleamed down at me in the warm, flickering light.

The fire sparked as he pressed his length inside me. Deeper and deeper.

Slow but determined. Slow enough and patient enough to not hurt me, though I felt the energy inside him coiling tighter and tighter.

Though he was slow, he was unyielding. I gasped, which was followed by his groan, and he rolled his hips deep. I stretched around his solid heat, tight.

Too tight.

"*Vok,*" he cursed, feeling me clamp down around him. He fell forward, bringing the fronts of our bodies together. His head hovered over mine. His lips touched my ear when he pleaded, "*Relax for me, seffi. Let me in.*"

He continued to roll those hips, making little circles that pinched but felt *good.*

When I caught my breath, I tried to do as he asked, letting my muscles release. Letting him in.

"*Ahh,*" he grunted, followed by a long slide of his cock inside me that made my whole body tingle. "*Lysi,* that's it, *seffi.* Perfect. *Rei leika seffi.*"

His beautiful *seffi?*

I bit my lip, the words blooming inside me before I could stop them.

Nik, nik, I thought, desperate to stop that warmth from spreading, tightening around him again.

He groaned and seemed unable to stop the quick punch of his hips into me. Sinking deeper still.

"Look at me, Maeva," he growled. His tone was so *Kiran*—dominant and authoritative—that I couldn't *not* heed his order.

And though it was what I feared, my eyes locked onto his—when he was seated so deep inside me that I felt his heartbeat throb in his cock, felt it throb *against* me—and then I couldn't look away.

It was then that he thrust fully inside me, as pleasure and pain mingled, the mixture strangely *sublime.* Goose bumps exploded across my arms as he stilled, as we were joined so completely together.

We were sharing the same breath, and he wouldn't let me look away.

"Maeva," he murmured, his voice hoarse and deep.

"*Don't,*" I pleaded, my voice barely above a whisper.

Frightened of him. Needing him. Needing *more.*

His brow drew together.

"*Hanniva.*"

Please.

Whatever he heard in my voice made his jaw tighten. His expression changed.

Darkening. Hardening.

And I was relieved to see it. I wouldn't have survived if he had looked at me with awe, with reverence and affection a moment longer.

With a gasp, I felt him pull out of me. My flesh felt cold without him heating me.

"You don't want this to mean anything, Maeva?" he asked, his tone hard.

I swallowed, looking at him as he lifted away, going to his knees again between my thighs.

"*Nik.* It *can't,*" I whispered. "You know that."

A dark, almost mocking smirk crossed his face…but I *swore* I caught a flash of hurt before he covered it. Which didn't make me feel good. Even after all this time, I cared that I hurt him. I didn't want to.

A startled sound emerged from me when his hands came to my waist and he flipped me on the furs. Then he pulled me up, maneuvering me onto my hands and knees with his large, wide palms. He wasn't gentle. A part of me needed that roughness. Another part felt like I'd lost something.

But this position meant I couldn't look at him. I was facing the shadowed part of the *voliki*, behind the bed, and I stared into that darkness when I felt his cock brush my slick folds.

Then a deep groan fell from me, making my arms tremble where they were supporting my upper body, as he thrust inside me. Deep and hard. The force of it shook my breasts below me, made my whole body jolt forward…though Kiran had a strong grip on my hips and he forced me back.

Seated deep inside me, I felt him cover my back, leaning

over me until his lips brushed my ear. Briefly, he nipped at the shell of one—he'd always *known* my ears were sensitive, had often teased me for it—and a shiver racked me *hard*.

This position made him feel deeper. Even though I couldn't see him, this position somehow felt even more intimate than before.

"I'll make a liar out of you, *seffi*," he vowed, his voice rough. "Because it will always *mean something*."

I bit my lip, my throat tightening, even as my clit throbbed and all I wanted was for him to move inside me.

"This is *us*, Maeva," he growled, thrusting into me *hard* as if to highlight his words, as if he'd read my mind. A ragged cry filled the *voliki*. My own. "It always *has* meant something. And you cannot escape that, no matter how hard you try. *Trust me—* I know."

His voice was all around me. His scent coated my skin. His cock felt like a brand inside me.

Maybe he's right. Maybe I can't escape this, I thought, lips parting as I stared down at the furs, as I saw his black hair tangle with strands of my own as his thrusts started to shake the bed.

Sounds of mating, of sex soon filled the *voliki,* so words weren't necessary anymore. Kiran hissed, gripping my hips tighter and harder. He leaned away from me, straightening, so that he could use the leverage of his grip.

And then he was fucking me hard and fast, stealing my breath from my throat, his claws digging into my flesh, though I didn't mind it. I savored it. I needed it to anchor me.

Sounds I'd never heard before were pulled from my throat. Mewing, desperate sounds, which seemed to make him even more *ravenous*.

When my arms could no longer support me under the onslaught of his strength, he pulled me up until my back was plastered against his chest. His arm wound low around my hips, holding me in place, and his other hand came to my throat. His touch was possessive and claiming, and he wanted me to know it.

"You want to see?" he rasped against the side of my neck, where he pressed a kiss.

My brows pulled down, and I was hardly capable of words at that point. But I still managed to ask, "S-See what?"

He held me tight against his body as he shifted us on the bed, stirring his cock inside me all the while, turning us toward the eastern wall of the *voliki*, close to where the fire was burning in the basin.

"You and me, *seffi*," he growled, punching his hips into me, making him slide against new places inside me I thought he'd already found. "And why this is right where we are *meant* to be."

That was when I saw it.

He'd faced us toward the only mirror in the *voliki*. The mirror that I'd sat in front of just that morning as Hinna had brushed out my hair. Though it was faded around the edges, the fire illuminated us well enough.

And I saw us. Me, wrapped in his arms, naked and flushed, my eyes half-lidded from pleasure. And *him*, so big and strong behind me. His arms were like tree trunks holding me close, his *Vorakkar* cuffs hot against my skin.

For that brief moment, I saw myself how Kiran did. He'd told me I was beautiful, and right then, I felt like it.

I whimpered, feeling him pick up speed between my thighs as his hand moved, running down my body with a proprietorial touch, like he owned me.

In the mirror, I saw him thumb my nipples—back and forth —and I felt the zapping of that sharp pleasure.

"Tell me you're mine," he murmured in my ear. "Tell me you're mine, *seffi*."

My eyes met his in the mirror.

"You know I won't," I panted, my voice hoarse and husky. A stranger's voice.

His hand dropped down my belly. And I cried out, my body jerking in his hold, when his fingers pressed into my clit, rolling.

And I was just about to orgasm, just about to lose control, when he stopped.

"*Nik!*" I cried out, frustrated, squirming against him.

"You want to come, Maeva?" he growled in my ear.

"*Lysi!*"

"Then tell me you're mine," he taunted, though I heard an edge to his voice. He was losing control too.

"*Nik,*" I whispered.

His chuckle was deep and rough. Wonderful.

"*Nik?* Then tell me you're mine for the frost," he amended, rolling his hips. "You never gave me my answer."

My breath was robbed from my lungs when he slowly and lazily began to pet my clit again.

"Isn't this answer enough?" I hissed out.

I saw his smile in the mirror—hard-edged but all Kiran.

"*Nik,* I want to hear you say it."

My sex rippled around him, but it was he who groaned, a sharp exhale tearing from his throat. His forehead dropped against my neck, his own breaths coming hard.

"*Lysi,*" he rasped.

His thrusts deepened, and I huffed. His hips slapped against my backside, the sound almost violent.

"Tell me!" he commanded.

"For the frost," I choked out, catching his eyes in the mirror before I felt that hand come to my throat again. He turned my head so I was forced to meet his gaze. Right there. So close. Looking deep into those beautiful golden pools, I whispered, "I'm yours."

Something sparked in his gaze. Breath seemed to fill him, making him straighten.

I gasped. In disbelief, I began to come around him, my belly clenching tight and hard. And as I began to orgasm on him, he never let me look away. I came around him as he held my eyes.

He growled when he felt me. His expression pulled tight, and those golden pools turned to molten fire.

A roar bellowed from his throat, and I cried out, feeling his hot seed burst from his tip inside me. So *vokking* powerful it felt like a thrust from his cock.

The pleasure was intense and incredible.

I'd never felt anything like it before.

It went on and on, drawn out by Kiran's wild and relentless thrusts as he found his own pleasure between my thighs.

And when it was done, I might've collapsed forward. I couldn't remember. Time seemed to leave me briefly, and when I surfaced again, we were lying next to each other on our sides. Kiran's arm was curled under my head, those eyes trailing over my face, his other hand brushing long strokes down my body.

I still felt him inside me. Still hard. Hot and thick.

"I'm not done with you, *seffi*" he murmured, his voice hoarse from his bellowing cry. "I will never be."

I gasped when I felt him begin to move again.

"K-Kiran," I whispered, shocked. Perhaps even more so when I felt my body respond in kind, especially when I felt his seed coat my thighs.

His grin was dark and a little feral.

"You're mine now," he growled.

CHAPTER 35

"I-I can't, Kiran," Maeva whispered, her eyes wide, though her flushed lips were parted. "*Hanniva.*"

I growled, stilling inside her.

"I need rest," she continued, breath huffing out of her, perspiration dotting her brow.

A rough sound made its way from my chest and out my throat.

"*Lysi,*" I murmured, reaching forward to stroke her cheek. "Of course, *seffi*. I forgot myself."

She was human. Unused to the lusts and attentions of a Dakkari male. She would be soon, I knew...but I felt how tight she was around me now. How tight she'd been when I'd first entered her. The last thing I wanted was to hurt her. And if I continued, I just might.

I caught her slight intake of air when I gently pulled from her body, and when I looked between her legs, a deep scowl etched its way onto my features.

"You're bleeding," I rasped. My eyes flashed up to hers. "I *hurt* you."

My heart seemed to triple in speed. I wasn't sorry about what we'd done—I could *never* feel regret for what had just happened between us—but I should've been more gentle! I should've taken more care.

Maeva frowned, peering down between her legs before she seemed to relax, lying back among the furs.

"I'll heal, Kiran," she told me simply.

"Were you…" I trailed off, not entirely sure if I had the right to know or the right to ask. "Were you untried?"

A deep silence settled between us as I waited for her to give me an answer or to tell me to *vok* off.

"*Lysi.*"

Did it make me a callous bastard that her answer relieved me?

Because if she'd said *nik*, hot jealousy would've reared its head though I had never been a jealous male before. I would've tortured myself endlessly by wondering which males from the *saruk* had known her, if she still thought of them…if she had loved them.

Because there wasn't a doubt in my mind that any male that knew her would love *her*.

With a tight chest, I pushed from the bed, standing. There was a fresh bath in the corner, though the water had cooled. I went to the fire, ignoring my aching, slick cock, and used the metal scoop to lift glowing rocks from the basin. I brought them over to the washing tub, dropping them inside, hearing them sizzle as they met the water.

Soon, steam rose from the surface, and I returned to the bed.

Maeva was propped up on her elbow, watching me. She seemed embarrassed for a brief moment when I caught her eyes on my backside before her chin lifted.

Maddening female, I thought, feeling something pull in my chest. Something I was all too familiar with because I'd felt it over half of my life.

"Come," I murmured, leaning down to scoop her from the furs. "The bath will help the pain."

"I'm not in pain," she protested softly, though I knew she was lying for my sake. "And I can walk, you know."

"Mmm. And I can carry you, you know," I replied easily.

She bit her lip. There was a strange energy rolling off her, one I couldn't read.

When I stepped into the washing tub and lowered us both inside, she swallowed but didn't say anything. She hadn't expected me to bathe with her, however—that much was clear.

My lips twitched, and I positioned her across my lap, shifting my legs. The bath was made for a Dakkari, so the water came up to her collarbones, whereas it only came up to the middle of my chest.

A small sigh escaped her, her eyelids fluttering shut for a brief moment. The hot water was relaxing, and I sank back against the head of the washing tub.

"I am sorry, *seffi*," I said softly, watching her. "I did not mean to hurt you."

The moment I said the words, I knew they could be taken in a variety of ways. For our past. Our present.

Maeva seemed to realize this too. She was quiet, her eyes flickering back and forth between mine, one of the few beings who dared to meet the gaze of a *Vorakkar*.

"I know, Kiran."

I couldn't keep my hands off her. My palms stroked her arms, running up to her shoulders, brushing over my bite mark on her neck, which that filled me with supreme masculine satisfaction whenever I spied it.

When I reached around her to stroke her back, another small sigh escaped her. Her head lolled forward. She seemed to at least enjoy my touch, though prior, she'd always been very hesitant to touch *me*.

When my fingers brushed the long scar over the back of her shoulder, I traced it, feeling the raised, hardened flesh.

"Are you ever going to tell me how you got this?" I murmured.

She wouldn't before. I'd first seen it on the journey from the *saruk* to my horde. And seeing it had...*disturbed me.* Because it was then that I realized I didn't know everything about her anymore. That she kept things hidden and secret from me when she had always been so open before. That something had hurt her and I hadn't been there to help her, to ease her pain, to protect her.

"You'll be angry if I tell you," she said. Though her words made me frown, made my fingers still over the scar, my mind reeling with possibilities, her lips quirked at the corners.

That wasn't what I'd expected her to say.

"It was foolish," she finally said, her smile dying, looking down into the bath water, her toe poking at one of the stones from the fire basin, though it wasn't glowing red-hot anymore.

I scowled, a rough sound emerging from my throat, as realization punched me right in the gut.

What else would *I* be angry about?

"You got it from the cliffs, didn't you?" I growled.

She didn't seem surprised that I'd guessed it. She watched me process it, her head tilted slightly.

"*Vok*, Maeva," I rasped, my fists clenching across her back, trying to keep my temper in check. "You *promised* me you'd never do it again."

And Maeva had never broken a promise in her life.

So why this one?

Why break her promise to me when I'd asked it of her only to keep her safe? Because she'd almost hit that rock diving off the cliff the first time. And I'd nearly lost my mind with worry when I saw her leap. To this day, I still remember that dread—

dread so potent I wanted to vomit when I realized I couldn't keep her safe.

"Like I said, it was foolish," she said quietly. "And I wanted to make you hurt."

I paused, my nostrils flaring.

"I wanted to hurt you," she admitted quietly. "Even though you'd probably never find out. But I thought that if I did it, maybe you'd come back. And you being angry with me was better than you not coming back at all."

Her words were soft but achingly vulnerable. Sad.

They made the air in my lungs freeze, made an invisible blade plunge into my chest, over and over again.

"*Seffi*," I whispered, anguished.

A tired laugh huffed from her throat, and she shook her head, leaning against me. And though I was angry and raw from her confession, I still wrapped my arm around her and held her tight.

"And then when that didn't work, I stopped doing all the things that reminded me of you. I stopped running in the mornings. I stopped going to our place on the cliffside. And though I was untried, I attempted to forget our kiss by kissing any male I could in the *saruk*."

My jaw tightened, as did my arms around her.

"And there was a male I liked kissing, who made me smile again," she whispered. "Kikoni. Do you remember him?"

In my mind, I saw the flash of a male I might always be jealous of now, even as I felt...gratitude toward him. Because he had made my *seffi* smile again, something I hadn't been able to do. And she'd always deserved to smile.

"But when we did more than kiss," she continued, "I couldn't..."

She cleared her throat, leaning away from me a bit, though I wanted her to stay right there.

"I couldn't go through with it. Because all I could remember was *you*," she said, her eyes glassy even as her lips quirked in a hopeless, sad smile. One I never wanted to see again. "And that must've scared Kikoni because he never looked at me again."

It was hard for her to tell me these things—these vulnerable parts she'd kept hidden—and it was hard for me to hear them. But I wanted to hear them. I needed to.

"But it wasn't you it was hurting," she said, meeting my eyes, wiping at her cheek as she brought her knees to her chest across my lap. She pressed her cheek into one knee and kept my eyes. "Because, of course, you knew none of this. You were far away, Kiran, somewhere on the plains or in the mountains or wherever you were. All I knew was that you were away from me. Away from *home*."

Which were one and the same, I knew as I stared at her, as I watched the tears drop from her eyes into the bath.

Because I loved this female and I had for most of my life. I'd never felt *right* in the wildlands. Early on, it had made me doubt that this had been my destiny. That I had made the right choice to become *Vorakkar*.

It took me years and years to realize that I had never been *right* because I'd been away from *her*.

Because I'd needed her. Leaving her had been like losing a limb. It was an ache I had felt always, an emptiness that could never be filled, no matter what I'd tried to fill it with.

I'd found my mate, my *kassikari*, my queen, my wife when I was thirteen years old, barely old enough to understand what love was.

But it had happened. And it had taken years and years to understand what that meant. For my life. For hers.

I'd wasted so much time.

"It wasn't you it was hurting," she continued. "It was me. And it was my family."

"Your *lomma*," I said quietly.

"*Lysi*," she whispered, sniffing, raising her head off her

knees. "She understood, I think, this need in me to be angry and to be hurt. She let me be both, at least for a while. But then she brought me back and probably saved me from some very foolish decisions. She told me I was meant for better things. She helped me relearn my purpose, my calling. To heal instead of wound. To help instead of destroy. To learn instead of be angry. And I wanted to do *those* things instead of all the others. And so that's what I did."

I swallowed, reaching under the water to catch her hand. She seemed surprised by my touch, by that small affection. But she didn't pull away. She stroked her thumb across the back of my hand instead, gently.

In all my life, she'd been the only one to ever hold my hand.

"Your *lomma* was always a wise, wonderful female, *seffi*," I rasped, my chest aching, knowing how much the loss of her must've *cut* Maeva, Laru, and their father.

And I hadn't been there, I knew. *She believed I'd turned my back on her.*

"The world is darker without her in it," I murmured.

She nodded, looking at me.

"I wish...I wish I would've been there. For you. For her. For your family. For the *saruk*," I said softly.

"*Lysi,* I know, Kiran," she said softly, squeezing my hand. She didn't hesitate, and that relieved me. "I know that now. Which was why it always filled me with so much confusion, so much *hurt* before. Because it never made sense to me. Because I *knew you.*"

That was a difficult conversation I intended to have with my own *lomma* in person. About why she'd chosen to deceive Maeva in such a callous way. Maeva, no doubt, had her own questions for my *lomma*.

"Why do you think she did it?" she whispered, looking to me for the answers.

With my other hand, I reached out to stroke the side of her

face, brushing my thumb across her nose, her lips, her cheek, feeling how *vokking* soft she was. I would need to dull my claws from now on so that I didn't cut her.

"That year," I started gruffly. "That year when your *lomma* passed...it was the most difficult time for my horde. I made a mistake, claiming land too close to another horde, and as such, they had the rights to most of the game. It was near the frost, so we couldn't leave. But we also couldn't store rations for the cold season. And my horde suffered for it. All because of me. Because of my judgment. On top of that, the other horde king led an attack on my *darukkars*, killing two who were hunting too close to his territory in the process. Sometimes...sometimes I still hear their wives' cries in my sleep."

All because of me. And the *Vorakkar* of Rath Dulia...that bastard. My fists clenched around Maeva's palm, but she stroked it, soothing the tension.

"I'm sorry, Kiran," she said quietly, her brow furrowed, lips pulled down into a frown. "I didn't know."

"But my *lomma* did," I finally murmured, raising my gaze.

Maeva nodded, understanding what I was saying.

"Even still, Maeva," I said, swallowing, "I would've come."

Even at the risk of losing my horde.

The knowledge of that was frightening. Realizing that *that* was the power of our relationship.

"Knowing that now," she said, "I would have never asked in the first place."

Blowing out a breath, I dropped my forehead onto hers, and she let me. My eyes flickered down to her lips. She wouldn't let me kiss her. Every time I'd tried, she'd turned away from me.

But this was comfortable and I would take anything I could get from her. However much she wanted to give me. Being with her this way...it was easy. It made me remember how easy it had been. How *right* it had been. She'd been vulnerable and open and giving tonight. Honest. It was all I could ever ask from her.

"I want there to be peace between us again, Kiran," she whispered. "I'm tired. So tired of fighting."

My chest felt tight as I said, "I want that too."

But I knew she meant in friendship only.

She wasn't ready to give her heart to me again, no matter how much I desired it. But this time...I would cherish her love. I would treat it right. I would let it grow wild, without feeling the need to cull it back. I would return it in its entirety because I finally felt like I was *worthy* of it.

She might've been tired, but I knew my *seffi* would continue to fight against me if I demanded that love again.

She didn't think she was capable of that love anymore?

I could love her more than enough for the both of us.

And I intended to.

CHAPTER 36

Hinna's giggle filled the *voliki*, and I saw Essir glare over at Gabe for the fifth time that afternoon, over the pile of stitched-up *lobbas* root mounded up on the table in front of him.

I sighed, giving the *bikku* a tonic I'd just finished bottling—brown in color but the perfect consistency. The older female had come into the *voliki* a few moments prior, complaining of a headache from all the meat smoking they'd been doing in preparation for the frost.

"I'll make a large batch of this today, *lysi?*" I told the *bikku*, handing her the small vial. "Any others that begin to have headaches too, send them my way because I will have plenty. You can drink half of this if the pain becomes too much, but no more."

The *bikku* nodded, peering at me with an intense curiosity. I bit back a knowing smile, turning to gather my supplies for that particular pain tonic, as I heard the female nonchalantly ask, "During the warmer months, I also get terrible aches from the humidity. Will you have more of this then?"

In the corner, Gabe whispered something to Hinna,

charming her easily with his impression of a horde member I didn't yet know. Essir scowled.

That morning as I strode out of Kiran's empty *voliki*, I'd felt the stares. Heard the whispers. The rumors had already begun, as I'd known they would.

A horde was just like a *saruk*. Everyone was in everyone else's business. It couldn't be helped. I'd accepted this, knowing it would happen.

"I do not believe I will be here then," I replied to the *bikku*, trying to answer her unspoken question. When I turned back to her, her eyes dropped to my throat, where Kiran's gifts lay—both his bite and his necklace. "But my apprentice will master all the potions and tonics for the horde, so there is no need to worry. Isn't that right, *ruhna*?"

Essir's brows furrowed and he gave me a hesitant smile. I sighed. His expression didn't exactly inspire confidence, and the *bikku* huffed.

"So you will be returning to your *saruk* after the frost?"

A prick of annoyance bit at me, but I kept my smile light and my voice even. "*Lysi*, I intend to."

"Hmmm."

The *bikku* seemed to realize she'd get nothing else out of me, and I wondered if she'd had a headache at all.

"*Kakkira vor, Mokkira*," she said, beginning to step toward the *voliki's* entrance just as I saw the flap push inward, and a familiar figure straightened on the threshold.

I ignored the way my belly flipped with a jolt of excitement or nerves. I wasn't quite sure which it was, but the *bikku* couldn't contain her surprised gasp.

"*Vorakkar*," she greeted, immediately dipping her head in respect as Kiran strode inside my *voliki*.

In the corner, Hinna rose and Essir had a *lobbas* root frozen in his palm. Gabe grew silent, though I felt his eyes on me, watchful after what I'd revealed to him yesterday.

"*Bikku,*" Kiran greeted, his eyes running over the inhabitants of the *voliki* before his gaze settled on me. Those eyes turned molten, trailing over my body, before his voice came out rougher and he ordered, "*Rothi kiv.*"

Leave us.

Immediately, the *bikku* squeaked and skirted around the *Vorakkar*. I could only imagine what she'd report back to the others. Hinna, Essir, and Gabe left as well, though the human male lingered in the entrance briefly, catching my eyes, before he finally turned away.

Kiran noticed. When we were alone, he approached where I stood with my backside to one of my work benches. He made my *voliki* seem three times smaller, taking up space that only he could take up.

"*Mokkira,*" he greeted, inclining his head, a small smirk perched on the edges of those lips.

I quirked my brow, but my voice sounded a little breathless when I returned, "*Vorakkar.* To what do I owe this visit? Are you ill?"

I gasped when he pressed me back into the bench, stepping into my space. My hands gripped the edges of it tight, as sudden heat bloomed between my thighs, dizzying and quick.

This morning, I'd woken to an empty bed, though the fire had been lit. Hinna had woken me, coming into the *voliki* like a *piki* would. I'd been disappointed to wake alone, especially after last night.

Because last night had been...

Intense. New. The sex had been indescribable, though I'd had to apply some *uudun* salve between my thighs this morning since I'd been a little sore.

And after the sex...in the bathing tub...

That had felt familiar.

It had felt...nice. Wonderfully nice. Comforting. It was the first time I'd felt comfortable with Kiran in a long time, even with what we'd spoken about.

It had been easy to fall back into the way we used to be with one another—honest and open and without fear—if only for those brief moments. And it did feel different between us yesterday. Like something had been lifted.

Kiran leaned down now, and he pressed a kiss just below my ear.

My knees actually trembled, embarrassingly enough. Didn't he realize it would be easier on me if he wasn't being so *sweet*?

"Not ill," he finally answered. "I was passing and simply missed my *alukkiri*."

His lover.

A small sigh escaped me when his hands came to my hips. And I felt him hard when his hide trews pressed into my apron. He'd been hard since last night. I'd felt him against me as we drifted off to sleep and when I'd woken briefly in the middle of the night.

His nostrils flared, and he picked me up and sat me on the work bench, moving between my thighs, bringing us to eye level.

"Kiran," I whispered, wide eyed, my gaze flickering to the entrance flap. Thankfully, I'd kept the windows sealed today since a cold wind had blown in through the night. "We shouldn't—"

I stifled my moan when his hand drifted to the seam of my trews, sliding underneath my apron. He stroked—up and down, up and down—with just enough pressure to tease me.

"I had to leave early this morning and didn't want to wake you," he murmured, "but I wanted to make sure you were not hurting today."

Some of the compacted, hardened old dirt filling the space around my heart shifted and loosened.

He'd wanted to check on me?

"I'm fine," I assured him.

"You are certain?" he grunted.

"*Lysi*," I whispered, biting my lip when he pressed his fingers a little harder. "I-I applied some *uudun* this morning. I don't feel sore anymore."

"Good," he murmured, pulling back. His eyes flicked down to my lips, and they seemed to glow when I licked them nervously. "You'll be able to take me again tonight?"

I swallowed hard.

"*Lysi*," I whispered, anticipation coiling, remembering the feel of him inside me, the delicious fullness and heat and *pleasure*. I wanted to feel it again. Soon.

Kiran leaned forward slowly, but I turned my head after a slight hesitation. He paused, stiffening for a brief moment, then dragged his tongue up toward my ear. I shivered when he suckled on the sensitive lobe and let out a small, breathy moan when his teeth grazed it.

I was panting and flushed by the time he stepped away. I barely kept my hands from reaching for him. It was on the tip of my tongue to tell him I wanted to take him *now*…but that was madness. Hinna, Gabe, and Essir were just outside. Passing horde members would hear. I didn't need to give them any more reason to gossip about my relationship with their *Vorakkar*.

And him fucking me in the *mokkira's voliki*—my *voliki*— would certainly give them a lot to gossip about.

With a trembling hand, I pushed my hair back, trying to get control of my suddenly racing pulse. My body felt hot and shaky. Cheeks flushed, eyes glassy.

And he'd only touched me for a mere moment.

Kiran watched me. The only indication of his own arousal was the obvious—*quite* obvious—outline of his massive cock in his trews. But his expression was careful and observant. I wondered if he was upset that I'd rejected his kiss again, but a moment later, he said, "I'll be heading out on patrol with some *darukkars,* but I will be back tonight. And I will be looking forward to you naked in my bed, *lysi?*"

Arrogant, magnificent male, I thought, sliding off my work bench onto shaking legs.

"I suppose it depends how late you'll be," I said, quirking a brow. "I plan to go running in the morning, and I do need my rest."

Kiran huffed out an amused breath. If he'd been hurt I didn't take his kiss, only warmth shone in his gaze now.

"Then I'll endeavor to return to you as quickly as possible, *seffi,*" he murmured, reaching out to stroke my cheek, tilting my face up toward him. "Because I know how prickly you get without your sleep."

I couldn't help my laugh, which only made his eyes shine brighter.

He's doing it again, came the sudden thought. *He's making me remember how easy it is to—*

I cut off my thoughts quickly, my laugh dying. I cleared my throat.

"Your run may have to wait, however," he told me.

"Why?" I asked, playing with a loose thread on my dirtied apron.

"A storm is coming," he informed me. "The wind is bringing it closer."

"You think it brings the frost?" I asked.

"It may," he said. "That is why we are heading out into the wildlands. To track it and ensure there are no beasts close to the horde."

The frost would be coming earlier than expected, then. No more running. Soon the days would be too frigid.

His hand lifted to my cheek, so I met his eyes.

"Any news from the *darukkar* you sent to Rath Tuviri's horde?" I asked next.

Kiran shook his head. "*Nik,* but I expect his return soon. Do not worry, *Mokkira.*"

I nodded. Just...with the frost coming, travel would become more difficult. On foot and for the *thespers.*

"I must go," he finally said, seeming loath to do so. His hand left my face, and cold air rose to take its place.

"Kiran," I murmured when he turned from me.

At the entrance of my *voliki,* he turned his head and raised a brow. Looking at him hurt sometimes. Because he was so handsome. So...*everything.*

"Be careful," I said quietly. "I'll be really angry if you encounter another *ungira* and I have to stitch you up again."

His chuckle filled the *voliki.* "I wouldn't dream of tempting your wrath, *seffi.*"

After he disappeared, I stood rooted in place before pressing a hand over my heart.

It was beating fast. Thunderous.

Waking.

For him.

Again.

Chapter 37

Maeva's back was arched off the furs, a silent cry on her lips.

I growled, pushing my tongue deeper, only to be rewarded with a flood of her juices, sweet and tantalizing. *Vok*, I'd needed this all day. I'd pushed my *darukkars* hard on patrol so I could return to her more quickly, so I could be between these thighs and lick every part of her body.

I wouldn't be satisfied until I did.

She was panting and squirming on the furs, her sudden orgasm riding her hard. I kept her hips clamped down, however, so she couldn't wiggle away from my tongue, laving against her, lapping at everything she gave me.

When she grew sensitive, she pleaded, "*K-Kiran, hanniva.*"

Licking my lips, I decided she'd had enough, and my cock felt like it'd tripled in size with need. It bobbed against my abdomen as I crawled up her soft body, all lush curves and smooth skin. I marveled at how soft she was, how I couldn't keep my hands off her.

How did we go so long without this? I wondered—and not for the first time.

This need was biting and intense. It had nothing to do

with the fact that I hadn't taken a female for close to a year. Nothing to do with my self-imposed celibacy. This was Maeva and me, and it was *always* going to be like this between us.

I wrapped her relaxed legs around my hips, tugging her down the bed, which elicited a gasp from her. I couldn't wait any longer, I knew, perspiration dotting my brow, a constant low growl rising from my throat as my tail flicked rapidly behind me, restless.

If I worried my touch was too rough, Maeva's desperate moans when I pushed inside her helped assuage that fear.

"*Lysi,*" she whispered, biting her lip, her wild curls spread beneath her. My chain was around her throat, just above her mother's pendant. The small vial of sand from the *saruk* had slid into the notch between her collarbones. Her breasts shook as I pounded deep, and I felt her legs tighten around me, anchoring me to her.

Groaning, huffing, I felt her tight sheath ripple around me, hot and dizzying. *So* vokking *tight,* I thought in disbelief. She would undo me before I was ready.

My hands came down on both sides of her head, bringing our chests together. I felt her hardened nipples dragging against me, and my mouth watered for them.

Maeva looked up at me, and I spied what I saw last night. Trepidation. Dawning fear. It was mingled with her desire, with her eagerness and excitement. My *seffi* had never explored this with anyone. Mating. What she needed, what she *wanted* in the furs.

And even though a part of her feared me—and I knew why she was frightened—she *wanted me.* She wanted my cock deep inside her. She wanted my tongue between her thighs and my kiss on her breasts. She liked when I bit her neck and whispered wicked things in her ear as I fucked her. She liked when she made me lose my mind with pleasure, when I bellowed it toward the ceiling of my *voliki*, when she felt the hot flood of it against her.

Perfection, I thought, looking down at her, running my gaze over her face before settling on her lips.

Well, almost perfection, I amended, thoughts darkening as my spine tingled, as I rolled my hips and alternated my thrusts. Some shallow, some deep.

Her little, dull claws dug into my shoulders, but I hardly felt them over the scar tissue there.

Kissing to the Dakkari was a valued intimacy—almost more intimate than sex in some ways. Maeva would know that. She'd been raised Dakkari, after all.

I made a rough sound. I wasn't hurt often. Not many *could* hurt me because there were very few I let close. But Maeva…

Maeva could destroy me if she wanted to. That was how deeply I felt for her.

And her refusal to kiss me was another barrier that she'd placed between us. Another barrier I would break because I was determined to ensure that nothing came between us.

Not now. Not ever.

"*Seffi,*" I rasped.

I felt her warm gasp drift across my lips when I slid *deep*. Our flesh slapped together, filling the *voliki* with the sounds of our mating, as the fire sparked in the corner. I felt her legs tightening, felt her breaths come quick, felt her sex tightening and squeezing around my cock, making me groan.

Seed began to rise in my cock, hot and thick. My *dakke* thrummed and pulsed, that hardened bump above the root of my cock aligning perfectly with her clit, pressing against it every time I stroked inside her.

"*Seffi,*" I growled, one of my hands going to her exposed throat as I fucked her faster, harder. A purely Dakkari instinct, a possessive touch meant for one's mate.

She couldn't move her head, and I felt her swallow hard

against my palm. Felt the rapid fluttering of her little heartbeat, and I felt mine rise to match it.

Her cunt began to clench around my cock. Her breath left her in a rush and her whole body tensed beneath me.

"*Vok*, how beautiful you are when you come on my cock, *seffi*," I purred to her, though my voice was rough. A gasp came, and another wave shuddered through her, rippling around me, squeezing me as I gritted my teeth. "You want my seed, *kassiri*? You want to feel me flood you with it?"

Her eyes went wide though they were dazed with pleasure. Perhaps because I'd called her *kassiri*. Love. *Rei kassiri*.

My palm tightened slightly on her throat, and I lowered my head.

"*Bnuru tei lilji rini*," I murmured. *Give me your lips*. "Give them to me, *seffi*."

"*Kiran*," she whispered, still coming around my cock.

I pounded my hips harder, making her grunt and squirm through her orgasm...but I kept her in place, pinning her down like any Dakkari male would, at her throat and at her cunt.

White hot pleasure flashed and spasmed through me. Groaning helplessly, I felt my *deva* draw up tight beneath me, and then I felt my seed begin to shoot from the head of my cock.

My roar seemed to shake the entire *voliki*. Everything was a haze as my vision blurred. As my strength *unleashed*. My hand tightened at her throat, and I lowered my head, determined to have her kiss.

She'd given it to me once, and I'd thrown it away callously. I wouldn't make that same mistake again.

Her sudden intake of breath met the rushing of blood in my ears.

"Kir—"

Then my lips met hers, cutting off her words.

Maeva froze, her body stiffening, as I kissed her deep. As I emptied my seed inside her and found my pleasure between her thighs, where I never wanted to leave.

And when it was over, I brushed my lips against hers, breathing her in, and licked at her tongue. Her taste was sublime, her lips soft and giving.

Then she was breaking my grip on her neck, tearing my palm away, turning her face.

My lips met her cheek, and I growled against her, feeling the last pulses of my orgasm jerk my body.

Then she was pushing at my chest, breathing hard. When I frowned, pulling away to look down at her underneath me, I found she wouldn't meet my gaze.

"Why did you do that?" she asked. "You know...you *know* I..."

She trailed off, her jaw pulsing in...*anger*.

Maeva pushed at my chest again, harder than I anticipated, and I rolled off her, sliding from her body.

"*Seffi*," I growled, watching as she squirmed off the bed, as she snatched up a cloth she'd used to dry off with after washing. She used it to wipe at my seed between her legs.

"How could you do that, Kiran?"

Her voice was shaking, though I couldn't tell if it was from anger or because she was on the verge of tears—both possibilities tearing at my chest.

I hadn't expected this reaction. My brow furrowed, and I stood from the bed, rounding it to approach her.

"*Nik*," she snapped, still not quite meeting my eyes. "I—I need you to not...*vok*."

She was flustered. Overwhelmed. And I didn't understand why. Unless she thought kissing me was offensive, *wounding*.

I felt my temper prick though I kept the simmer of it low.

"So I am allowed to fuck you, *seffi*, but I am not allowed to have your kiss?" I rasped, watching as she hurriedly tugged on a dress from her chest, which I'd had brought in from her own *voliki* before I'd had it dismantled.

As if she couldn't stand to be bared to me.

"That's...that's not what this is about," she argued, finally lifting her eyes to meet mine. Her cheeks were still flushed from our bed play, which made this confrontation all the more... hurtful.

"That's right," I murmured softly, crossing my arms over my chest, leaning against the stabilizing pole in the middle of my *voliki*. "You don't want this to mean anything. You don't want *us* to mean anything."

Just last night, there were moments during our mating where I knew she was trying to *detach* from me. Like she wanted to take her pleasure, *feel* the pleasure that I was stoking inside her, but she didn't want it to be with *me*.

She'd closed her eyes last night, like she'd been trying to ignore it was me that was fucking her. For the first time, I wondered if she wished it had been someone else.

"If you just wanted sex, you could have fucked any male you wished to, Maeva," I growled loudly, ignoring the jealousy that the words brought, hot and tight in my chest. "Yet you're in *my* furs. No one else's."

"Like you would've let any male in your horde touch me, Kiran," she hissed.

I stepped toward her, towering over her height.

"That's *vokking* right," I snapped back, staring straight into her gaze, letting her see my own anger, my own hurt, my own pride. "No one would dare."

Her lips parted, her brows furrowing.

"You're mine, Maeva, and you always have been. Anyone can see that," I rasped. "And I've always been *yours*. Don't you understand that?"

A sharp, surprised exhale escaped her.

Suddenly another voice cut in, small and gruff outside the *voliki*.

"*Vorakkar.*"

"*Vok*," I cursed, thinking this was the *worst* time we could be interrupted. But the night was late, the horde quiet. Whatever it was must've been important. "*Lysi?* Enter."

One of the *darukkars* on the night watch ducked inside. He kept his gaze carefully averted. No doubt he'd heard our raised voices, had heard the tail end of our argument.

"*Vorakkar*, the messenger that you sent to Rath Tuviri's horde just returned."

Maeva's head snapped toward him. When the *darukkar* held out a rolled up piece of parchment, I approached, not caring that I was still naked and half-hard, and took it from his grip.

"This is what he brought back," the *darukkar* said.

"How is he?" I asked, barely glancing at the rolled note.

"Tired from the journey, but he reported no incidents. I sent him to rest, but if you would like me to bring him—"

"*Nik*, that won't be necessary. Let him sleep," I said, cutting him off. "I'll speak with him in the morning."

The *darukkar* inclined his head and left quickly, backing from the *voliki*.

I stared at the entrance, jaw tight. The heat from the fire felt like it was prickling my skin, pinching it.

Looking down at the rolled note, I turned back to Maeva and handed it to her, though she didn't look at it. It hung limply in her hand. She was watching me as I pulled on my discarded trews, as I laced them quickly.

Silence stretched, heavy and tense.

I needed air. Cold, icy air that would sear me from the inside out. *Vok*, how I wished we were close to *Drukkar's Sea*. Because then I could swim in that icy, nourishing, crisp water.

Perhaps the lake would do. Or a ride out on Roon to clear

my head, though the storm was coming. It would hit later tonight.

"Where are you going?" she asked quietly. "It's cold out."

I blew out a breath. Just last night, we'd decided to move forward. And now we were fighting again.

"You're the last female I ever kissed, Maeva," I told her softly.

"What?" she whispered.

"That night on the cliff with you...that was the last time," I said. "Until tonight."

"But Hinna said..." She trailed off, swallowing.

I could only imagine what her *piki* had told her about me.

"There were other females, *lysi*," I told her. She already knew that. And if she wanted to talk about it, I would. "But I never took their kiss. Or offered them mine. That was an intimacy I was never going to give to them. It was an intimacy that wasn't *theirs*."

"But...*why*?"

"Because it never felt right with them," I admitted. "*I* never felt right after I left, Maeva."

Her expression went stricken.

"After *you*...nothing felt right," I confessed.

My words lingered in the space between us. I didn't know how else to explain my reasons. I didn't know how to explain it to her when I didn't understand it myself. Just like I didn't understand the dream Kakkari had given me or why I'd stopped taking females to my bed or the feeling that had *eaten* at me, the feeling that it was *time*.

Time to return home. Time to return to *her*. When I had already wasted so much of it.

"Maybe now I'm beginning to understand," I said softly, my fists clenching at my sides. "What I put you through. Wanting someone, *needing* them, loving them so fiercely...and not having those feelings returned."

Maeva froze, staring at me with those mirrored hazel eyes. They were reflecting the fire light, which made them glow.

"*Vok*," I breathed, needing to get my head on straight. Softening my tone, I said, "I need some air. I'll return later. Get some rest, *lysi*?"

I didn't wait for her reply. I left the *voliki* after pulling on my boots.

The tension between us was tight, and I worried that I'd pushed too hard.

Perhaps in kissing her I'd crossed a line that she wouldn't be able to forgive.

Chapter 38

I wanted Laru here.

That was what I thought as I stood in Kiran's *voliki*. Suddenly, I felt so incredibly lonely and homesick. I wanted to kiss Rasik's cheeks and hear his squealing laugh. I wanted to fret over my sister when she complained about her aches from pregnancy. I wanted to take my evening meals with my father. Not alone. Even the quiet between us had been comforting—for my *pattar* had always been the quiet sort.

I sank down onto the edge of the bed.

I wanted Laru here because she would make me see what I couldn't now. She would tell me if I was being a fool. She would call me out if I was being unfair or vindictive or a hypocrite.

"I hurt him," I whispered, needing to hear the words out loud.

I saw it.

In his gaze.

I didn't think...I didn't think I'd ever seen that expression on Kiran before. Anger, *lysi*. Amusement. Affection. Annoyance. Lust...

But hurt?

Maybe when we were younger. When his father—the

Sorakkar—had publicly called him a "weak fool" after one of his peers had bested him on the training grounds. Kiran had only been fifteen then. I remembered the hot shame that swept over his face, though he'd hidden it quickly, morphing his expression into a blank one as his father turned away.

But I saw it. The lingerings of that jab, hidden behind his eyes. He'd been quiet the rest of the day after his training session, even though I'd tried to cheer him up.

Kiran and his father had always had a tumultuous relationship.

But it was *me* who had caused his hurt this time.

That realization felt like a stab in my chest, making it a little difficult to breathe. I licked my dry lips, staring unseeing into my lap, where the scroll of rolled parchment lay innocently.

When I opened it, I read the scrawling but hardly absorbed it. *Head down...birthing position...begalia root,* which made my brows furrow.

Sighing, I rolled it back up, knowing I would pore over every detail in the morning, when my head wasn't muddled with guilt and bewilderment and...tentative hope.

The last of which I didn't want to dwell on.

Laru would tell me I *was* being a fool. That Kiran had been right. That I *had* been using him. That I had cared for only *my* comfort and that I refused to acknowledge that *he* might need more than what I was giving him.

I had tried so hard to keep him at arm's length. I had tried so hard to treat our relationship as if it were locked away in a chest. Separate. Out of sight. Something I could take out when I needed it.

It had been selfish and wrong to think that Kiran was doing the same. Especially when he told me his intentions, had hinted at them since the first day I arrived. To make me his wife, the queen to his horde.

And...he might've just confessed that he loved me, I thought, feeling my cheeks warm.

I would be lying if I said it didn't scare the life out of me.

Especially when I had already begun to feel the stirrings inside me. Those old feelings, like old friends since they had been with me for so long, hesitantly peeking out from their hidden places, places I had stuffed them so deeply into because I had hoped and prayed to Kakkari that they would never be found again.

My eyes alighted on Kiran's fur pelt.

He'd left in such a hurry he hadn't taken it with him.

I had a decision to make. I realized that. I could either move forward with him, knowing what was at stake, knowing that he wanted to keep me as his wife, in his horde.

Or I could end this.

Right now.

Then I wouldn't even have to risk being completely destroyed by the end of this.

Or maybe there doesn't have to be an end, I thought quietly.

My first instinct was to push that thought away, but I refused. I let it linger, let the possibility of it settle. I tried on that thought like a dress to see how it would look, how it would *feel.*

Blowing out a shaking breath, I stared at his fur pelt, draped on a hook close to the fire basin.

Rising from the bed, I walked over to it slowly, reached out my hand to touch it. It was warm from the fire. I paced away, biting my lip. But my eyes always came back to it.

You're not a coward.

I stilled. Words that my mother had once said to me, when she'd pulled me from heartbreak and loss. She'd made me believe those words. She'd made me remember how brave I could be. How, no matter what, I didn't run from anything. I would always *try.* And when that didn't work I would try again.

I'm not a coward.

And as the words flowed through me, so did my decision. I couldn't run from this. I didn't want to. I would give it a chance.

I would give *us* a chance.

I nodded to myself in the quiet, swallowing as my belly began to flutter, and then I went to put on my boots. Though my dress was thin, I draped my own furs over it, wrapping them tight around my shoulders. They'd keep me warm enough.

And then I went over to the hook near the fire, lifting the heavy pelt, bundling it tight in my arms.

I left the *voliki* in search of Kiran.

Of a passing *darukkar* I found wandering near the center of the encampment, I asked, "Have you seen the *Vorakkar*?"

He peered at me curiously, seeing Kiran's pelt in my arms before frowning. "*Lysi, Mokkira.* He went down to the lake. But he would not want you outside the—"

"*Kakkira vor,*" I said quickly, already turning from him.

"*Mokkira!*" the *darukkar* called after me before I heard his quiet curse.

Once I reached the gates, I saw two night watch guards on duty. The gates were open, however, and I slipped past them before the *darukkars* could say otherwise, hearing them call out quietly behind me, voices strained, uncertain. They let me go though. Probably because they knew Kiran was close, that he wouldn't let anything happen to me.

The lake was in sight, though the field between it and the horde was dark. I spied a figure on its shore, and I walked, determined, toward it.

Kiran had to have heard someone approaching, but he didn't turn. He was sitting on the sandy shore, the moonlight glistening over the water. His legs were stretched out in front of him, his hands behind him, holding his weight. His *Vorakkar* scars flashed, lining the entirety of his back, though I spied little red marks too. I flushed when I realized they were from my own nails.

I'd found him in this position often, though it had been at the *saruk* and instead of the lake stretched out before him, it had been the sea. His eyes always on the horizon line like he was wondering where it ended and what the world looked like there.

When I stepped in front of him, he straightened slightly, a strand of his dark hair whipping across his face. It was freezing out. *He* must have been freezing. My fingers were numb, and a dark cloud passed over the moon, darkening the shores. He'd said a storm was coming—one that might bring the frost—and I believed him.

"What are you doing out here, *seffi*?" he asked, his voice gruff. He was frowning. "It's—"

His words stopped abruptly when I lowered myself into his lap, hitching up my dress and sliding my legs on both sides of his hips. His nostrils flared, and he straightened completely, his hands hovering close to my thighs.

I slid his furs over his shoulders, fastening the clasp in the front, all too aware that he was studying me carefully, trying to read me.

"I know what you want, Kiran," I told him softly.

His brow furrowed.

"You truly want me as your *Morakkari*?" I asked, needing to hear the confirmation. Because at first, I'd thought he hadn't been serious.

"*Lysi*," he murmured, not hesitating, his honesty flowing from him easily. Kiran had never been a liar.

And I wanted to be honest with *him*.

"And I don't know if I can give you that yet. I don't know if this life is for me. I don't know if I can be apart from my family because I miss them so terribly that it aches," I whispered, watching his jaw flex. Swallowing, I added, "But I will try, Kiran. I want to *try*."

"*Neffar?*" he rasped, his gaze suddenly intense, eyes flickering back and forth between mine.

"I'm not agreeing to it yet," I told him softly, wanting him to understand. "Because being your *Morakkari* is a lot more than agreeing to be your lover."

I slid my arms around his neck as an icy breeze swept around us, making me shiver, drawing me closer to him.

Our faces were close. His hands came to grip my hips, holding me in place on his lap as realization dawned in his eyes.

"But you will think about it," he rasped. "You will consider it."

"*Lysi,*" I said, feeling lighter as the word fell from my lips. "I will. I promise."

A relief, perhaps.

Permission, I realized.

Permission to explore this again. Permission to...love him again.

And I wouldn't think about the cost.

I wouldn't think like that anymore.

This was what Laru had been trying to tell me, I realized. That I needed to put myself in situations where I might get hurt because those were the situations that were worth fighting for. For so long, I'd protected myself, building up walls, never letting anyone in.

And it had worked. With the exception of the loss of my mother, I had never been hurt by anyone again. Until Kiran came back and he opened that festering wound I thought had healed.

He'd poked at it, prodded at it. Making me realize that protecting myself from hurt, numbing myself to *possibilities* had not necessarily been a healthy choice. It had kept me safe, *lysi*. But it had also kept me trapped and afraid.

Kiran made me angry. He made me hurt. But he also made me smile, made my belly flutter with anticipation, made me gasp with need, made me feel safe and wanted and protected.

I hadn't realized it, but *those* were the things I'd needed to make me feel *alive*.

My gaze trailed to his lips. My fingers curled around his neck.

Without hesitation, I leaned forward and pressed my lips to his.

A gruff sound emerged from his throat. His hands tightened on me.

And then he was stealing my breath straight from my lungs, angling himself so I could take from him freely. My head swam, and I pressed closer, my eyelids falling shut.

Everything about it was familiar. Only this time, I wasn't worried he'd push me away.

Warmth spread from my lips, down my throat. It rushed through my blood, warming my icy fingers and wind-stung flesh. Kiran radiated heat, and I greedily lapped at it, taking what he offered.

I smiled when I made him groan, when I nibbled at his full bottom lip and sank into him. I felt him, hard and ready, beneath me. The dark cloud covering the moon shifted, and blue light flooded us, making his golden eyes flash.

He ate at my mouth, his grip tightening, his lips becoming more demanding. And I gave him everything he wanted.

My hands went to the laces of his trews, and he hissed when my hand found what it sought. My fingers were no doubt chilled as they wrapped around his cock, but if anything, he seemed to pulse hotter at my touch.

"Get me inside you, *seffi*. Now," he rasped. "*Hanniva.*"

Please?

My *Vorakkar* was begging now?

How could I refuse him?

Sliding up, I shifted my dress and positioned his cock between my thighs. Biting my lip, I sank down, rocking and wiggling my hips until I felt the pressure of him. Heat so searing it was almost painful.

But *vok*, I wanted it. I wanted him.

"*Lysi*," he hissed, his throat bobbing.

When my lips returned to him, I didn't close my eyes and neither did he. We watched one another as he thrust up into me, his strokes so powerful, and I gasped into his kiss. And our eyes watched it all.

I didn't care that the guards at the gate might guess what we were doing. I didn't care that it was the middle of the night and we were exposed on the wildlands with a dark storm coming.

I slid and ground down, this new position making me feel so full of him. My fingers dug into the back of his neck, and he groaned, rough sounds I loved vibrating his chest, falling across my lips.

I wanted him.

And finally, I gave myself the freedom to have him without fear.

CHAPTER 39

Later that night—or rather, in the early hours of morning—Kiran's hand was stroking down my naked spine, trailing his claws over the little bones.

The furs of his bed tickled my cheek. I was drowsy but sated, watching him on his side as he looked at me and touched me. Touched me like he couldn't stop touching me. His hands had been on me since the lake, and they hadn't left.

Outside the *voliki*, the wind was howling. In the distance, I heard the frost sweeping over the land, drawing closer and closer. I wondered how my *pattar* was. I wondered if he was living with Laru and her husband now.

"What are you thinking of?" Kiran rumbled, his voice rich and thick.

I didn't want to tell him the truth. I didn't want him to know how much I missed home and my family, not when I'd just agreed to give this a chance between us.

"The storm," I whispered, a half-truth. "And you."

That was a full-truth. Because Kiran was always on my mind these days.

His grin stole my breath straight from my lungs. Kiran had always stolen things from me, the thief.

But as I felt that grin melt me from the inside, as his fingers made goose bumps spread across my arms and made a pleasurable shiver race down my spine, I thought that maybe he was giving things back to me now.

He'd hinted that he loved me earlier.

Did he mean that?

Or had they just been words?

His grin slowly died, and those molten eyes trailed to my lips.

"I did not tell you before," he murmured, "but I will need to leave the horde in a few days. Only for a little while."

I frowned, blinking.

"Leave?" I asked, incredulous. "But the frost is coming. If it's not here already."

His hand went to my hair, brushing a strand off my cheek. He rubbed the curls between his fingertips and shifted closer, propping himself up on his elbow.

There was a peace about him, I thought. Something steady and calm. Certain. So much like the Kiran I'd once known, before he'd gone to *Dothik* and come back a little harder, a little colder.

"The *Vorakkar* are to meet in the Dead Lands."

Alarm made me still.

"The *Dothikkar* demands it."

My jaw ticked. I didn't know much about the *Dothikkar*. Our *saruk* was not terribly far from *Dothik,* but the *Sorakkar,* Kiran's father, had never once said anything pleasant about the king of Dakkar.

All I knew was that he had never traveled to the wildlands. A king of Dakkar who had never stepped beyond the walls of his city.

"Will it be dangerous?" I asked quietly.

The Dead Lands were where the Ghertun lived. In the Dead Mountain. Which, as Kiran said, had been cloaked in a strange, dark fog after the events that had transpired there earlier in the year.

"Worried for me, *seffi*?" he teased softly, but I saw through his attempted deflection.

"Kiran."

His breath huffed from him.

Quietly, he said, "I am more worried about the journey—about how the journey during the frost will drain Roon—than I am about the East Lands. Though, truthfully, I do not know what we will discover there."

"Maybe you should stay," I whispered softly. "It's safer here."

His jaw tightened.

"I cannot," he murmured. "Because no matter how I feel about the *Dothikkar's* orders, I am still a *Vorakkar*. I still made an oath to uphold his wishes and to obey his commands. He is still our king. For now."

I sighed. "And will his reign be over soon? Maybe a better king should take his place now more than ever before."

"He has bastards, I am certain, born from his mistresses' wombs. He took a wife long ago, but she never bore him a child and she's long passed into the next life," he told me, and my heart started pounding in my chest just from the way he was looking at me. "He never experienced the gift of a child from his chosen queen."

I swallowed, the tension between us changing into something more electric.

"Kiran," I whispered.

He leaned down to kiss me, taking it freely now that I had offered it to him. His arm slid around my waist and his warm palm spread across my belly.

He broke the kiss just as my sex began to tingle and warm. In my ear, he growled, "Perhaps I should get you with my child, *seffi*. If there isn't one already."

My breath hitched, my eyes flying to his.

I was shocked at the way my body *throbbed* at the idea.

"Then you would stay with me," he continued. He pulled back to look in my eyes, deeply. He kissed me again as I began to shift on the furs. A sigh escaped his throat. "But I want you to choose me. I want you to choose this life freely. Not because there is a child."

Swallowing, I realized I needed to steer this conversation away from talk of us having babies.

"So the king has bastard children?" I breathed, feeling his palm trail away from my belly, even though I felt his continued warmth there, a phantom touch. "Could one of them become his heir?"

Kiran blew out a long breath. The corner of one side of his lips quirked up because he knew what I was doing.

"I suppose so, *lysi*," he murmured. "But the only one I know of that would make a good king might never take the throne. *That* throne, at least."

I frowned. "Why not?"

"Because the *Dothikkar's* Trials recently ended and a horde king was born from them."

Lysi, I'd heard the news. A couple moon cycles ago, a new *Vorakkar* had been victorious in the Trials. He would take to the wildlands soon with a new horde.

"This new horde king *is* one of the *Dothikkar's* bastard sons, though not many know that."

Surprise made me stiffen. "Truly?"

"*Lysi*," Kiran said. "And from what I have heard, this new *Vorakkar* wants nothing to do with his father or his throne, though he would be the best choice for his heir. The better king for Dakkar."

I had no idea. I had no idea about the happenings in *Dothik*. For obvious reasons, I had never been there. No one outside the *saruk*—and now Kiran's horde—knew that a human girl had been raised among the Dakkari, as one of their own. Though my father had traveled to the capital once or twice and he'd told Laru and me about it. He made it seem like such a grand, opulent place.

But...if I were to become Kiran's wife, if I were to accept his offer, these were things I *would* need to know.

I must've been quiet for a long time, wondering about all the things I *didn't* know, because Kiran tipped up my chin and ran an assessing look over my expression.

And because I couldn't hide anything from him, I teased softly, "Perhaps a female in the horde is better suited to be your wife. Because all I know is how to suture a bloody wound and how to deliver babies. I know nothing of the politics of *Dothik* or of the other hordes. All I've known is the *saruk*."

The more I talked, the more I realized it was true. I had always been confident in my abilities as a healer. And I took pride in what I did.

But I was a healer. I'd studied to become one. I'd poured nearly half my life into the pursuit of it. I knew nothing about being a *Morakkari*. I knew nothing about being a horde king's queen.

Kiran didn't hesitate.

"I don't want any other female but you," he rasped, and I felt more of that compacted dirt in my chest loosen. I imagined my heart beginning to peek through, shifting more of that dirt as it pumped harder and faster, exposed. "And I never will."

"You don't know that," I whispered, swallowing.

"I do," he returned without hesitation. "And you will learn how to be a *Vorakkar's* wife. And you will be great at it, as you are at everything you put your mind to. *Lysi?*"

I couldn't help my tired smile. "You are relentless, you know that?"

"You've always known that," he replied. "Do not act surprised now."

A small laugh burst from my throat.

"Do not think of these matters now, Maeva," came his voice, a subtle change in its tone. I sobered when I saw how serious, how focused he looked. "Do not worry about being my *Morakkari* now. Just be with *me*. Let me touch you and kiss you. Let me warm you in this bed. Let me make you smile again."

I took in a deep breath, feeling his words burrow their way into my chest.

"And if you find yourself loving me again," he continued, pressing closer, his arms coming around me, "if you find that at the end of the frost you do not want to leave me, that you want to stay by my side, that you want to be the *mokkira* to my horde and my queen in our furs, that you want to bear my children..."

His voice went a little gruffer at those words as a sharp inhale whistled through my nostrils, imagining *that*.

"If you find all that to be true, *then* allow yourself to worry about being my *Morakkari*. But even then, I will see you through it. Because you'll find you have nothing to worry about. Not with me, *seffi*. You have nothing to worry about with me—ever again."

Later that night, as I lay in Kiran's arms, as I listened to his steady, even breaths as he slept beside me and felt his warmth pour into me, I heard the storm reach the horde.

As his words continued to ring through my mind—feeling more and more like a premonition than a possible path to where this would lead—I heard the stones of ice begin to rain down from the sky.

And when those little pelts of ice ceased suddenly, I knew the frost had taken their place, soft and slow yet already chilling the air inside the *voliki*.

In the morning, I would wake to a new Dakkar. But for now, I closed my eyes and slept in my horde king's arms.

CHAPTER 40

"What did the healer say again?" Addie asked, perched on the table in my *voliki*, nervously nibbling her lip. "Because something feels different. I noticed yesterday, after I left here."

"What feels different?" I asked, approaching her with the note from the healer of Rath Tuviri. A note that I had pored over in the last few days, ever since the frost had blown in.

Addie had come in every day since the note arrived. She asked me to read it to her again and again. I knew she was just nervous. The baby would be coming soon. Sooner than the previous *mokkira* had believed, that much was obvious, and there was always a hint of panic in her face whenever I saw her.

"I'm not sure," she said. "Just a...heaviness. Sometimes pain. I woke Jurin last night because it frightened me, but he calmed me back down."

Jurin must have been her mate, and Addie was in too much of an anxious state to realize she'd given me his name.

"Addie," I said quietly, lowering my voice so Essir couldn't hear us where he was in the back section of the *voliki*, pounding away at *terruni* root in the mortar. I had sent Hinna to the *bikku* tent for some fresh water, and Gabe had gone with her. "I know you're nervous. But this stress won't help the child, *lysi*?"

Still, she fidgeted on the table. "I know," she whispered. "It's just...ever since the frost, it's really hit me hard."

"What has?"

"That this baby will come soon. Very soon," she said, and tears welled up in her eyes. "And what if something goes wrong? You said the baby was in the wrong position and—"

"*Lysi*, but I maneuvered the child into the right position yesterday, remember?"

"Yes, but what if he was in the wrong position for a reason? What if something is wrong? What if..."

She trailed off, her lip quivering, looking away from me.

"Addie," I called softly, reaching out to squeeze her hand. I was relieved when she squeezed back after a moment of hesitation. "I have delivered many babies. A few had difficult labors, *lysi*, but in the end, all the children were healthy. And this fear you feel is normal."

"Is it?" she asked, tentatively meeting my eyes.

"*Lysi*," I said, nodding. "Every mother I have ever encountered has voiced these same concerns. It is a universal fear."

"It's just..." She trailed off, licking her dry lips as she shivered in her bundle of furs. "My mother died giving birth to me."

I pressed my lips together at the admission.

"I never knew her," she said, quiet tears leaking from her eyes. "And I stay up at night and worry that that will happen to me. That I will never know him. Or her. That Jurin will have to—"

She broke off, her expression crumbling, and she pressed her face into her hands. Her shoulders shook, and my chest twisted. I reached out to embrace her, the note from the healer crumpling in my hand, and she sobbed as I tried to soothe her.

"I'm s-sorry," she finally gasped out, leaning back from me quickly, wiping at her reddened cheeks and swollen eyes. "I know I'm a mess. I'm just scared. And I'm human. And Jurin is Dakkari. And you say you've delivered a lot of babies, but you've never delivered a child of two different worlds before."

"You're right, I haven't," I said softly. "And until you give birth to this child, that will be so. I wish I could tell you differently, Addie. I truly do."

Addie took a deep breath, seemingly embarrassed by her tears. But I frowned, just wanting to comfort her and soothe her fears in any way I could, though I didn't know how.

Once her shoulders stopped trembling, she gestured to the note. "What does it say again? I know I've asked so many times, but can you read it again for me?"

I gave her a small smile. "*Lysi*, of course."

I read the note to her—almost in its entirety except for a small portion at the bottom—for the tenth time in three days. It was long, but the *mokkira* of Rath Tuviri had graciously written out every detail of the *Morakkari's* delivery. The *Vorakkar* of Rath Tuviri—rumored to have golden hair, which was rare among the Dakkari—had taken a human as his queen. She'd given birth earlier in the year, after the last frost.

The human queen's actual delivery hadn't been complicated. Everything had gone perfectly that night, according to the *mokkira*, which seemed to put Addie at ease whenever she heard it. So I would read the note to her every moment until she gave birth if necessary.

One thing that had made me pause, however, was that the *mokkira* claimed he used *begalia* extract for the pain and to lower the risk of bleeding during and after delivery.

And I didn't translate the part of the note for Addie where the *mokkira* said the human queen had been bedridden with sickness for a few days after the birth. I didn't want her to needlessly stress when she was already so tightly wound.

However, I suspected it was the *begalia* that had made the human queen sick. The root extract was perfectly harmless to the Dakkari. It was a dark-colored root that grew deep underground over most of Dakkar. The root was ground, dried, and then powdered. Mixed into water, it could help Dakkari with most pains that ailed them.

I'd taken *begalia* once. My mother had given it to me when I first began my bleeding cycles, when my abdomen had cramped so badly that I cried and cried for hours. And the *begalia* had seemed to work...at first. The pain had disappeared. But then it returned with a vengeance and I had become so sick from the powdered root, vomiting for days, my flesh hot to the touch, feeling like I couldn't breathe, like I was being stabbed continuously, all over my body.

I had thought my reaction a fluke, though I had never touched the root again. After hearing that the human queen was bedridden after taking *begalia*, however, I wondered now if the root was poisonous to humans.

If it *was*, that was problematic. Because *begalia* was how many Dakkari delivered their babies safely...because the root dramatically lessened the risks of bleeding and infection after the birth.

I remembered my reaction to *begalia,* how I wondered if I was actually dying, how my mother didn't sleep for those days, watching over me, whispering to Kakkari when she thought I was asleep. My mother had given me a small amount. For births, the amount given was almost tripled. I couldn't imagine how sick the human queen must've been after her birth.

Did I risk poisoning Addie with *begalia*, knowing she'd be in a weakened state, though it would dramatically improve the chances of a successful delivery for her child? Or did I risk a natural birth that would be safer for the mother?

"And this human queen and her baby are fine now?" Addie asked when I was done reading the letter.

"As far as I know, *lysi*," I said, moving to place the letter back onto my workbench, my mind working. There was something in the back of it, something that was bugging me, something I was trying to remember and couldn't. Something that might help. I knew the story, the one my *mokkira* had told me, but I couldn't remember the *detail* I sought.

The tent flap pushed open, a chilly gust of icy wind blowing in, making the fire in the basin flicker. It always amazed me how quickly the frost came. One day it could be warm. The next, as cold as ice.

Instead of Hinna and Gabe as I expected, it was Addie's mate who stepped inside. Jurin.

His expression warmed on Addie, and already I sensed that the human female's shoulders relaxed. Like just being in her mate's presence made her fears lessen and melt away.

I watched the two of them as Addie hopped off the table and approached him. He wrapped his arm around her, holding her close, and she breathed in the scent of the furs draped across his shoulders.

"*Mokkira,*" the *darukkar* greeted, inclining his head. I bowed mine back, briefly, as Jurin looked down at his mate. "Everything is all right?"

"Yes," Addie replied, though he no doubt saw her reddened eyes. "I'm just worrying too much."

Jurin's lips pressed together. His eyes came back to me, and I met them steadily. I wondered if he saw my own worry. But I hoped he didn't.

He nodded and said something to Addie about making certain she was eating. With a brief wave, I watched as they left my *voliki* together. And then it was just me—and Essir toward the back, the rhythmic sound of the pounding mortar and pestle filling the space.

I turned back toward the bench and placed my hands on it, my eyes drifting down to the letter. Closing my eyes, I listened to Essir working, thought of Addie's fear, and I prayed to Kakkari to guide me. To help me.

I let my thoughts go blank. I only listened to the mortar and pestle. In the back of my mind, I felt that thing pushing forward, that thing that was eluding me. Then I thought of Kiran, and I felt strength burst in me.

I swore I felt Kakkari respond to the prayers I'd been silently whispering in my mind for the last few days.

And suddenly I remembered what I'd been trying to find. The name.

Adiri.

The rare fungus that grew on *adir* trees in the South Land forests.

"Essir?" I called out.

The rhythmic grinding of the *terruni* root stopped suddenly.

"*Lysi, Mokkira?*" he asked.

"Do you know if *adir* trees grow in the forest next to the lake?"

"*Adir?*" Essir asked, frowning. "I have never heard of them before."

Kiran will know, I thought. He was from the South Lands, after all. He would know the *adir*. But he had gone out on another patrol earlier that morning. He wouldn't be back until later tonight, and if there were *adir* trees in the forest, I would still need to gather them, clean them, grind them, and powder them. The process could take days.

Was *adiri* extract the answer to Addie's worries? Could it help her deliver the baby safely while not poisoning her in the process? It was already a risky pregnancy.

But maybe it could help.

My *mokkira* had told me the story of it, after all, though it was only a rumor that he had heard from another healer, who'd heard it from a healer who had delivered a hybrid child nearly thirty years ago. The first hybrid child on Dakkar, though not many knew about her. A child who would be around my age, if she still lived, wherever she was, whoever she was.

"I'll be back later," I told Essir.

"Where are you going?" he asked in slight alarm.

I remembered, briefly, his frazzled state when I'd first arrived at the horde. How relieved he'd looked when I stepped in. And I knew that he still had many years of training ahead of him. He wouldn't be ready to be a *mokkira* in a few short moon cycles. How had I ever believed differently when it had taken me nearly ten years of constant study?

Giving him a small, hopefully comforting smile, I reached for my blade I kept tucked in the cabinet and then swung my heavy furs around my shoulders.

"I have to go find something," I told him.

CHAPTER 41

This might be incredibly foolish, I acknowledged as I stepped into the forest.

Kiran would be furious when he found out. Because he *would* find out upon his return, and if I thought he wouldn't, that would make me incredibly naive.

The only reason I felt a *little* less fearful was that the guard that Kiran had assigned to me—ever since I'd arrived at the horde—had trailed me. And this time he didn't bother to keep his presence a secret. I heard his crunching footsteps behind me.

"*Mokkira*," he said quietly, his voice echoing in the quiet, still forest. Ice hung off deadened branches in long shards, and the ground crunched underneath me. Just a few nights ago, as I rode Kiran on the edge of the lake, the boughs had been dry and clear. "The *Vorakkar* would not like you away from—"

"*Lysi*, I know," I called back.

"*Hanniva*," he called out, "let us return to the horde. When he returns, he can escort you here himself if you need to find whatever it is you're looking for."

He sounded fearful. Not of the forest, but of *Kiran*. Of his wrath, perhaps, if anything happened to me under the *darukkar's* watch.

"It cannot wait until then," I replied simply, hurrying forward. "I'll be quick. I'll be even quicker if you can tell me if there are *adir* trees in this forest."

Behind me, I heard the *darukkar* say, "*Adir* trees?"

I sighed.

"Are you from the South Lands?" I asked.

"*Nik,*" he replied. "I was raised in a *saruk* in the North. Then I lived in *Dothik.*"

That explained it, then.

"They are different trees than these," I pointed out. "More blue in color. The trunks, I mean. And they grow taller, though they tend to grow in the denser areas of a forest. You won't find them near the outskirts."

"You will not return to the horde until you find these trees?" the *darukkar* asked, his tone resigned.

"*Nik,* I will not. I need to find one."

A deep huff came from the *darukkar.* "Then we better hurry. Because if the *Vorakkar* finds you gone and outside the gates, he will banish me and send me back to *Dothik* without hesitation."

"*Nik,* he won't," I told him. "I promise."

It seemed like we trekked through the icy forests for days, but in reality, it was only a portion of the late afternoon. Though the skies were dark and overcast with heavy, smoky clouds, it was still early enough in the evening to allow us more time to search before we were forced to turn back.

"*Mokkira,*" the *darukkar* called after another stretch of time.

And I knew what he was going to say.

That we couldn't remain in the forest past dark and we were beginning to lose the light quickly, especially this deep in the forest.

"If we don't turn back now, we won't reach the horde until

long after dark," he said. "*Hanniva.* We can return in the morning."

I knew he was right.

But somehow, I *knew* that we needed to keep going. That we were close. I swore I spied a deadened *adir* sapling not too long ago, but the branches were too shriveled and sunken to tell.

"Just give me a little more time, *lysi*?" I pleaded.

He sighed.

And we continued.

As the last of the daylight was beginning to drain from the forest, I worried that I was out of time. I worried that there were no *adir* trees in this forest, though it was large enough and we were in the South Lands.

"*Mokkira,*" the *darukkar* urged for the third time. His tone was hardened. I knew he'd reached the end of his patience and that he would drag me from the forest if he needed to. "We must—"

My breath hitched.

"There!" I cried out.

I raced forward, catching sight of a blue trunk that peeked out from behind a larger tree. And as I got closer, even in the dimmed light, I saw another blue trunk. And then another. And another.

A small, stretched-out grove of *adir* trees grew in the middle of the forest, and I knew there would be more deeper. But this little grove was all I needed. Just one tree was all I needed.

I dropped to my knees in front of one, though the soft, powdery ice that covered the springy moss stung even through my hide-lined trews. At the base of one frost-covered *adir* tree, I saw the fungus that I sought. Thin, sprouting, flattened blue strings were reaching toward the sky. Given the season, however, they were a little softer than I anticipated.

But they would have to do.

"These are them?" the *darukkar* asked in disbelief. "These

are the ugliest trees I have ever seen. You should see the trees of the North. They grow so high you cannot see their tops."

A laugh burst from my throat, his comment unexpected, and I took out my blade, swiftly slicing through the fungus. A dark blue liquid seeped out, but I was careful not to get it on my prickly, icy fingers.

A shrill cry—a familiar one—suddenly echoed around the forest.

I froze, my heart stuttering in my chest. The *darukkar's* hand flashed toward the hilt of his sword, and I saw him freeze, though his eyes flickered around the darkened trees.

That cry hadn't been far away. And I recognized it. It was a *polkunu,* that taloned creature that had attacked one of Kiran's warriors close to the *saruk.* Another one, so far south.

"*Mokkira,*" the *darukkar* hissed. "Quickly. We need to leave. *Now.*"

I nodded, my breath coming shallowly, and I finished sawing at the fungus of the *adir* tree with my blade, filling my carefully lined satchel. It would be enough for now. If I needed more, I could return—though I'd do it in broad daylight and perhaps with a few more *darukkars* for protection.

Foolish, foolish, foolish.

But I'd needed to come. And it had to be now. Addie was so close to giving—

Another hissing cry came, and that was when I saw it. Glowing red eyes, peering at us from the darkest place in the forest, coming toward us. Fast. *Polkunu* looked like *pyrokis,* except they had massive wings that sprouted from their backs, meant for speed, and larger talons.

It would outrun us easily.

"*Run,*" the *darukkar* hissed at me.

What other choice did we have?

I didn't hesitate.

We sprinted from the clearing, dodging around trees, the

darukkar nipping at my heels, shielding my back. I heard the ground began to shake, heard jittering from the ice that hung from the boughs of the trees around us, and I felt fear pierce me when the *polkunu* began to give chase.

Nik.

My heart was trying to pound its way from my chest, but I kept my grip on my satchel tight. We ran and ran, but the *polkunu* was not letting up. We were able to weave through the trees, but we would never be able to outrun a creature like this.

Just as we rounded another tree, my feet slid across hard ice at the base. My breath whooshed from my lungs as I fell hard. I heard the *darukkar's* surprised curse. I heard the *polkunu* closing in on us.

Closer and closer.

My breath was jagged as I tried to catch it, gasping.

Then those red eyes burned into me. I saw it racing toward us. It was all I could see, coming from the darkness. Night had fallen quickly. How long had we been gone?

Was Kiran back? Had he already discovered my absence?

The *polkunu* moved quickly. For a moment, those red eyes were all I saw. They seemed to glow like fire in the night.

Aggressive. Too aggressive, came the thought.

Just like the *ungira.* I'd never heard of *polkunu* giving chase like this. They lived in packs and kept to themselves. That was what my father had told me.

Those eyes glowed. Before the *darukkar* could defend me with his sword, the *polkunu* reared back and brought those clawed talons down toward me.

I shielded my body with my arms, squeezing my eyes shut.

Hot pain bit at me hard. Searing and sharp.

My scream echoed through the forest.

CHAPTER 42

Her scream made familiar chilling fear sting my chest and squeeze my breath from my body. Familiar fear from when I'd watched Maeva jumping off the cliff in the *saruk*. Fear that made me want to fall to my knees. Fear that made me feel like I was spiraling.

Only this fear was so much worse because I couldn't see my *seffi*. And I knew what dangers lurked in this forest. In the darkness, the forest was too dense. Below me, Roon charged forward faster, as did the group of *darukkars* I'd brought with me, though they were having a difficult time of navigating the trees.

When I'd returned to the horde from my patrol to find Maeva gone, her apprentice, Essir, told me she'd gone. The poor male went a sickly white when I growled at him, demanding where. He'd told me she'd mentioned something about *adir* trees, though he'd stammered out that he'd never heard of them.

She'd left the horde with only a single guard for protection, had ventured into the forest, and night had fallen. There had been no sign of her since.

Hanniva, Kakkari, let her be unharmed, I prayed, gritting my teeth, ice spreading through my veins. *I will do anything for you, if only she is unharmed.*

Adir trees. I knew where they grew. And as we approached the clearing, with Roon's hot breaths billowing silver in front of him, I heard the hissing of a *polkunu.*

I heard the ringing of Dakkari steel scraping off hardened scales. Heard a male grunt and smelled the metallic stench of blood. Maeva's? *Nik*, it couldn't be.

But as we drew closer and closer, I spied her lying on the ground, and my fear tripled until I felt like *I* couldn't breathe. The only reason I didn't lose my *vokking* mind was I saw her moving, trying to push up from the ice though something dark was spilled on the forest floor, making it slippery.

Her blood? Or the *polkunu's?*

"*Maeva!*" I bellowed, and her head snapped up. I saw the fear in her eyes, coupled with pain.

The *darukkars* swarmed the clearing just as the *polkunu* whipped Maeva's guard across the chest with its long tail. The guard went flying, hitting a tree trunk before slumping to the ground, his sword dropped.

The *polkunu* hissed and roared when it saw us. I saw its hesitation, its red eyes flickering at all of us, snapping its jaws to warn us away. I didn't even need to steer Roon toward Maeva. Our loyal beast put himself between my *seffi* and the *polkunu*, stomping his clawed hooves into the ground, letting out a warning all his own.

Like me, Roon would die for Maeva. He would do anything to protect her because he was bonded to her just as much as he was bonded to me. *Pyrokis* had long memories, and once bonded, they would never forget their true masters.

When the *polkunu* charged Roon, my *pyroki* reared back, going up onto two legs, and with a swiftness that didn't surprise me, he stomped his own clawed hooves right across the approaching beast's face.

The *polkunu* shook its head, a cry echoing around the forest, bright claw marks across its face, just missing its eyes. It stumbled back, but it didn't look like it was backing down.

With a grim realization, I called out, "*Darukkars, venuri ji vorak.*"

Protect the horde.

The *polkunu* was a danger so close to us. And it was... changed. This was the second *polkunu* we'd encountered that seemed strangely aggressive and violent. The first had been farther south, near my father's *saruk*. The beasts were usually very difficult to hunt if we were in their territory because they were timid creatures and ran when they spied potential predators.

I didn't watch the efficiency of my *darukkars* as they circled the *polkunu*. I took no pleasure in giving that order, but the horde came first. And this *polkunu* had attacked Maeva and her guard. It was a danger to us all.

I jumped off Roon's back, hearing the *darukkars* as they drove the *polkunu* away from the clearing. Roon stood guard as I sank down toward Maeva, taking her face in my palms.

Her cheeks were so cold, and her eyes were round and glassy with fear when I met them.

"*Seffi*, are you hurt?" I demanded, feeling a shiver rack her body, so I drew her closer, wanting to crush her to me in relief that the *polkunu* hadn't taken her.

She shook her head, her eyes flickering to the opposite side of the clearing. "Where's my guard? Is he all right?"

Always worrying about everyone but herself, I thought.

Maeva hissed when I touched her arm, and my fingers came away with hot blood.

"*Vok*," I breathed, looking down at the wound, my chest tightening with worry and more fear. The back of her forearm had a long slash down the flesh. It was a clean slice, but it needed to be mended. And soon. Blood was dripping from it, wetting the earth and the furs that hung from her shoulders. "We need to get back."

"The guard, Kiran," she said hurriedly. "*Hanniva!*"

"I'll check on him when I get you on Roon," I said, hearing my *darukkars* in the background make the killing blow to the *polkunu*, quick and efficient. The weight of its slackened body shook the ground as it fell.

All at once, the forest grew silent. Even Maeva seemed to be holding her breath as I lifted her carefully in my arms. Roon went to a kneeling position on his front legs, and I deposited her onto his back easily.

I was loath to leave her side, but I hurried around Roon to check on her guard, Danir, one of my best warriors. Just as I reached him, the pack of *darukkars* returned.

"It's done, *Vorakkar*," one of them called out.

Danir was breathing, which was a relief. He didn't appear injured or bloodied, but that tail whip from the *polkunu* had knocked him unconscious.

"Should we take the creature back to the horde?" my *darukkar* asked.

"*Nik*," I rasped, thinking of the red fog in the East. "The meat might be tainted."

"Should we bury it?"

"*Nik*, burn it," I told him, standing from my crouched position over the *darukkar*. Burning a creature of Dakkar was not common practice, but I wouldn't take the risk. "Danir lives. One of you take him back to the horde. The *mokkira's* apprentice can check on him."

"*Lysi, Vorakkar.*"

When I returned to Roon, my gaze immediately landed on Maeva. She was looking forward, into the darkness of the forest, where the *polkunu* now lay.

My breathing still felt ragged and uneven. I couldn't shake the fear that swam through my entire body, like I'd been plunged into it. Like fear was *Drukkar's Sea* and I'd jumped off the cliff. Those waves threatened to pull me under, but I needed strength.

When I swung onto Roon behind my *seffi*, I wrapped my arm around her waist, holding her close and tight, though I was careful of her arm. She was shaking in front of me, and my jaw tightened.

"*Ji vorak*," I ordered to Roon, and he began to run through the forest, back the way we came.

With my fear came my fury. Fury at myself, for not protecting her from harm. Fury at Danir, for putting her in danger.

Fury at Maeva.

I'd explicitly told her to stay away from the forest unless I accompanied her. And she'd gone out to seek the *adir* trees, which were so deep inside it.

We didn't speak on the ride back to the horde. Maeva's shaking finally ceased once it came into view, the golden glow from the fire basins lighting up the sky around it. The gates were closed, but I heard the yell of a *darukkar* when he saw my approach and opened them.

To one of the posted guards, I growled, "Bring me the *mokkira's ruhna* now."

I didn't wait for his reply. The eyes of the horde were on us. Most had come out to see the commotion because they knew I'd left and taken a pack of *darukkars* with me into the forest.

Maeva stiffened with the attention even as her blood dripped over my arm. Her red blood. Blood I'd hoped to never see again because I knew how slowly *vekkiri* healed.

I brought Roon to a halt outside the *mokkira's voliki*, and my *pyroki* kneeled, letting me slide Maeva off his back, swinging her into my arms as I strode forward.

"Kiran," came her soft voice. It had regained some of its strength on the ride back to the horde. She was no longer shaking. She was no longer panicked now that she knew her guard hadn't been seriously injured. Only she had been.

My jaw ticked, and I ducked under the flap of the domed tent. I placed her on the table where she tended to the members of the horde, then went to the dark fire basin to light it.

Then I returned to her, my movements quick and efficient as I stripped her of the furs around her shoulders. I needed to see her, needed to make sure that she was all right, that she was *here* with me and not lying on a cold forest floor.

"Kiran," she said softly, reaching out to take my hand. I'd avoided her eyes thus far, but when I looked into them now, my breaths came faster. My tail was flicking restlessly behind me, and I couldn't shake that fear and fury. I wanted to, but it stayed with me. It stuck to me.

The *voliki's* entrance flaps slapped back, and Essir, Maeva's apprentice, dove inside, his eyes wide, breathing hard.

"Are you all right?" he asked hurriedly, coming toward us. I stepped back, trying to drag in breath, trying to *vokking breathe* properly.

I still felt Maeva's eyes on me, watching me carefully, when she replied to Essir, "*Lysi*. I—"

"*Nik*, you are not," I growled, turning to Essir. "She has a deep wound on her arm. Clean it and get it sutured quickly. She's already lost enough blood."

Essir inclined his head, not meeting my eyes. Then his gaze went to Maeva, who nodded.

"You'll do well, *ruhna*," she said quietly. "I know you will. It's just like the *lobbas* root, *lysi?*"

Essir straightened and went toward the cabinet to gather his supplies quickly. He brought back an armload of supplies just as Hinna, Maeva's *piki*, ducked inside.

Relief was evident on her features. "Oh, *Mokkira*, I was so worried!"

"I'm all right," Maeva said quietly. I knew how much this

embarrassed her, how much all this attention discomforted her. "I'm sorry I worried you."

I began to pace the edges of the *voliki,* and Hinna stopped suddenly when she noticed me inside.

"I need fresh water," Essir said.

"I'll get it from the *bikkus,*" Hinna said, and before anyone could say a word, she left, running.

"Essir, you'll need to work quickly. My guard..." Maeva trailed off. "I need to check on him once he arrives."

"You will do no such thing," I growled from the corner.

Maeva ignored me. "And this, Essir."

She loosened her satchel from around her shoulders. When Essir took it from her and opened it, I saw *adiri* fungus, long and flat and blue, inside. It was filled to the brim.

And I hated them on sight because I knew that they were the reason she'd gotten injured, why she'd ventured into the forest.

"I need you to clean these off as I look over the guard and mash them to a very fine pulp. We need to start powdering it tonight."

Essir was confused, but he nodded and took the satchel. "I'll do my best, *Mokkira.*"

"I know you will."

Essir went to work, and Maeva's eyes returned to mine as he began cleaning the wound. Even when Hinna returned, Maeva never took her eyes off me. Even when I saw her expression pull into a pained one as Essir cleaned, salved, and began suturing her wound, she never took her eyes off me.

And the longer I looked at her, the more I felt that tight fear begin to loosen in my chest. The more my lungs opened. I was still *vokking* furious with her, still so *vokking* worried...but at least I could breathe again. At least she was safe and being tended to. She was calm. And though she was in pain, I knew her wound could've been so much worse than it was.

Swallowing hard, I heard the *voliki* entrance open once more, and I saw Maeva's guard limping into the *voliki*. Though another *darukkar* was behind him, Danir was standing on his own, and I couldn't describe the relief in Maeva's eyes when she saw him.

It was the same relief as in the guard's eyes.

I felt my temper begin to rise all over again.

"I need to speak with you," I rasped, stepping toward him.

I heard Maeva's sharp inhale. "Ki—*Vorakkar*, it can wait. I need to look him over, and I need to speak with you before—"

"*Nik,*" I growled out, watching the blood drain from Danir's face though he inclined his head. "Now."

When we both stepped out of the *voliki*, alone, he began to apologize. Roon was still standing outside, waiting, ignoring the *mrikro* who was pulling at his reins, trying to lead him back to the enclosure.

"*Vorakkar*, I take full responsibility for what happened," Danir said, his tone grim and tight. "I...I cannot express how relieved I am that she is..."

"She was still injured," I growled, my fists clenching at my sides. "I assigned you as her guard, Danir—do you know why? Because you are one of my best *darukkars* in the horde."

His eyes widened slightly. Then came his shame.

"And I would only trust her safety with those *I* trust," I told him. "If anything had happened to her tonight...if her wounds had been fatal...*vok!*"

Danir stood still, no doubt hearing the worry and fury in my voice. Very rarely did I lose my temper. Very rarely did those in my horde witness emotion from me. But if my father taught me anything, it was that a horde king needed to be cruel sometimes.

"You broke my trust tonight. After I trusted that you would protect her at all costs," I said, trying to keep my voice even. "That you would keep her *safe* when I was not here."

"I know, *Vorakkar*," came his low voice. "And I will accept any punishment you decide to give me. I never should have let her step out of the horde. If you wish to send me back to *Dothik*, I will go."

I was tempted.

I'd be lying if I said I wasn't tempted.

Because looking at him right now made me so *vokking* furious.

In the end, I said, "I will not send you back to *Dothik*."

A relieved breath escaped him—one he probably didn't mean for me to hear. He straightened.

"But I am removing you as her guard and dropping you in rank among the *darukkars*," I growled.

His face paled further, but he nodded. "I understand, *Vorakkar*."

I tilted my chin toward the *voliki*. "Go. Get out of my sight."

Danir didn't hesitate. He ducked inside the *mokkira's voliki*. I couldn't hear anything within, but I couldn't go back in quite yet. The frigid air stung my nostrils, froze my flesh, but it was welcome to the stifling heat inside.

I almost lost her tonight, I realized, tilting my head back toward the stars in the sky.

And it was something I never wanted to experience again.

"Go, Essir," I murmured late into the night. "I'll finish up here."

"*Nik*, you go, *Mokkira*," Essir replied. "I'll clean up. Rest."

I hesitated but only briefly. It was hours after we'd returned from the forest. My arm was throbbing though I'd taken a pain tonic. Since it didn't have *begalia* in it, it wouldn't work as effectively, but it still helped to dull the sharpest of the pain.

"*Kakkira vor,*" I told him. "You did well tonight."

He flushed with my praise, and I gave him a tired smile, seeing him spread out the mashed *adiri* on the workbench. We would keep the heat high in the *voliki* as it dried.

When I stepped from the *voliki*, I froze. Because Kiran was still there and I thought he'd left. Roon was gone, but Kiran was leaning against the *voliki*, his arms crossed over his chest. When he saw me, he didn't say anything. Instead, he swung me up into his arms as I gasped. He was careful of my left arm, however, being sure not to jar the tight bandages Essir had wrapped around the wound.

"Kiran," I whispered.

He didn't say anything as he strode through the quiet

encampment. His fur pelt was icy against me. He'd been standing outside the *voliki* all this time? In the cold?

My heart began to pound once we reached his *voliki*. I couldn't read him. For once, I had no idea what was running through his mind, and that made me nervous.

Inside, the fire was burning hot and the heat was welcome. A bath, still steaming, was in the corner, and food was laid out at the table. But Kiran didn't go toward the food.

Instead, he began to undress me carefully until I was naked and exposed before him in nothing more than my bandage. Afterward, he undressed himself too and brought us both to the bath. Though I kept my arm along the edge of the washing tub, I sighed as the heat enveloped me.

He had my back to his chest. He had me tucked between his broad, massive thighs. Safe. Warm. For the first time all night, I relaxed, feeling that bundle of tightness in my chest begin to unravel.

The only sounds in the *voliki* were the trickling water as he gently scrubbed at my flesh and the intermittent sparks that popped in the fire basin.

Licking my lips, I asked softly, "Are you angry with me?"

"*Lysi*," he rasped. "*Vokking* furious."

I bit my lip, guessing as much.

"In case it wasn't obvious, Maeva," he continued, "you have my *vokking* heart in your hands. *Lo kassiri tei.*"

I love you.

My breath whooshed out from my lungs. Unexpected tears pooled in my eyes.

How long have I wanted to hear those words from him? How long have I dreamed of it? I wondered.

"And ever since we were young, that love has taken many different forms. It's shifted and changed, but it has *never left*," he told me. "Not for a single moment."

And I knew exactly what he was trying to tell me. That

maybe he hadn't loved me in the way I wanted him to before…
but he loved me in that way now. He *had* always loved me.

"Remember when you jumped from the cliff?" he asked. Then he amended gruffly, "The first time."

Of course I did.

"You were furious with me then too."

"*Lysi*, because I'd been so *vokking* frightened!" he burst out, and I felt how hard his heart was pounding at my back. "I don't think you understood how much that day. Because that was the first moment when I realized that you had more power over me than *anyone*. Because when I saw you drop away from that cliff, it was the first moment when I was forced to imagine a life without you in it. And I couldn't, Maeva. *I couldn't.*"

Tears dripped down my cheeks when I heard the *rawness* in his voice.

"And tonight…*vok*," he cursed. "Tonight, I felt that same fear all over again. Only this time, it was so much worse."

I turned in his arms, shifting in his naked lap because I *needed* to see him. I *needed* to look into his eyes to know that he was all right.

"I'm sorry," I whispered, my eyes blurry with tears. "I'm so sorry, Kiran."

His nostrils flared, and his arms wrapped around me tighter. He wanted to crush me to him. I sensed that. But he was trying to be gentle with me because of my wound.

"It was foolish," I whispered, wanting him to understand. "And I'm angry with myself. I'm angry that I put myself *and* my guard in that position. I should've waited until you returned from the patrol. I realize that."

"Then why didn't you?" he growled softly.

"I remembered something. A story from our *mokkira*. I wanted to help Addie, and I think the *adiri* is the best way to. But it takes days to powder, and I fear that we are running out of time."

Kiran shook his head. "*Adiri* is useless. Why would—"

"For a Dakkari, perhaps," I told him. "But not for a human."

His nostrils flared.

"The *mokkira* told me a story a long time ago," I said. "About the first hybrid child, born shortly after the humans settled on Dakkar."

His brow furrowed. "That was over thirty years ago."

"*Lysi*," I murmured. "And if the story is true, then there is a hybrid female somewhere on Dakkar. The first. The first of many to come," I added, thinking of Addie, of the human queens who had already given birth.

In the back of my mind, I caught a flash of a thought. Of a child that Kiran and I could have. Together.

For once, I let that thought—that want—linger. And maybe Kiran saw it in my eyes because I felt his hands tighten on me.

Clearing my throat, I told him, "The *mokkira* told me that *adiri* was used during the birth. And I strongly believe that *begalia* is poisonous to humans, so I don't want to use it with Addie. I needed to find a different option."

Understanding dawned in his eyes, but I saw that Kiran wasn't pleased with it.

"You still risked your life, *seffi*, put yourself in danger."

"For a necessary reason," I told him, reaching out to touch his face, stroking my fingers over his high, cutting cheekbones. "But I know that I should have waited. I should've brought more guards with me. I can't change that now."

Kiran's shoulders sagged in the washing tub, and I watched as his eyes closed, as he took deep, even breaths as I stroked his face.

"Forgive me," I whispered, watching his eyes shift beneath his closed lids. Leaning forward, I pressed my lips to his. "*Hanniva*, Kiran. *Hanniva*."

A slow rumble vibrated his chest, strong and low.

Finally, his lips moved against mine, and relief sparked

inside me. The stitches on my wound tugged painfully when I moved my arms around his shoulders, sliding closer, but I paid them no mind. I could handle my own pain. I couldn't handle Kiran's, however.

"Forgive me," I whispered, my voice a little more breathless as his kiss made my head swim.

He deepened it briefly, moving that tongue against mine, nibbling at my mouth almost desperately. And even with my injury, I felt myself begin to respond, though he pulled away.

Leaning his forehead against mine, he rasped, "Promise me. Promise me that you will not do that again. Promise me you won't put yourself in danger like that again."

"I promise," I murmured, my tone somber. And with one exception, I'd never broken a promise to Kiran. He knew that. I knew that.

A deep growl emerged from his throat. Relieved. Some of his anger had drained away. The muscles in his shoulders began to loosen.

And maybe it wasn't the right time to bring it up, but I murmured, "About my guard..."

"*Nik, kalles,*" he growled. "My mind is made up."

My guard hadn't wanted to tell me what punishment Kiran had given him, but eventually I'd dragged it out of him as I checked him over. With the exception of a nasty blackened bruise all across his torso and a sprained leg from his fall, he was mostly unharmed, which brought me such relief.

"Then let's unmake it," I murmured.

His eyes sparked with sudden heat. "You think to convince me to see your way, *seffi?*"

"I can try," I suggested, pressing closer.

A roughened sound emerged from his throat. Between us, his cock was hardening, rising from the bath water.

"*Nik,* Maeva," he said, and I sensed the determination in his tone. "As much as I want to, you are injured. I will not hurt you further."

"You don't hurt me," I argued.

"I might. Sometimes I forget myself with you. I will not risk it when what you really need is rest to recover."

I sighed but knew he was right. The past few days had been...intense. Every moment we'd been alone, every chance we got—morning and night—he'd been between my thighs.

Going without him for a single night seemed excruciatingly long. Already I was dreading when he had to leave the horde in a couple days to make the journey east.

"How else can I convince you, then, to retract your punishment for my guard?" I asked softly. His eyes darkened. "Because short of throwing me over his shoulder, which I'm sure you wouldn't have liked either, he was trying to convince me to return to the horde the entire time. He kept saying how angry you'd be, and he was right. But I didn't listen. My mind was made up. You know how I am."

Kiran bit out a sharp sigh. He knew me better than anyone. He knew how stubborn I could be.

"He shouldn't be punished for this, Kiran," I added. "*Hanniva.* I want him as my guard. And I don't want his *darukkar* rank stripped away because of *my* mistake. He doesn't deserve that. He was trying to keep me safe."

With bated breath, I waited.

When the silence stretched, I added, "I promise to never leave the encampment again. Not unless it's with you or an entire horde of *darukkars, lysi?* Just don't take it out on him."

I saw when he broke.

I could almost read his thoughts, and they were something like, *You know I could never say* nik *to you.*

Because he'd never been able to.

I was his weakness. I was beginning to understand that. I was beginning to understand everything.

"If he puts you in danger again, I *will* send him back to *Dothik* next time. Do you understand?"

And I knew he was serious. He wouldn't change his decision for me again. This was the last time.

"*Kakkira vor,*" I breathed, tucking my head into the crook of his neck, leaning my cheek against his chest.

His sigh stirred my hair. Then I felt his hand stroke down my bare back, running over the scar across my shoulder.

Softly, he said, "You'll be the death of me, *rei kassiri.*"

My love.

And for once, those words didn't fill me with fear.

CHAPTER 44

"R in nekanevexi rei kakkiva, rei kassiri," came his husky, roughened voice. It seemed to thread down my spine, making my flesh tingle in its wake.

You ride my cock so well, my love, he'd told me.

It was two nights later, and Kiran had *finally* given in to my pleas for mating, though he'd still been worried about my healing arm.

A moan escaped my throat, breathy and full of need, as his hands dug into the cheeks of my buttocks, his claws pricking into my flesh. Using his grip, he brought me down harder as I rocked over him, rolling my hips desperately.

"*Ahhh!* Kiran," I breathed, my hands spanning his broad chest, curling into the scars there.

"Come for me, *seffi*," he ordered, snapping his hips up, perspiration dotting his flesh, his brow furrowed in concentration and pleasure.

So, so close, I knew. *Right there!*

"*Lysi*," I gasped. "*Lysi!*"

A sound came from outside, but I paid it no mind. Kiran's gaze flickered away from me, toward the *voliki's* entrance, but he groaned when I snapped my hips down hard over him.

Then I heard a voice, and I froze.

"*Mokkira.*"

For a moment, I was confused, my mind muddled with sex and pleasure and the enticing scent of Kiran. Usually when we were interrupted, it was because the *Vorakkar* was needed. Not *me*.

"*Mokkira*, you are needed at your *voliki*," came the hesitant voice again, no doubt knowing what Kiran and I were doing.

Vok.

I gasped out, "I'll be right there!"

Hearing my words, Kiran's hands gripped my buttocks tighter. As the footsteps hurried away, Kiran growled, "*Nik*, it can wait."

A breathless laugh rose from my throat even as disappointment crashed down on me. I slid off Kiran's cock, making him exhale sharply, his body slumping against the furs.

"You know it can't," I told him. "I have to go."

On trembling legs, I rose from the bed. My arm twinged from my healing wound when I tugged on my tunic. I'd put too much pressure on it, I knew. But with Kiran, I always forgot myself.

"*Maeva.*"

As I dressed hurriedly, I looked back at Kiran, my heart doubling its already rapid speed when I saw him there.

Magnificent male, I thought.

He was watching me, those golden eyes molten and smoldering in his lust. He was on his back, one hand cradling his head, the other moving toward his cock. His cock, which was still so hard and swollen, glistening with my own arousal and the beginnings of his seed.

I pulled on my trews just as he began to stroke his cock, his arm flexing.

For a moment I froze, regret curling in my belly. I wanted to watch him pleasure himself. I wanted to watch him *finish* himself. Between my own legs, I was throbbing, wet. I felt heavy with the ache of wanting him, of being denied my own orgasm when I'd been so close.

But I couldn't.

I had a duty to the horde, just as Kiran did.

Biting my lip, I hurriedly wrapped my furs around my shoulders and tugged on my boots. And because I couldn't help it, I rushed back to the bed where Kiran lay. Leaning over him, I kissed him, pouring my frustration and want into that kiss, and he licked at my tongue greedily. I heard his hand quicken over his cock.

"I'll be back later," I whispered, pulling away, catching his dark eyes.

Then I rushed out of the *voliki*, leaving him groaning behind me.

The slap of the icy air helped clear the fog in my mind, and I hurried through the encampment, running to make up for lost time.

Kiran had to leave in the morning for the East Lands. Self-ishly, I wished I could be back in bed with him, in his warm *voliki* and furs, because a part of me missed him already...and he hadn't even gone yet.

When my *voliki* came into view, my stomach dropped. Because Gabe was pacing outside it. And just like that, my desire was replaced by determination, mingled with a little bit of trepidation.

"Is it Addie?" I asked quickly, rushing past him.

"Yes," he replied.

"Where's Essir?" I asked.

"I don't know," he said, his voice pinched with panic.

"Go find him for me. Quickly. *Hanniva!*"

Gabe nodded and took off as I ducked inside the *voliki*.

Addie was hunched over and trying to walk around the *voliki*. Jurin, her mate, was hovering at her side, a hand on her arm. My heart broke a little at the helplessness on his face, but he looked relieved when he saw me.

"What's wrong, Addie?" I asked quietly, approaching them both.

"I—I think the baby is coming," she gasped out, her teeth gritted in pain.

My lips pressed together, my eyes immediately flickering to the drying *udlrl* still on the workbench. It had been two days since I went to retrieve it in the forest, since the *polkunu* had attacked us.

The *adiri* wasn't ready. It would be another couple days before it could be powdered. But we were out of time.

"Let me look at you, *lysi*?" I murmured. With Jurin's help, we steered her over to the table, and she cried out, her body tightening, her eyes squeezed in pain. I quickly washed my hands in the water basin, rubbing dried *honira* over them before I returned to Addie.

Placing my hands over her belly, I pressed deeply. Then I crouched, lifting her dress.

"I need to check inside, *lysi*?" I murmured quietly to her.

She nodded, breathing deeply.

I pushed inside her as gently as possible, reaching toward her womb. When I felt the lining, my brow furrowed.

"How long has she been in pain?" I asked Jurin.

Guilt crossed his expression when I looked at him, as I pulled my fingers away from Addie and went to wash again. "She says since earlier in the evening. But she..."

"I didn't tell him," Addie gritted out. "I thought it was fine. I felt the contractions yesterday, remember?"

Lysi, Addie had come in early in the afternoon, though her womb hadn't started to open yet.

"But tonight they got worse," she said, panting, in between her contractions.

Essir raced inside the tent, huffing and out of breath. His eyes widened when he saw Addie and Jurin.

"Is it time?" he asked me. He'd never seen or experienced a baby's birth before. The last *mokkira* had done them alone.

Addie turned her gaze on me, and I met her eyes.

"*Lysi*, I believe so."

My words sparked fear in her gaze. I would be lying if I said I didn't feel fear myself, but I wouldn't show her it.

Smiling, I squeezed her hand and helped her up from the table. "Keep moving. Some females find squatting helpful."

"How long until the baby comes?" Jurin asked, his expression suddenly frantic, taking Addie's hand.

"It's hard to say," I told him. Especially since I'd never delivered a hybrid child before. "It could be soon. It could take all night or even into the morning."

The mother was human, not Dakkari. I didn't know if humans tended to have shorter or longer labors. Sometimes it was strange, not knowing much about my own race.

Turning back to Addie, I said, "Don't exert yourself too much. Save your strength because you'll need it. I'll have furs brought in so you can lie down if you need to."

"Thank you, Maeva," Addie said quietly.

Poking my head outside the *voliki*, I saw Gabe still continuing to pace, though Hinna had arrived as well and seemed to be keeping him company. The two of them had been close the past week. It wasn't the first time I wondered if something would become of them.

"She should be delivering tonight," I told them. "But I would like to keep the *voliki* clear. Only her and her mate, *lysi*? Go rest."

Gabe hesitated.

"You can come by to check on her, I promise," I assured him.

Finally, Gabe nodded, and I watched him begrudgingly leave with Hinna, disappearing from view. When I came back inside, I told Essir, "Get a mound of furs, a lot of clean water, and clean cloths, *lysi*? I'll start boiling the water we have."

"*Lysi, Mokkira,*" Essir said quietly.

Watching him leave, I knew it would be a long night.

CHAPTER 45

"Addie, push," I urged, my own brow dotted in sweat. "You need to push now! *Hanniva!*"

Dread pinched my belly, but I tried to keep calm. Before me, Addie was lying down on a bed of furs I'd had brought in for her. Jurin was cradling her between his legs, and he was constantly wiping away the sweat on her forehead with a cool cloth. His expression was tight and drawn. Scared, I knew, though he was trying to be strong for her.

As for Addie, she was pale, trembling...and nearing exhaustion quickly. Blood covered my hands. She'd just begun bleeding. And I couldn't even see the baby yet.

It was the early hours of morning, nearing dawn I knew. Next to me, Essir was still and quiet. He'd been a steady presence throughout all of this and did whatever I needed of him without question.

Addie's next contraction came, and her body seized up.

"Push," I pleaded.

She cried out, squeezing her eyes shut, and bore down.

"That's it, Addie," I breathed, finally seeing the head emerge. "I can see the baby."

"Really?" she rasped, her voice husky from her cries. Though she was fading, my words seemed to give her renewed strength.

"*Lysi*," I murmured, wiping at my forehead. "You're so close. I need you to be strong. Just for a little while longer."

She nodded, resting her head against Jurin's chest, breathing in deep, resting in between the contractions. She looked up at her mate, who murmured words of love and praise down to her, words that made tears well up in her eyes.

"You'll hold our child soon, *kassi*," Jurin murmured, stroking his wide palm down her small face. "*Lysi?*"

"*Lysi*," Addie whispered, tears falling down her cheeks. Then her body tensed. Jurin's face drew tight, and I saw helplessness on it. A loud, pained cry fell from her lips.

"Again," I murmured.

Addie pushed, a silent scream on her lips. Then she fell limp, her breath ragged.

"I—I c-can't," she breathed. She closed her eyes. "I need to rest. I need..."

"Addie," I called out, my tone sharp. "Addie, you need to stay awake."

Jurin murmured something down to her, something I didn't hear. He roused her, and she blinked up at him, her lids heavy. She was too pale. She'd already lost a lot of blood, and I feared she'd lose much more by the end of this.

"I'm so dizzy," she whispered, shivering even though it was blazing hot in the *voliki* and she was sweating.

Her next contraction came swiftly and without mercy.

"Push!"

Addie bore down again, teeth gritting together, a low scream emerging from her throat.

Relief pierced me when the baby's head pushed forward, and I worked quickly, guiding the head through, reaching inside, stretching Addie further to gently guide the shoulders out.

"One more," I urged, my eyes flashing up to meet hers. "Quickly!"

With one last cry, she gave the last of her strength. And it was enough.

The baby slid out easily with my pull. Into my waiting hands.

Addie was crying and exhausted. The little thing in my hands looked like any other Dakkari child I'd ever delivered. Wrinkly and dark, with a scrunched up face and a budding tail. But there was a softness in the features. More human than Dakkari.

Gently, I patted the baby's chest, rubbing.

After a few breathless moments, I heard the baby gasp.

Then a strong cry filled the *voliki*, bright and relieving.

"You did it, Addie," I told her, tears pricking my eyes. "And she's beautiful."

"A girl," Addie breathed, head lolling though she tried to hold it up. "Let me see her."

I nodded. Motioning to Essir, I watched as he cut the cord leading from the baby's abdomen, and then I placed her in her mother's arms.

It was one of my favorite things in the world. Watching a mother hold her child for the first time. Jurin pressed his lips to Addie's forehead, his expression awed as he looked down at his daughter. As for Addie, her eyes never left her child.

I spied movement near the entrance, and to my surprise, I saw Kiran there, standing on the outskirts of the *voliki*. My lips parted, wondering how long he'd been there. He listened to the baby's cry—the newest child of his horde—but his eyes never left me. And with that gaze, I felt my own strength return to me. Though it was early, he was here. And I knew it was for me.

"*Mokkira,*" came Essir's quiet voice.

Something in his tone made me break Kiran's gaze and look down.

My belly pinched. Swallowing, I saw the blood. I saw the afterbirth push out. Addie was so wrapped up in her baby that I doubted she even felt it. But it was the continued flow of blood that worried me. It was the excess of it that was abnormal, and it was everything that I'd feared.

Rising from my place, I hurried over to my cabinet and pulled it open. My eyes landed on the *begalia* extract, my fingers curling around it.

But then I hesitated. She was too weak. She could barely keep her eyes open, could barely hold herself up. The labor had cost her much. The *begalia* would only take more. And this time, it might take her life. She might not have the strength to fight the poison, even if it helped stop the bleeding.

But if I didn't use it...I risked her bleeding out.

My eyes landed on the *adiri*, the mashed fungus still in the process of drying.

"What's wrong?" Jurin's voice came, sensing something that his mate didn't. In the corner, I saw Kiran straighten.

At her mate's voice, Addie looked at me. "Maeva?" she asked, her voice trembling.

I unstoppered the *begalia,* but my hand hesitated before pouring it over a clean cloth.

"*Vok,*" I whispered.

Nik, I thought. *This isn't right.*

My gut was telling me that this *wasn't right.*

Perhaps *Kakkari* was.

And I needed to trust my instincts. I needed to trust *her.*

With a soft, frustrated growl of my own, I flung the *begalia* back into the cabinet and went to the *adiri.* It wasn't ready, but it would have to be.

"Clean water," I told Essir, and he immediately went into action, bringing me a basin of it.

"Maeva?" Addie asked again, fear in her voice.

I mixed the *adiri* quickly in the water, though I was

guessing how much to dilute it. Then I dropped clean cloths inside the basin—cloths I would need to pack into Addie's womb—and Essir brought it over to the furs, setting it down.

I didn't have much time.

"You're bleeding, Addie," I told her quietly, a strange calmness coming over me. "I'm going to try to stop it."

"And will you be able to?" Jurin asked, tone pinched and tight, over his daughter's cries.

My *mokkira* had always taught me to never to give false hope as a healer. Because the will of Kakkari was always an unknown.

But right then, I felt *knowing* spread within me. I felt the goddess's presence. I felt her will.

My eyes went to Kiran. His expression was darkened with worry, his shoulders tense, but he stayed out of my way. He trusted me. He had faith in me. Even from the beginning.

"I will," I told Jurin, nodding at the *darukkar*. My eyes went to Addie, gaze bright and glassy. "I know this will work. It will be painful. But I just need you to trust me. *Lysi?*"

"I do," she whispered.

I nodded.

Then I went to work.

Just as dawn broke over Dakkar, I stumbled from the *voliki*.

Dragging in lungfuls of icy, stinging air, I let it replenish me. I'd left my furs inside. All I was wearing were my trews and my bloodied tunic. Red blood. Just like mine. Not black like a Dakkari's.

My skin felt overheated, but the cold season cooled it quickly and rapidly.

Tilting my head back toward the sky, which was just lightening with streaks of blue and purple, I whispered, "Kakkari, *kakkira vor. Kakkira vor.*"

I was so exhausted that my eyelids were threatening to droop, though I was not as exhausted as Addie. The new mother was inside, sleeping soundly after a seemingly never-ending night. In her arms was her daughter. And Addie herself was in the arms of her mate, who was watching over both of them as they rested.

The *adiri*...it had worked. I had stopped the bleeding. It had likely saved Addie's life.

And right then I knew that the stories of the first hybrid female were true. I wondered about her. I wondered what had happened to her.

A sense of peace descended over my shoulders, as if Kakkari heard me and my thanks.

And right then, under that icy sunrise in the dawn of a new day over Dakkar, I had a pure flash of clarity.

My lips parted.

And I realized that—in that moment—I was exactly where I was supposed to be. I was exactly where Kakkari had always meant for me to be...where I'd always needed to be.

Destiny, I knew.

I found immense comfort in that. I found immense purpose in that. I found a sense of *place* and *belonging* in that realization.

"*Seffi,*" came Kiran's quiet, steady voice.

When I turned, I saw him approaching me, coming from the front of the encampment. In his hands was a large tray of food, covered in thick hide to keep it warm.

My chest squeezed at the sight, and I tilted my face up to him when he stepped close.

"I broukht you food," he murmured. "You should eat, to regain your strength. You must be starving."

"That's not your duty, *Vorakkar*," I teased softly.

His expression softened.

"Of course it is," he said. "It is my duty to take care of *you*. However I can."

My breath hitched.

He set the tray down on the ground and came closer, as if he couldn't stop himself from touching me. Even though my tunic was covered in blood, he dragged me into his arms. He'd been a quiet presence during the labor and in the aftermath, when my hands and arms were soaked in blood that wasn't my own. For a moment, I'd feared I wouldn't be able to save Addie.

"You were incredible, *seffi*," he murmured in my ear, embracing me hard. It was exactly what I needed.

His praise made my throat tighten, made tears well in my eyes.

And because I could tell no one else, I told him.

"I thought I would fail, Kiran," I admitted. "I thought I would watch her die. I thought I would have to look into Jurin's eyes and tell him that I couldn't save her, that their child would never know her."

That had been my worst fear. Even remembering that moment made agony burst in my chest. It had been the most difficult delivery I'd ever experienced.

"But she didn't, *seffi*," he said quietly. "She didn't. The *adiri* saved her life. *You* saved her life because you trusted yourself and your abilities as a healer. *Lysi?*"

I blew out a long breath.

"I'm proud that I can call you the *mokkira* of my horde, Maeva. Because I believe I have the best one on all of Dakkar."

Pulling back to look up at him, I studied him, silhouetted against the dawn sky. His sharp features were so familiar to me —and always had been. Those golden eyes met mine and made my chest warm and loosen.

That feeling washed over me again. That sense of belonging.

Like I was right where I was meant to be...in his arms. With Kiran, in his horde.

And I knew right then that I was falling in love with him. *Back* in love with him. Fast and hard.

Maybe it was the exhaustion. Or maybe it was the happiness and joy on Addie's face when she first held her daughter. Or maybe it was because Kiran had stayed in the *voliki* all night, silently giving me strength, like he knew I needed it.

But this morning, I didn't try to fight it. I let it happen.

I felt my heart burst with that old, deep love I remembered... only now, it somehow felt hopeful and new.

"Maeva," he murmured, brow furrowing, seeing something in my gaze. His hand stroked down my cheek. "What is it?"

I blew out a breath and gave him a small, wavering smile.

"I'll miss you" was what I told him. Because he would be leaving soon. Just this morning. He was planning to leave with the dawn. He should've been gone already.

He pulled me back into an embrace, and I buried my face in his chest, breathing him in deeply. I was certain I smelled like sweat and blood and afterbirth—but Kiran didn't seem to mind.

"Be careful," I pleaded with him.

"Worried for me, *seffi*?" he teased gently.

"*Lysi,*" I replied, seeing no reason to lie.

His arms tightened around me. His lips pressed into my hair on the top of my head.

"I'll come back to you soon, Maeva. Never worry about that."

CHAPTER 46

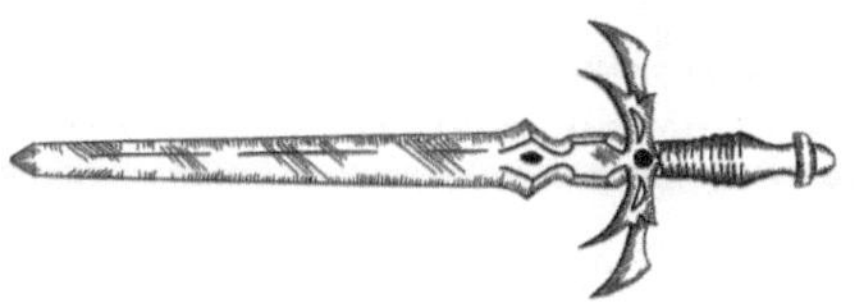

The East Lands were quiet. All I could hear was the irregular, roughened pants of Roon and the crunch of his hoofed talons as they crunched into the dry, rocky, crumbling earth.

It was eerie.

The air seemed electrified, crackling and tight. Like one of Drukkar's storms was coming, bringing with it explosive lightning and torrential rains.

But it wasn't the season for that.

Perhaps most strangely of all...the frost hadn't reached the East Lands. The icy ground had cleared suddenly as I navigated my way through the Blood Forest, towering high with *irruna* trees, all gangly limbs and rough, bleeding bark.

The trees should've been frozen over, the ground covered in frost, the bleeding sap from the trees momentarily still. Instead, the tree blood covered the forest floor, thickening around Roon's talons, making my poor beast irritable.

As we finally broke out from the forest, the hush in the air seemed more obvious. We ventured toward Rath Kitala's horde, which lay somewhere east of the Dead Mountain, closest to the river pass of Konilo.

I'd encountered no beasts along the way. Not a single soul, though I usually passed a messenger or two from *Dothik* on such journeys. Not a *Vorakkar* either, though our hordes lay in different directions.

It had been three days since I'd left my horde, since I'd left Maeva. I had been loath to leave, especially when I saw her in such a state after Addie's birth. But I knew Maeva. She was strong. She could handle anything in my absence, I had no doubt about that.

Still, I missed her. Craved her. I marveled that I had gone nearly nine years without her, without waking to her in my furs, without touching her whenever I pleased, without seeing that smile or hearing that laugh I'd longed for.

Those nine years, I'd been merely existing. Waiting.

I could wait a few days more to see her again. Though it would be the purest form of pain and longing and frustration.

It took me the rest of the afternoon to reach Rath Kitala's horde. When I saw the towering gates, my brow raised. They were perhaps even higher and stronger than mine, and yet I hadn't encountered a single creature on my journey that would threaten the horde. It was as if the land was emptied of game, of life.

Darukkar calls rang up in the air when they saw me approach. I saw the gates open.

Urging Roon into a gentle run, we made for the horde.

Only, just as I reached the entrance, I saw the *Vorakkar* of Rath Kitala and the *Vorakkar* of Rath Drokka step out to meet me.

At Rath Drokka's side was a small human female with white hair, carrying a bundle of something in her arms.

The white-haired sorceress, I knew. The one who had nearly brought the Dead Mountain down with her rumored power. And Rath Drokka's, the Mad Horde King, wife and queen. The one I had last seen in *Dothik*, when the *Dothikkar's* guards had captured her after she'd broken into the capital.

I pulled Roon up short when the three of them stepped out to meet me.

"Okkili," Rath Kitala murmured, inclining his head but never breaking my gaze. "Any troubles on the journey?"

"*Nik,*" I replied, quieting Roon when he began to stomp. "What in Kakkari's name has happened here? The frost covers the rest of Dakkar, and yet there is not a single indication of it here."

"That is what Rath Drokka said," Kitala murmured, cutting his gaze to the male at his side.

When I met Rath Drokka's eyes, his reddened gaze was mistrustful and hardened. And I couldn't help but notice that when I looked to his female, a low growl built up in his throat, his arm curling around her waist.

"Don't worry, Drokka," I rasped, stilling Roon again, who was no doubt sensing the sudden tension between us. It was always like this when *Vorakkar* came together. "I have already chosen a queen for myself. I am merely curious about yours, for I have heard the stories."

Drokka's jaw tightened and pulsed. However, whatever he heard in my voice made his grip loosen on his female. The large bundle in her arms began to struggle, and my gaze sharpened on it.

A cry filled the air, strong and robust.

I'd known the queen was pregnant with Drokka's child, but what I hadn't expected was for her to already have given birth. Though, it made sense, I realized. It had been nearly half a year since the events of the Dead Mountain. I'd just...lost track of time.

"My congratulations on your offspring, *Morakkari,*" I murmured to her in the universal tongue, catching sight of not one but *two* hybrid children squirming and kicking in her arms.

Twins were rare on Dakkar. Extremely rare.

The human queen was a lithe thing, and the half-Dakkari children were strong...but she was stronger than she looked and calmed them with ease.

"*Kakkira vor, Vorakkar*," she replied. Rath Drokka took the bundled twins from her, and the children immediately settled in their father's arms. "We don't have much time this evening if you wish to see the mist. The sun seems to set quicker here in the East."

They wanted to take me to see it now?

"Leave your *pyroki* here," Rath Kitala rasped.

"Why?" I asked. "Surely it would be a faster journey than on foot."

"Trust me," he murmured. "I'll have my *mrikro* see that he is well cared for."

"Very well," I murmured, dismounting from Roon. Kitala motioned for a *darukkar* hovering nearby, who took the reins from my grip, and I watched a reluctant Roon being led away, though he craned his neck to look at me until he couldn't anymore.

The human queen's lips were quirked as she watched the exchange. "Even still, I am always amazed by a *pyroki's* loyalty and love."

"He was born of my mother's *pyroki*. I have raised him since," I told her. Raised him with Maeva. We were both there when he was born.

She smiled, nodding. "Shall we go?"

"*Nik, leikavi*," Drokka growled. "You will stay."

"I will go," she said calmly, reaching out to touch his forearm. "I need to feel how much it has grown. You know that, my love."

My brow furrowed.

How much it has grown?

"Where are Rath Tuviri and the others?"

"On their way," Kitala replied, and I watched as Drokka handed his offspring off begrudgingly to a waiting *piki*, watched as the human queen pressed kisses to her children's round faces. "Rath Rowin arrived this morning, but he is resting. He has been traveling mercilessly the past week, has hardly slept."

I nodded and fell into step with the *Vorakkar*. Rath Drokka and his wife trailed behind us as we began to head east of the horde on foot.

"I know you probably wish to rest as well," Kitala added. "But I wanted you to see what we face."

"The sooner I can return to my horde, the better," I told him honestly.

Kitala huffed out a small breath. "To this new queen, no doubt."

I grunted. "She has not agreed yet."

"Intriguing. I like her already," Kitala murmured before barking out a small laugh. "How that must fester for someone like you."

Ignoring his dig, I rolled my neck, feeling the muscles pinch there. "Where is your own queen, Kitala?"

He sobered. He flashed me a quick look. "Safe in the horde. You will meet her later. But she is pregnant with our second child, and I want her nowhere near *this*."

Whatever *this* was…I could see how uneasy it was making the *Vorakkar*. The one most at ease seemed to be Drokka's queen.

"What is your chosen queen like?" came her voice from behind us. "I do love stories."

Kitala's breath huffed from his nostrils. I knew he would prefer to talk about the mist now that I'd arrived, but I wouldn't deny the *Morakkari* her innocent request. There would be time for talk and strategy later.

"She is the *mokkira* to my horde," I told her. "An accomplished healer. Intelligent and strong. She is…"

How to even describe her? I didn't know.

"She was my friend. For a long time," I finally said. Then I added, catching the human queen's gaze when she walked next to me with Rath Drokka flanking her, "She is human, like you."

Surprise went through her gaze, and Kitala made a sound next to me.

"She is?" the queen asked, her brow furrowing. "Is she one of the human females from the Dead Mountain that your horde took in?"

"*Nik*," I murmured. Kitala flashed me another long look, assessing. Clearing my dry throat, I told them, "She lived in my father's *saruk*. One of my father's hunters found her abandoned in a forest when she was a child. That hunter took her in with his wife and daughter, raised her as his own. I grew up with her. Like I said, I've known her a long time. We were…close."

"How romantic," the human queen said softly, smiling.

"Did the *Dothikkar* know about her being raised in the *saruk*?" Kitala asked, his brow still furrowed.

I sobered, casting him a sharp look. "*Nik*. And if you breathe a word about it to anyone, I will gladly cut your *deva* from your body and shove them down your throat."

Drokka barked out a loud, raucous laugh, tossing his head back. His wife put a hand on his arm, sighing.

To me, Drokka said, "Maybe I can be convinced to like you after all, Okkili."

"*Kakkira vor*," I said, sarcasm laced heavily in my tone. "I would be most honored."

Drokka continued to laugh. Mad Horde King, indeed.

The silence afterward was tense, though mostly between Kitala and myself. Rath Tuviri wasn't here to make peace between the *Vorakkar*. He'd always been the most…*calm* of us all.

"Through here," Rath Kitala murmured, cutting through a narrow passageway of tall rocks and boulders. The East Lands were littered with small mountains like these. "This leads to the ridge of the Dead Lands. You can see the Dead Valley below. You'll be able to see the fog."

"The *pyrokis* could have made it through here," I said, frowning. The passageway was wide enough for two *pyrokis* to pass side by side.

Kitala shook his head, taking the lead ahead of us all. Over his shoulder, he said, "Any creature that passes close to the fog...it tires them. Exhausts them. It takes days for them to recover their strength. The first time I came to see the fog after a report from my scout, I nearly had to drag my own *pyroki* back to the horde."

Grimly, I thought of the *thesper* that had returned to my horde after coming from Rath Kitala's. It had flown itself into the ground, crashing just outside the gates. And it had taken days for the poor flying beast to recover.

"And what about us?" I asked. "We are creatures of Kakkari, after all."

"We feel it as well, though perhaps not as strongly," he told me. "Still, we will stay as far away as possible. Though Drokka and his queen do not feel its effects as we do."

I frowned, casting a look over my shoulder at the both of them. "Why not?"

The white-haired queen paused, looking over at her husband.

"Tell him," Kitala ordered. And I saw the way his order made Rath Drokka bristle and scowl. His expression calmed again when his mate stroked her hand down his arm.

"I have always possessed..." the queen started before licking her lips, "a power. One I cannot describe. I believe I was born with it, for whatever reason."

"And this power is how you harnessed Kakkari's heartstone under the Dead Mountain?" I asked.

She hesitated. "Yes. Though it left me afterward. It is only now beginning to return."

My brow furrowed, and then I looked to Drokka. "And what of you?"

Drokka scowled at me.

His wife sighed and then told me, "He has had a gift too. All his life."

Drokka bit out a sharp laugh. "I would not call it a gift."

"What is it?" I asked.

Drokka looked me right in the eyes, grinning. "I can see the dead."

Somehow...those strange, jarring words didn't surprise me.

"I can speak with them. And they can speak back."

I swallowed, turning around to face forward, seeing the end of the passageway beginning to loom.

"That is why we believe that this fog is somehow tied to Kakkari's own power. We have a portion of her power, and because of that, we are immune to this fog," the human queen murmured quietly. "Or ...or maybe I unleashed something that I shouldn't have."

I heard a guilt in her voice. A worry.

"*Leikavi,*" Drokka murmured, his voice softening. "You know that's not true. The fog only just appeared. It has been many moon cycles since the heartstone. Enough time for our children to be born."

A shuddering sigh escaped her.

Silence fell once more as I processed their words. There had been recorded histories and accounts of Dakkari who possessed gifts from Kakkari. I was not surprised by that, though many believed that the tales were made up, that they were lies.

Our booted feet crunched over the dry, rocky gravel of the

East Lands. The end of the passageway was growing nearer and nearer.

"We're here," Kitala announced quietly. "Come see for yourself, Okkili."

The passageway led to a wide ledge that overlooked the Dead Lands below. The cliff we were on was high up, giving an unparalleled view of the valley. The sun was sinking in the sky, casting golden swirls and glittering streaks across it.

Ordinarily, it would have been a breathtaking view.

Only now, it stole my breath for an entirely different reason.

The red fog I'd heard so much of was dense. So dense that it seemed like a thick blanket shrouding the land from sight. I couldn't see the Dead Mountain. It covered that high peak in its entirety, swallowing it up like a hungry beast.

The Dead Valley was *erased*. Gone. The forests beyond it were not visible. The craggy outcroppings of the pillars to the east—where the *polkunu* nested—had vanished from sight. The land was quiet. *Dead.* Not even a rustle of wind could be felt.

My chest tightened, my nostrils flaring.

"Now you see," Rath Kitala grunted, just as Drokka's queen stepped forward to the edge of the ledge, "what we face."

I watched as she closed her eyes. I heard her long, slow breath.

After several quiet moments, something strange prickled my skin. It made my scalp tingle. I saw her long hair move, though there was no breeze. I heard a humming begin to buzz in my ears.

It went on and on, until that humming sound made my jaw tighten and clench.

Then, all at once, it stopped. The human queen turned and opened her eyes. For a moment, those violet eyes flashed a bright blue and then the sudden color faded.

"It's grown," she said slowly, her voice calm and even. "Not by a lot. But still, it extends a little every day. Its reach is spreading."

"*Vok*," Kitala cursed, his fist clenching at his sides, looking over the vast fog with a scowl, as if he could glare it into submission.

"We need to send for the priestesses of the North," I murmured, my eyes raking over the reddened mist.

"That was what Rath Rowin suggested, though we thought it would be best to discuss it with the others first," Kitala replied.

"The priestesses won't come, even if we send for them," Drokka argued. "They're forbidden to leave their temple."

"They will make an exception for this," his queen replied. "Surely, they must. Maybe they know what this is. Or what can be done about it."

Fear burrowed its way into my chest the longer I looked at the fog. I had...I had *hoped* that the stories of it had been exaggerated in Kitala's messages, though I knew better. He was a good *Vorakkar*, a chosen protector of Dakkar like us all. He wouldn't lie about this.

When I met Kitala's eyes, I was certain he saw the grim trepidation in my gaze. His own lips pressed together, and he nodded once, as if to tell me he felt the same.

"The priestesses must come," I said quietly. "Or else I fear we are all in danger."

CHAPTER 47

The week that passed since Kiran's departure was long and excruciatingly slow.

It was the early weeks of the frost, which hadn't yet thickened and hardened across Dakkar. Soon, however, it would be so frigid that merely walking from the warm safety of one *voliki* to another would become a daily chore. Dakkari seemed more immune to the cold than humans, something I'd always been jealous of, especially since the frost had always kept me inside, away from my runs, away from the fresh air.

In Kiran's absence, I filled my days in the *mokkira's voliki* with Essir and Hinna—and, more often than not, Gabe. Twice a day, I checked in on Addie and the baby to ensure that she had not begun bleeding again, though the *adiri* seemed to do its job perfectly.

A week out from her labor, I was confident that her recovery would be smooth, something I thanked Kakkari for every single day.

It didn't stop the nightmares, however. The terrible thoughts that somehow wiggled into my mind as I slept of a reality where Addie had died beneath my hands, of a reality where her baby would grow up without a mother, just as she had.

The relief when I woke, gasping for air, was so profound that it almost brought me to tears. The dreams seemed to be tapering off, however. And I knew that if Kiran slept beside me, they would be more manageable. But there was no indication of his return, no *thespers* from the hordes of the East, and no sign of Roon bringing his master home.

"This is very good," I praised quietly, studying the *pova* potion that Essir had made in its entirety, tilting the small, dark bottle toward the light of the fire. The contents were thick but silky. There were no lingering remnants of *pova* root. The way the potion clung to the sides of the bottle before sliding down was a good indication that Essir had properly boiled, simmered, and thickened the mixture. "*Excellent.*"

Essir flushed with my praise. My apprentice might not have been confident enough to suture wounds—or deliver offspring—quite yet but he had a natural talent for potions and medicines. The former would come with time and experience.

Gabe was helping Hinna wash and dry cloths on the far workbench. I saw the way Gabe smiled at the Dakkari female, reaching out to touch her arm, murmuring something low that no one but they could hear.

In the last week, Essir had seemed resigned to the fact that Hinna would never see him as more than a friend. He'd listened as Hinna giggled at Gabe's jokes and watched when she helped Gabe brush lingering frost from his hair whenever they came in from the outside, letting her touch linger. Her eyes glowed whenever she looked at him.

I'd asked Essir earlier if Gabe's presence was a distraction, if he would rather that I send him away. Because *he* was my apprentice, not Gabe, and his well-being was important to me. Though Gabe had been a great help around the *voliki* now that he had retired from the crops for the frost, if Essir asked it of me, I would send him away to another task without question, though it would no doubt disappoint Hinna.

But Essir had told me quietly that he was thankful Gabe helped Hinna, thankful he helped us all. He asked me not to send him away, though he gave no further explanation. I didn't bring it up again.

"We will need a healthy stock of *pova* through the frost. Especially once hunting season begins again," I told Essir, handing the bottled potion back to him. "You should start on the next batch. And after the frost, I will teach you how to make a potion for expecting mothers to help with their nausea. We will need much of that, but I need to procure more *hakin* blooms first. I usually get them from hordes that come down from the North."

His face drew into an expression of...tentative hope.

"So you mean to stay with the horde after the frost?" he asked quietly.

I stilled, my eyes flashing up to his in surprise.

I hadn't even realized I'd said that.

Someone ducked under the *voliki* entrance. It was Kiran's *pujerak*, I saw. I frowned when his eyes sharpened on me and he strode forward.

"*Mokkira.*"

A heavy sheet of ice hung from the tips of the furs around his shoulders, and for a moment, anticipation and excitement went through me.

I met him halfway. "Has the *Vorakkar* returned?"

My belly sank briefly when he shook his head. "*Nik.* But a *thesper* came for you."

My brow furrowed in confusion. "From the *Vorakkar*?"

He shook his head again and held out a frosted piece of hide to me, tied together tightly. "*Nik,* from the *saruk* of Rath Okkili. The *thesper* had a red string tied to its leg."

Which meant it was an urgent message.

My heartbeat picked up, and I snatched the hide from his hands, untying it to reveal a slim, rolled, slightly damp parchment underneath.

My breath became shallow. An urgent message—which couldn't be anything good.

Was it *Pattar*? Or was it Laru? Or Rasik? Nevir?

Trying to calm the panic, I was careful to unroll the message, not wanting to tear it in its state. I sensed that four pairs of eyes were on me—Essir, Hinna, Gabe, and the *pujerak*—but I paid them no mind.

The ink was blurred, but I read:

Father was injured in an attack on the saruk. *Many were injured, but we are safe now. Come if you can, but be careful on the journey. I will watch for you.*

I recognized Laru's script easily. And as I read the message a second time over, my lungs felt so tight I couldn't breathe.

It sounded like my voice was millions of lightyears away when I murmured, dazed, "My father has been injured. There was an attack on the *saruk*."

I felt a touch on my arm. When I looked up, I saw it was Hinna, her expression sympathetic and gentle. I felt tears prick my eyes. Because I knew that Laru wouldn't write to me unless he'd been seriously injured. She wouldn't have me risk the journey during the frost unless she knew that he was in danger.

"An attack?" the *pujerak* said, his voice hardening. "From what?"

"She doesn't say," I whispered, my eyes tracking around the *voliki* silently.

A stab to my chest came, followed by the memory of grief. The memory of loss. Was my father dying?

"I will help you pack supplies for the journey, *lysi*?" Hinna murmured quietly.

Her words made me snap out of the stupor I was in. "I can't leave."

"*Mokkira*," Essir murmured quietly.

"Addie just gave birth. What if there are other complications? What if another child comes early? I—I have a duty to the horde. I can't...I can't..." I tried, feeling something in my *soul* break. And with it came the tears. "Oh Kakkari," I whispered.

And I'd promised Kiran that I would never leave the safety of the gates without him or a group of *darukkars* as protection. I'd seen how shaken and frightened he'd been when I'd encountered the *polkunu*. I couldn't do that to him again.

But if I didn't go...I might never see my father again.

Duty or family?

Family.

Always.

I closed my eyes, my fist curling around the note.

What had I been thinking?

"I can watch over Addie," Essir murmured. "You told me what we can expect and what to do if complications arise. But it has been a week already and she is stable. The child is healthy."

I bit my lip. "I could be gone for a week, maybe more. I—I just...I—"

Essir reached out to squeeze my wrist, catching my gaze. "I can do this, *Mokkira*." His expression was serious and sober. "You taught me how to stitch wounds. I know to pack *runiri* in deeper ones. We have a full stock of medicines and potions that will last us well through the frost. And there are no other females that are close to giving birth for another moon cycle at least. There is time."

I took in a deep breath before exhaling slowly, meeting his gaze.

"Let me do this, *Mokkira*. I know I can. Go to your father and be with him. Because if anyone can heal him, it will be you," Essir finished.

With those words, I felt hope rise. I saw that Essir believed that, truly.

What if...what if I can help him? I thought.

I could look after him day and night. If there had been an attack on the *saruk*, the *mokkira* and his healers would have their hands full. I could help where needed, but my priority would be seeing my father well.

That was enough reason to go.

I knew my decision.

"*Kakkira vor,*" I murmured quietly, reaching out to take Essir's hand.

"It will be my honor, *Mokkira.*"

"I'll run ahead to get you rations from the *bikkus,*" Hinna said hurriedly.

The *pujerak* reached out to take my shoulder, stilling me when I tried to reach for my furs.

"He would not want you without the horde's protection," he growled. "He would have my head for it."

I met his gaze. Guilt and regret swarmed my veins because I knew that I would need to break my promise to Kiran.

"I need a *pyroki,*" I told him. "Will you allow me one?"

His jaw shifted and clenched. Whatever he saw in my eyes —my determination, my fear, my resolve—made his hand tighten.

"*Kalles...*" he rasped, shaking his head. "*Vok.* He will never forgive me for this."

"He knows me," I argued, feeling the tight pinch of time pricking my skin. I needed to leave soon. And I would do it with or without the *pujerak's* help. "He knows that once I make up my mind I will not be swayed from it."

His nostrils flared. Finally, he released my shoulder and stepped away.

"You will have your *pyroki,*" the *pujerak* said, filling me with relief. "But I will also send you with a pack of *darukkars* for protection on the journey. No less than eight."

Surprise went through me, but I knew it was the *pujerak's*

own loyalty to Kiran that had him helping me. That and possibly the fact that, had Kiran been here, he would have sent *darukkars* regardless to help protect his father's *saruk*. Our home. Though Laru had said they were safe, what had attacked them? More creatures?

I would find out.

"*Kakkira vor.* I am in your debt, *pujerak,*" I murmured, tying my furs tightly. With one last look over my shoulder, I nodded at Gabe and then finally Essir. "I'll return as soon as I can."

CHAPTER 48

Closest to *Drukkar's Sea*, the frost was still mild, though the ground was covered in soft ice.

It didn't settle in deeply until the middle of the season, and it reared its head with a vengeance then. The sea frosted over, the waves solidifying into peaks, with ice so thick you could walk over it, though no one from the *saruk* dared. Because if the ice cracked, it would mean a certain death. Even Dakkari couldn't withstand temperatures that cold.

The *pyroki*'s breath billowed silver in front of her. I was in the middle of a pack of *darukkars*. Two in front of me, two at my sides, and four trailing behind us. As we raced closer and closer to the *saruk*, there was a peculiar stench in the air. Of raw meat but not of rot. The stench grew more and more potent as we traveled onward.

And finally, when the *saruk* came into view, my breath left me. Because in the field outside, between the Forest of *Isida* and the newly fortified gates of where I'd grown up, there was a pitted battlefield. Large, ice-covered mounds lay between us and the *saruk*, surrounded by deep, deep holes in the earth.

Ice-covered mounds that—as we drew closer—I saw were

slain *ungira*, their innards spilling out, which accounted for the smell. The chilled air kept most of the stench tolerable.

The *darukkar* next to me breathed, "What in Kakkari's name happened here?"

A battle, I thought grimly.

And my father had been fighting in it, defending his home.

I'd known the *ungira* were moving south. As were the *polkunu.* But judging by the deep holes in the field before the *saruk*, it looked like the beasts had chosen to *nest* here. And *ungira* were territorial creatures—that was what Kiran had told me. They would have defended their land, their homes in the ground, even if they'd chosen to reside next to an outpost.

But why had the *ungira* been drawn to the *saruk? Our saruk?* When there was so much land to nest in?

I froze, realization going through me.

Could it be...could it be that they'd been attracted to the heart-stone? I wondered.

Kiran's father was one of two *Sorakkar* that possessed one. A portion of Kakkari's own power was rumored to be contained within each one. It had been a heartstone that the white-haired human sorceress had used under the Dead Mountain, after all. The *Sorakkar* of Rath Okkili had been tasked with a heartstone's protection when he'd retired from the wildlands and settled in the South.

Was that why the eastern creatures were journeying here? Because they were drawn to Kakkari's power and influence, as if *they* needed protection?

"*Draki,*" I murmured to the *pyroki* underneath me, my eyes set on the gates. All the *pyrokis* began to run faster, as if sensing that their reprieve was close. We'd been riding straight through since we left the horde. I hadn't wanted to stop and rest, but the frost was difficult on the poor beasts. It had been difficult on us all.

The gates began to churn open as we approached, and we rode straight through, into a very quiet *saruk*.

Nevir, my sister's mate, was one of the guards posted on duty.

"Maeva?" he rasped, coming toward me quickly when I dismounted.

I embraced him when he reached me. He smelled like my sister, like the soaps that she made for us all, and I drew in that scent deeply.

When I pulled back, I asked hurriedly, "Is *Pattar*...is he—"

"He's resting," Nevir told me. The relief made my knees shake, and Nevir reached out to catch me when I began to sway. I'd been riding on the *pyroki* for so long that all the blood was rushing downward, stinging my numb, cold limbs.

"And what does the *mokkira* say?" I asked, hearing the *darukkars* from Kiran's horde dismount. But I was walking with Nevir already, heading to my family's *soliki* toward the back of the *saruk*.

"There is infection in the wound, Maeva," Nevir told me quietly, his hand on my arm as if afraid I'd fall over as we walked. "He's had a fever for three days now. It has not broken, and we fear he is losing his strength to fight it."

I swallowed.

"*Nik*," I whispered. "I will see him well."

I had to believe that. I felt Nevir's hand squeeze my arm in comfort.

It was strange as we walked toward the *soliki*. Everything seemed just as I'd left it. The same roads, the same buildings. But the *saruk* was quiet. A hush had fallen, heavy and thick.

"Were any killed in the attack?" I asked quietly.

Nevir nodded. "Five males. More wounded."

My chest squeezed.

"And were you all right?" I asked.

"I got a slice down my arm but nothing worse. It's healing

quickly," he told me. "We were...unprepared. The *ungira* moved in so quickly. One night they were not there. In the morning, one was battering itself against the gates. I've never seen an *ungira* act like that before."

Thinking of the *polkunu* that attacked my guard and me, I pressed my lips together.

"I'm glad you're all right, Nevir," I murmured, seeing my father's *soliki* loom. When I saw the inside was lit, a warm gold flickering through the windows, a piercing stab of longing and ache went through me.

At the base of the stairs, Nevir said, "I'll see to the *darukkars* and inform the *Sorakkar* of your arrival."

"*Kakkira vor,*" I said, tossing the words over my shoulder as I scrambled up the stairs.

"Maeva."

When I turned to look down at him, he was staring up me, a peculiar expression on his face.

"I'm glad you are home."

His words made my chest pinch tightly.

Am I home? I wondered.

I gave him a small, sad smile, and then I pushed open the door to my father's *soliki*. The little stone stable home—not domed or made of hide—greeted me. The smell was the same, though an underlying stench of *begalia* root tinged the air. This home...where I had grown up. Where we had all been happy... until we hadn't been.

A ragged gasp came from the corner.

When I turned, I saw Laru rising from a cushion. My heart thudded in my chest, tears swelling in my eyes.

Laru came to me and embraced me tightly. Her pregnant belly pressed into my abdomen. Over her shoulder, I saw Rasik asleep on a cushion close to the fire, bundled tight in furs, his sweet little face scrunched up, his tail twitching with his dreams.

Tears leaked onto my sister's shoulder, and I pressed closer to her, wrapping my arms around her, my hand tangling into her silky hair I'd always been jealous of.

"I have missed you so much," she breathed, her voice already shuddering with sobs. When I pulled back, we studied one another. Her hand came to my cheek, her eyes glassy with tears too. "You're crying," she said in surprise.

I couldn't help the small, sad laugh that bubbled from my throat. "I do that these days."

She hadn't seen me cry since *Lomma's* burial, after all.

Laru looked exhausted. She hadn't been sleeping—that much was obvious.

"You need to rest, Laru," I murmured to her quietly. Especially since she was pregnant. "I'm here now. I'll do whatever I can to help him, I promise."

A tight sob burst from her throat and her face crumpled. I soothed her, pulling her taller frame into me, stroking her hair. I could sense the weight that had been on her shoulders.

"I've been worried sick about the *thesper* message I sent," she whispered once she calmed slightly. "I shouldn't have done that. The wildlands are so dangerous now. I thought...I thought you would get hurt or attacked, and I couldn't sleep. I just—"

"It's all right, Laru," I murmured. "I'm glad you sent me the message. You did the right thing."

She blew out a short breath, lifting her watery gaze to mine.

"I need to see him," I said.

She nodded, and we pulled away. Taking a deep breath, I followed her toward the room our father had once shared with *Lomma*. She pushed open the door—the one that had always creaked loudly—and there he was. Sleeping. In the middle of his bed, the furs piled around him.

His breaths were shallow, however, and his face was pale. Sweat ran down his forehead, rolling onto the furs underneath.

The whole room smelled of sweat and the acrid stink of infection.

I blew out a breath, dropping the satchel I didn't remember carrying from my *pyroki* at the door. I went to his side, kneeling beside the bed.

Tears wavered in my vision, blurring him, but I blinked them away quickly. I needed to be strong for him. I knew that I needed to be focused in order to best attend to him.

I felt guilt and sorrow now because in the weeks prior to this, I'd been angry at him. Angry that he'd kept Kiran from saying goodbye and lied to me about it. And denied me the closure I had desperately needed at the time.

All of that seemed silly now. None of it mattered. All that mattered was that I did my best—and I would do anything I could—to see him healed.

I lifted the furs covering him. Underneath, his chest was bare and a large slash that ran nearly the entire length of his torso was visible, covered in a light bandage soaked with green *uudun*. Black veins ran out from the infected, weeping, pus-filled wound.

I swallowed, my stomach sinking.

Lomma, I whispered quietly in my head, *please give him strength. We still need him here. We are not ready to say goodbye.*

I cleared my throat, taking *Pattar's* hand, turning his palm over in mine. He roused at my touch, his eyes flickering underneath his lids.

A breathless moment later, his eyes slitted open. His gaze was bleary and glassy. His face scrunched in pain, and I knew he needed more *begalia.* I wondered how long it'd been since the *mokkira* last tended to him.

"*Pattar,*" I whispered.

His brow furrowed. In a weakened, quiet, raspy voice, he asked, "Maeva?"

"*Lysi,*" I whispered, giving him a soft smile. "I'm here."

A rough sound emerged from his chest. He shook his head, though even that took effort.

"You're home," he whispered. True to himself, he commented softly, "I must truly be dying if Laru sent for you."

He was trying to be amusing, but his attempted, pained joke fell flat. Laru made a squeaking sound in the threshold of the doorway, no doubt trying to muffle a sudden sob.

"Oh, *rei kassiri*," my father murmured, his gaze going to Laru, his brows drawing down deeper, pained. "I'm sorry."

"I'll see you well, *Pattar*," I breathed, squeezing his hand gently.

His gaze flashed to mine, flickering between my eyes that looked nothing like his own.

"I swear it to Kakkari."

Three days.

It took three more days for my father's fever to finally break, and when it did, I went outside to a private, icy corner of the *saruk*—though it was in the dead of night—and cried with relief until my throat was raw.

Three days and nights of little sleep. Of constant wound cleaning and fur washing so he didn't have to lie in a puddle of his own sweat and grime. Of trying to keep my *pattar's* fever down with ice I collected from outside, though he thrashed in the bed and claimed it felt like fire was crawling over his flesh.

Three mornings and nights of nausea that racked his body until he was weak and gasping. Of increased pain because I didn't want him to be dependent on the *begalia*—which was known to be addictive—and his foul mood because of it.

Laru helped me as much as I would let her. But I could see why she'd been so exhausted and overwhelmed. And she'd had to shoulder this responsibility alone.

And as my father slept during those three days and three nights, as I cleaned the furs and kept the *soliki* tidy and aired out, as I *waited*, whenever I was alone with my thoughts and had time to think about myself and my own well-being, I missed Kiran with a stinging acuteness that surprised me.

I couldn't help but wonder if he'd returned to the horde safely. I couldn't help but wonder what he'd encountered in the East Lands, if he'd seen this mysterious—and possibly dangerous—red fog that covered the land. If he had, I prayed to Kakkari that he'd kept far away, that he was safe and protected.

Now, as Laru and I quietly sat in the common room of the *soliki*—where we had often taken our meals in the evening and relaxed when we were younger—I was praying again to Kakkari that Kiran was all right. And I hoped that he'd be able to forgive me once he found me gone from the horde upon his return, if he hadn't returned already.

"You're thinking about him again," Laru commented softly.

The doorway to my *pattar's* room was open, and I could hear his gentle snores as he slept. It was the first time all day I'd allowed myself to *sit*.

I straightened on my cushion, peering across the space to Laru. Rasik was sleeping, with his head on her swollen belly, and she was stroking his hair. He'd fallen asleep trying to listen for his sibling, who he was convinced was a sister.

I swallowed and pushed back a strand of hair that had escaped my braid. I was tired. I felt like I could sleep for a week after this.

"You love him. Again," she whispered. "Don't you?"

Laru and I hadn't talked about Kiran. But she was my sister. Even with the distraction and the stress of my father's recovery, I could sometimes feel her watching me, as if she knew something was different, as if she could *see* it written across me, invisible to me but never to her.

She'd always been able to see me best. Sometimes even better than *Lomma* had been able to.

I licked my lips, staring into the fire basin when it crackled. In my lap was a plate of food I hadn't been able to eat. It was cold now, a waste of Laru's cooking. But the stench of my father's wound wouldn't leave my nostrils, though the injury was now draining clear. I hadn't been able to eat much since I'd arrived.

Quietly, I said, "He wants me to be his *Morakkari.*"

Laru's sharp gasp almost roused Rasik, but she held her breath until he settled once more.

Her eyes burned into me. The longer I looked at her, meeting her gaze steadily, the more her expression changed... morphing into *understanding*. And perhaps...sadness.

"And you will accept him," she said quietly. "You will leave the *saruk* again. And then you will be gone. Gone from us. Lost to the wildlands with your horde king."

I thought back to the dawn of Addie's birth. I recalled that feeling of *knowing*. Of purpose. I had never been more certain of my decision. It had flowed from me, freeing and bright.

But of course, with that decision came pain. Because I couldn't have the *saruk and* Kiran. He was a horde king of Dakkar. It was his duty to help protect it. It was his duty to travel across the wildlands, to patrol for threats and to uphold the ancient laws of Kakkari.

I would never expect him to give up his title, his own destined purpose, to resettle in his father's *saruk* simply because I missed my family. It would kill him. And I knew that my *pattar* would never join Kiran's horde because it would mean being taken from my mother's burial place, which he visited almost daily.

My father would feel like he was leaving my *lomma* behind. And he'd remained loyal to her all these years, waiting for the day when he would join her, wherever she was.

I heard Laru sigh, a deep aching thing. Then I saw her smile. It was soft and knowing.

"It has always been him," she said, nodding. "It was always

going to be him, Maeva. Wasn't it? You've known since you were a child. You were always so certain."

I bit my lip, feeling my throat tighten.

"Not always," I felt the need to remind her.

She shook her head. "*Lomma* knew. And she was right."

My brow furrowed, my gaze sharpening on her. "What do you mean?"

"It was before she died," Laru murmured, stroking the entirety of Rasik's back, picking something off that clung to his flickering tail. "She told me that you would never be truly happy again unless he was by your side."

Something about those words made it difficult to swallow. Because I didn't want Laru to think that I had been *unhappy*. How could I ever be unhappy with my family, whom I loved dearly, with me?

"But I *was* happy, Laru," I argued. "I was happy here. As happy as I could be without *Lomma*."

And without Kiran, I thought, but I kept that to myself.

"*Nik,*" she said, shaking her head once. "You were content here, Maeva. But I always saw it in your eyes. Your loneliness."

I stilled.

"You tried not to think about him, but I could always tell when you were wondering about him. About where he was. If he was safe. If he had found another. If he would ever come home. If he ever thought about you."

Now I knew that he had. He'd thought about me all the time, missing me, just as I'd longed for him, even when I'd tried not to.

"*Lomma* knew," she finished. "She knew that you were meant for one another. That Kakkari had always meant for it. She believed that you would find your way back to one another. She believed that, even at the end. And she was right. Everything she believed came to pass."

The fire sparked loudly, as if our *lomma* was in the room with us now and announcing her agreement.

We both fell quiet, and my gaze dropped to Rasik, watching him sleep in my sister's lap, under her gentle touch. Why hadn't *Lomma* ever told me this herself?

"I hate him," Laru whispered, though it was entirely without malice. "But only because he is taking you away from us. For good this time. I think I knew that though. When you left. I think I knew that you wouldn't be coming home."

Later that night, I was changing my father's bandages. Laru and Nevir were talking quietly in the common room. I'd left them cuddled up, warming by the fire, with Rasik sleeping between them.

Ever since the attack, Nevir was away almost all waking hours of the day—helping bring in fresh water from the wells, watching over the gates, and today, he'd begun helping with the disposal of the *ungira*.

Though it was the frost, most of the *ungira* had already dug their nests deep into the earth outside the gates. Nevir and the rest of the *saruk's* warriors who were able and unwounded were heaving the dead beasts back into them, where their bodies would rest and nourish the earth once the frost passed.

However, it was difficult and grueling work, especially with so few *darukkars*. And I'd counted at least fifteen *ungira* outside the gates. It would take the better part of the week to erase all evidence of the battle.

But everyone who was able to was pitching in around the *saruk*. Whenever my father was resting, I returned to the *mokki-ra's voliki*, offering him my help, which I could tell he was thankful for. Even Nebrik, the *mokkira's* nephew and the male who would be taking over his position eventually, seemed thankful for the extra hands.

Though Nebrik and I had never gotten along, he'd still inclined his head in respect. I was, after all, a *mokkira*. A *mokkira* of a horde. I was not simply Maeva anymore, a healer. A *kerisa*.

But as the days blended, as the sun rose and then set, I felt an anxiousness rise. Because I was a *mokkira* of a horde...and I had left. I couldn't stay at the *saruk* forever. Once my father was healed, once I was certain that he would be all right, I had to leave. I knew that. I worried for Addie, for the baby. The nightmares of watching her die had returned. I worried for Essir, for placing so much responsibility on his shoulders when I knew he wasn't ready.

The guilt was overwhelming. The shame. But I could do nothing else. Not until my father was well...because I wouldn't abandon him. Not for my duty, not for anything.

Tonight, once I had a fresh bandage on my father's wound, once his furs were clean and I'd wiped him down with a soft cloth and brushed out his hair, I kneeled on the floor next to his bed and memorized features I knew like the back of my hand.

His spirits had returned—his color too—and today was the best he'd been feeling since the attack, which I thought boded well. When he was awake and not in pain, we talked of the horde, what life was like there...but of course, he knew. He'd been a *darukkar* for Kiran's father, after all, before he became a hunter. Most of his life had been spent in a horde.

I'd almost asked him, as we talked earlier. I'd almost asked him if he would consider horde life again. But I couldn't make the selfish words come. Not when he'd been so anxious to visit *Lomma's* burial site, which was near the Forest of *Isida*, though protected along a coastal path. He'd been so worried that the *ungira* had destroyed her grave.

"I wish you would come with me, *Pattar*," I whispered though he slept soundly. "I wish you all would."

There was noise in the common room, noise that made me pivot my head and frown down the hallway, though I saw nothing, only the flickering of the fire against the walls. Laru and Nevir were out of sight, though I could hear their hushed voices.

I turned back to my father. He was sleeping, and though I was exhausted, I knew I should take advantage of that time and see if the *mokkira* needed any—

Heavy footsteps came down the hallway. Too heavy to be Nevir's.

Before I could react, a large body was stepping over the threshold of the doorway, silhouetted in the darkness.

Even if I were blind, even if all my senses were taken away from me, I'd still be able to recognize Kiran anywhere.

Stunned disbelief and a bright burst of relief—overwhelming and wonderful—made me gasp for air, made tears immediately flood my eyes as I clamored hurriedly from the ground.

"*Seffi*," came his gruff, quiet voice, those golden eyes glowing in the darkness.

All my emotions came flooding to the surface. My worry for him, my guilt for leaving, my fear that my father wouldn't be able to survive this, my exhaustion, both emotionally and physically. With it also came my need to be near him, my need to hold him, to feel his arms around me, his heartbeat against my cheek. With it also came my surging love, love that had never died after all. He'd been right. I had just buried it so deeply I couldn't feel it anymore...until he'd unearthed it again.

I tumbled into his arms, but he held me steadily. He was warm. He smelled of Roon and the frost. He was safe. He'd come to the *saruk*. Looking for me?

He was in my family's *soliki*, where it was so easy to remember him, remember us.

My tears unleashed, silent, happy, relieved sobs shaking my

shoulders. His arms tightened around me, his head dropping to press his lips into my hair.

"I'm here, *seffi*," he murmured. "Let me take care of you now, *lysi*?"

CHAPTER 50

Maeva slept soundly in my arms, dead to the world.

With my back to the stone wall, I was sitting on the floor of her father's room, listening to his even, steady breaths and feeling my female's heart pump against my chest. Down the hallway, I could hear Nevir and Laru whispering to one another, though I couldn't make out their words.

The longer Maeva was in my arms, the more I felt the thick, heavy, tight knot loosen in my chest.

It had been a long, nightmarish week. Made even longer when I'd finally returned from Rath Kitala's horde to find my *pujerak*—with a grim, knowing expression—telling me that Maeva had returned to the *saruk*.

The only reason I hadn't eviscerated him where he stood was that he'd sent her away with eight *darukkars* as protection and he'd told me that the *saruk* had been attacked, Maeva's father injured.

And I had known right then that nothing would've stopped her from leaving. I'd been back at my horde for scarcely an hour, long enough for Roon to eat and rest briefly, before I was on his back again, riding south. He'd seemed to sense my urgency, and he brought us quickly to the *saruk* in a little over a day.

Now, my beast rested, reunited briefly with his mother—my *lomma's pyroki*—in the small enclosure of the *saruk*. And I was holding Maeva in my arms.

"*You,*" came the voice.

My head snapped up, and I met the eyes of Maeva's father, careful not to wake her.

"*Terun,*" I murmured softly, inclining my head. It meant *elder*. It was the respectful title I'd always greeted him with. It didn't matter that I was a *Vorakkar* now.

The last time I saw him, he'd been so mad he was spitting and cursing my name. Furious that I'd broken Maeva's heart, that I'd rejected her love. And I remembered the words—the last words he'd ever said to me.

One day, you will regret this. I hope it haunts you. I hope she haunts you so that you will understand what you threw away. But if you ever dare to hurt her again, I will gut you and throw you into the pyroki *enclosure,* Vorakkar *or not. Do you understand me? Now leave. Don't you dare come back.*

My title had been a sneer on his lips. I'd been pained and astonished by the malice I'd heard in his voice. Maeva's *pattar* had been a *darukkar* once, *lysi*, but I had never so much as heard him raise his voice. Ever. He'd always been kind to me. Quiet.

Even then, I'd known he spoke the truth. Even then, I'd known that Maeva would haunt me, that I would regret that night for years to come.

"I am glad you are recovering, *terun,*" I murmured in the darkness. There was a fire basin in here keeping Maeva's father warm, but it needed to be rekindled.

"*Nik,* you are not," he rasped, a large huff falling from his lips.

I frowned, my jaw tight.

"Your death would destroy her," I rasped quietly. "And I know what you think of me, but if it destroyed her, it would destroy me."

Her father grew silent, his eyes narrowing on me. His gaze flickered down to Maeva sleeping across my lap, her cheek pressed into my chest. Realization made that gaze stricken, and his eyes flashed back up to mine.

"She deserves better than you."

The quiet words bit at my chest.

"I know," I replied quietly, which surprised him. Gruffly, I said, "She does. But have no doubt, *terun*, with the exception of yourself, there is not a male in this entire universe that could love her as much as I do."

Maeva's father stared me down for a long time, the silence stretching tightly between us. Finally, he let out a small huff through his nostrils, his gaze straying back to his daughter, his face softening.

"Go put her in her bed," the *terun* ordered me. "She has barely slept and needs her rest."

I rose carefully, trying not to jostle her. I turned back to her father, but his eyes were closed, as if he didn't wish to speak anymore.

Quietly, I walked from the room to Maeva's own. Being back inside a *soliki* after so long was strange, but I remembered this place so well. Maeva's bed was small, and I carefully laid her down on it, brushing her hair from her cheek. Her cheekbones were sharper, the area around her eyes darker. She'd lost weight, and it was obvious she hadn't slept. She was always so consumed with helping those around her that sometimes she forgot to take care of herself.

But that is my duty, I thought, leaning down to brush my lips across hers. I breathed in her scent, letting it soothe the wild thing inside me, the wild thing I'd felt ever since I first saw the dark fog in the East Lands.

I was loath to leave her, but I would return shortly. With one last look at her, I left the room and went back into the common space, where Laru and Nevir were resting.

Both of their eyes flashed to mine when I appeared.

Laru rose. She reached out to touch my forearm, cradling her other hand underneath her belly.

"How are they?" she asked softly.

Laru had always been kind to me. She'd always been understanding. Nevir too, though he had no reason to be.

"She's exhausted," I told Laru quietly. "And your father still hates me."

A small laugh chuffed from Nevir's throat.

"And he probably always will," Laru said with a sheepish, tired expression. "Sometimes *Pattar* is still mistrustful of Nevir. It's in his nature to be protective. And he remembers everything. He holds on to memory."

I nodded, grimly.

"I need to go speak with my own father," I told them. The guards would've alerted both my parents to my arrival already. "But I'll return shortly."

"You...you will be staying here?" Laru asked hesitantly.

"*Lysi,*" I said, knowing it was nonnegotiable. "I stay with her."

Something knowing flashed in Laru's gaze, and she nodded, dropping her touch from my forearm. I wondered what Maeva had told her about us. The two sisters had always been close.

With one last look at Maeva's door, I left the *soliki*, pulling my furs tighter around my shoulders, and threaded down the main stretch of stone road that would lead to my parents' home.

Just as I was ascending the steps, the door flew open and my mother was waiting on the threshold. My eyes locked and held on to hers, and I felt her arms come around me, pulling me into the warmth.

"The guards said you'd come. I could scarcely believe it," she whispered. "Twice you've come in a single moon cycle, when I have not seen you for two years."

The guilt that crept up on me was familiar. A son's guilt. But I was a *Vorakkar*. *Lomma* understood that. She knew the sacrifices that needed to be made.

Sacrifices that she had perhaps made for me, though it had not been her right to, I thought quietly, leaning back to peer into her eyes.

"I came to collect my *mokkira*," I murmured to her.

"Maeva?" she asked quietly, knowing. "*Lysi*, I'd heard she'd returned."

My brow furrowed. And she hadn't gone to see her? To lend her support to Maeva's family?

Disappointment spread in my gut.

"I need to speak with the *Sorakkar*."

She hated when I called him that, but he had always been a *Sorakkar* to me. I couldn't remember when I'd last addressed him as *Pattar*, and he seemed to prefer it that way.

His presence loomed behind her, emerging from the doorway of their room. I paused when I noticed his limp, a padding underneath his trews that signified a bandage.

"You were injured in the attack?" I rasped.

"It is a small thing," he grunted. My mother sighed, casting my father an impatient look over her shoulder.

I doubted that, considering he still wore bandages nearly a week after the attack. Dakkari healed quickly. The wound must've been deep.

"Why didn't you send for aid?" I asked him, walking toward him, skirting around my mother to reach him. "You know my *darukkars* would have come. They could've been here in a day."

His shoulders straightened as I studied the face that looked so much like my own. A stubborn brow, pursed lips, wide, rough features. A scar tracked down my father's cheek—an old battle injury.

"The *ungira* moved in quickly. There was no time," my

father snapped. "I didn't expect aid from a horde. I can handle the defense of my own *saruk*."

Impatience rose.

"I'm not just a *Vorakkar*, I'm your *son*. This is about your pride, not about your *saruk's* protection," I growled. My father's gaze narrowed, and he stepped toward me at the insult, though he knew there was truth in it. "When was the last time your *darukkars* had need of their swords?"

His expression was dark, and I saw my mother moving toward us, felt her hand rest on my forearm.

"That's enough," she said quietly. "Both of you."

My jaw pulsed. A moment into seeing one another and we were already at each other's throats. Perhaps we were more alike that I cared to believe.

I blew out a rough breath, knowing my mother was right.

"You don't think I care about what happens to the *saruk*?" I asked quietly, gentling my voice. "You don't think I care about what happens to you? To *Lomma*?"

A huff left his nostrils. He looked past me to the closed door. Finally, he said, "I know you do, Kiran. Of course I know."

I nodded, feeling my mother's hand squeeze my arm.

"But the *ungira* came in the night," my father said, limping toward a raised cushion before he lowered himself with some effort, hissing slightly. He rubbed at the bottom part of his leg as I took the cushion opposite him. "There truly was no time to send for help."

His voice was suddenly so tired. It was a side of my father that I saw very rarely.

There had always been tension between us, which had seemed to double once I'd become *Vorakkar*.

"We lost five *darukkars*. Dozens more were injured. The *ungira*..." My father trailed off. "I've never seen anything like it."

"I've just come from the horde of Rath Kitala," I told him

quietly, finding his gaze, as my mother sat beside him, running her hand across his broad shoulders in comfort.

"Kitala?" my father asked, surprise in his voice. "Because of this red fog that plagues the East?"

"*Lysi*," I said, swallowing. Hesitantly, I said, "I've seen it."

"And what do you make of it?" my father asked in a hushed voice, leaning toward me. "What was discussed among the *Vorakkar*?"

"It is growing," I told him. "Every day, it grows, consuming more of the land."

"And what is it?" *Lomma* asked, her brows furrowed in confusion and concern.

"We do not know," I told them. "All we know is that we haven't seen a Ghertun emerge from the Dead Lands. No one has. And that this fog...it drains our energy, it drives beasts from their homes. It makes them violent. Changed. Scared."

My father had already guessed this. There was no other reason why the *ungira* would journey so far south, why they would attack so viciously, unless they felt threatened.

I saw my mother's hand tighten on my father's shoulder.

"The *Vorakkar* have decided to call for the priestesses of the North. To summon them from their temple. The *thesper* is already on its way."

"The priestesses?" *Lomma* breathed. "You think they will answer?"

"If anyone knows what this is, it is them." I looked at them. "I want you to be prepared, *lysi*? Prepare the *saruk*. Send for more *darukkars* from *Dothik*. Recover your strength, and then begin training again. Because something is changing on Dakkar. And we need to be prepared for whatever it will bring."

* * *

In the early hours of morning, I was preparing to leave my parent's *soliki*. In the time I'd been there, I'd gone over every detail of my journey to Rath Kitala's horde, every detail of what I'd learned there, and my father had soaked up every piece of knowledge he could.

But now, it was time to return to Maeva. And I was eager to hold her again. Already I felt that tightness growing in my chest, and I needed to make sure she was all right, sleeping, resting.

"You will not stay here?" my mother asked, frowning, watching me swing my furs back over my shoulders.

Though I caught her eyes, I sensed my father studying me, though I saw fatigue pulling at the edges of him. He was still recovering from his injury. And despite his pride, I knew that the attack against the *saruk*—the lives lost—weighed on him heavily. He felt responsible for them, as any leader would.

"I will be with Maeva," I told her, told them both.

There was a flicker in *Lomma's* gaze. A flicker of guilt?

"Kiran," she said, stepping forward when I made for the door. "Wait."

This wasn't something I was planning to do tonight, but I would if she pushed the subject.

"You should both know something," I said softly.

"*Lysi?*" my mother whispered, though she knew. She knew what I was going to say.

"I have asked Maeva to be my *Morakkari*," I informed them both. My mother froze. My father didn't look all that surprised. "She has not given me an answer yet. But I had already chosen her long ago. It just took me this long to realize that. It was always going to be her. But you already knew that, didn't you?"

My mother's eyes were soft yet pained.

"And I know," I told her. "I know what you did, *Lomma*. I know that you lied to her. Lied to *me*."

"What is he talking about, *rei kassiri?*" my father asked quietly, but my gaze never left my mother's stricken face.

Her shame kept her from answering. It was obvious, however, that she'd kept it hidden from even my father. Or perhaps she hadn't thought it was serious enough to warrant a discussion or to bring it to my father's attention. That thought alone made my anger surge, but I kept my voice calm.

"I even understand why you did it, *Lomma.* You thought you were helping me. You thought I didn't need the distraction," I said.

"*Lysi,*" she whispered. "I was only trying to..."

She trailed off, as if she couldn't bring herself to say the words.

"Maeva trusted you. She had no reason to think you would lie to her about something like that. But it was her mother's *burial, Lomma.* Her mother had just *died.* And I wouldn't have cared what it took or what it cost. I would have wanted to be there for her. You had no right to make that decision for me, *lysi?*"

My mother's gaze strayed to the ground.

"I did what I thought was best at the time," she whispered. "I'm sorry, Kiran. I'm sorry I lied to you."

I shook my head. "If you were, *Lomma,* you would have told her the truth a long time ago."

Her eyes flashed up to mine.

Blowing a breath, I inclined my head to her. I didn't want to fight. But it needed to be said.

"I'll see you in the morning."

And with that, I left.

When I woke, blue light was streaming through the small, circular window of my room, casting prisms across the wall through the heavy, wavy glass.

Warm flesh was pressed completely against me. A steady, strong heartbeat against my chest. Black, straight hair trailing across my shoulders, tangling with my own.

My eyes drifted up, and I studied Kiran's face. His expression was slackened and relaxed with sleep, his chest pushing against mine with every breath he took.

We were wedged beside one another in my small bed. It was cramped and probably uncomfortable for Kiran, but it was the first time I'd slept through the night since arriving. It was the first time I'd slept more than a handful of moments at one time, truthfully.

He's here, I thought, still in disbelief though I shouldn't have been surprised. *He came for me.*

He must have been exhausted. He'd probably ridden straight here from the East Lands after stopping at the horde. I wanted to ask him about his journey, about the horde, about Addie and Essir and Hinna, if he'd had enough time to speak with them.

I'd fallen asleep crying in his arms last night. There had been no time to talk.

I knew that Kiran was especially tired because he didn't move when I slid out from his arms.

A violent shiver racked my body when my bare feet touched the icy cold floor of the *soliki,* and I dressed quickly, watching Kiran sleeping as I did, my heart so full that it felt like it could burst.

I walked over to his side and pressed a kiss to his chin, though he didn't stir. Then I left the room, walking quickly down the hallway to *Pattar's* room.

I stopped short when I saw his bed was empty, the furs flung back. Panic rose, but I quickly pivoted, going to the common room, only to find it empty. Nevir was already gone. Laru and Rasik were gone too, back to their own *soliki.*

At the door, I toed on my boots and tied my furs across my shoulders. I opened the door and raced down the steps, and relief bit me when I spied my father leaning heavily on a cane, standing in the middle of the quiet road, looking toward the front of the *saruk.* Toward the field beyond...and beyond that the coast, where my mother's grave lay.

"*Pattar,*" I said softly, racing toward him, my breath billowing out in front of me when the frosty air bit hard. "You should not be out of bed. Not in this cold. You need to be resting."

He waved a hand, his eyes coming to me.

"How did you get dressed?" I demanded, looking him over.

"I can dress myself," he pointed out, his tone without sharpness. "I have done it most of my life, *rei kassiri.*"

I sighed. "Still, you are healing and—"

"Maeva," he said, "allow me some fresh air. I have my strength this morning. Don't make me feel older than I already am."

I sighed again, and though I bit my lip, worrying that the

cold would be too much for him, I stood at his side and turned to look at the view with him.

I felt...refreshed this morning. Good. My spirits had brightened, and Kiran had kept my nightmares away. My father's fever had broken, his wound was beginning to heal.

"The *Vorakkar* slept in my *soliki* last night," he said, his tone decidedly more cranky than it had been a moment prior.

I didn't know what to say to that.

All I could manage was "*Lysi*, he did."

Another long stretch of silence came between us. I wondered if they'd even spoken yet or if my father had gotten a shock when he'd seen us sleeping together through the open doorway when he'd snuck out here.

"He came during the night and—"

"This is the most beautiful place in all of Dakkar," came my father's voice, soft and reverent. "Your *lomma* always thought so too."

Perhaps he didn't want to speak of Kiran. My shoulders sagged a little.

"And you've seen most of Dakkar, *Pattar*," I said, reaching out to take the hand which wasn't clutching his cane. "I have missed the sea. It's so strange not living next to it. Not hearing the waves at night. The air smells different on the wildlands too."

"This may be my favorite place, Maeva," he continued, "but make no mistake, there is plenty to see on our planet. Plenty to marvel at and many of Kakkari's creations to be in awe of. There is not just the sea. There are many things that you will find beautiful. And I want you to see them all."

My brow furrowed, and I turned to face him, turning my gaze from the waves that still shimmered across the sea.

He turned to meet me, his expression sober. Sad.

"*Pattar*," I whispered.

"Have you chosen him?"

I took in a deep breath, but I didn't break his gaze.

"*Lysi*," I whispered. "I believe I have."

My heart was pounding ferociously in my chest, so loud that I wondered if my father would hear it on that quiet, still, frosty morning.

Pattar closed his eyes. He clutched his cane harder, but he squeezed my hand too.

Eventually, he shook his head and a rueful sigh drifted from his lips. When he met my gaze again, he said, "Your mother told me it would happen. Sometimes I believed that female had the gift of foresight. She always knew."

Just as Laru had said.

"I have had years to prepare for this moment, and yet I find the years have not been long enough. No amount of time could prepare a father to say goodbye to his daughter."

The words made my heart squeeze, made tears swell in my eyes.

"It's not goodbye, *Pattar*," I whispered. "It doesn't have to be."

His cold hand cupped my cheek, and I clutched at his wrist, feeling his pulse underneath my fingertips.

"When I found you in that forest, I knew that you were a gift from Kakkari herself, Maeva," he told me, his own eyes going glassy. He'd never been ashamed of his tears. "The warm wind led me to you that day, and that wind will take you far from here. It will lead you where you need to go."

He leaned his forehead against mine.

I didn't expect it to hurt *this much*. I knew it would be diffi-cult, but this made my heart feel like it was being shredded all over again, just in a different way. Because I knew my father was hurting too.

"Kakkari will lead you where you need to go. But the *saruk* will always be your home. You can always come home, Maeva. Remember that."

"It's healing well," I told the *darukkar*, inspecting the incision where the *mokkira* had needed to extract a broken *ungira* talon that had imbedded itself inside the poor male's leg. "Another day and you'll be able to walk on it, *lysi*?"

The relief in the *darukkar's* eyes was vivid and bright. "*Kakkira vor, Kerisa.*"

Healer.

Not Mokkira.

Hearing my old title was strange, made me feel like I'd gone back in time, like the last month hadn't happened at all.

I gave the *darukkar* a small smile. "Rest for today. The *mokkira* will check on you later tonight."

He nodded, and then I left the *soliki*, nodding at the *darukkar's* mate as I left the small home. It was late afternoon already. The day had seemed to fly by after my conversation with my father earlier. After I'd ensured he made it back to his bed safely, him grumbling the entire time, I'd left to assist the *mokkira*, making rounds around the *saruk*.

I hadn't seen Kiran since I'd checked in on him sleeping before I left, though I thought I'd spied him near the front of the *saruk* earlier.

I had a break, however, and wanted to see him. So I ventured down the main road, and I asked a passing *darukkar*, "Have you seen the *Vorakkar*?"

His chin lifted, and he looked out beyond the gates. "He's out in the fields."

He is?

But that was just like Kiran, wasn't it? Even though he was a *Vorakkar*, a king in his own right, he was helping the *darukkars* with a filthy, laborious, difficult job out in the frost-bitten fields.

"*Kakkira vor,*" I murmured and headed the rest of the way,

winding down the road, and then I had one of the guards open the gates.

There were dozens of males working around the field, but most of them were centered around the next *ungira* they were trying to drop back into its nest. Others were trying to break through the frosted ground, to cover the nests that were already filled.

I spotted Kiran easily. He was tethering a strap to Roon out in the field, which was wrapped around an *ungira*. They were using the *pyrokis'* strength to help shift the massive beasts.

His head came up, as if sensing me near. I heard him call out something to the other males—who seemed relieved for a break—before he strode toward me.

When he was close, he said, "I have to warn you, *seffi*, I am certain I smell like rotting *ungira*."

My heart stuttered when I saw his quirked smile. Something that felt like relief spread through my chest.

"I'm a healer," I told him when he stopped in front of me, stepping closer. "I've smelled worse, I assure you."

His low, husky laugh slid down my throat and into my belly.

And though there were eyes on us, he reached out to embrace me, pulling me close. And though he smelled like *ungira*, he also smelled like *Kiran*, and I'd missed having that smell all over me. I dragged in that scent greedily, falling into his arms, burying my face into his wide chest.

Some of the tension that had started to build from that morning—from the sadness and impending grief I'd spied in my father's eyes—loosened.

"I missed you, *rei seffi*," he rasped, his voice thick and gruff. "I missed you so *vokking* much."

My face softened, and I craned my head to look back at him.

"How's your father?" he asked quietly. "I checked on him before I left, but he was sleeping."

"*Kakkira vor*," I murmured. "I found him outside this morning. So I'd say he's feeling more like himself."

Kiran nodded, studying me.

"And you?" he asked next, his voice serious. "How are *you*, Maeva?"

My chest warmed at his worry.

"It hasn't been a good week," I told him truthfully. Hesitantly, softly, I added, "But I'm happy you're here."

Those golden eyes heated, and it made my belly flutter.

To distract myself, I said quickly, "Were you able to check on Essir when you returned to the horde? On Addie?"

He nodded, his hands sliding to my shoulders. "Essir was handling it well. And Addie was upset that you were gone, but she understood. She and the child are healthy."

Guilt mingled with my relief. Before I'd left the horde that afternoon, I'd gone to see Addie, gone to explain to her why I needed to leave. She'd been worried, naturally, and upset that I was leaving. But I hoped that she'd forgive me. One day.

"I'm sorry I broke my promise to you," I said quietly.

His brow furrowed.

"I left the horde. I chose my family over my duty as *mokkira*," I said. "And I—I understand if you wish to send for another from *Dothik*. I—"

"Maeva," he growled in warning.

I bit my lip.

"You cannot be perfect all the time," he growled. "I gave that up long ago. I learned that in my first moon cycle as *Vorakkar*. You will always disappoint someone with your decisions. But you are worth it, *lysi*? You have not failed in your duty."

I kept his gaze.

His lips quirked, his face softening. "But you would not be my Maeva unless you worried about this. You care so much about others that you forget to care for yourself."

I let out a shuddering breath.

A cracking sound filled the air, sharp and sudden. Males cried out in alarm when one of the straps tethered to a *pyroki* snapped from the cold air and the *ungira* slid forward.

"*Vok*," Kiran cursed. "We will talk later, *lysi?*"

I nodded. "Go."

His warmth left me, and I watched him jog back to the *darukkars* who were trying to secure the strap again, though the sound had spooked the *pyroki*. I turned and headed back to the enclosed safety of the *saruk*.

Just as I stepped through the gates, I spied the *Arakkari*. Kiran's mother.

She was walking with her *piki* down the road, talking quietly to her, dressed in her white furs. Once, it had been my *lomma* at her side. The two of them had been great friends.

The *Arakkari* hadn't come to see me after I'd arrived, and I hadn't made the effort to see her, knowing what I knew now. I watched as she nodded and stopped to speak with a few female members of the *saruk*, smiling all the while.

I'd forgotten just how beautiful she was. How engaging and kind she seemed.

Her eyes caught on me, and she stilled. The females bid their goodbyes, but the *Arakkari* was frozen on the road, meeting my gaze.

I might never be able to understand why she lied to me.

But I realized right then that it didn't matter. She thought she was doing what was best for Kiran, even if she'd lied to us both. And maybe she'd taken me under her wing after my *lomma* died because she felt guilty about that. Maybe that had been why she'd been so kind to me.

Still, it didn't stop the betrayal and the hurt from simmering in my chest.

I met her gaze steadily, and she met mine. I wondered if

Kiran had confronted her already. I wondered if she would approach me.

My question was answered in the next moment when she turned her face away, her lips subtly shifting downward. Then she smoothed the furs around her shoulders and turned, heading back up the path she'd just come from, leaving me to stand there, looking after her.

A small, sharp sigh burst from my lips. I looked down at my feet, and then I looked up, staring at her back as she walked away.

Kiran confronted her. He told her about us, I suddenly knew.

And this was her answer to it all. To turn her back.

I nodded to myself.

Then I lifted my chin. And I made for the *soliki* of the next *darukkar* on my rounds.

Then I would go home to my *pattar* and savor the last moments with him that I could.

That was what really mattered.

CHAPTER 52

I paused when I spied a familiar figure lingering on the road just outside his *soliki*.

I had just come from the common baths, where I'd washed away the *ungira* stench that had stuck to me all morning and afternoon. Intending to find Maeva, I hadn't expected to encounter her father first.

"*Terun*," I said, frowning. "Does Maeva know you're out of your bed again?"

A derisive huff left his nostrils, and he turned to narrow his eyes on me. "*Nik.* Are you going to tell her, *Vorakkar?*"

I sighed. Then I couldn't help it when my lips quirked up. I wasn't used to being spoken to like this...but Maeva's *pattar* knew that he would be able to get away with it.

He was dressed again with his heavy furs over his shoulders, though his back looked sunken in from the weight of them. His breathing was a little labored. He was still in pain—though probably not nearly as much as before—but he'd still taken the journey outside the *soliki*, risking his daughter's wrath for fresh air.

They were more alike than they probably believed. Because Maeva hated being trapped inside as well.

"I cannot lie to her if she asks," I told him. "But until you decide to return to your *soliki*, I will need to stay out here with you."

Which, no doubt, would have him scurrying back sooner than he wanted to, if only to escape being in my presence for long.

With a soft curse—something I didn't think I'd ever heard him utter—he rummaged around in his furs for something, his hand tightening on his cane. It was a quiet night in the *saruk*. I'd found that most were still in shock from the attack, that there was a morose and somber air that had settled, one that might not lift until after the frost.

Because the attack showed the *saruk* that even near *Drukkar's Sea*, in the peaceful South Lands, they were not immune to the outside world creeping in. I'd often felt that way about my father's *saruk*, especially after I'd journeyed to *Dothik*. That this place was separate from Dakkar and all the turmoil our planet faced. A little haven next to the sea, when the rest of the planet experienced fear and greed and suffering.

Maeva's *pattar* pulled something from his furs and uncapped it. It was a skin of brew, I realized, listening to him take a long swig of it.

Then, to my surprise, he held it out for me after a moment of hesitation. I met his gaze before I took it, feeling the burning, fiery liquid make a path down my throat. It was strong brew, some of the strongest I'd ever had.

I handed it back to him, feeling it warm my belly and keep the chill away.

"I told you that if you hurt her again, I would—"

"Gut me and toss me into the *pyroki* enclosure. I know, *terun*. I remember. Everything."

He grunted, seemingly pleased that his threat had stayed with me all these years.

It was quiet between us, and a wind rustled our hair briefly before it calmed.

"I love her," I rasped. "I always have."

He surprised me further by saying, "I know."

I'd expected him to fight me on it.

"No one regrets what happened here almost ten years ago more than I do," I told him, meeting his gaze. "I need you to know that. I need you to know that not a day went by where I didn't regret it. Not a day went by where I didn't miss her."

"*Pattar*," came a gasp, and I turned from his grim expression to see Laru hurrying up the pathway, coming from the direction of the *soliki* she shared with her mate. "What are you doing out here?"

"Breathing," he replied, still a little cantankerous, probably from my continued presence. "Is that all right with you?"

Laru's eyes went wide, and she huffed out a strong breath.

Then he sighed. "I'm sorry, *rei kassiri*. You know how he makes me."

Laru's gaze went to me, her brow raised, her tail flicking with anxiousness behind her.

"You were apologizing," Maeva's *pattar* reminded me, expectation on his face when he turned to me. "Go on."

An amused but rough huff left my nostrils. But I would beg on my knees if it was what he needed to see. I would do anything for Maeva.

"I am sorry," I said, meeting his eyes before flickering to Laru, who looked uncomfortable and shocked to have a *Vorakkar* speaking to her like this. "I am sorry for what I put her through. I am sorry for hurting her, for putting strain on your family."

The *terun's* jaw tightened.

"You turned your back on her," her father stated. "Not once but twice."

The first had been when I'd broken her heart, I knew. But the second...

"I didn't know," I rasped.

His scowl was deep. "*Neffar?*"

"You have no reason to believe me except that you know I'm not a liar, *terun*. And you have known me almost my entire life," I said quietly, holding his gaze. "I did not know about your mate's passing until mere weeks ago when Maeva told me herself. The messages never reached me."

Disbelief went through his gaze. I kept out the fact that my mother had been responsible for that.

"And I am sorry that you felt the loss of her too early," I continued gruffly, feeling Laru reach out to touch my forearm. "But trust that I would have come had I known. Nothing would have kept me away."

Something flickered deep in the *pattar's* eyes. Stunned realization. Because he knew me. Despite the fact that I had hurt Maeva all those years ago...I was not a liar. He believed me when I said I hadn't known.

And maybe his hatred of me dampened slightly because of it.

His lips pressed together.

"I love her," I said again, my voice quiet. "And I have asked her to be my *Morakkari*, though she had not given me her answer yet."

Part of the reason, I knew, stood right in front of me.

"And I know that Maeva will never truly be happy without her family close to her."

The *terun's* eyes narrowed. Laru's went wide.

"And I want her to be happy. She deserves to be happy. I do not want her to feel torn between us when she does not have to be," I said, reaching out to clasp her *pattar's* shoulder. "So I am asking you both...if she decides to accept me as hers, if she decides to take her place as *Morakkari* to my horde, will you join it? Will you leave the *saruk* for her?"

My gaze shifted to Laru's. This was uncommon, certainly, but not unheard of.

"I know I ask a lot," I said quietly. "But you would honor me if you accepted my horde as your home."

My eyes returned to Maeva's *pattar*. In his own, I saw his fear, his indecision, his sorrow. But I also saw his love. His love for his family, for his daughters and their happiness.

"Will you come with us?"

CHAPTER 53

Drukkar's Sea was stretched out before me, and I breathed in that air I'd missed so much.

The frost dulled the crisp scent slightly. It made it sting my lungs, but I didn't care. I needed this. I needed a moment to remember this place. This beautiful place.

I didn't know how long I'd been out here. But the view was breathtaking. The wild, violent beauty of the sea...my eyes feasted on it. Kakkari was the earth, and Drukkar was the sea. Where they met was the cliffside, the waves crashing and tumultuous below, as if nothing would stop Drukkar from reaching her. That was what my *lomma* always told me. That Drukkar would always come for Kakkari.

The base of my neck prickled. And I sensed his presence before I heard his low voice call my name.

"Maeva."

When I turned, I saw Kiran heading down the small pathway that led to our private little cliffside. The one that was hidden from the main pathway.

When he reached me, his gaze flickered over the cliff before it settled on me. I knew what he was thinking because I'd thought the same thing myself. It had been years since we'd been here together. It had been years since *I'd* come to this cliff —well, with the exception of when he'd first come to the *saruk* weeks earlier. But I hadn't ventured down here. I'd stayed on the pathway.

I took his hand, drawing him toward me.

"I was looking everywhere for you," he murmured, dragging me into his arms, wrapping them tight.

I listened to the steady thump of his heart, and when he tilted my face back and gave me his kiss, my eyelids fluttered shut.

His mouth moved over mine, and I tasted his tongue when it stroked inside me. He tasted of Kiran and…strong brew. Brew that only my father could create.

That made me pause. I pulled back and asked, "You were drinking with my father?"

A huff escaped him. "*Lysi.*"

"Was he in pain?" I asked, frowning. How long had I been out here? "I'm sorry. I lost track of time. I should go and check—"

"He's sleeping, *seffi*," Kiran murmured, brushing his hand across my cheek, smoothing back my unruly curls. "And Laru is at the *soliki* with him right now. Don't worry. Take a moment, *lysi*? Take a moment with me. In this place, especially. *Our* place."

I met his eyes.

"Our place?" I teased softly, feeling my shoulders relax and loosen. He was right. I could take a moment—*more* than a moment. I deserved to take time for myself. "I haven't been back here for a long time," I confessed.

His expression sobered, but I reached up to smooth the lines that suddenly cut through his forehead.

"I broke your heart right here," he murmured, his eyes glowing with memory. "I made the biggest mistake of my life right here."

I heard the ragged, grim regret in his voice. It stole my breath. I didn't want to remember those times. We had agreed to move past them.

Sliding my arms across his shoulders, I stared into those eyes I knew so well and felt that *knowing* burst in my chest again. Because it felt so *right* being in his arms.

"There were more happy times here though, Kiran," I told him, giving him a soft smile that momentarily made his expression go slack. Like I'd dazed him.

"Mmm," he murmured. "And is this one of them?"

His question made my lips part. It made me go a little shy, truthfully.

But I knew it was past time that I told him. It was past time that I told him my decision.

The choice I'd made.

The choice that had become more clear to me with every passing day.

The choice I'd told my father just that morning, the choice that Laru had read in my eyes. My family knew already, but Kiran didn't. Not for sure.

A rumbling purr rose from his throat. He gave me a small, crooked grin that had me swallowing.

"Why are you looking at me like that, *seffi?*" he whispered, leaning his forehead against mine just as a wave crashed on the cliffside below, loud and booming, sending icy spray around us that stung my very bones.

But I didn't care.

"I love you," I told him softly, my gaze flickering back and forth between his eyes. "*Lo kassiri tei.*"

He stilled under my touch.

"I don't know how you did it, Kiran," I whispered, "but you made me love you all over again. And maybe it's made up of remnants of the love I had for you before...but this also feels new. Different."

"Maeva," he growled against me, pulling back so he could see me clearly. "*Lysi?*"

I smiled, though I could tell that it wavered with nerves. Because I'd told him I loved him before…and maybe there were parts of that frightened girl within me still.

But I knew better.

I had loved the Kiran I'd *known* for nearly half my life.

But *this* Kiran, the *Vorakkar*, the one I'd fallen in love with all over again—this confident, maddening, wicked, certain, magnificent male—I trusted that *he* wouldn't break my heart. I knew he wouldn't. He would take care of it.

"I don't need the frost to be certain that I want to be by your side," I told him. "I am certain right now. I was certain before you left for the East Lands."

Which we still need to talk about, I knew. But it would wait.

"I just…" I trailed off, not knowing how to explain it to him. "I had this feeling the morning after Addie gave birth." His gaze sharpened. "I felt like Kakkari was with me. I felt her with me when I looked at you that morning. And I knew that I would be yours. And you would be mine. I knew that like it had already come to pass."

Kiran went quiet.

Then he said, "I have felt the same, Maeva."

My breath hitched. "*Lysi?*"

"During the last frost, Kakkari gave me a dream," he murmured. "And I felt her presence in it so strongly that I *knew.*"

Dreams from the goddess were rare but not unheard of, I knew. My own mother had told me she'd been given one, though she hadn't told me what it had been of. Only my father knew.

"It was of us," he murmured, reaching out to cup my cheek. "In my horde, though we had traveled far to the North. It was a slice of a memory that hasn't happened yet. But it will. I know that with certainty now. I saw this future so clearly that it couldn't have been anything but a vision from Kakkari herself."

"What was it of?" I whispered, wide eyed and breathless.

His expression went soft. His eyes warmed. "Us. In our bed."

My breath hitched.

"And your smile," he rasped, "as I felt our child move in your belly."

Tears pricked my eyes.

"*Lysi?*" I asked, my voice wavering with *want*. Because Kiran had always known that I wanted children, a family of my own.

Only I had thought that that future was lost to me. Because I couldn't see myself ever loving another male, not like I'd loved him.

"And I'd never felt such peace," he continued. "I'd never felt such...*purpose*. Because in that moment, it was my purpose in life to make you happy. To love you. To protect you. To protect our child."

He pressed a kiss to my lips, slow and soft. My head swam.

"I made the biggest mistake of my life right here," he repeated, "but I will spend the rest of our lives together proving to you that I am worthy of your love, Maeva."

"You have nothing to prove to me, Kiran," I told him gently. "I know who you are. I chose you a long time ago. And now I've chosen you again. Not the male I used to love. But the male you are *now*."

His gaze slid past me, straight out to *Drukkar's Sea*. He took in a deep breath, his arms tightening around me.

"I spoke with your father earlier tonight," he said slowly before meeting my gaze again. "And Laru. And eventually Nevir once he came in from the fields."

I cocked my head, hearing something in his voice that made my heart begin beating faster and faster.

"About what?" I asked.

"I asked them to join the horde."

My hands clenched against his chest, but I never took my eyes off his.

"I told them that I only want to make you happy. And I know that being separated from your family would slowly eat away at you."

"Kiran," I whispered, my eyes widening.

He gave me a little grin, one that made me swallow. "They accepted my offer."

A ragged gasp escaped my lips. "*How?*"

"I am very persuasive, *seffi*. Or have you forgotten?" he teased.

I shook my head, a laugh bubbling from my throat. "*Neffar?*" I asked, incredulous, in happy disbelief.

"They accepted. With one condition," he added.

"What is it?"

"You father wishes to return to the *saruk* for one season out of the year," he told me. "During the season of life. He wants to be here when the sea is warm and the forest is coming alive. Because he said it was your *lomma's* favorite time of the year, and he wishes to be close to her during it."

Tears dripped down my cheeks. "And Laru? Nevir?"

"They will remain among the horde permanently but visit the *saruk* on occasion, as I'm certain you will as well. Nevir will become one of my *darukkars*."

I was overwhelmed with happiness.

I couldn't breathe, I was so overwhelmed.

And he'd done this. He'd done this for me. Because he knew I needed my family close to me.

I wondered just how persuasive Kiran had needed to be when it came to my father. Because I got my stubbornness from that male. And I knew the grudge that he held against Kiran, though I hoped this was the first step in moving forward for the two of them.

"*Kakkira vor,*" I rasped, going up to my tiptoes as another wave crashed into the cliff. Against his lips, into our kiss, I whispered, "*Lo kassiri tei.*"

I love you.

"Anything for you," he murmured. "Always, Maeva."

When we finally pulled away, he leaned his forehead against mine, his breath ragged. As was mine. There was quiet as we listened to one another, as I still reeled in disbelief.

My family would be with me. In Kiran's horde.

Was this a dream?

If it was, I hoped it was one from Kakkari.

Kiran's mood shifted subtly, the energy between us changing. I felt it prickle against my skin.

"There is one thing you should know before you take your place as my *Morakkari, seffi*," he said.

His quiet voice had me sobering. The sudden seriousness of it.

And I knew. I knew it was about whatever he'd encountered in the East. I read him so easily.

"The Dead Lands?" I guessed softly, curling my fingers into the furs at his chest.

He nodded against me.

"I do not know what will come, Maeva," he confessed. "None of us do. But to stand at my side means being at the forefront of the dangers that might come."

Was that what he was worried about?

That I'd turn away from him in fear?

Nik, he knew me better than that.

"Whatever comes, Kiran," I whispered, looking up into his eyes, "I will stand by your side no matter what."

His eyes glowed. His nostrils flared.

"Never fear that," I told him. "*Lysi?* Because I'm not afraid. When I'm with you, how could I be?"

With a growl, he was kissing me again, and all I felt was relief. I leaned into that kiss, gripping his shoulders tightly, anchoring him to me along that cliffside where I had spoken his name for the first time, where I had first fallen in love with him.

And right there, I bound myself to him. I poured everything into that kiss. Our past, our future, no matter how uncertain it seemed at present given the dark fog in the Dead Lands. Into that kiss, I poured every hurt and ache. Every delight and joy.

I gave it all to him.

And he gave me everything too.

"*Seffi,*" he whispered against me.

A plea.

A promise.

That feeling washed over me again, just as the spray from *Drukkar's Sea* swirled in my hair.

And I knew that no matter what came next...I was right where I was supposed to be.

This was where I belonged.

With Kiran.

Always.

Three moon cycles later...

"**M**orakkari," he rasped under me, his eyes like embers from a fire. "*Finish me.*"

I felt the curl of my smile, though everything was focused on the place between my legs where he was buried so deep, where his heat pulsed into me, and I tightened around him.

"Is my *Vorakkar* begging now?" I teased, though it was punctuated with a small, breathless moan.

"*Lysi,*" he growled. His claws dug into my hips, but I didn't mind the sharp prick of pain. I knew that sometimes he forgot himself with me. "*Hanniva!*"

A small laugh bubbled from my throat. Then I tossed my head back, working my hips harder, rocking over his cock. His deep, sensual, skin-tingling groan made my pace quicken. His hands tightened, and I felt the soft glide of sand across my legs, caressing me in an unexpected way.

My eyes quickly scanned the cliffs above us, but I saw no one. Kiran and I were somewhat hidden on the small beach below, but conceivably anyone that walked past would be able to see us.

Kiran tugged me forward—until our chests were pressed to one another, my nipples dragging across his scarred flesh. Until his *dakke* pressed and thrummed against my clit, hurtling me toward an orgasm that I had long teased and drawn out. For the both of us.

"*Seffi,*" he rasped, one of his hands leaving my hips to curl in my hair. His grip was firm, keeping me in place, as he began to take control. He used the position to keep me still as he began to piston his hips, fast and hard and wild. "More. *Lysi!*"

Our eyes caught and held, and then I was kissing him, hearing the slap of our flesh, feeling the warmth of the sun across our bare bodies. Behind us, I heard a wave crash against the shore, heard the hiss of it as it approached us before retreating.

"Kiran," I whispered breathlessly, my eyes wide.

"*Vok,* you feel so good, *rei Morakkari*. Come for me," he ordered before he licked at my tongue. "Let me feel you come around my cock."

Then I was doing just that.

The pleasure racked up my spine like lightning across my back.

"*Lysi,* Maeva," he growled. "*I feel you.*"

His hips moved faster. Deep, long strokes that sent shudders through my body. Then I felt him push deep, I felt his cock spasm...and then I felt the flood of him. Hot, thick seed coated inside me as his loud bellow met my ears, as it echoed around the cliffside, bouncing off the stone walls.

My own orgasm went on and on, *so vokking good*. Then again, with Kiran, it always was. Every time, it felt new and sublime. Every time, I thought it couldn't get any better and somehow he proved me wrong.

When it was over, I collapsed onto his chest, breathing

hard, panting into the crook of his neck. I felt—rather than heard—his groan rumble across my breasts. I felt the slide of his heavy arm coming around my back.

Another wave crashed and rolled toward us. This time, it reached high, and I felt the water against my bare toes—warm and inviting. It always amazed me how quickly the South Lands warmed after the frost.

The frost had passed a few weeks ago, and the season of life was here. The days were warming. The ice caps on *Drukkar's Sea* had long melted. The Forest of *Isida* was coming to life—though just yesterday, Kiran and I had walked through it and noticed that there was a *lack* of life. A strange, hushed quiet.

With the end of the frost, we were back at the *saruk* of Rath Okkili to make good on the promise Kiran had made to my father. He would be returning here for the coming season, to be close to *Lomma*, to return to the place where he had shared much of his life with her.

As for the horde, we were tasked with venturing far to the north, a decision that all the *Vorakkar* had come to together. The dark fog in the Dead Lands continued to spread every day, though it was a small amount of land. The entire valley was swallowed up now, based on the continuous reports from the scouts that were assigned there, and the fog was moving in all directions. It might take a year for it to reach the borders of the North and the South, but its pace was steady and constant and alarming.

Kiran's horde was assigned to make contact with the priestesses of the North, who had ignored every *thesper* message that had been sent to them. Though, truthfully, it was possible that the *thespers* had never reached them. None had come back, so it was difficult to be certain.

As such, it was Kiran's task to speak with the head priestess, and that required a long journey north, to one of the coldest places on Dakkar—though my father had told me the mountain ranges were breathtaking and that frozen lakes stretched for miles.

I wasn't eager for the cold again so soon after the frost had passed. But I knew this was destined. It was time to go north. If only because that was where Kiran's dream—the vision he'd received from Kakkari—had taken place. Far to the north.

And I'd been pregnant in his dream.

More pregnant than I was now, at least.

And that was how I knew everything would be okay.

When another wave broke along the shore and hissed its way toward us, I raised my head, propping my chin on his chest.

"I always hate to say goodbye to this place," I told him, smiling. "Maybe after we go north, we can bring the horde near here and settle along the coast for the hot season. I know the children of the horde would be delighted. Most have never seen the sea."

His soft smile met my eyes, and I felt his hand drift across my cheek.

"Our child will be born then," he commented, sliding his hand down, slipping it between where our abdomens touched. His warmth spread across my growing belly when he stroked there. "Will you bless her in *Drukkar's Sea*?"

"I would like that," I whispered, my eyes going a little misty with the sentiment. And the fact that Kiran was so certain the child would be a girl. A princess of the horde.

"It is settled, then," he told me, leaning forward to take my lips. After a slow, languid kiss that made my head spin, he murmured, "And once my time in the wildlands is over, I will build you a *saruk* by the sea. Then you will never have to leave this place again."

My breath hitched, and I pulled back to look at him properly. With the red fog, our future was so uncertain. What dangers we would face, what decisions would need to be made, the changes that would come on our home planet, changes we were already feeling.

Like the new horde king—the bastard son of the *Dothikkar*—taking to the wildlands with his battle-bred horde. Though I had yet to meet him, there were rumors circulating that he was destined to become the greatest horde king of all time, that the priestesses had foreseen it since his birth.

And while *Vorakkar* never truly got along—for their personalities and wills clashed too much—Kiran had voiced that this new horde king was a welcome addition to the wildlands, that they needed him if they had any hope of defeating whatever would come.

And perhaps Errok, Kiran's former *pujerak* and close friend, would become the next horde king to take to Dakkar. The next Trials were already starting in *Dothik,* and he'd been allowed entry. It would be many moon cycles before we would know anything. If he was triumphant, however, he could be out in the wildlands with his own horde shortly after the harvest.

Two new horde kings, taking to the wildlands within a year of one another...that was practically unheard of.

With all the changes that would come, one thing I was certain about was that Kiran would be by my side throughout it all. And I would be at his, giving him whatever he needed in order to lead his horde best. That was my duty as *Morakkari* now.

Our child would not come for the next three moon cycles. We had time before her arrival to get settled in the North—though the journey would be long. But I was eager to see more of Dakkar because I knew that my father was right. There was more than the South Lands.

I wanted to see it all.

And then, when we were old and tired and wanted peace, we would settle next to *Drukkar's Sea.* Our time in the wildlands would be over, and new hordes would take our place, to begin their duty to Dakkar and Kakkari.

Leaning forward, I kissed my *Vorakkar* again and then sat up, feeling the sun stroke its way down my back. Slowly, I rose from his cock, making him groan, and I bit my lip when I felt a rush of wetness flood between my thighs.

"Let's clean up, *lysi*?" I teased.

He growled, his gaze tracking over my exposed body, settling on my growing belly. His eyes were hot and needful when they met mine.

I grinned and pushed off his chest, standing on somewhat shaking legs. But the sea was waiting and the water would be warm. I intended to soak up every last bit of sun I could before we journeyed back to the horde and began our journey north.

Kiran stood, watching me walk back into the sea. The water splashed up my calves, the sand silky and smooth beneath my feet. My mate, my husband, my love began to follow, that crooked smile he wore making my heart thump in my chest.

When the water reached my waist, brushing over the child that grew in my womb, I turned and dove into *Drukkar's Sea*. The world went quiet underneath the water, just for a brief moment. I swore I felt Drukkar's fingers threading through my hair, accepting me into his sea. I felt at peace. I felt belonging.

I smiled, and then I surfaced.

When I did, Kiran was there, his hair wet, his eyes bright and golden in the sunlight.

Magnificent male.

"*Seffi*," he called, grinning.

I went into his arms.

And as long as I was in them, there was no place on all of Dakkar I'd rather be.

Taken by the Horde King

Horde Kings of Dakkar #5

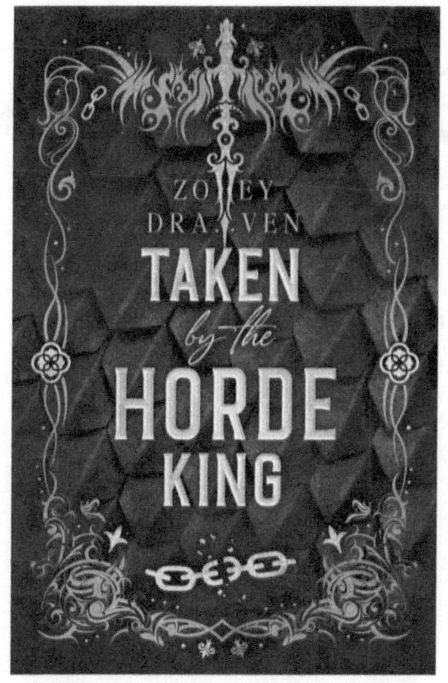

OUT NOW!

To save Dakkar, she must lure him to his deadly prison. Instead, she finds herself wearing *his* chains...

As a fatal curse continues to spread over the planet of Dakkar, I make a deal with an alien witch who claims she can stop it.

Her price?

The heart of a horde king.

Only the horde king in question is the fiercest male I've ever seen, with glowing demon eyes, a god-like body crafted in battle, and a cold, cruel grin that promises destruction.

Yet when I offer myself to him, all under the premise of luring him back to the witch, his touch sets my blood on fire. His dizzying kiss makes the world spin. Instead of fear, I feel hot and unwanted desire, awakening instincts that tell me I'm *his*.

When he discovers my ultimate betrayal, the enraged horde king vows he will take me as his prize, that I will wear his chains, and that I will serve him in *whatever* way he wishes.

And as the dangers on Dakkar loom, I find myself craving my wicked, wicked ruin...all at the hands of a horde king I should've never crossed.

Want to hear about new releases, exclusive giveaways, and get access to **bonus content,** like extended epilogues and character art?

Sign up for **Zoey Draven's newsletter**:

www.ZoeyDraven.com/newsletter

If you're already subscribed to my newsletter, access all bonus content here:

https://zoeydraven.com/bonus-content/

Connect with Zoey

Scan the QR code with your phone to access her links:

Also by Zoey Draven

Horde Kings of Dakkar:

Captive of the Horde King

Claimed by the Horde King

Madness of the Horde King

Broken by the Horde King

Taken by the Horde King

Throne of the Horde King

Warriors of Luxiria:

The Alien's Prize

The Alien's Mate

The Alien's Lover

The Alien's Touch

The Alien's Dream

The Alien's Obsession

The Alien's Seduction

The Alien's Claim

Warrior of Rozun:

Wicked Captor

Wicked Mate

The Krave of Everton:

Kraving Khiva

Prince of Firestones

Kraving Dravka

Kraving Tavak

<u>Brides of the Kylorr:</u>

Desire in His Blood

Craving in His Blood

Hunger in His Blood

<u>Hordes of the Elthilu:</u>

The Horde King of Shadow

About the Author

Zoey Draven has been writing stories for as long as she can remember. Her love affair with the romance genre started with her grandmother's old Harlequin paperbacks and has continued ever since. As an Amazon Top 50 and USA Today bestselling author, now she gets to write the happily-ever-afters—with an otherworldly twist, of course! She is the author of Sci-Fi and Fantasy Romance books, such as the *Horde Kings of Dakkar* and the *Brides of the Kylorr* series.

When she's not writing, she's probably drinking one too many cups of coffee, hiking in the redwoods, or spending time with her family.

Website: www.ZoeyDraven.com
Facebook group: Zoey's Reader Zone